THE JANES

Praise for *THE JANES*

'*The Janes* has everything—a plot ripped from the headlines and darkly twisted, explosive action, original characters, a dash of humor, and memorable settings. The story grabs the reader like a steel band of cold tension tightening with each new development. Investigators Alice Vega and Max Caplan deserve a long career with many more cases ahead.'
Anne Hillerman, author of the Leaphorn, Chee & Manuelito mysteries

'*The Janes* is a timely, gripping thriller with an ending that will leave you utterly satisfied but wanting more of Alice Vega. Get to know her now, because she and her partner, Max Caplan, will be around for the long haul.'
Alafair Burke, bestselling author of *The Better Sister*

'Packed with thrills and heartache, *The Janes* kept me up way past my bedtime to see what rule-bending, jaw-breaking, no-fools-suffering P.I. Alice Vega would do next in her relentless pursuit of justice for the victims of a border sex trafficking ring. An absolutely rip-roaring read from a fantastic talent.'
Amy Gentry, bestselling author of *Good as Gone*

'Luna's gripping sequel to 2018's *Two Girls Down*… A plot as dark and twisted as one of the tunnels used for smuggling between Mexico and the U.S. This dynamic duo has a long run.' *Publishers Weekly*

'An intricately plotted, adrenaline-fueled conspiracy thriller…Luna's latest entertains while subverting gender stereotypes and confronting the politics of immigration.'
Kirkus Reviews

Praise for TWO GIRLS DOWN

'Opening this book is like arming a bomb—
the suspense is relentless and the payoff is spectacular.
Lead character Alice Vega is sensational—
I want to see lots more of her.'
Lee Child, #1 *New York Times* bestselling
author of *The Midnight Line*

'From its haunting opening to the pulse-pounding final
sequences, *Two Girls Down* delivers a gripping read. Alice
Vega and Max Caplan are characters I'd follow anywhere,
and Louisa Luna is a writer to watch. Highly recommended.'
Michael Koryta, *New York Times* bestselling
author of *Those Who Wish Me Dead*

'This is such a terrific read. High stakes, relationship-
driven, perfectly paced. *Two Girls Down* has something else
worth noting: three-dimensional female characters. Alice
Vega could give Jack Reacher a run for his money. Maybe
Louisa Luna should write all the thrillers.'
Chelsea Cain, *New York Times* bestselling author of *Heartsick*

'A knockout, read-it-in-one-sitting novel…
Gripping, emotional, and tautly written, with a
wonderful cast of memorable characters.'
Jeff Abbott, *New York Times* bestselling author of *Adrenaline*

'Louisa Luna is an incredibly talented writer
with a bewitching gift for storytelling, and *Two Girls
Down* fairly crackles with energy and suspense from the
first page to the last. I can't ever recall a time before now
that I lost sleep as a result of reading a crime thriller.
This one, I just could not put down.'
Donald Ray Pollock, author of
The Devil All the Time and *The Heavenly Table*

'Sensational…One of the book's great pleasures is seeing Caplan and Vega's initially testy entanglement develop into a true partnership. But there are many other aspects in Ms. Luna's story to savor as well: a host of sharply sketched characters, from spaced-out dopers to distraught parents and grandparents; action sequences startling in their sudden violence; and quick psychological revelations that pierce the heart.' *Wall Street Journal*

'I'm always looking for a good thriller, and this just was perfect. It's exactly the kind of thriller that I most enjoy… You really want to spend time with these two main characters. It was one of those things where the plot was great and it was complex enough to keep me interested, but what I loved most was the way these two very, very different characters— complicated with complicated lives—interact.' NPR

'To the pantheon of unforgettable noir detectives, add Louisa Luna's bounty hunter Alice Vega and her partner, P.I. Max Caplan, one of the best and most original duos to grace crime fiction in many years. *Two Girls Down* is a breathlessly gripping journey into the dark heart of America: I couldn't put it down.' Elizabeth Hand, author of *Generation Loss* and *Hard Light*

'A real nail-biter…The brisk plot combines psychological suspense with solid action, while providing a realistic look at a family under siege, as it builds to a shocking finale.' *Publishers Weekly* (starred review)

'An outstanding neo-noir, introducing enigmatic bounty hunter Alice Vega, a perfect female incarnation of Jack Reacher… Vega springs to life in the hands of this immensely talented writer… This is a must-read for fans of strong female protagonists.' *Booklist* (starred review)

'This one is a beaut, not only suspenseful but with some real embedded truths about how hard it is to be a mother.' Anna Quindlen, author of *One True Thing*

'This thriller is so full of suspense it'll make the hairs on the back of your neck stand on end!' *Woman's Day*

'An engrossing mystery bulging with so many memorable characters...The writing is superb and the witty repartee between Vega and Cap, even as they deal with society's lowest, is a delight. The ending is as shocking as it is unexpected. It's a truly gripping read.' Michael Rowland, *ABC News*

'This was so good, unforgettable characters (Alice Vega is brilliant), couldn't put it down.' Chris Whitaker, author of *Tall Oaks* and *All The Wicked Girls*

'Loved *Two Girls Down* by Louisa Luna. Tense, measured, spare writing, badass but relatable heroes, and a payoff that's worth every word of the wait. Whoever this Lee Child fella is on the cover, he's not wrong.' Rod Reynolds, author of *Black Night Falling*

'A turbulent, razor-sharp book... A beautifully taut firecracker of a read.' *Readings*

'Equally good at the Christie-twisty stuff and at giving us characters to relish...this flawless performance is captivating.' *The Times* [UK]

'High drama, humanity and not a hint of sentimentality.' *HuffPost*

'A tense and intelligently written thriller.' *New York Journal of Books*

'This tautly written thriller balances suspense with strong characterisations and insightful reflections on motherhood. The story unfolds quickly, and it will hold your attention until the end.' *Canberra Times*

Louisa Luna is the author of the novels *Brave New Girl*, *Crooked*, *Serious as a Heart Attack*, *Two Girls Down* and *The Janes*. She was born in San Francisco and lives in Brooklyn with her husband and daughter.

louisaluna.com
facebook.com/LouisaLunaAuthor

THE
JANES

LOUISA
LUNA

TEXT PUBLISHING MELBOURNE AUSTRALIA

textpublishing.com.au
textpublishing.co.uk

The Text Publishing Company
Swann House, 22 William Street, Melbourne, Victoria 3000, Australia

The Text Publishing Company (UK) Ltd
130 Wood Street, London EC2V 6DL, United Kingdom

First published by Doubleday, an imprint of Penguin Random House US, in 2020. This edition published by The Text Publishing Company in 2020

Cover design by Text, based on the original by John Fontana
Cover photograph by Nils Ericson/Gallery Stock/Snapper Images

Printed and bound in Australia by Griffin Press, part of the Ovato group, an accredited ISO/NZS 14001:2004 Environmental Management System printer

ISBN: 9781922268495 (paperback)
ISBN: 9781925923100 (ebook)

A catalogue record for this book is available from the National Library of Australia

At some point I was asked what's the one thing you need to know about Alice Vega, and I said, "She's not afraid of pain or death," and in that moment, I realized I was also talking about my mother.

This is for my mom, Sandra Luna, once again.

1

MEET OUR GIRL: SEVENTEEN, ARRIVED HERE A YEAR AGO FROM A rough and dusty town in Chiapas, considered pretty by most standards because she is young, her face unmarked by scars or wrinkles, her body boasting the tender snap of fresh muscle. Our girl's brain, on the other hand, is at war with itself and others: with memories of her mother's worry and her father's pain, subtle with her own simmering meditations on sex and violence, with fear of all the men that come through the door with their eyes so stark and full of want it's like they've eaten her up before they've even selected her from underneath the butcher's glass.

Our girl walks in bare feet, unsure if she is dreaming. Her dreams these days are collisions, collages, bursts of fire and color that all start normally enough—she is playing paper dolls with her sister on the porch under the umbrella with one panel missing, or fluffing up yellow rice in a pot right after it's done steaming. But then they turn; the dolls become scuttling cockroaches in her hands; the rice bowl fills with blood; her own teeth grow into blades and shred her tongue to streamers.

The house is divided, two floors: the ground floor, where she and the other girls sleep on towels side by side in the bedroom they share, and watch TV and wait in the living room; and there's downstairs full of boxes that pass for rooms—no windows, no air. The working rooms.

Then there is the garage, which is separate from the house, but there are no cars inside. There is just a table and some machines and tools. Our girl hasn't been there yet but this is what she's heard. Only girls who cry and act stupid are taken there and our girl keeps her head down and does what she's supposed to do. She doesn't ask questions and doesn't make trouble, but she watches everything.

She avoids the bosses. Coyote Ben is easy to avoid because he comes and goes, although when he's around and there's no work he grabs the hair at the back of her neck and whispers in her ear. He speaks English so she doesn't really understand everything he says, but she knows he doesn't expect her to respond. He lets her make the drinks.

Fat Mitch is always there, and he's got the gun on a belt that looks like it's strangling all the fat on his stomach. He has named the gun, Selena, after a singer, and he is always reminding the girls the gun is there. He'll say things in Spanish like "Selena got a lot of sleep last night and wants to have some playtime today." And then there's Rafa.

Rafa is the one who takes the girls to the garage. Fat Mitch tells them Rafa only does what he does because he has to, but our girl doesn't buy it. She knows Rafa does it because he likes it. It's not like on a farm when they make the runtiest worker shoot and drown the sick animals to toughen him up. The house may be a farm but Rafa's no runt—he's bigger and stronger than Fat Mitch, and our girl has heard he smiles when he does what he does to the girls in the garage. That is what they get when they act stupid.

Our girl's not stupid, and she stays away from the stupid girls: Isabel, Chicago, Good Hair. They cry and try to steal food. Stupid. The girl called Maricel is new, one of the girls from the city, and while it's usually not a good idea to get to know the new girls, our girl actually likes her and Good Hair both. In another time and place they may have all played card games and shared secrets about boys in their class. Instead they wait to be picked. Which is better than the alternative. If a girl doesn't get picked from the TV room for a month, she's out, not taken to the garage—*out* out, out of the house and dropped somewhere in the desert because she's not worth the Wonder bread.

Our girl has learned a little English here and there from TV. She pays attention to the American news. Police, homicide, catch, release. She watches a news show about a boy who looks her age, and Mexican too, but American. She tries to wrap her mouth around a word the newswoman keeps repeating, which sounds like something about a duck flying up. Duck-ted. Up-duck-ted. The boy talks to the newswoman, points to a picture of a fish tank. Then there is another woman, not the newswoman; 2014 it says in the corner. Her name is at the bottom of the screen. Our girl notices: American first name, Mexican last name. She looks like she is police. Or a lesbian. Or a gangster. She wears black clothes and sunglasses.

Back to the boy. Over and over he says the same thing: "She safes me, she safes me." Our girl watches the boy's top row of teeth, the way they scrape his bottom lip as he cries. The word is not "safes." It's "saved." "She saved me," the boy says, again and again.

Our girl watches Maricel get up close to the TV. Maricel doesn't take her eyes off it. The boy on the screen says, "She saved me. Alice Vega, she saved me." Maricel begins to cry, along with the boy. Our girl watches her and realizes her own hands are shaking.

Our girl has a thought out of nowhere: you treat us like dogs; we're going to act like dogs. A map unfolds in her mind, square by square. She saved me, the boy says. She saved me.

2

ALICE VEGA WATCHED THE DOGS, AND THE DOGS WATCHED THE meat.

There were six different kinds, some shaky fluff balls, some big with long jaws, all tied by their leashes to the same bike post outside a Reno's Coffee, all watching the couple at the table nearest them eating breakfast sandwiches. Mouths open, tongues flapping like flags. Vega didn't know much about dogs, about what variations in their gene pools led to different breeds, but they all wanted that bacon, even if they weren't hungry.

Vega sat at a table without an umbrella, and it was hot and just after nine in the morning. It was pretty and bland here. The streets were clean; the people were attractive in a nonflashy way; the dogs were groomed. It was not unlike where Vega lived, except in her town there were a few more homeless people, a few fewer luxury car models. A little rougher by only a couple of ticks. California was its own planet, and Vega had lived there her whole life, so most of it felt like familiar terrain to her. San Diego was not an exception.

When the time on her phone read 9:50, she threw away her cup, took one last look at the dogs, and left. Drove the half mile to the County Medical Examiner's office and pulled into the lot. It was a building made of sandy yellow brick, looked like half hospital, half elementary school. Vega scrolled through the email on her phone, the name, the address.

She stepped out of the car, cracked her neck, twisted her back one way and then the other like a licorice stick. Felt better. Thirty-five isn't that old, she thought, not defensively to anyone in particular.

Through the automatic doors, where it was cool inside, clean, a diamond pattern on the linoleum underfoot. A guard sat on a folding chair at a desk watching the feed from the security cameras. He was not surprised to see Vega; he had seen her walk from the parking lot.

"Can I help you, ma'am?" he said. He was young and black, the faint line of a mustache on his upper lip.

"I'm here to see Emilia Paiva," said Vega.

"Your last name Vega?"

Vega nodded, produced her driver's license. The guard took it and wrote down her information on a log in front of him. He pressed two buttons on the phone and handed her license back to her. Vega glanced at the screens: clipped office park lawn, cars parked, a line of white vans, two staff wearing scrubs unloading the contents—gurney and bag.

Then a woman's voice: "You're Alice Vega."

Vega looked up, and there she was, Latina, with a youthful face, a line of straight dark bangs over her forehead. She was a little shorter than Vega and weighed about two fifty. She wore her blue lab coat unbuttoned, a Deadpool T-shirt underneath.

"Ms. Paiva?" said Vega.

"Mia," she said cheerily. "Everyone calls me Mia."

They shook hands.

"That's Sam," she said, nodding to the guard. "He smiles once a week."

Sam smiled.

"There it is," said Mia, pointing. Back to Vega: "This way."

Vega followed her through gray swinging doors, into a hallway with a long window on one side, facing a line of parked cars. They walked toward another set of swinging doors at the other end. Mia moved surprisingly fast for carrying so much weight on her hips.

"How long've you worked with Rowlie?" she said to Vega.

"Roland Otero?" said Vega. "I haven't met him yet. He wanted me to see you first."

"Ohhh," sang Mia, pushing through the second set of doors. "I get it now."

Vega didn't ask what it was that she got. Now the hallway split—on one side were transparent sliding doors; inside were technicians at counters and desks with microscopes, boxy analysis equipment, laptops. TOXICOLOGY, read the small sign. On the other side was a narrower hallway than the one they just came from, a set of stairs leading down. Vega followed Mia, who kept talking.

"Hot out there, huh?" she said, and then without pausing for a response, added, "It's supposed to get up to ninety today. At least we're inside, right?"

Vega put on a smile when Mia turned around. Better to keep her offering information, but Vega had a feeling it wouldn't be difficult; Mia seemed to be a chatter. She pushed through another door at the bottom of the stairs, and here the doors in front of them were steel, a large red biohazard sticker on the left. Mia held her ID up to a key card reader, and the pinpoint light turned green. The doors slid open in front of them.

It was a big room, metal racks with six shelves apiece lined the walls, white polyethylene bags with a black zipper down the middle on every one, each containing a dead person. Vega recognized the smell. The vinegar tang of formalin, the heady odor of a meat counter.

"Here you go," said Mia, handing her a pair of safety goggles. "The chemicals might get to you after a while."

Vega put them on, watched Mia put on her own. Then Mia pulled a pair of purple latex gloves on her hands.

"It gets to me, too. I'm one of those people who tear up at everything, not because I'm emotional or anything like that, I just have sensitive eyes," said Mia, as she walked to the back of the room.

She stopped at two gurneys side by side, a bag on each. Vega stood at the short edges of the gurneys, what she suspected were the feet.

"Cutting onions, forget it," Mia added. And then, "Okay. This one was the first."

Mia unzipped the bag. There was the body of a girl, Latina, long curly hair that probably hit midback when she was standing, slender with small breasts and narrow hips. The Y-cut of the autopsy incision, with the two tines on either side of the neck and the line down the middle of the torso. Mia pulled the bag off the body's shoulders so Vega could get a better look at what she was there to see: a cluster of clumsy cuts above the left hip.

"Female, age twelve to fourteen, came in last Thursday. Cause of death was myocardial infarction due to bleed-out due to multiple stab wounds," said Mia, lifting the hip with two fingers to show Vega where the cuts continued. "I estimate she was dead about a day before getting to us. No sign of recent sexual assault, per se, but some labial and anal fissures, as well as absence of hymen tissue. And, notably, a functional IUD in her uterus."

Vega walked around the body so she stood next to Mia, to see what she saw.

"Organs all relatively normal, except one puncture in the kidney."

"Is that what did it?" said Vega.

Mia shrugged.

"Kidneys bleed a lot, so it probably accelerated the process, but it's not like she would've definitely lived if the stabber missed the kidney. No food in the stomach. Here's something for you," said Mia, somewhat bubbly. She pointed to the stab wounds. "You see this scraping, here?"

Vega leaned closer. Between the cuts on the hip and the cuts on the back were scabs close together, some shorter, some longer, like a bar code.

"My guess is that Jane's moving around, Stabber drags the blade, but you see how some are shorter than others?"

Vega nodded.

"Serrated blade, right?" said Mia.

"Right," agreed Vega. "Anything else about the knife?"

"Not really," said Mia. "Probably sixteenth of an inch, but most knives are."

Mia stood up straight, surveyed the whole body.

"Some bruising, contusions here and there. This one down here," she said, pulling back a bit of flesh on the upper right thigh to reveal several small sunburst-shaped scars. "Looks like cigarette burns to me."

Vega looked at the hands and arms, saw small red gashes near the wrists and on the fingers.

"Defensive wounds," she said.

"Totally," said Mia, wrinkling up her nose. "Stabber comes from behind, girl reaches around and back."

Mia mimed it, wiggled and waved her fingers to the sides, a weird little hula.

"And these," Mia said, moving up to where the girl's head lay. "You see?"

Vega joined her on the other side of the body and saw an egg-shaped, dark red mark on her left temple.

"Some sort of blunt trauma," said Mia. "But I can't think of an object that would make a shape like that. Wooden spoon, maybe?"

Vega tilted her head to get a better look. The skin was raised slightly, looked a little puffy. It reminded Vega of an allergic reaction, a rash from poison oak or ivy but strangely concentrated.

"You want to see the new one?" Mia said.

"Sure."

Mia walked around to the second gurney and unzipped the bag, Vega right behind. This girl had a different smell. Vega took it in at first, didn't fight it. It was strong, musty, had dampness to it. Almost like this one was fresher.

She, the girl, was either older than the first girl or just more developed: fuller breasts, rounder hips, darker and more hair in between her legs. Her eyes were closed, but she had an expression: brow pushed down, off-center lips, an unmistakable scowl. The body was also beat up much worse than the first girl. She had dark brown bruises the size of plums covering her arms and legs, and again, above the left hip, stab wounds, not as sloppy as those on the first girl and more toward the back, only four that Vega could see. No scraping.

"Stabber got better," said Mia, seeing where Vega was looking.

Vega nodded.

Mia waved her hand over the girl's crotch. "Jane Two. Also twelve to fourteen. Also plenty of fissures, lacerations on the labia." She lifted the hip with two fingers again. "He got three in the kidney this time."

Vega leaned down to look at the wounds, but let her eyes wander to the hand. Dirt was encrusted under the short nails and in the pockets of the cuticles. The fingers were long and slender and appeared to be resting so lightly on the table Vega almost had the impression they were hovering just above the surface. She glanced at the other hand, wondering if it looked the same, and oddly, it did not. The fingers on the right hand were slightly tucked under the palm, as if the girl were just starting to make a fist.

The smell filled Vega's nose again; this time it was all meat, and Vega tried not to think of food, of the dogs and the breakfast sandwich, turkey on Thanksgiving, fish sticks. She bent over, hands on her knees, breathed through her mouth.

"You sick?" said Mia, not unkindly. "Happens to me sometimes, too. Happened last week. I was really hungover, but still."

Vega barely heard her, fuzz filling her ears.

"Try this," Mia said, holding something in front of her face.

Vega squinted at it: a bright white pill.

"Altoid," said Mia.

Vega took it, placed it on her tongue. The mint spiked through the roof of her mouth, and she could breathe again. She exhaled and stood up straight.

"Thanks," she said, lifting her goggles to wipe the wet corners of her eyes.

"NP," said Mia. She looked back down at the body. "Where were we?"

"Were they found in the same place?" said Vega, pushing the mint to her back teeth with her tongue.

"No," said Mia. "Rowlie will give you those details, crime scene stuff. We didn't have any of our people there. But no. Different days, different places. Jane Two we had to clean a lot more. Lot of dust."

Vega walked between the two bodies, looked from one to the other.

"Cause of death, type of victim, but that could still be random, right?" said Vega. "So what makes us think they're definitely linked?"

Mia smiled, round cheeks pressing up against the bottom of the goggles. Brainy squirrel, thought Vega.

"The new girl had an IUD, too," she said, pleased.

Mia paused then, and Vega sensed more was coming.

"I bagged them," she continued, and she pulled two plastic evidence bags from the shelf below the gurney, held one up in each hand. "Copper. From the same company."

"How do you know?" said Vega.

"Name's printed on the coil. Health-Guard."

Mia paused another moment and looked almost giddy, like she had a secret.

"Can I show you something?" she said.

Vega nodded.

Mia grinned, lifted her goggles to her forehead.

"Come."

She went to a counter in the corner of the room, where there was a desktop monitor and a microscope. Vega followed and watched as Mia removed one of the IUDs from its bag and placed it on a small plate under the lens of the microscope. She flipped on the monitor, and the screen was white with a blurry image of the IUD.

"I'll make it as sharp as I can," said Mia, peering through the eyepiece and adjusting the lens.

The image grew clearer and Vega stepped closer to the screen. The lettering on the IUD was visible now, the words HEALTH-GUARD engraved on the tines at the top.

"Take a look here," Mia said, not lifting her head away from the eyepiece.

She turned the plate that held the IUD sideways, so the longer tine was lengthwise across the screen. There was something written there as well.

"Numbers," said Vega.

"Yeah," said Mia. "Eight numbers, but you only have to remember the last three."

Vega studied the numbers.

Then Mia removed the plate, and the screen was blank white. She slid the second IUD under the lens, focused again.

"You remember the last three?" she said to Vega.

"79433530."

Mia raised her eyebrows, impressed.

"Very good," she said, tightening the focus as close as she could.

Vega put her face very near to the screen. Identical make of IUD, HEALTH-GUARD printed on the top coil. She stared at the number on the long tine.

"79433525," she read aloud.

Mia lifted her head from the eyepiece and looked triumphant.

"Almost sequential," said Vega.

"Yep," said Mia. "Rowlie always tells me if I notice something, not to wait for him."

Vega listened to her as she walked slowly back to the new girl. Jane 2. IUD 79433525.

"That's smart," said Vega, studying the body.

The scowl, the breasts, one hand with fingers curled, the other reaching out. Vega crouched a little to get a closer look, her face near the girl's shoulder, and thought, Somewhere there's four more just like you, or not like you at all.

Max Caplan wedged a finger in the knot of his tie as he waited for the client, attempting to loosen it. He'd worn a tie most days as a cop but they were always loose back then, always halfway-to-happy-hour style. Then when he stopped being a cop and started as a private investigator he threw most of them away, only pulled them out for weddings and funerals. But now, working for a lawyer, it was jacket and tie on the days he came to her office to hand in reports.

Vera Quinn was a one-man shop, just like Cap. No-nonsense, polished, attractive in a senatorial sort of way. She was possibly the most well-known attorney in Denville, PA, had produced a series of print ads boasting the only sentiment a potential client needed to know: I don't get paid until you do. The classiest ambulance chaser this side of the Allegheny.

Work had been steady for Cap for almost a year and a half now, since he'd enjoyed a brief stint of notoriety after finding two local abducted girls, the Brandt sisters. But no one paid more or as frequently as Vera Quinn, and the work, though not exactly exciting, when Cap was being very honest with himself, watching the numbers of his direct deposits run up, was so damn easy. No skips, no cheaters, just desert-dry interviews with insurance companies.

And he was helping people! On top of everything, Vera Quinn was out to help the little guy. Medical malpractice, car manufacturing negligence, dead bugs in the French fries. The only price was he had to wear a tie once a week, and hell, Cap could do that for no black eyes or pulled muscles, for eight hours of sleep a night. Win-win all over.

"You can go on in, Cap," said the receptionist, in her sixties, a smoker with a voice like a buzz saw.

"Thanks, Martha."

Cap walked into the office, where Vera leaned against her desk and spoke into a headset with a microphone the size of a pencil eraser. She smiled and waved emphatically to Cap while she wrapped it up.

"You can expect the memo tomorrow . . . I appreciate your time. Cheers."

She clicked a button on the headset and removed it.

"Whoo," she said energetically.

"Good news?" said Cap, sitting in the chair opposite her desk.

Vera held her hands up above her head like she was presenting a banner.

"Turino settled," she said.

"Already?" said Cap.

"Already," said Vera, laughing. "If I weren't on the Paleo diet, I'd say let's get a margarita."

Cap laughed, in part because Vera was funny, self-deprecating and humble, but also because the job he'd just started was over and won. Easy.

"I guess we won't need Double G's statements," he said, dropping a manila envelope on Vera's desk.

"Hey, let's hold on to those. Paperwork's not signed up yet. Anything of interest?"

"I got two day laborers saying the foreman told them to work fast and cut corners."

Vera sat in her chair behind the desk and rolled forward.

"Just what you expected them to say," she said, pointing at Cap.

He shrugged.

"Makes sense. Those guys don't have a dog in the fight. Should we call Mr. Wyse, tell him he can pay for his medical bills and maybe a little trip to Atlantic City?" said Cap.

"Try the Bahamas," said Vera, grinning.

"No shit," said Cap. "That's fantastic. Let's call him."

"In a few," said Vera. "I wanted to run something by you first."

She had a look in her eye like she had a nice juicy secret. It was silly for Cap to be nervous but he couldn't help it. The only other person in the room knowing something you didn't never felt good.

But he smiled congenially and said, "Shoot."

Vera put her hands together and rubbed them a tiny bit.

"This is good, don't you think? Us working together?" she said.

"Yeah, of course, Vera," said Cap right away.

She nodded.

"Your work is impeccable, Cap. Thorough, fast, you have more experience and ethics than anyone in the field I've worked with, certainly."

Cap was embarrassed; he didn't like compliments because he never believed them unless they were coming from his daughter, and then he allowed them to wash over him in a gentle mist.

"I appreciate that," he said. "You know the feeling's mutual."

Vera didn't respond to that sentiment directly, just presented a tight smile and kept talking.

"I've been thinking about our arrangement, and I think we could consider making it a little more permanent."

She let that sink in for a moment. She was a lawyer, after all. Let the other guy do the thinking and the talking; maybe he'll say what you want to hear. But if she was a lawyer at her core, Cap was a cop, and he could play the quiet game too, maybe even better than she could.

He just kept smiling, allowed a marginally confused expression to cross his face.

"I'd like to make you an offer," Vera said finally. She continued: "To become a full-time employee. You could make your own hours, just like you do now. All you have to do is keep doing the work you do. Health benefits, vacation, sick days. All I would ask in return is your word that you'd stay on for two years, and then we'll reevaluate."

Vera then handed Cap a gray envelope. He took it and stared at the blank face.

"Vera, I . . ." he began.

"Please. You don't have to answer now. Take a couple of days. Talk it over with Nell."

Cap smiled because everyone knew his daughter, Nell, was his most trusted adviser. Even though there had been a seismic shift in her personality since she'd been held at gunpoint for two hours during the Brandt case. Whereas before there had been boundless energy and eager curiosity, now there was burgeoning anxiety and uncharacteristic sullenness.

His ex, Jules, still held an impressive grudge about Cap having put Nell in danger. When Cap had confided in Jules that he had the distinct feeling Nell was hiding things from him, Jules responded, via email, "What the hell do you expect? She's been through a trauma and now God forbid she acts like a normal teenager!! Stop feeling sorry for yourself."

"I'm not sure what to say," said Cap, feeling like an idiot.

"Think about it," said Vera. "We make a good team."

"Thanks, Vera. This is really something," he said, good-natured and vague.

"I hope that's good."

"It is," said Cap. "It absolutely is. It's just I've gotten so used to worrying about where the next job is. I'm not sure what I'll do with all that excess energy."

Vera smiled and said, "Well, there's always CrossFit."

Cap laughed, and Vera laughed, and then they talked politely and professionally for a few more minutes about the Turino suit, another project in the pipeline, other possible business prospects. Then Vera walked him to the door and opened it. Cap tucked the gray envelope into the inside pocket of his blazer, and they said goodbye.

Vera said, "Speak soon, then?"

"Yes, thank you, Vera. Thanks," said Cap, shaking her hand with both of his to convey his gratitude.

"I got your two-o'clock holding," said Martha.

"Be there in a sec," said Vera.

Vera gave a last wave to Cap and retreated into her office. Cap stood still for a moment, a little dazed.

"See you when I see you, Cap," said Martha, idly scrolling on Facebook.

"You take care, Martha."

Cap started slow and then hurried to the front door, where he fumbled with the knob and then was out, onto the sidewalk, choking on the humid August air. Come on, Caplan, he thought. No matter what's inside that gray envelope, this is a solid offer with a good shop and a first-rate boss and a health insurance plan that will make you salivate over its reasonable deductible like it was a medium-rare cheeseburger.

Then what was the problem? He grabbed hold of the knot in his tie and yanked it side to side until it loosened up. What was that movie, he thought as he bent over to catch his breath. Who was it—Brad Pitt? George Clooney? When he rips the tie off and throws it to the ground to reject corporate job security? Cap didn't want to do that.

He had only two ties.

3

VEGA WAS THE ONLY PERSON WAITING. IT FELT MORE LIKE A DOC-
tor's office than a police department, a young black woman with her
hair in a neat bun and starched uniform behind the desk, the landline
beeping inoffensively. Magazines fanned out on small tables in the corners. Clean floors, no dust.

Vega read news about the tunnel while she waited for Roland Otero.
She scrolled on her phone, looking at the photos—the lights, venti-
lation systems, appliances, and the tracks for the carts. Entrance was
a hole in the ground on a construction site near the airport, just big
enough for a large dog or an average man. Or, Vega thought, two girls
side by side.

A Latino man emerged from a door behind the reception desk. A
few inches taller than Vega and with a slight build, dressed in a black
button-down shirt and gray suit pants, a patch of white in otherwise
black hair.

"Ms. Vega," he said, walking quickly to shake her hand. "Roland
Otero."

They shook, said nice to meet you. Vega noticed pockmarks on
his cheeks and forehead, smelled musky cologne on his skin as they
returned to the door he'd come from.

"Thank you for coming on such short notice," he said.

Vega nodded and put on a small, gracious smile. She glanced at the
officer answering the phone, the Glock 19 tucked into her belt holster.
Then she followed Otero through the door to a room the size of a high
school gym. There appeared to be no offices, or even cubes, just pairs and
clusters of desks, conference tables, vending and coffee machines—no
walls or doors anywhere, just a long clear window wrapping around the
whole space showcasing the brilliant sky outside. The room wasn't that
loud either, just the ambient hum of people speaking simultaneously.

"You met Mia?" said Otero as they weaved through the aisles of the desks.

Vega saw cops, most of them plainclothes—mostly men with some women. White, black, brown.

They came to a long desk in the back of the room, almost flush with the window, what Vega assumed was the corner office equivalent. Otero offered Vega a seat and then went to his chair on the other side. The surface of his desk was sparsely covered: a yellow legal pad, a pen, a slim desktop monitor.

"You were saying," he said. "About Mia."

"I met her," said Vega.

Otero waited a second, quickly realized she wasn't adding anything. He nodded.

"What did you make of our Janes?"

Vega wasn't sure if she was at a job interview, wasn't sure if she wanted a job, but there was no sense in holding anything close. As of now she wasn't hired or fired, just a regular citizen being asked for her opinion.

"Similar cause and manner of death," she began. "Similar age, ethnicity. I'd guess the first girl was found indoors. Second girl outside."

Vega paused, remembered the dirt under the second girl's nails, the scowl on her face. She pushed the images from her mind and continued: "Both showed signs of recent intercourse, both with IUDs in their uteruses; considering their ages, I'd say they were commercially sexually exploited and possibly victims of human trafficking."

Vega looked over Otero's head, out the window, which seemed for a moment to be without glass, the sky so blue it looked liquid, like it would soon start flooding the panes and spill onto the floor where they stood.

"The IUDs with serial numbers five apart," she said. "Would imply there are other girls somewhere with IUDs numbered 526 through 529. At least."

Otero studied her for a moment and then stood.

"That's our conclusion as well. If you wouldn't mind coming around, I can show you some photos."

Vega joined him on his side of the desk. He typed his password into his computer and scooted the mouse around. Screens opened, and he double-clicked on a file labeled "JD1 8-16."

"This is Jane One," he said.

Vega recognized her from the medical examiner's morgue: curly hair, slim build. It was a tight shot of her, curled on her side in the backseat of a car, naked except for a lacy bra and underwear, fresh stab wounds leaking blood like oil.

"Found in a parked car on a street in El Centro."

"That in San Diego County?" asked Vega, trying to picture a map of the state.

"Imperial," said Otero. "Sheriff passed it to us because we have more resources, facilities. We have pathologists like Mia."

"Car registered?" said Vega.

"Yes, reported missing six a.m. on Friday."

"Does the owner's story make sense?"

"On the face, yes."

"Prints?"

Otero nodded. "Partial from the wheel, didn't bring anything up on past offenders."

He moved the mouse over the screen and closed the photo.

"Would you like to see the second girl?"

"Sure."

He double-clicked, and another photo came up: it was the second girl in a ditch outside, wearing boy shorts and a white tank top with a flowering patch of blood on the side where she'd been stabbed. Dusted in dirt, bare feet.

"A trucker spotted her in a ditch near Brawley and called 911. This was yesterday morning."

"Assuming the trucker checks out," said Vega.

Otero nodded.

"We can trace his route to where he started in West Texas. Plenty of alibis," he said, with a quick sigh. "Not much to say about the second girl besides what Mia already told you. Similar stab wound pattern."

Otero closed the files, and Vega took that as a sign to return to her side of the desk.

He smiled politely with just a dash of something fake in it, and Vega felt like there was something he wasn't saying. She didn't necessarily mind. There were things she wasn't saying either.

Finally he spoke.

"Do you have any questions for me?" he asked.

"Sure," said Vega. "What was in the second girl's hand?"

If Otero was caught off guard, he did well in hiding it, just barely tilting his head so his chin pointed in another direction.

"Not sure what you mean," he said.

"Her right hand," said Vega, holding up her right hand to demonstrate. "Looked like it was starting to close in rigor. Either trying to make a fist or holding something. I doubt she'd try to defend herself with her fists—not many women do. They use"—Vega opened her hand wide again—"nails. So I'm guessing she was holding something."

Otero nodded almost imperceptibly, then pushed his chair back from the desk.

"Would you like to see our evidence room, Miss Vega?"

"Sure."

She followed him out a side door, down a flight of stairs. They came to a vestibule with an armored door next to a transaction window, an officer standing on the other side. The officer passed a tablet to Otero, who typed in a number and passed it back. There was a tissue box of latex gloves on the ledge below the window. Otero took four gloves and handed two to Vega.

The officer reached down and pressed a button, and the door buzzed. Otero pushed through.

It was a clean evidence room, blue archive boxes on shelves, at least ten aisles. There were two long steel tables with folding chairs at the front of the room.

"I'll be honest," said Otero, walking toward the stacks. "That wasn't the question I'd thought you'd ask."

He grabbed a box from a shelf on the aisle closest to them. Most recent toward the front, thought Vega. He placed the box on the table between them, and they stared at each other for a minute.

Otero smiled and said, "I thought you'd ask why you're here."

Vega leaned on the table, pulled herself a little closer to the box, and kept the stare.

"Why am I here, Commander?"

Now the smile went away, and he avoided her eyes, suddenly sad and almost nervous. But perhaps that was just the appropriate expression for the work he did all day.

He opened the box and began to remove the transparent evidence bags, one by one. Each was labeled with a six-digit number and the date, 08-21. Two of them appeared to contain boy shorts and a white tank top.

"You are right, of course," said Otero. "The second girl was holding something."

He picked out the last bag, which had a scrap of paper inside, no bigger than the palm of the second girl's hand, Vega thought. Otero opened the bag and reached inside, pinched the scrap with two fingers and pulled it out slowly.

He handed it to Vega and said, "As you see, it answers both questions."

Vega read it a couple of times, examined the shapes of the black letters blurred by sweat, smeared by dirt and blood, and it all made so much sense.

Otero and Vega sat across from each other, again, at a table in a large conference room on the third floor. The room was bright, another wall-wide window on one side exposing another blue sky. Vega felt like she was in a Silicon Valley start-up instead of a police department.

"Any minute," said Otero, glancing at his phone. Small jittery shake of the head.

They sat a few more minutes in silence. Vega did have more questions but got the impression that Otero couldn't say much more. So they waited.

Soon the door opened, and the two men they were waiting for came in. Vega stood slowly and looked at them down and up. One was tall, broad-shouldered, blondish. His hair looked wet with a sculpted little wave in front.

The other was shorter, not fat but fuller in the face, with small eyes, brown hair that was a little too long and absolutely not sculpted in any way. They both looked about forty.

"Christian Boyce, DEA," said the blond one. "This is my partner, Mike Mackey."

"Alice Vega."

She shook their hands, and they walked around to the opposite side of the table and sat on either side of Otero.

"Commander Otero's briefed you on what we know about the Jane Does?" said Boyce.

Vega nodded.

"There was something on *48 Hours* last week, an anniversary, where-are-they-now piece about kidnapped kids," he continued. "There was a segment on about the boy in the tank, what was his name?"

Vega didn't respond right away, and Otero said quickly, "Ethan Moreno."

"Right," said Boyce. "We think the second Jane sees the show, gets stabbed, knows she's going to die, and writes your name down. Questions," he said, touching a finger on his right hand with his left as he listed them. "Are the Janes foreign-born or domestic? Was the first Jane killed in the vehicle where she was found or just dumped there? Are there more? If they're being trafficked for prostitution, are they also being used as mules?"

On that last question, Boyce paused and linked his index fingers around each other. He looked to Vega for a response.

Vega looked back at him, waited.

"Nothing found in organs or cavities of either girl, as far as narcotics go," added Otero.

Though he addressed Vega, she had the feeling he was correcting Boyce indirectly.

"Labial and vaginal lacerations, right?" interjected Mackey, his voice a little nasal.

Vega nodded.

"And IUDs in the uteruses of both girls," he added.

Vega glanced at Otero, who looked away from her, his gaze falling on his phone. What did people do before phones when they wanted to avoid confrontation? Vega thought. Must have been a lot of clean fingernails in the world.

"So," Boyce said, not acknowledging that his partner had spoken. "Here is where you fit in."

Then he smiled, flashing straight white teeth. Vega pictured him with an enamel strip across the top row.

"We could use your help. We have a significant tunnel problem in this part of the state, as I'm sure you're aware. Three this year alone. Difficult to know how long they'd been operational, but we estimate about a hundred thousand dollars' worth of meth, cocaine, and marijuana coming through per week, per tunnel. With an overwhelming degree of certainty we can say it's either Eduardo Montalvo or the Perez cartel. We've got DEA, FBI, police," he said, tilting his head toward Otero. "All of us working to contain this. You understand?"

He nodded at her, his eyes a little too big and glassy, the way he looked in his pressed shirt and sleeveless fleece vest a little too much like a dad trying to get Princess to brush her teeth nice and good. Just a dash of patronizing.

"I think so," said Vega. She folded her hands and leaned forward. "So, to clarify, if the girl had written down Bugs Bunny instead of me, you'd be looking to hire him?"

Otero looked up from his phone. Boyce turned a little pink in the cheeks. That's the shitty part about looking like a Ken doll, thought Vega. Can't hide any color in the creamy skin. Vega thought she saw Mackey repress a grin.

"You're more than qualified for this type of work, Miss Vega," said Mackey quietly.

"Sure," she said. "You know about me, right? I don't do a lot of charity."

"I think you'll find the compensation adequate," said Boyce. "You'd be a consultant for the DEA, but we need to keep it quiet, keep out the media. You'll report to Commander Otero, and he'll report to Mackey, who'll report to me."

"We'll share findings," added Mackey.

"Right, share findings," said Boyce.

Vega restrained a smirk and said, "Are you paying me by personal check?"

"Cash, actually," said Boyce.

"Huh," said Vega. "You going to tell me how much it is or do we have to pass a chit back and forth?"

Boyce appeared to take a short breath in and hold it.

"Ten K for two weeks," he said. "Then we evaluate and decide how to move forward."

They stared at each other a minute. Vega rapped her knuckles twice on the table softly and said, "No thanks."

"Sorry?" said Boyce.

"No thanks," said Vega, louder now, standing.

Boyce and Mackey both stood up too, then Otero. Boyce was too polished to stammer, but Vega thought she saw him flinch a little in the eyes. Mackey licked his lips.

"How much then, Miss Vega?" Boyce said quickly. "How much is acceptable?"

"It's not the money," said Vega. "It goes without saying I'll keep everything we've discussed confidential. Pleasure to meet you all."

She turned and left the room, took the stairs down at an efficient pace. The stairwell spit her out in the big room on the ground floor, and she took a last look around at the panoramic windows, then went through the door leading to the lobby, then out the front doors.

She could feel the heat in the air even though the sun wasn't directly on her. It was hot where she lived too, up north, but it was far more aggressive here; the air had a weight she could feel, pressing on her chest. She put her sunglasses on and walked down the paved path toward the parking lot.

Vega was halfway to her car when she heard someone behind her. Between five and ten feet, she thought. Rushing, not running, steps on the ground hitting almost at the same intervals as her own.

She reached her car and pulled her phone from her jacket pocket, opened up her map app and let it load. The steps behind her stopped. Between four and five feet behind her, she guessed. She did not turn around.

"Forget something, Commander?"

Otero didn't say anything at first. She turned to face him. He scratched the back of his head and squinted.

"I get it," he said. "Why you might not want to take this job."

"Yeah?" said Vega, leaning against her car. "Why I might not want to take a cash payment under the table from the DEA for busting a sex trafficking ring?"

Otero nodded.

"Then?" she said, barely shrugging.

"Then," he said with a sigh. "There are things I can't tell you. What I can tell you is that Mackey wants to get it taken care of. Since we have no weeping mothers coming forward, no missing persons reported fitting the description of the Janes, it hasn't been difficult to keep it quiet."

Otero paused. Something dark crossed his face and put a frantic twitch in his eyes.

"I've followed your career," he said. "Ethan Moreno, Christy Poloñez, the Brandt sisters."

Vega felt ice on the back of her neck at the mention of the Brandts, which was the way it had been for some time. If Otero hadn't kept talking, she might have corkscrewed down and landed right back in the woods in northeastern Pennsylvania, living through those long, cold minutes again.

"Jane Two," he continued. "I think she knew she was going to die and wanted to find you so that you could help the others."

Vega was glad for her sunglasses. Otero took a step closer, and Vega didn't move a thing.

"I think you could make this right."

Vega held her breath when he said that. It hit her in a certain way.

"I can loan you one of my detectives. All my contacts here and in Imperial," Otero continued, sensing that she was listening close. "I'm tied up on the tunnels like everyone else, but I'll help you any way I can."

Vega took off her sunglasses.

"Is Boyce paying out of pocket?" she asked.

"I'm not at liberty to say," said Otero, firm and polite.

"Right," said Vega. "Tell him I'll do it if we start with twenty, not ten. Your detective can do research? Stitch up loose threads?"

"Sure."

Vega got into her car and started the engine, the door still open.

"Can I tell them you're in?" Otero said, leaning on the door.

Vega pulled her belt on.

"The money, the resources, your contacts, all the photos and reports," she said. "I'll be back in a couple of hours."

Otero seemed humbled, his eyes soft. Unusually grateful, thought Vega. As if this was a personal favor to him. Maybe he just took his job that seriously.

"Thank you," he said.

Vega nodded at him, then at the door, implying he should stop leaning on it. He backed away, and she shut it, powered the window down.

"One more thing," she said. "I need to bring in someone else. He can keep quiet. I'll pay him."

"I have to clear it with Boyce," said Otero.

"Deal's off without my guy," Vega said, shifting to reverse. "So clear away."

She pulled out of the space, then the lot, didn't look at Otero anymore, kept her window rolled down and felt the hot wind hit her skin. She was thirsty as hell but didn't want to stop. She had an unusually good feeling; it was like suddenly finding the exact thing you wanted in a store where you'd been a million times.

4

THE TEMPERATURE ON CAP'S DASHBOARD READ 84, BUT THE HIGH
dew point was the real killer, the thickness in the air. Everything was
sticking—his shirt to his back, pant legs to thighs, drops of sweat on his
scalp threading through his hair.

But once the car cooled from the AC, he had an urge to turn it back
off and open all the windows. The air was still hot and still wet, but
he suddenly wanted to feel all of it, let his skin get slick as a tropical
plant leaf. So he did, stuck his head out the window like a dog and even
opened his mouth to feel the condensation bud on his tongue.

Then his phone buzzed.

"Ralz cell," announced the Bluetooth lady.

Cap squinted at the name on the screen, thought what reason could
Detective Brad Ralz have to call him. They'd parted ways after the
Brandt case with a mutual respect they'd never fostered as colleagues
at the police department, but Cap wouldn't call what they had a friend-
ship, exactly. Must have been a misdial. He let it ring out, drop to voice
mail.

He tilted his head again toward the window. He thought about Vera
and her offer and tried to make sense of what he was feeling, his tepid
response. ALLERGIC TO SUCCESS blinked an off-ramp motel sign in his
head. He wasn't sure where he heard that; it sounded like something
Jules might have said in one of her more passive-aggressive moments,
or a book title by a celebrity shrink.

But he wasn't, he hadn't been—the last sixteen months he had
embraced the work and the respect and the money. No bad reaction to
any of it, no rash, no itchy eyes. Then what, he thought.

Again, the phone buzzed.

Again, the Bluetooth lady: "Ralz cell."

"Goddammit," Cap muttered.

He tapped the Call Answer button on the screen.

"Ralz," he said loudly. "Stop calling me."

"Cap, that you?"

"Yeah?" Cap said, confused. He had been sure the phone had been in Ralz's pocket. "Uh, how're you doing?"

"Okay. You going to be home soon?"

"Yeah, about five minutes away. What's going on, Ralz?"

"It can wait five minutes. See you then."

"What? Where?" said Cap, but Ralz had hung up.

"Call Ralz cell," Cap said to the Bluetooth lady.

It rang once, then straight to voice mail. Cap had a bad feeling, shook his head. He let up on the brake and sped up a little. Slowed when he took the corner to his block, and as he got closer to his house, he knew he wasn't imagining what he was seeing in his driveway, but still the picture didn't make sense.

It was definitely Brad Ralz, leaning on his car, and the person he was talking to was definitely Cap's daughter, Nell, in front of the permanently loaned hatchback from Jules's parents. She stood in what Cap considered a standard teenager pose, arms crossed, the knee of one leg bent to the side, slightly bored expression. When she saw Cap approaching, though, she stood up straight.

Cap felt a surge of panic but talked himself down quickly. She's right in front of you, safe, breathing, uninjured. Cap parked across the street from his house and stepped out. Ralz lifted his hand in a wave.

"Hi," said Cap, crossing the street. "What's happening?"

He shook Ralz's hand and kept his eyes on Nell, who looked away.

"That roundabout off Highway 30," Ralz began. "I noticed this car taking it a little quick, so I tailed. Then down Lowell I had to go forty to keep up, so I pulled her over."

Cap felt his heart rate spike and took an aggressive breath through his nose. He stared at Nell while Ralz continued.

"I didn't recognize her at first," said Ralz. "Then I saw her name on the license."

Nell still wasn't looking at Cap, gazing over the roof of her car. She'd cut her own hair and dyed it black a few months ago, in the downstairs bathroom. Now it was short, just below the ears, the strands splitting off in different directions like falling fireworks. And her personal dress code had changed too; instead of the sportswear that used to be her uniform—khakis and baggy hoodies—now it was jeans with gaping holes in the knees and fitted tank tops or T-shirts, also with jaggedly ripped seams and edges. Winehouse-black makeup on the eyelids. Cap didn't have a problem with her dressing more maturely (or so he liked to tell himself) but was periodically disturbed at the signals her fashion choices were sending about her mental state: shredded into strips and pieces.

"I said no harm in a warning," said Ralz.

Cap's mouth was too dry to form a proper thanks so he put on a tight smile and nodded.

"I just escorted her here so I could tell you face-to-face."

Cap swallowed and finally spoke: "How much would the ticket be?"

"Street speeding?" said Ralz. "It's one fifty."

Cap glanced back at Nell. She was still doing the freeze-out thing, looking straight ahead.

"Issue it," said Cap.

That got a reaction from her. She jumped back from the car like it was hot and stared at Cap, shocked.

"What's that now?" said Ralz.

"Issue the ticket," Cap said, slower.

He and Nell kept their eyes fixed on each other. The same eyes, really, acorn brown with an amber glint in the light.

"Dad," Nell began.

Cap held out a hand to stop her.

"Don't," he said.

They were all quiet but it didn't last. Ralz looked from Nell back to Cap and spoke.

"I'm not going to do that, Cap," he said. "Nell and I had a talk. It's a warning this time."

"Thanks, Detective," Nell said calmly. Then, as if she were the parent making an excuse for Cap, she added, "Sorry about all this."

"It's okay," said Ralz, even keel. "Just make friends with your brake."

She nodded quickly, hiked her backpack from her hand to her shoulder, and hustled up the stairs into the house.

Cap let out a breath and pinched the sweat from his upper lip.

"I couldn't give your kid a ticket. Sorry, Cap," said Ralz.

Cap shook his head, said, "I appreciate it. I just wanted to make her sweat for a second."

"She was real polite," added Ralz helpfully.

"Yeah, she can be," said Cap, looking toward the house.

Ralz put his hand out to shake Cap's.

"Take care, Cap," he said.

"Thanks."

Ralz got in his car and pulled out of the driveway, drove away. Cap flexed his fists, open and closed, and said aloud to himself, "Watch it, watch it." He walked up the stairs to the porch and then went inside the house, felt the wave of AC douse him.

Nell was in the kitchen, leaning into the fridge. She emerged a moment later holding a slice of leftover pizza and glanced at Cap before heading for the stairs.

Cap summoned whatever scraps of patience he could gather so he wouldn't yell.

"Nell," he said quietly.

She stopped and turned, had a look that reminded Cap of Jules: it was the I'm-too-exhausted-by-the-day's-events-to-be-annoyed look.

"Can you tell me what happened, please?" he said.

She sighed undramatically.

"It was just like Ralz said, Dad," she said. "I didn't realize how fast I was going."

"That's not good enough," said Cap. "There's Jonas Middle on Lowell, do you realize that?"

"There were no kids around; school hasn't started yet," she said.

"That's not the point," said Cap, his voice rising. "You can't speed ever. *Ever.* It's not just about you. There's a whole world of people you could hurt."

"But I didn't hurt any of them," said Nell, still calm but growing defensive.

"No, see, that's the problem—you get cocky and think, I'll never hurt anyone, I'll never get hurt—"

He realized too late what he'd said, and Nell stared at him, her eyes glassy, perhaps with tears.

"I said I was sorry," she said, almost whispering.

Cap got quieter as well but still struggled to keep it together.

"That's not enough," he said.

All the features on Nell's face flared.

"What's enough then, Dad? You want me to send written apologies to all the middle schoolers I *didn't* hit?"

"Let's watch the tone."

Nell made a sound of frustration, somewhere between an "ugh" and a scream.

"You know what?" she said through locked teeth. "I've had about a half a beer in my life and a puff of one cigarette. Never tried weed." She cast her eyes down and added, "Never had sex."

Cap was shamed by her honesty. He felt himself begin to calm down. She was fine. She was alive. The evening would turn peaceful, and they might watch some TV. Then there would be tomorrow and the next day. She would not die before him.

"It felt good to punch the accelerator today," she said. "So maybe you can give me a little break and let me off with a warning like Ralz."

He didn't know what to say, so he nodded.

Nell turned and loped up the stairs, and Cap felt like a bunch of shit. When Brad Ralz, who had never been a model of restraint, was the voice of reason, it gave one pause.

Cap went to the kitchen, got a can of beer from the fridge, and trudged to his office, feeling like he'd been awake for a couple of days.

The AC was weaker in his office—to save money he'd shut the room off from the central air in the rest of house and used an old window unit instead. He felt fresh sweat gather on the back of his neck and cranked up the AC to ten.

He went to his desk and sat, finally took the tie off over his head and threw it on top of some papers. He opened the beer and sipped the foam off the top. He tapped the keyboard on his desktop; his computer woke up. He saw that it was 3:22 and could not believe the day wasn't almost over. He knew he had to wait a little bit before he approached Nell again, figured he would go up at 4:00. For now, just email.

Eleven new emails since this morning. He squinted to see clearly, trying to remember where he left the reading glasses that Nell had finally convinced him to buy, decided his eyes were just fine without them, and scooted his chair back another inch so he could see the type on the screen.

Mostly junk. One from Vera with the subject "Great speaking with you." Cap skipped over it, put a mental bookmark on it. Another from Nell, obviously sent before she'd been pulled over, forwarding him an article from the *Denville Tribune* about the increase in hate crimes. And then one with a time stamp of 2:54 p.m. from A. Vega. Subject: "Job."

Alice Vega, his partner in the Brandt case. The elusive, the conundrum, the deviously lovely. Right after she'd left town she'd communicated through a steady flow of emails for about a month as they cleaned up details, filled out paperwork, answered the FBI's questions, made statement after statement. But since then, not much, or more accurately, hardly anything at all.

Every once in a while Cap sent her an email out of desperation for some contact with her, anything, to hear her voice if only in his head as he read the words in front of him. His messages to her were lame ducks, links to stories about missing or found persons, cases that ended unexpectedly or cold cases finally solved.

MaxCaplan74 thought you might be interested in this story. Cap never knew what to write and usually just added, "Thought you'd like this. Cap." Her response was always the same. Just "Thanks."

But here it was. A. Vega. Job.

Double-click.

Cap didn't realize he wasn't breathing until his vision began to cloud and then he took a quick inhale and began to read:

"Hi. Got a job here in San Diego for you. 10K to start. Let me know if you can make it.

—Vega."

Cap read it a couple of times, then stood up and read it again from a standing position. Then he read it aloud. If he'd known another language, he might have translated it and read it aloud in that language. He started to laugh, then covered his mouth as if he didn't want to wake anyone.

He took a large sip of beer.

Then he clicked PRINT on the message and grabbed the sheet of paper from the printer, left his office, went upstairs, and knocked on Nell's bedroom door. She didn't answer at first, and he knew she had her earbuds in. He pounded with his fist.

She opened the door and appeared annoyed, one of the earbud wires thrown over her shoulder. She held a rind of pizza crust in her hand.

"Hi," said Cap. "I know we're arguing, but I really need to talk to you."

She raised her eyebrows, her face brightening up.

"I just got this," he said, handing her the paper with Vega's message.

Nell read it, chewed on the pizza crust. She turned the paper over to see if there was any more.

"I don't know if I should do it," said Cap.

"Sure you should," said Nell, holding the crust in the corner of her mouth like a squirrel. "It's Alice."

"Vera Quinn also offered me a permanent position."

Nell gaped at him. "When?"

"Today."

"Why didn't you say anything?"

"We've been a little preoccupied."

Nell almost allowed a smile, then said, "What do you think you're going to do?"

Cap thought for a moment.

"Vera's offering a good job with health insurance."

"No way," said Nell.

"Oh yeah," said Cap. "Everything. Benefits, vacation, sick days, probably some kind of retirement plan."

Nell's eyes searched the wall behind Cap as she thought.

"I gotta get some water," she said, walking past him. "And Alice is offering what—ten K? How long?"

Cap followed her down the stairs.

"You read it. She's not big on details."

In the kitchen Nell pulled a bottle of water from the fridge.

"You should probably call and ask her," she said, pointing the bottle at him. "And then you should probably take it."

"I have no idea how long I'd be gone," he said.

Nell shrugged.

"How long do her cases usually last?" she asked before offering her own answer. "A month?"

"Something like that," said Cap. "What about you?"

"I can stay with Mom. She'll be thrilled."

Cap knew she was not being completely cheeky. Jules actually would be thrilled to keep closer tabs on their daughter, a luxury she couldn't afford the days Nell was at Cap's.

"She won't be thrilled with me," said Cap.

"What else is new?" said Nell, unimpressed by his argument. "Tell you what, I'll handle Mom if we can maybe keep the speeding thing between us."

Cap's mouth fell open and then he laughed.

"Are you kidding me?" he said. "Can we just play out that scenario? I don't tell Mom, and you don't tell Mom, and then one day she runs into Brad Ralz—"

"Where the hell would that happen?" Nell interrupted. "Your scenario doesn't have legs!"

"Immaterial," said Cap. "She runs into Brad Ralz *somewhere*," he enunciated. "He says, 'How's Nell? Still speeding?'"

"So unrealistic," muttered Nell. "Brad Ralz doesn't talk like that."

"Are you aware of the storm of shit that will rain down on me?" Cap said, running his hands through his hair as if to stretch out his scalp. "They do not make a big enough umbrella."

Nell was quiet, tapped her toe against the base of the counter.

"Withholding information isn't as bad as lying," she offered.

"So not true."

"But it will just worry her to death, and you know it," said Nell.

Cap knew she was right. But he also knew he and Jules had maintained a relatively congenial relationship since the divorce. He'd seen and heard of so much worse—ugly custody battles, long-term harassment. What a bit of good luck it was that he and Jules just naturally agreed to stay out of each other's way. But it was a tenuous accord, which had been rattled by the Brandt case the previous year, and every small fracture since felt like a rift in the earth.

"I'm not trying to snake out of it," said Nell. "I swear."

Cap shook his head, felt himself running out of gas.

"I can't keep it from her," he said. "And besides, that never works. I'm the king of It'll-just-worry-her-so-don't-tell-her."

Nell looked at him skeptically, knew she was winning a little.

"Yeah, but you were never good at it. You could never hide it. *I'm* good at it," she said.

"Goddammit, you're right," Cap said weakly, rubbing his eyes. "Okay, Bug, just this once I will not tell your mother."

Nell smiled now, wide as a lake.

"But just because I'm not squealing doesn't mean you're off the hook. We still have to talk about consequences from today."

Nell's smile dissipated and she furrowed her eyebrows, confused.

"You mean, like a punishment?"

"Yeah, like a punishment," said Cap, sounding unsure of himself.

"What, like, ground me?" she said, before erupting in laughter.

Cap felt disarmed.

"What's so funny?" he said loudly, over her. "I could ground you. It's within my rights as a father."

"Dad, you've never grounded me, ever. I don't think you'd even know how to do it."

"Sure I do. Don't I just say, 'You're grounded'?"

"Yeah," said Nell, wiping her eyes. "I think you have to add, 'Young lady.'"

"Okay, now you're just making fun of me."

"Little bit," said Nell. Then she breathed deeply through her nose. "How about if I just say I won't do it again ever-ever?"

Cap looked at her face. No combination of cop training and dad training would lead him to find a lie in her earnest eyes.

"I honestly feel like shit about it," she said. "I wish I could just replay the whole day, you know?"

Cap nodded. He knew. Wanting to replay the day was a ritual of at least a third of his days.

Then Nell hugged him around the neck and kissed him on the cheek. She smelled like the oregano from the pizza.

"Call Alice. Then you should go to California."

She let go and went up the stairs, shut her bedroom door gently.

Cap was cold suddenly, the sweat cooled on his forehead and back. He went back to his office, sat at his desk, tapped the keyboard.

The message from Vega was still there; it had not evaporated. A thin line pulsed horizontally through the letters in her name. Cap knew it was because the screen was old, something to do with the monitor's magnetic field, but it made the word look alive, like it had a shaky little heart.

5

IN EL CENTRO, VEGA DROVE TO A STREET CALLED APPLE. THERE
was also a Cherry and a Berry nearby, Vega recalled from the map on
her phone. The street was residential, the houses all small ranch styles
painted faded pastel colors, sun bleached. There were regular trees with
not a lot of leaves and palm trees with crisp brown fronds. Across the
street was a small, shoddy strip mall—China Buffet, Lucky Upholstery,
which appeared closed at the moment, and Cash Advance and Vision
Plaza, which seemed permanently closed, façades boarded and signs
chipped.

She typed a quick email to the Bastard before getting out:

"Hey. Need info on a pharmaceutical accessory company called Health-
Guard. Any way to get into their shipping/purchase logs? Let me know."

Vega locked her car and walked once up and down Apple Street.
She stopped in front of a salmon pink house with a slightly beat-up car
in the driveway. There was a light on behind the curtains in the window. She backed up to the curb and then turned around, 360, slowly.
When she came to face the house again, there was a boy on the path
with a scooter. He had black hair, was a little chubby, wearing a T-shirt,
basketball shorts, flip-flops. He watched her.

"Hi," she said.

He didn't answer, kept watching her.

"You see anyone steal a car from right here?" she said, pointing down
at the curb.

The boy looked at her finger. He still didn't answer.

Vega tried Spanish. She asked the same thing. The boy scratched his
ear, then answered in Spanish.

"No, but a man saw."

"What man?"

"The can man," he said in English. He pointed to the recycling bin in the driveway behind him. Then back to Spanish: "He takes all the cans. Sometimes he sleeps over there, by the garbage."

Now he pointed across the street, to the China Buffet.

"Is he there now?" said Vega.

The boy shrugged.

"Okay," said Vega. "Thanks."

She pulled her wallet from her pocket and took out a ten, handed it to him.

He stared at it and said in English, "Just ten?"

"Yeah, just ten," said Vega. Then she remembered what her old boss in fugitive recovery, Perry, used to say when there wasn't any money on the table. "This isn't a charity operation. Take the money."

The boy's eyes widened at her tone but he didn't seem upset, and he took the bill and held it in his fist, flattened it around the handle of his scooter, waved with his other hand, and away he went.

Vega waved too. Then she crossed the street. The China Buffet was low on charm, the fake stucco exterior punctuated by streaks of water damage and bird shit. CHINA BUFFET was in red block letters that looked like they might glow at night, if the bulbs worked. She walked to the back of the restaurant through the empty parking strip.

There were overgrown weeds and grass back there, still patches of green fluff left over from the spring rain but plenty of brown too. Beyond it was a chain-link fence about ten feet tall. Directly in front of the fence was a steel orange dumpster with a rusted bar.

Vega crossed the dirt to the dumpster. Next to it on the ground was a flattened box under a sheet with a red bandanna print. Vega squatted, peered under the dumpster, and saw nothing, then looked up and realized with the dumpster lid flipped open, there would be a nice bit of shelter against rain or bird shit.

She stood up, gripped the lid, and pushed it up, glanced inside at a cluster of stuffed black garbage bags, circling flies, and slowly composting food. She set the lid down and wiped her hands on her pants.

Her phone rang.

She pulled it from her pocket and saw the name. She felt the muscles around her mouth surge into a smile, and then she answered.

Cap took the car key from the desk agent in a daze. He noticed her healthy tan, turquoise earrings with matching necklace, white-stripped teeth.

"Enjoy your stay in San Diego, Mr. Caplan."

As he drove away from the airport, the glare was so bright off the bay, he had to flip the sun guard down and put on sunglasses so his eyes wouldn't water. He headed east and saw three pelicans on a street corner. He reached for his phone, tried to get a picture for Nell, but the light turned green before he had a chance, and the Tesla behind him gave a quick, polite honk.

Then he was on the freeway, trying to read signage and focus on the GPS instructions, but it was proving difficult. He'd never been west of Chicago and was easily distracted by the sky, the palm trees, matching up what he was seeing with the imagery he'd been fed from TV and movies about the West Coast for forty-three years. So far, there didn't seem to be much of a gap. He started whistling "California Girls." Beach Boys, not Katy Perry. Wish they all could be.

Soon he was at the exit he needed, and the GPS told him which streets to take, until he got to the four-lane road a half mile out from the clinic where he was supposed to meet Vega. As he turned in to the small lot, he took off his sunglasses, glancing quickly from one end of the lot to the other, looking for Vega, but she wasn't there. There were a handful of other cars parked, but no one appeared to be inside them.

Cap parked and got out. It was hot but not humid, and it was glorious. Hot but *not humid*. Did everyone on the East Coast know about this? He wasn't even sweating. Only the back of his shirt stuck a little to his skin but that was just from driving and sitting on a plane for six hours. He ran his hands through his hair and turned toward the sun, closed his eyes. He couldn't believe his luck.

Vega sat in her car at the curb and watched him for a minute or two. She caught a glimpse of her reflection in the side mirror and didn't recognize her own expression. Her mouth was closed but she could see the outline of her teeth through the skin. She straightened her face out, rubbed her mouth hard with her fingertips like there was a mark she was trying to wipe away, and got out.

Cap opened his eyes at the sound of a car door shutting. And there was Vega, walking toward him. She was exactly the same except her skin was tanner, and she had a look on her face that was now familiar to him—pleased but not showing off about it.

"Alice Vega," he called to her, not attempting to hide how happy he felt. In fact, he let the smile take over his face like he was in an advertisement for the health benefits of smiling.

As she came closer, he saw some lines at the edges of her eyes that hadn't been there before. Even you get older, he thought.

"Hey, Caplan," she said, glancing up and down at his face, body. "You're thinner."

Cap patted his stomach gently.

"Well, I've been running," he said.

"How much do you run?"

"About four miles," he said, picturing his route around Calhoun Park. "Every other day. More or less."

Vega nodded and kept staring at him, like she was expecting more.

"I, uh, hate it," he said.

She laughed. It was quick but it took over her face like a sneeze.

Cap went on: "I really fucking hate it. Every second."

They both laughed now a little bit, and then Vega began to walk out of the parking lot toward the front door of the building.

"Did you get a chance to read what I sent you?" she asked.

"The highlights," said Cap. "You want to tell me why we're here?" he said, pointing to the BAY FREE HEALTH CLINIC sign.

"Not really," she said. "You'll understand as soon as we get in there."

"So I'm talking first, right?" Cap said, deadpan.

Vega raised her eyebrows at him. He felt soon she would shift into eye rolling. He grinned, so happy that he'd successfully teased her, that she didn't land an upward elbow jab into his neck, that they were in the same place at the same time and that she still had a few stubborn strands of hair that would not stay in the short ponytail she always wore and that he still, more than anything, wanted to reach out and slip them behind her ear.

Elizabeth Palomino seemed in a rush, her dark eyes large and intense. She shook hands with Vega and Cap briskly and sat behind her small desk in a small office. She wore nurse's scrubs, and there was a poster on the wall behind her that read KNOW YOUR CHOICES.

"You're police, is that right?" she said, looking at a printed email in front of her. "And you have questions about the staff here?"

"We're not police," said Vega, handing her a card. "But we're working with them on a case."

"Ah, okay," said Palomino, glancing at the card. "So what can I do for you?"

"Have you had any staff leave within the past year?" said Vega.

"Sure, there's always turnover," said Palomino. She looked at Cap then and said, "It's not for everyone."

Cap nodded politely.

"Anyone stand out?" said Vega.

Palomino paused.

"How so?"

"In a way that might justify having us here asking you questions," said Vega, adding a little smile.

Palomino smiled too, but it was tense.

"I'm sorry," she said, brushing a spot on her blouse, as if there were crumbs there. "No one comes to mind."

Vega nodded again, slower.

"Would we be able to take a look at their personnel files?" she asked.

Now Palomino stiffened up in her chair and said, "I don't think so."

She breathed heavily in the silence that followed. Vega met Cap's eye and gave a near-invisible nod toward the door.

"Excuse me for a minute," he said to Palomino, and then he left, shutting the door very quietly.

His departure seemed to galvanize Palomino even more, as if now she could really say what was on her mind. She leaned across the desk and planted her fingertip on the surface, tapping it hard.

"Let me tell you something," she said sternly. "The people who work here get their tires slashed, houses vandalized, death threats, you name it. I'm not about to give away their contact information."

Vega had the feeling if she didn't say anything, Palomino would keep talking, so she let her.

"You said you're working *with* the police, but you're not police— I don't know what that means," she said, incredulous. "I'm not giving you a thing, not a goddamn postage stamp, without a warrant or a subpoena."

Palomino paused and sat back in her chair. The corner of her mouth puckered, chewing her lip on the inside.

"I've been doing this a long time," she added, sounding tired and somewhat apologetic.

Now Vega leaned forward and perched on the very edge of her chair.

"I understand," she said. "You've logged twenty IUDs missing from your inventory within the past year, right?"

"We didn't report that. How do you know about our inventory?" said Palomino, angry again.

"Don't worry about it," said Vega.

"Don't tell me not to worry about it," snapped Palomino. "We have a great deal of sensitive—"

"Information," said Vega, finishing her sentence. "Got it. I don't care about it. I'm not interested in harassing your former employees. I'm interested in finding the guy who took your IUDs and put them inside underage girls for the purpose of sex work."

Everything on Palomino's face got bigger—eyes, nostrils, mouth, which she covered with her hand.

"Sonofabitch," she muttered into her palm.

"Yeah, that," said Vega. "Now, please tell me, anyone stand out?"

Cap followed Vega out, a ream's worth of personnel file copies under his arm. As soon as the doors sealed shut behind them, Cap sped up so he was next to her.

"Anything come up?" he said.

"Two guys," said Vega, keeping the pace quick. "One was fired four months back—an X-ray tech. The other was an MD, left about three months ago."

They came to Vega's car. She turned to face Cap.

"You going to tell the Bastard to go fishing?" he said.

She nodded. She seemed to be examining all the parts of his face except his eyes, quizzical. Cap surfed a small wave of panic internally, worried about errant nose hairs.

"How's your ear?" she said finally, nodding up at it.

Cap touched it, felt the spiny ridges on the top of his disfigured helix. It was numb there, where a bullet had skinned him while he'd been working the Brandt case. Cap tapped it like a roadie testing a microphone.

"Not too pretty but still works," he said.

Vega nodded, kept looking at it.

"How's Nell?" she said.

Cap paused and then said, "Good. She's good."

Vega reared back, concerned.

"What's wrong?" she said.

"Nothing's wrong. Nell's fine."

"You're lying," said Vega. "What's wrong with Nell?"

Cap rubbed his eyebrows and sighed hotly.

"She's fine, ultimately. She's just exhibiting typical behaviors of having undergone a traumatic event."

"Drugs?" said Vega.

"No, not drugs."

"Boys?" said Vega with a hint of aggression, as if she wanted to locate these boys immediately.

"No," said Cap. "She . . . dresses differently, wears a lot of eye makeup. Dyed her hair black. She got pulled over for speeding, by Ralz, no less."

Vega stared at him.

"So eyeliner and a speeding ticket," she said.

Cap laughed a little.

"Actually, she didn't even get a ticket."

Vega narrowed her eyes and said, "She'll be okay then."

"Yeah, she will," Cap said, exhaling.

It was nice to hear it from her and nice to believe it.

Vega put on her sunglasses, and Cap sensed that was it for the small talk.

"We going to look through these for the two candidates?" he said, holding out the stack of paper Palomino had given them.

"No, it's Wednesday," Vega said, heading for her car at the curb.

"What's Wednesday?" said Cap, feeling like he was missing something.

Vega opened her driver's side door.

"Comes before Thursday," she called over the street traffic.

"Right," said Cap, raising his voice. "And what's Thursday?"

"Recycling day," she called back to him. "Follow me, okay?"

Cap said okay.

They drove for about two hours east, away from the water and the airport. Cap watched as the buildings disappeared and the land surrounding the interstate got brown with bursts of desert shrubbery. On the East Coast you could go from New York to Jersey to Pennsylvania, see the same kind of ash trees, drive two hundred miles without any discernible change in the landscape. Here the progression happened so quickly, he thought: ocean, city, desert.

Cap followed her as she took the exit for a town called El Centro. As he got to street level, it felt a little more like Denville than San Diego had—more run down block by block, more vape pipes, fewer macchia-tos. But still palm trees, glass blue sky, the mild heat that rested on the surface of his skin.

Vega led him to the parking lot of a strip mall that appeared aban-doned, or getting there. She pulled into a row of spaces facing a two-way roadway and, past that, a residential street. He parked alongside her, and they both got out.

"Late lunch?" he said, eyeing the China Buffet.

"Looking for a witness," said Vega, locking her door. "Evidence sug-gests Jane One was killed and then dumped in a car, stolen from the street over there."

Vega pointed.

"Apple Street, right?" Cap said, remembering.

"Right."

"PD said no witnesses," said Cap.

Vega ignored that and started to walk away, toward the China Buffet.

"We're going back here," she said.

Cap followed, around the restaurant, where there was some wild grass and a dumpster. Vega cut through the grass on a diagonal and stopped on the far side of the dumpster, where there was a blanket on the ground and a stuffed black garbage bag. Vega tapped the bag with her foot. Cans.

"Let's get in my car," she said.

"Okay."

Vega's car was a gray Honda, and nothing about it gave Cap any fur-ther clues to her inner workings. Nothing hanging from the rearview, no bumper stickers, no noticeable dents, no debris from pets. It was moderately clean, the paint scratched here and there, dirt and gravel scrapes on the tires and wheel wells.

She pulled out of the lot and drove across the divide to Apple Street. She slowed to ten miles an hour and turned the corner onto another residential block. Cap read all the houses as lower middle class, one floor with front yards and hacienda-style details.

"Who are we looking for?" he said.

Vega peered over the wheel to the sidewalk.

"The Can Man," she said.

"The Can Man," Cap repeated.

Around and around they went. Not a lot of people on the street. A couple of kids on bicycles, a couple people flipping through mail. After about twenty minutes, Cap saw who he assumed to be the Can Man. The guy was short, dark-skinned, and Asian, a bandanna over his head pirate-style and jeans rolled up to his knees like he'd been wading in a lake. He was sifting through a blue recycle bin on the side of a driveway and picking out cans and bottles, placing them in a wheeled cart lined with a black garbage bag.

"That him?" said Cap.

"Think so."

Vega parked at the curb, and they got out and watched the Can Man work. He glanced at them.

"They know me," he said, not looking up from the cart. "People who live here. Not trespassing."

"We're not handing out tickets," said Cap.

The Can Man ignored them then. Cap caught Vega's eye. How do you want to do this?

"You know anything about a blue Ford Focus?" Vega said to him.

The Can Man continued to sort and said, "Nope."

"You didn't see a car like that get stolen last week?" said Vega. "From Apple Street?"

He leaned over his cart and pressed the cans down with open palms. It sounded like little keys scraping little car doors.

"The fat kid tell you?" he said, not looking up.

"He wasn't that fat," said Vega, a little protective. "But yeah."

The Can Man tied the top of the bag up in a loose knot.

"He's got an imagination," he said.

Then he started to roll out of the driveway, pushing the cart past Cap and Vega to the next driveway.

"Do you want some money?" said Vega.

The Can Man stopped.

"Sure," he said.

He flipped the lid on the recycle bin and opened the bag inside. Vega pulled out her wallet, counted five twenties. She folded them in half and walked a few steps, held it out to him.

He peered at the money in her hand and said, "Got any more?"

Vega didn't move, stood right there with her arm extended.

"No."

The Can Man wiped his eyebrows with his forearm, pinched and tugged the edge of the bandanna down.

"Okay," he said, taking the money.

He tucked the bills into the back pocket of his jeans.

"Driver door was unlocked. Big Mexican. He just got in and drove away."

The Can Man stopped talking, turned back to the recycle bin.

Cap glanced at Vega. She was staring at a point past the Can Man's head and waved her hand at Cap like she was directing traffic. Telling him to talk now because she needed to think.

"Do you remember what he was wearing?" said Cap.

The Can Man shook his head.

"Nah. I only noticed him 'cause I know the guy who owns the car and that wasn't him."

"You tell the owner?" said Cap.

"I thought he knew Duffy. 'Cause he opened the door. Thought Duffy knew him."

"Duffy's the owner," said Cap, clarifying.

"Yeah."

"You remember anything else about the Mexican—how tall do you think?"

"Over six foot. Big this way, too," he said, holding his arms out to the sides. "More muscles than fat."

"Okay," said Cap. "You remember anything else about him? Haircut, tattoos?"

The Can Man shrugged.

"Nah," he said. "I didn't see him too well. I was pulling my cart in for the night across the street."

"By the China Buffet?"

The Can Man nodded. Cap got the feeling he wasn't lying. Some people, few people, had no reason to. The Can Man struck Cap as one of them.

"Could you say that again?" Vega said.

Cap and the Can Man looked at her.

"About the hair?" said the Can Man.

"No, no," said Vega.

Cap knew her expression—she was impatient, annoyed, but only at herself for not finding the answer quicker.

"Before," she said. "What you said to me. Exactly what you said to me about how you thought the big guy knew Duffy."

The Can Man glanced at Cap, a little confused. Cap rolled one shoulder in a shrug. I don't know where she's going, Can Man.

" 'Cause he opened the door?"

"Yeah," Vega said, pointing at him. "That's it."

The Can Man tugged at his bandanna again.

"I thought Duffy left it unlocked for him," he said slowly.

Cap watched Vega's face for clues. All three of them were quiet. The Can Man did not return to the recycle bin. He was waiting now too, to see what Vega would do next.

"So you saw the big Mexican walk up to the Ford Focus and open the door?" she said.

"Yeah."

"He walks up to the car and opens the door."

"Yeah," said the Can Man, getting a little irritated.

"What did he do right before that?" Vega said, moving her hand, directing traffic again. Back it up.

"I . . . you know, he went up to the car."

Suddenly Cap understood where Vega was going. Why it took him so long he didn't know.

"Where did he come from, though?" said Cap. "Did he get out of another car?"

"Ah," said the Can Man. "I didn't see that. I was pushing the cart around to my place, and when I look up, I see him walking. I don't know where he came from."

"You don't remember hearing another car door shut," said Cap.

"No, I don't know. I just happen to look over there and see him go up to the car."

"He goes up to *that* car," said Vega.

"That one car," said Cap.

"Yes, Jesus," said the Can Man, exasperated. "That one car."

He went back to the bin, and Cap and Vega looked at each other, and there was the old click. Cap thought if he were to ask Vega to describe it, she would say it was like a magazine locking into place after reloading rounds. Cap's was a littler gentler—a child's wooden puzzle piece, peg for a handle, the chicken or the barn or the fire truck landing in a space cut just for it.

At the Hampton Inn, Vega stood in the room she had booked for Cap next to hers. She leaned against the door and thought as he unpacked basics from his small wheeled suitcase. She was watching him in the sense that her eyes were following his movements but she wasn't paying too much attention, her mind skittering across list after list.

Cap was talking, rattling off narrative, which was his way to get a handle.

"Big Mexican walks right up to the car, doesn't try any other doors on any other cars, as far as the Can Man sees, and this door on this car happens to be unlocked."

"Yeah," said Vega, pushing off the door with her elbows.

"So someone left it unlocked for him," said Cap, holding a jar of vitamins. "And PD didn't figure this because . . ."

"Duffy the owner reported it stolen," Vega said.

She sat at a small table against the wall.

"And PD didn't push because they don't know the thief walks up to that one car specifically," said Cap.

"No evidence of forced entry, but they figure user error," said Vega. "And they don't have the Can Man."

She pushed aside the binder full of ads for local attractions and began to sort through all the paper that Palomino had given them.

"They don't have the Can Man," repeated Cap. "Still . . ."

He stopped speaking and stared at the vitamins.

"Still?" said Vega.

Cap did the thing where he let his head wobble side to side on top of his neck, as if he were literally bouncing between two ideas.

"Let's say Duffy knows the Big Mexican and leaves the door unlocked for him. Don't you think PD would get to that if they asked the questions they were supposed to ask?"

"Maybe," said Vega. "They're rushing, couldn't dedicate a lot of time to it."

"Right, they're busy," said Cap. "Maybe they weren't asking because someone told them not to look too hard at it."

Vega almost said, "That's what we're here for," but she didn't have to. Cap sat on the edge of the bed and yawned. Vega shot him a stern look, and he closed his mouth and raised his hands like he was behind a bank counter in the Old West and she was Jesse James. Which made her laugh just a little bit.

6

DYLAN DUFFY OPENED THE DOOR FOR THEM WITH DRIPPING WET hair and a towel around his waist. He apologized, saying he just got home from work, invited them in, and offered them a seat on the couch in the living room. He introduced them to a girl of about ten or eleven lying on the floor with a pillow over her face.

"That's Jaylin. Jay, say hi."

Jaylin gave a wave, kept the pillow over her face.

"I'll be right back," said Duffy. "Do you want anything to drink?"

Cap said no thanks, and Vega shook her head.

Duffy jogged out of the room. Cap and Vega sat on the couch, which had wicker armrests, patterned with big tropical flowers. It squeaked under their weight.

Cap watched the girl on the floor. Her legs were crossed at the ankles, relaxed. Cap turned to Vega, but she wasn't looking at him or the girl. She was surveying the room, taking in the nubby carpet, the soft IKEA bins filled with magazines, shoes, markers, papers.

"You talk," said Vega.

"Sure."

Another few minutes passed, and Duffy returned in jeans and a muscle tee.

"Sorry," he said, putting his hand through his hair. "I work for a tree doctor. I'm a real mess when I get home."

"Thanks for taking the time," said Cap.

"Sure thing," said Duffy. "I want to help. Like to get the guy who put me out of a car."

"So the police didn't tell you the conditions in which they found your car?" said Cap.

"No, just said it was part of an investigation, like evidence, so they had to keep it. Insurance is getting me a loaner. I'm not sure how it works."

Duffy nodded as he talked, his hair dripping onto his shoulders. The girl on the floor uncrossed her ankles.

"Mr. Duffy," said Cap quietly. "Could we speak to you alone for a minute?"

Duffy appeared confused. Cap nodded toward the girl.

"Oh, yeah," said Duffy, realizing. "Jay, go practice in your room awhile." Then, to Cap and Vega, "She's really into sensory deprivation."

The girl removed the pillow from her face and stood up.

"Now I have to start over," she said to Duffy.

"They're with the police," said Duffy emphatically. "Official police business!"

The girl remained unimpressed. She glanced back at Cap and Vega and left the room, dragging the pillow behind her.

After she had gone, Duffy said, "You were saying, about how they found the car?"

"They found a body in it," said Vega.

"No shit," said Duffy with an appropriate degree of awe. "That's fucking crazy, excuse me."

"Yeah," said Cap. "We don't know if the thief is the murderer but he is certainly a suspect. And we have reason to believe he knew your car would be unlocked."

Duffy nodded at him and kept nodding as the idea snaked around his head.

"Wait," he said. "My car wasn't unlocked. I always lock my car."

Cap continued: "There wasn't any substantial evidence of forced entry, and we have an eyewitness who says the thief opened the door without a problem."

Duffy stared at Cap, his hand on his head, processing. Cap could see him start to question himself.

"Look," he said hoarsely. "If I didn't lock my car, it would've been the first time, okay?"

"So you think the thief got lucky?" said Cap, only a little skeptical.

"No," said Duffy, sounding pained. "I don't know. I know it doesn't make sense."

Cap smiled at him. He sounded honest and confused.

"That's why we're here, Mr. Duffy," he said. "To try and figure it out. Why don't we start somewhere else? Why do you park the car on the street to begin with and not in your garage or your driveway?"

"My wife, she's an RN, she works second shift. I don't want to block her—I like her to park her car in the garage so she can come straight into the house. I don't want her walking around outside at midnight, one a.m., you know?"

Then he turned to Vega.

"It looks like a nice neighborhood, but we had a lot of crime the last couple of years. Carjackings, stuff like that."

Vega gave him a small commiserative nod.

Then she said, "Could we talk to your son?"

Duffy looked from Vega to Cap and wiped his hands on his jeans.

"My son?" he repeated.

"Yeah, your son," said Vega. "He's about fifteen, right?"

"Um, yeah. But he's not here—he's at a friend's house, you know?"

"When will he be back?" said Vega.

"I think he's sleeping over, so tomorrow morning probably," Duffy said, squirming around in his chair. "He doesn't even drive yet. I don't know what he could tell you."

"Probably nothing," said Cap generously. "Sometimes we notice things and we don't realize we're noticing them."

Duffy smiled, grateful.

"We'll come back then," said Vega, standing up. "Tomorrow morning."

"Oh, okay, sure thing," said Duffy, jumping to his feet. "I'll, uh, walk you out."

He followed them to the door, and they all shook hands and said goodbye. The temperature had dropped at least ten degrees, the sun rolling down fast, sky lit up with pinks. Cap waited until they were in Vega's car to speak.

"How'd you know he had a son?" he said. "I didn't see any Shakespeare."

"The paper recycling outside," said Vega, starting the car. "I saw it as we went in. There was a drug-test box in there, over the counter. I don't think it's for the girl."

"No," said Cap. "And not for the parents. But how'd you peg fifteen-year-old boy?"

"Figured it was a teenager under sixteen because police might have covered that if there was another licensed driver in the house," she said, pulling away from the curb. "Had to be a boy."

"Why?" said Cap. "Girls smoke pot, too."

Vega peered at the upcoming intersection and moved her jaw from side to side.

"Teenage boys, even the smart ones, are led around by their dicks.

Unless they get into drugs. Girls are more likely to binge-drink and have eating disorders."

Cap almost began to argue and then thought better of it.

"Goddammit, you're right."

Vega rolled down her window and stuck her hand out, wiggled her fingers in the warm air.

"You think Duffy's telling the truth?" she said.

Cap thought about it, remembered the eager nods, the genuine shock. "I do."

"I do, too," said Vega.

"So first thing tomorrow morning we go back?"

"Yeah."

"And wait for the Bastard," Cap added.

"Heard from him already," Vega said, glancing at her phone. "Got some addresses. X-ray tech, Antonio LoSanto, in Santee—suburb of San Diego. Dr. Scott Miller's in Escondido—nicer suburb."

They stopped at a light, and Vega leaned back, stretched her neck out, took her hands off the wheel.

"We could split up tonight and go see them," she said. "If you think you can stay awake."

Cap turned to her and saw she was giving him a side eye, waiting for his response.

"I truly appreciate your concern," he said. "I think I can handle it."

She nodded, didn't smile but didn't scowl, eyes on the road. The light changed to green, and she drove.

Cap didn't tell her he actually did feel the weight of the jet lag coming down on him as if it were the end of the night on the East Coast and not the beginning on the West, his lower back and foot arches aching, throat scratchy, eyes dry and heavy. But being with Vega while her brain snapped and curled like flames in a fireplace was enough to keep him awake for at least the next few hours, he thought. Better than Red Bull.

Vega got to Santee around eight. The sun had just slipped down, the air light and cool. The X-ray tech lived in a condo complex on a quiet block. Vega parked in a spot marked SUNRISE TRAILS APARTMENTS—VISITOR, got out, and began to look around.

Vega walked along a small paved path, saw the flickers of TVs through windows, noticed all the ground-floor units had small walled decks; second- and third-floor units had narrow balconies. The X-ray tech's condo was on the ground floor. Number 107. Vega followed the path to the door, thought she smelled something sweet. Powdered sugar and frosting floating around the air like in an amusement park.

She pressed the bell, heard it buzz inside. When there was no answer, voice, footstep, she buzzed once more. Then she knocked, lightly at first with a tap of her knuckles, then pounded her fist. Still no one, nothing. She tried to peer along the sides of the synthetic bamboo blinds hanging in the window.

A text from Cap came through: "Here. No one home. Staking out."

Vega backed up off the path, thought about how long she wanted to wait. She tilted her head and let her eyes drift to the three-sided cinder-block wall to the side of LoSanto's condo, which, Vega assumed, must be surrounding LoSanto's deck.

She crossed the small strip of grass separating the path from the parking lot and came to the deck wall, about six feet tall. She reached up and touched the top. It had been a long time since she went up a wall, but the principles had to be the same. Run, drive hard through right leg and push, grab the top, jam, and run up with the left leg to avoid the dead hang.

Then she heard a cough.

"Hello?" Vega called.

There was no answer.

"Mr. LoSanto?" she said, stretching her hand up and waving so that whoever was on the other side of the wall could at least see her fingers.

Vega could sense motion. Then she heard the catch of air through the person's nose, the scrape from a patio chair on the ground.

"Who's there?"

The voice was female, young, high-pitched.

"I'm looking for Antonio LoSanto," said Vega.

"He's not here," said the girl.

Vega took her wallet from her pocket.

"I'm a private investigator with the SDPD," she said, holding up her PI license.

She didn't flash it often. Usually there was no need if she could see the person's eyes, and the person could see hers. Usually people just tended to believe her.

The girl paused, then said, "Come around front."

Vega went around, across the grass to the path, up to the front door. She heard the snap of a sliding door, footsteps, lock clicking open and then the door.

The girl was in her twenties, Latina, pudgy in a babyish way with a round face, hair pulled tight back. She held a phone, earbuds still connected and dangling.

"Sorry I didn't hear you. Headphones," she said, holding them up.

Vega nodded with a tight smile.

"Alice Vega. Is Antonio LoSanto here?"

"No, he's not home."

"Do you know when he'll be back?"

"In a while," the girl said. "He's at work."

"Can you tell me where his place of business is?" said Vega. "I need to speak with him right away."

The girl flipped her ponytail up, as if it had been caught inside the collar of her hoodie. She laughed nervously.

"I'm just, I'm really not supposed to bother him at work."

"Got it," said Vega. "If you have a minute, could I ask you a couple of questions?"

"Me?" the girl said. "I don't know anything."

Scared, thought Vega. Be nice. Cat with a feather.

"Look," said Vega, bending her knees, letting her head fall an inch to one side to appear casual. "I'm staying out in El Centro. Do you mind," Vega hedged. "Just a couple of general questions, and then I won't have to come back and bother either of you?"

The girl blinked a few times, eyelashes fluttering.

"They're just some timing questions, like when he worked certain places."

The girl turned her phone around in her hands.

"You wouldn't even have to tell him about it," Vega added.

"What's it about?" said the girl shyly.

She was almost there, thought Vega. Saying to herself, This is something I can take care of, take a load off his tense shoulders. Which meant she, the girl, thought of other people before herself, at least sometimes. So make it easy for her. No big deal.

"Taxes," said Vega. "One of his past employers may not have paid all their taxes. We're questioning all the employees, see if they have any knowledge of it either way." Vega shrugged. "Just standard procedure."

The girl nodded, seemed pleased at how standard it sounded. She opened the door and let Vega in. The furniture was nice enough but not a lot of it. Suede couch, low table with unopened mail, flat screen, handheld Nintendo. Clean beige carpet. Blank walls except for a big framed watercolor of the ocean crashing onto a beach. Blurry blue swirls on a tan swath.

The girl sat on the couch, and Vega stood, staring at the painting. The girl glanced at a vape pipe on the table, a small pink bottle next to it. She seemed self-conscious, maybe embarrassed about vaping in front of someone official.

"You can, um, sit," she said. "Do you want a Diet Coke?"

Vega shook her head and sat, pulled out her phone and scrolled through her emails, pretending to read and remember things.

"So let's see," she said. "Your name, please."

"Sarita Guerra."

"Ms. Guerra. You've been living with Mr. LoSanto how long?"

"Oh, I don't live here," she said emphatically. "We're just boyfriend-girlfriend."

"Okay," said Vega. "That makes sense."

She kept scrolling down the screen, squinting. She took the pen from her inside pocket and clicked it. She had a feeling Sarita wouldn't notice she didn't have anything to write on. Nervous respondents just want to talk and defend themselves; they are not noticing details.

"So did you, were you together with Mr. LoSanto when he worked at Bay Free Health Clinic over on Mission?"

"Yeah," Sarita said. "Well, we met, like, six months ago, so I didn't know him when he started that job but I knew him when he quit."

She nodded along with her own memory. Truth, thought Vega.

"Okay," said Vega. "And do you remember when he left that job?"

"Yeah, it was like, right before Easter, so April, I guess?" Sarita said, ending with a question to herself perhaps.

"April, okay," said Vega.

Then she looked up, cocked her head to one side, and feigned confusion.

"Why did he leave?" Vega said.

Sarita stared at her blankly.

"Seems like a good cause and everything," Vega added with a shrug.

"I don't think they gave him enough hours?" Sarita asked again.

Vega nodded, in case the girl was asking her if that was a sufficient answer.

Sarita went on: "He just bought this place and wanted to pay some of it off, and he was only part-time at the clinic, I think."

Vega tapped the pen on her phone, gave the girl time to think about it.

"He really didn't say," added Sarita.

"And he didn't mention anything strange he noticed when he worked there?"

Sarita shook her head, crimped ponytail swinging.

"No, I don't think so. He liked some of the people he worked with. It just seemed like regular . . ."

She paused, searching for the right word.

Finally: "Um, work."

Vega's eyes drifted up to the watercolor above Sarita's head. Sarita kept chattering nervously.

"He works hard, you know?"

The painting was big, probably three by three and a half feet, and set squarely in the middle of the wall.

"Now he can get a double shift if he wants overtime," she went on.

"And where's that?" Vega asked, still staring at the painting.

"Kenner Orthopedic?" said Sarita. "It's in La Jolla."

"Uh-huh," said Vega. "Can I use your restroom?"

"Oh, yeah," said Sarita. "It's, uh, down there," she said, pointing to a small hallway off the living room.

Vega nodded and left, eyes combing the off-white walls as she went. At the end of the hall were the bathroom and the bedroom, side by side, both doors wide open. She stayed in the hall and peeked inside the bathroom, where it was peach and beige and relatively clean. She left the door open a crack and peered toward the living room, unable to see Sarita, which meant Sarita could no longer see her.

She stuck her head into the bedroom—standard queen bed, white sheets, turned down and messy. Small bedside table with just an alarm clock. Dresser with a lamp on top.

Nothing on the walls.

Vega walked on the balls of her feet back to the bathroom, stepped inside and flushed the toilet, ran the water in the sink for a few seconds. Then she went back to the living room to ask Sarita one more question.

Sarita still sat on the couch, sucking on the vape pipe. She pulled it from her mouth as soon as Vega emerged, like she'd been caught in the stall in high school.

"I'll get out of your way," said Vega.

Sarita stood up and smoothed out the legs of her pink sweatpants.

"Can you tell me, though, how long he's had that painting?"

Sarita corkscrewed her body around to look at the watercolor. Then she turned back to Vega.

"Um, I'm not sure?" she said.

"Take a second," said Vega, brisker than before. No need for the IRS taxman act anymore.

Sarita looked at the painting again for clues.

"Maybe a few months ago?" she said.

"Maybe around April, when he quit the clinic?" offered Vega.

"Oh yeah, I think so," said Sarita, remembering. "He said he was tired of staring at the wall."

Vega came closer so she stood next to Sarita, the couch between them and the wall. Vega glanced at the girl for only a moment, and Sarita backed away, a flicker of fear passing through her eyes.

Then Vega removed her gun from the holster, kept her eyes on the painting.

"Wait," said Sarita, breath catching in her throat.

Vega ignored her and flipped the gun in her hand so the nose pointed down, grip up. She stepped onto the couch, the cushions depressing under her weight, wound her arm back, and brought it forward hard like she was pitching a ball, cracking the butt of the gun on the glass of the painting. The sound was not loud but blunt; Vega could feel resistance from the other side. The canvas was not hollow.

Sarita let out a small scream and covered her mouth right away.

The glass had cracked, not shattered, a ring of crumbled bits and spiderweb threads splintering out from the center.

"What, what are you doing?" said Sarita, voice shaking.

Vega continued to ignore her and put the gun back in the holster. She grasped the sides of the frame and carefully lifted it off the wall, stepped down from the couch, and laid the painting down, back side up, on the table.

The back of the painting was covered with brown paper and crisscrossed with packing tape. Vega ran her fingers over the paper and pressed lightly along the edges.

"Do you have any scissors?" she asked Sarita.

Sarita was in a state of stun, her hands in a knot under her chin.

"Sarita, scissors," said Vega. "Could you get some?"

"Yeah," said the girl, and she hurried into the kitchen, running into the counter on the way.

Vega heard her opening drawers and rummaging. Then Sarita started to run back, scissors in hand.

"Don't run," said Vega softly.

Sarita took the order and stumbled to a walk. She held out the scissors to Vega, handle first. Vega took them and held them over the painting, pointing the blades near the top left corner. She punctured the paper with a quick stab.

Sarita made a squeak but didn't move, rapt.

Vega sliced the paper at the top of the canvas, then a few inches down either side and peeled back the paper.

There was money there, twenty or twenty-five stacks, small denominations, wrinkled, bound by rubber bands. Vega continued to tear the paper off, saw that the stacks took up about three quarters of the canvas hollow. When she was done she stood with the paper shreds at her feet and what she estimated to be a few thousand dollars in dirty bills in front of her.

Sarita's face appeared to expand, her eyes and mouth opening up in disbelief.

Vega paused before telling her this was probably a good enough reason to bother her boyfriend at work. Might as well let her have a minute to come up with it on her own.

It had been a while since Cap had been on a stakeout. It was dark now, the temperature down a few degrees, the air smelling sweeter and feeling somehow even more pleasant on his face than it had been during daylight. Cap sat in his car with the window open across the street from the house of the former clinic doctor, which was similar to every other house on the upper-middle-class block, two floors, ivory façades with sandy red roofs. The houses on either side of the doctor's had cars in the driveways, lights on inside, but the doctor's was dark, driveway empty.

Cap sipped an iced coffee, cracked his neck both ways, remembered he used to listen to Books on Tape in the old days when he'd stake out skips and cheaters. Nonfiction mostly, American history—civil war, lives of presidents. All about little decisions and big mistakes.

He wiped the condensation from his drink on his pant leg and wrote a text to Nell:

"Hope you're asleep already but if not good night!"

He sent it, and immediately the three dots flickered back.

Then, her response: "Almost. What's happening with the case?"

Cap smiled. He couldn't help having pride in a girl he'd raised to ask infinite questions even if sometimes those questions made him want to stab himself in the eye with a number 2 pencil.

"Nothing yet. On a stakeout. Boring," he sent back.

He glanced up at the house and the quiet street. Heard crickets and a strange bird. The phone buzzed in his palm.

"How's Alice?"

He typed and sent: "Good. The same."

The three dots flickered for only a moment, and her response came back:

If that was meant as a sentiment from Nell to him directly, or as a reaction to him describing Vega, he didn't know. He decided to change the subject.

"Hey—is 'emoji' plural?"

A brief pause, then, "Good night, dad. xoxo."

Cap grinned and set his phone down in the cup holder under the HVAC knobs. He waited. Every once in a while a car cruised by, and he ducked his head. It seemed like the type of neighborhood where a strange guy waiting in a parked car might get noticed.

Around ten he saw a dark SUV approaching in his side mirror. There was a reflective sunshade covering the windshield—odd at night, he thought. He started to slide down in his seat but quickly realized whoever was driving would easily see him if he was looking. So Plan B— Cap brought up Google Maps on his phone, put on a brow furrow like Bert from *Sesame Street,* and made like a lost tourist.

The SUV passed, and Cap watched it turn the corner up ahead. Then he waited some more.

Nine became ten, which was 1:00 a.m. on the East Coast, and Cap felt it in every muscle and joint. He sucked whatever moisture was left on the bottom of the iced coffee cup and rubbed his face up and down with his open palm.

His phone read 10:11. He opened up the CNN app and attempted to read. The letters crowded one another, and the glare from the screen stung his eyes. His reading glasses lay in their case on the bed back at the Hampton Inn.

He shut his eyes and pinched the bridge of his nose, tears beading at the corners of his lids, and his mind wandered quickly, breathing in the fragrant air nice and deep, thinking about how loud those crickets were, strange that he could hear them from his bed at home in Denville, window closed and the AC whirring. How he'd finally managed to hit the perfect temperature with the central air he had no idea—not too cold, not too hot, gentle fanning breeze on his face. Was that Nell on the phone in the next room, whispering, upset?

Cap shook himself awake.

The doctor was home.

Cap sat up straight and leaned back, staying hidden. The doctor, wearing a dark suit, and a woman in a blue evening gown with her hair pinned up in a delicate twist stood on either side of a silver Audi, doors open. It was the woman (the doctor's wife, Cap assumed) whose voice had spilled into Cap's half dream. She was whispering, but her voice was raised and strained. Instinctively, Cap pulled his pocket DVR from his jacket and rested it on the window runner. It was a holdover from his older PI days of tracking cheaters—always have tape. He considered himself old-fashioned, didn't want to rely solely on his phone.

The doctor tried to take his wife's arm as they walked up their driveway, but she yanked it away and stumbled. Cap couldn't make out exactly what she was saying, but he pulled the focus on their faces as tight as it would go, figuring later he could read her lips and jack up the sound. He wasn't sure but he thought the end of her sentence was "Trust you."

Now this really did remind him of the old days. Lovers' spat, faithless spouses, cuckolds, and "How dare you make a fool out of me." That always surprised Cap—when he broke the news Hubs or Sweetums was cheating, how the sharpest sting for the cheated-on was not actually being cheated on but the embarrassment, the shame, feeling stupid, silly, old.

The doctor got ahold of the wife's arm at the elbow. Cap couldn't quite read the expression on his face. It was blanker than he would've expected, like this was something rote. Business as usual.

The wife tilted back on her heels and then steadied herself. She struggled against the doctor for a moment but then didn't fight, allowed him to guide her. Motion lights flicked on at their feet as they proceeded up the path to the house. The doctor unlocked the front door, and in they went.

Cap tapped Pause on the DVR and checked his phone. 11:09 p.m. But also a text from Vega, which had come through twenty minutes earlier, when he'd been dozing.

"Brake on the doc. Got something here."

There was a photo. It appeared to be a box or a bag ripped open with a bunch of money inside. Cap chuckled to himself.

He wrote back: "That is something. You need backup?"

Her answer shot back quickly.

"No. Get some sleep."

Cap tapped the screen. Miss Vega doesn't need your help, thanks for asking. He stretched out his arms and legs quickly, like an oversize starfish, and released. Slapped his cheeks a little bit to get the blood flowing and started the car, turned on the GPS audio, and let the nice lady tell him how to get back to the hotel. He sped down the empty streets and spare freeways, his rental cutting through the warm air like a skiff on a river.

Sarita sat on the couch vaping sadly, wiping away the occasional tear. Vega stood with her back flush against the kitchen counter. Both of them stared at the money. Sarita had stopped speaking about a half hour before, after furiously texting and leaving multiple messages for LoSanto.

And then the shine of headlights flashed through the sliding glass doors. Sarita sat up at attention.

"That's him," she said.

Vega nodded and kept her eyes fixed on the front door. She heard a car door slam outside, then running steps, and then the door flew open.

Antonio LoSanto came inside, short and stocky with a buzz cut, dressed in navy blue scrubs. He was breathing heavily, his eyes bouncing from Vega to the money to Sarita, who didn't move.

"Sarita," he said between gasps. "Go in the other room."

Sarita stood and walked past Vega to leave the room. She peeked at Vega once, and then her head dipped down as she hurried away. You don't have to do everything he says, girl, Vega tried to tell her in the second their eyes met. But then she was gone.

Vega heard the bedroom door shut, and then she and LoSanto stood looking at each other some more. The scent of cotton candy stayed in the air. LoSanto's breathing slowed down, and he ran a hand over the back of his neck.

"You have a warrant, I'd like to see it," he said finally.

"I don't need a warrant. I'm not a cop," said Vega.

LoSanto moved his hands to his hips, stood up a little straighter. Gonna get tough now, thought Vega.

"Then I could call the cops right now. You're trespassing."

"Your girlfriend invited me in and offered me a Diet Coke," said Vega.

LoSanto didn't flinch.

"Who are you, then?" he said.

"Name's Vega."

"What do you want, Vega?" he asked, eyes drifting.

Vega followed his gaze to the money.

"I'm a private investigator working with the police," she said.

LoSanto sneered, bristling at his options.

"Then I could call the police right now and tell them you conned your way into my house, they gonna know all about you?"

Vega waited a second before answering.

"Yes, that's right."

"I don't have to tell you a damn thing," he said, as if he were convincing himself of the truth of the statement.

"Sure," said Vega. "You don't have to talk to me or the police or a lawyer or a judge." She nodded to the rows of money in the cut-up canvas on the table and continued: "You let the prints and serial numbers on those dirty dollars do the talking, and you can keep quiet when you're in Lompoc and the boys are arm-wrestling over who gets a shy flower like yourself first."

LoSanto froze, and he unlocked his gaze from Vega's. She sensed the intensity in the room siphoning out like a tire's slow leak. LoSanto ran his hands over his hair and sighed. His limbs seemed to loosen up as well, and Vega knew he was about to start talking. Sometimes all it took was a little hit of truth.

7

CAP SAT UP, AWAKE AND CONFUSED IN A STRANGE ROOM. HE KICKED the thin covers off and looked at the clock blaring 5:23 in red. California, he thought. You're in California, and your body thinks it's 8:23. He scratched his face and head all over and yawned theatrically, as if he wanted to prove to himself he was truly awake now.

He got out of bed and went to the window, pulled the curtains open. It was still dark outside, the sky only hinting at lighter shades of blue in the distance. He turned on the lamps on the table and by the bed and took a shower, shaved with the kit he'd bought in the airport. So small, he thought, why is everything so small; he could barely hold the razor. Then he grinned, thinking if Nell could hear him she'd say, "They sure don't make 'em like they used to, hey, Old Man Caplan?"

By the time he was done it was almost six, and he was in urgent need of coffee.

He stepped outside his room and leaned over the railing for a minute. The sky was brighter now, a yellow and orange pool gathering at the center, where the sun would be coming up soon. The air smelled like fresh, wet flowers.

He headed for the stairs, pausing by Vega's room on the way. He glanced at the window on the chance he might see a light on. He knew Vega was an early riser or, more specifically, a seldom sleeper, could just shut her eyes for an hour or two and then get to work and be efficient, was able to deduce and surmise and think rationally with the right amount of hunch.

The curtains were mostly closed, but there was a gap in the middle, a couple of inches wide. Cap looked in. He didn't even think about not looking in. His heart thumped and skipped—suddenly he was aware of it, and his eyes adjusted to what he thought he was seeing.

There, in the middle of the room, was Vega doing a handstand. The lights were off, but Cap could make out the shape of her body and could tell she was clothed. She was facing away from him, toward her bed, her hair draped onto the carpet below. And she wasn't moving.

Cap stood still and watched her five, six, seven minutes. How could she hold it that long, he thought. The sun crept up behind him as he stood there, Vega's bare arms wrapped in a soft gray light. He could see the contours of her muscles, and the taut tendons leading to her wrists.

Then she came down.

It was graceful but quick, one leg swung to the floor and then the other, and as she began to roll her spine upright, Cap panicked and jumped to the side, pressed his back against Vega's door, and held his breath. Please don't let her have heard me, he thought, letting the anxiety run a few laps. Please don't let her think I'm a fucking giant perv. He froze for a few minutes, and the sun was rushing up now, hot on his face.

Vega heard something.

She broke from the handstand and came down quicker than usual, felt the weird chill of the blood escaping her head and wiggled her fingers. She went to the window and peered through the gap between the curtains, then opened them all the way.

No one.

The sun was up and blurry with heat. Vega let it warm her face for a moment and then closed the curtains fast, making sure there wasn't any space between them this time.

She took a shower and got dressed, brushed her wet hair and tied it in a knot at the base of her forehead. Socks and boots. Shoulder holster, one arm, then the other. Springfield on one side. Mag on the other. Then she heard a knock.

She looked through the peephole and then opened the door to Cap. He held a cardboard tray with two cups and a white paper bag.

"Options," he said, shaking the bag.

Vega nodded and cracked a smile, moved aside so he could come in. Cap set the tray on the table and opened the bag, pulled out a small brown sack and a Clif bar.

"Egg whites, turkey bacon on an English muffin, I think," he said, flicking the lip of the brown sack open with his finger. "Or crunchy peanut butter power bar."

"Bar," said Vega, tightening the strap on her right shoulder so that the Springfield fit just under her armpit.

Cap tossed her the bar, and she caught it with one hand.

"How did I know?" he said, removing the sandwich from the sack. "And tea, China something?"

"Thanks."

She went to the wall rack in the corner, where her jacket hung, pulled it off the hanger, and slid it on.

"We just showing up at Duffy's?" said Cap, taking a bite of sandwich.

"Think so," said Vega. "Before anyone goes to work."

He nodded, mouth full, and chewed quickly, holding a fist over his lips. He swallowed and said, "What did LoSanto have to say about all that money?"

Vega tugged the bottom flaps of her jacket to straighten it.

"Six months ago, he got an anonymous email. Gave a handle, no name, knew who LoSanto was and where he worked, offered him a way to make some money. Gave him a number to call. Guy said he'd pay under the table for IUDs. LoSanto didn't get along with Palomino, thought this was a good way to stick it to her, and doesn't have a problem with making money."

"He take them all at once?" Cap said, sipping his coffee.

"Over a few months," said Vega, taking her keys and phone from the bedside table.

"Did he actually do the procedures?" Cap asked, wincing in doubt.

"No," said Vega. "Said he just provided the equipment."

"Why not bank the money?" asked Cap, handing Vega the tea as she passed him. "It didn't look like that much."

"It wasn't, but the payer told him not to. Said to stash it instead and spend it piecemeal. LoSanto didn't ask, didn't care."

Vega took a too-big sip of tea, and a few scalding drops landed on her tongue.

"He claims he never saw the payer, that it was a blind drop-off. Suitcase on a street kind of thing."

"You believe him?" said Cap, as they left the room together.

"Yeah. He wasn't going to lie to me," Vega said.

"He give you a name?"

"Yeah but might be a fake. Email and number too."

They headed to the parking lot, the staircase rattling under their weight.

"Ride together?" said Cap.

"Yeah," said Vega, walking to her car. "LoSanto claims he hasn't had contact in at least six months since he left the job. If that's true, doubtful we'll get any hits from the email or cell."

Vega unlocked her car, and she and Cap got in.

"I sent everything to Otero's detective, guy named McTiernan. He's going to pick LoSanto up."

"Everything?" said Cap, buckling his seatbelt.

The car was filled with the smell of Cap's egg sandwich. Vega didn't eat a lot and didn't care for the smell of food unless she happened to be eating it. She started the car and quickly powered down the windows.

"Almost," she said, taking another sip of tea.

It was only a little cooler now, but she didn't mind the heat on her throat.

"Almost?" said Cap, a little tease to his voice. "Holding back from the client, hmm."

Vega pressed her cup into the holder, put on her sunglasses and seatbelt. She allowed him to mock her a little, and still she knew she had to tell him the truth behind her thinking. She had brought him here, and he was the closest thing to a partner she'd ever had.

"There's a lot they're not telling me," she said. "They answered my questions, but there's still a lot that doesn't fit."

"Like why you, why the DL, why the cash," said Cap.

"Yes, yes, yes."

"So you figure," Cap said, lifting the edge of the lid off his cup, steam framing his face, "they hold back, we hold back."

"Something like that."

Vega had not matched her thoughts to words until that moment. She recalled Boyce's arrogance, Mackey's sheepishness, Otero's eventual complacency, the that's-the-way-it-is-ness. She knew she would tell them what they needed to know only when they needed to know it and use whatever resources they'd give her in the meantime.

She realized Cap was staring at her while he sipped his coffee. Studying her.

"You okay with that," she said, allowing the last word to inflect up just the tiniest bit to indicate a question instead of an assumption. Or an order.

"Me?" said Cap boisterously. "I'm the cop, remember. I don't tell anyone anything. Not a goddamn thing." He took a bite of his sandwich and held it up to Vega in a toast. "I'm great at that."

Vega pulled out of the space and turned the car around, headed for the lot's exit. She knew he was being funny but she didn't have an urge to reward him this time, so she didn't. She was thinking of the next thing, and the next, of Duffy and his son, the men that licked their thumbs and counted out the money for LoSanto, and the girls they were standing on while they did it.

They were at Duffy's door and heard yelling. Two voices—one male, one female. Mostly profanity. Cap and Vega glanced at each other.

"You can start," said Vega, pressing the bell.

"You planning to finish?" said Cap.

Vega dropped her arms to her sides, and the fingers on her right hand rippled like a little wave.

"Sure," she said, and then the door opened.

It was the young girl, still in pajamas. She wore Beats headphones and didn't speak, just stood to the side so Cap and Vega could come in.

The yelling stopped suddenly. Cap and Vega walked into the living room, and there was Duffy in blue coveralls ready for work and Mrs. Duffy in leggings and a windbreaker.

"Hi," said Duffy, his face flushed and glinting from a light sweat. "This is, uh, my wife, Tamsin."

"Max Caplan," said Cap, giving her a sturdy nod and wave.

Cap thought there were certain moments when it felt like an imposition to stick out his hand and expect physical contact, and this was one.

"This is Alice Vega," he said.

Vega nodded, didn't wave. Not a waver, thought Cap.

Tamsin Duffy had short blond hair with eyebrows and lashes so fair they blended with her skin, which was a pale pink, her eyes seemingly too big for their sockets.

"What is this about?" she said to Cap impatiently.

Cap quickly tried to unpack the moments that had come before he and Vega arrived. Duffy and Mrs. had been fighting, but why—either she was upset that Cap and Vega would dare question her angel or that the little shit had really stepped in it this time. Or maybe she was just a wheel gripper in traffic all the time, why-me-why-me twenty-four-seven-three-six-five.

"We think your vehicle may have been left unlocked on purpose," said Cap plainly.

Tamsin frowned, eyes became even bigger.

"We don't do that," she said. "We never leave our cars unlocked . . ."

"Understood," said Cap. "I don't either unless I'm very distracted. As we explained to Mr. Duffy last night, we'd like to ask your son if he might know anything about that."

Tamsin shook her head but not saying no. She huffed out a sigh and then screamed, "Logan!"

The house was silent except for a television on somewhere. The poppy tunes of toy commercials. No one appeared.

"Goddammit," she said through her teeth, then left the room, down a hallway.

Cap heard her yell again: "Logan! Get the fuck out here." Then, the slap of a palm against a door. Then, the door opened and Cap heard, *What the hell, psycho?*

Dylan Duffy rubbed his mouth and stared at the ground.

Whispering, then the boy in a high adolescent whine: "I don't even drive."

"They're the police and they need to talk to you!" yelled Tamsin.

"Yeah, heard you," said the boy dismissively, as he emerged from the hallway with his mother behind him.

Black T-shirt, blue jeans, cheeks speckled with acne. Tamsin's face was red, eyes about to pop like those of a squeezed stress doll.

"Hi, Logan," said Cap, congenial but not enthusiastic. "I'm Max Caplan. This is Alice Vega. We'd like to ask you some questions about your dad's car."

"I don't have a license," said Logan, pushing limp bangs off his face.

"Right," said Cap. He glanced around the room. "Why don't we all sit down?"

Cap glanced around at everyone, thought they looked about as friendly as a firing squad. Vega sat first, and Cap thanked her in his head, and then he sat next to her on the couch. Duffy leaned back on the one-shelf bookcase, and Logan dropped dramatically into the wicker chair. Tamsin Duffy wasn't moving and wasn't planning to move, arms crossed, angry at the wind.

"So," said Cap, clapping his hands together lightly. "Before we start, Vega, can you do the thing with the video?"

Vega didn't flinch, stuck her chin up to signal agreement, and then held up her phone, tapped the screen, and nodded at Cap, as if they'd done this many times before.

"Hope you don't mind," said Cap politely.

Duffy and his wife glanced at each other, and Duffy shrugged. Logan sat up a bit straighter.

It was a cop trick. Once you record people, they usually go one of two ways; either they panic and start confessing or they panic and ask for lawyers. Cap had a hunch the Duffys wouldn't think they needed a lawyer just yet.

"Okay," said Cap. "So, Logan, do you ever go into your dad's car without your parents for any reason?"

The boy clenched his jaw and forced air through his nose so hard Cap was surprised he couldn't see two streams of steam.

"I already told you," he said. "I don't have a license."

"Right, no license," said Cap, turning toward the line of Vega's screen, as if he wanted to make sure she got that particular detail. "But what if, say, you leave your phone in there or something, would you grab their keys maybe and go in there to get it?"

Logan shook his head.

"Sorry," said Cap. "Could you say the word 'no' if that's your answer? For the recording," he added, nodding back to Vega.

"No," said Logan quietly. "I don't have keys."

"Uh-huh," said Cap. "Mom, Dad, you ever give Logan the keys to get something out of the car?"

Duffy cleared his throat and said, "Sure, sometimes."

"Ma'am?" said Cap to Tamsin.

Get everyone to tell the same story, he thought. Tamsin's eyes reduced slightly in circumference while she thought about it.

"Yeah, maybe."

"I have this dish on a table by the front door. It says 'keys' on it. My daughter got it for me because I'm always losing them," Cap said, smiling fondly at his audience.

Duffy grinned politely, and the muscles around Tamsin's mouth softened.

"You all have a place like that?"

Duffy spoke: "Those hooks."

He pointed to a small silver hook rack next to the front door.

"Oh, wow," said Cap. "I'm going to have to tell my daughter about that. Now that is organized."

"We don't always get them up there," conceded Duffy shyly.

Cap squinted at it. "And the hooks are thin so you can hang the, what are they, the fobs on them."

"Yeah," said Duffy.

"So, Logan," said Cap, turning his attention back to the boy. "You ever recall a time, maybe once or twice, you took the keys from that hook there and opened the door to your folks' car?"

Logan shrugged. "Maybe."

"Any time recently? Last couple of weeks?"

"No," said Logan, right away.

"You want to think about it for a minute?" said Cap, pressing his palms together. "Because we'd like you to be sure."

Logan got a snotty look, as if he suddenly felt like picking a fight.

"Yeah, I'm sure. I said that already."

"You did, didn't you," said Cap good-naturedly. "Sorry about that."

Logan didn't respond, just gave Cap a bratty stare. Cap turned to Vega and said, "He said that already, didn't he?"

"Yeah, he did," said Vega, a little reproachful, like Silly Absentminded Caplan, always forgetting something.

For some reason her tone filled Cap with joy and made him want to laugh, but he stifled it.

"And you're fifteen, correct?" said Cap.

"Yeah," Logan muttered.

"You have your learner's permit?" said Cap.

Logan huffed out a sigh.

"No."

"Why not?" said Cap, feigning confusion. He looked to Duffy and Tamsin. "Where I'm from, they make kids wait until they're sixteen to get their permits. But it's different here, right? Fifteen, fifteen and a half?"

Tamsin glared at her husband, who said, "We're waiting till Logan's sixteen to get started. No point rushing."

Logan seethed, his mouth cinched up like a drawstring on a gym bag.

"Okay, then," said Cap cheerily. "No big deal. Where was I now?"

He turned back to Vega. She peered at him from behind the phone.

"You're asking Logan if he's sure he hasn't been in the car in the past couple of weeks."

"Right," said Cap. "That's right."

Cap was quiet. He stared at a spot above Logan's head. He could see Tamsin and Duffy fidget in their spots and imagined their internal dialogue: What's he doing? Are we done? Is he going to ask anything else? Logan started squirming. The TV was still on somewhere, blaring the sounds of car wheels screeching and windshields shattering.

"So," Cap announced, bringing his palms together in a soft clap. "No learner's permit, right, and no entry into the car in the past couple of weeks, correct?"

Logan stared at him blankly.

"If that's true, Logan, could you say, 'correct'? For the video, you know?" said Cap.

Logan rolled his eyes. "Correct."

"Right. So when the labs come back with the fingerprint results, yours won't be on the driver's side door for any reason. Or on the power door lock inside," Cap said, standing.

Logan sat up quickly, suddenly at attention.

"Guess we're done then, folks," said Cap.

"Wait."

Logan stood, panic lighting his eye. "Don't go yet."

Tamsin rushed to her son and grabbed his elbow, said, "What are you talking about?" The panic had spread to her now, and Duffy too, who came off the bookcase and stood behind his wife.

"Let me—" Logan began, shaking his mother off. He stood there and breathed heavily.

"If you have anything to add, Logan," Cap said, "this would be the best time. Because down the line, there'll be cops and lawyers and reporters all talking at once. It'll be harder to hear you."

As Cap spoke, Logan started touching his face, eyebrows and lips twitching. Tamsin's nostrils flared as she crossed her arms aggressively. Duffy placed a hand on her shoulder, and she wriggled out from under it. Vega was the only one in the room not standing or moving around. She held the phone calmly, watching the red dot and the seconds creep by as the video continued to run.

"The guy told me he just needed the car for a day," said Logan finally.

"You sonofabitch," Tamsin said, and she lunged at him.

Duffy caught her in a bear hug from behind.

"What guy?" said Cap, ignoring her. He approached Logan quickly, pointed a finger at his chest. "Speak fast and accurate, Logan. I don't have my partner here because she's good with a smartphone. She will get the truth out of you if she has to remove every one of your teeth to do it."

Logan, Tamsin, and Duffy gaped at Vega and seemed to notice her for the first time, their faces filled with a mix of shock and wonder.

Vega tapped the phone to stop the recording and dropped it into her pocket, as they all watched her every move, even Cap with a soft brow and curves around his mouth, giving up the game face just for her. She stared back at all of them and didn't smile though her eyes were bright and engaged as if to say, It's true, it's all true.

Vega powered her window down as she thought and waited for Cap. She squeezed a dime between her thumb and forefinger. It almost felt like it could split from the pressure. She thought about the rush of information that had spilled out of Logan Duffy's snotty mouth and tried to make it all fit in her head. She pinched the dime harder, until the tip of her thumb was numb, and the torch and branches had made a little imprint on her skin, and then she flipped it into the cup holder. Cap came out of the Dunkin' Donuts. He squinted in the sunlight and got into the car.

"You're sure you don't want anything?" he said, buckling his seatbelt. "I can go back in."

"No thanks," said Vega.

"You talk to Otero?"

"Sent him an email."

"You want to wait to hear from him before we move forward?"

"Why would I do that?" said Vega.

Cap smirked. "I don't know, he's sort of your boss."

"I'm not waiting for him to get back from lunch or the dry cleaner to call me."

"Got it," Cap said. He was quiet for a minute while he sipped his coffee. "Just saying, now we're talking about drugs, we're talking about dealers . . . If I was working for, say, a state or federal law enforcement agency, I would think that's the kind of thing they like to be updated on."

Vega shrugged both shoulders back, bristling.

"You're my consultant, remember?" she said, looking in the rearview.

"Absolutely," said Cap. "I look forward to my 1099."

"They hired me to do this my way."

"Of course."

"That is how I'm doing it."

"Yes, and I am consulting you."

Vega nodded, and Cap grinned dumbly at her. She took out her phone and began to text.

"So," Cap said, taking a gusty breath. "What's the best way to catch a dealer?"

Vega showed him her phone. He read, "I am a friend of Logan Duffy. Need supplies."

Cap answered his own question then: "Buy whatever he's selling."

Vega put her sunglasses on and pulled out of the parking space. "I knew I hired you for a reason," she said quietly, without humor.

Cap laughed, put a fist over his mouth to stop coffee from spraying. "Vega, do you know something?"

She nodded at him, indicating he should speak.

"I missed you."

She punched the gas and muttered, "Fuck off."

The dealer's house was narrow, Cap figured not more than fifteen feet wide, one-story with bars on the two front windows and door. The street was full of houses like that, built like railroad apartments stretching back on the dirt lots as opposed to toppling row houses on concrete like in Denville. Vega parked across the street from the dealer's house.

"I'm going in alone," she said, taking off her sunglasses and looking at her eyes in the mirror.

"Come on," said Cap.

She wasn't sure if he was protesting because he was worried about her or if he didn't want to miss anything. Either way she found it foolish.

"It's conceivable that someone who looks like me would want to buy drugs," she said. "You look like you're going to a PTA meeting."

Cap snapped his seatbelt off. "First," he said, "heroin, meth, yes, I agree, but this guy sells high-end hallucinogens and sedatives, which I could conceivably be into—I could pass for an old hippie."

"Not Rohypnol," Vega countered. "No way you are roofieing yourself or others."

Cap flipped his visor mirror down and glanced at his reflection. He ran his fingertips through the little black and gray curls above his ears. Below, on the sides, he was cutting it shorter than before, Vega noticed. The gray glinted in the light.

"Okay," he conceded. "I will wait here, available for consult whenever you need me. Do you want to come up with a signal, something to let me know if you need help?"

Vega slipped her jacket off, then removed her shoulder holster and placed it on the dash. She pulled the band from her hair, which fell to her shoulders in stiff waves. Then, two bobby pins from the hair behind her ears. She dropped all the accessories into the cup holder tray.

"You're not bringing the Springfield?" said Cap in disbelief.

"Don't need it," said Vega, getting out of the car. "He's a club dealer. Was probably a weed dealer until it became legal. Just sells to stoners, party boys. No hard stuff, like you said."

She shut the door, and Cap leaned across the driver's seat so she would hear him.

"Party boys who stole a car where a girl turned up dead," said Cap.

Vega shrugged, not concerned.

"Thirty minutes," she said. "Thirty minutes, I'm not out, I don't text, you take what's in the trunk and come and get me."

She began to walk away. Cap leaned further so his head was at the window.

"What's in the trunk?" he called.

"Don't look in there unless you need to," she said.

He retreated from the window and sat back in his seat.

"Sneaky," he said out loud, but she didn't hear, already on the curb on the other side.

He watched her go. Without her jacket, he could make out more of the shape of her body than he usually could, especially her ass in the fitted black pants she always wore. Stop looking at her ass, he said to himself halfheartedly. But he didn't. He looked at it, and it was a god-damn perfect thing.

Vega rang the buzzer, then knocked softly. She heard music inside, hip-hop. The door opened, and there was a guy in his twenties with brown hair in a messy bun on his head, wearing board shorts and no shirt.

"Hey, I'm Alice," said Vega, pushing her voice up to a higher register.

"Well, hey, Alice, I'm Corey."

He opened the door for her, and she came inside. It smelled like weed, incense, maple syrup.

"You want to sit down?" he said, gesturing to a navy blue velvet couch.

"Sure," said Vega.

She sat and took a quick visual inventory of the room: a barrel-shaped brass table in front of her with one ashtray on top. A stool covered in some kind of shaggy-dog fabric. *2001* movie poster on the wall. Thick beige shades over the windows letting in a couple of inches' worth of light, giving the room a gauzy, underwater feel.

"You a friend of Duffy's?" Corey said, a hint of doubt in his tone.

"Yeah," said Vega, twisting her hands in her lap.

"So how do you know him again?"

Vega examined his face to gauge his gullibility. He was still being casual but not hiding his skepticism. Fake crooked smile, eyes narrow but alert. Chill bro, but he's watching every move for a misstep.

"It's a little complicated," said Vega shyly, brushing hair away from her face.

"Yeah?" said Corey. "I like complicated."

Tell him just enough to make him believe you, she thought.

"I'm his, uh," Vega started, letting her eyes roll up to the ceiling. "His English teacher."

Corey's mouth bloomed into a smile.

"No shit," he said, charmed.

Vega shrugged, held her breath to force a blush onto her cheeks.

"I get it, I get it," he said. "Duffy didn't do his homework because he's partying too much, and you talk to him and say, 'Fuck it.'"

"Something like that," said Vega.

Corey laughed.

"Ah, I love it," he said genuinely. "Miss Alice, all right," he said, a little flirty. Just seemed to notice she was female.

There you go, Vega said to herself. Now you got him.

She shrugged again and laughed. "That's me."

Cap checked his phone. She'd been in there five minutes. No need to worry. He'd been so distracted by her ass he hadn't really considered what she'd said about the trunk. Last time she'd hid something in the trunk it was a guy Cap had been hired to find and couldn't. It had taken Vega about a minute to locate him and drop him into her trunk hog-tied with an apple stuck in his mouth.

This was not the case now, of course. Spare magazines, an extra fire-arm or two was his guess. One way to find out.

He leaned over to the driver's side, found the button for the trunk, and pressed it with his thumb. It pushed back with some resistance, felt like the mechanism had not been triggered. No pop, no sign of the trunk rising open in the rearview. Cap pressed the button again, for a few seconds this time, and still, nothing.

He got out of the car and went around to the trunk, which was definitely not open. He squeezed the latch but it didn't click or give. Looks like your trunk's busted, girl, he thought. He turned around and leaned back on it, closed his eyes in the sun.

He tried to remember her ass in the black pants but instead the picture that kept coming back was the sculpt and contour of her white shoulders in the dim light of the hotel room.

Corey had laid out the options for sale on the barrel-shaped table. There were sealed foil blister packs, miniature Ziplocs, and a small red lacquer suitcase lined with a gunmetal foam, all containing pills, white and yellow and green, round and oval, imprinted with numbers and letters and happy faces, none bigger than a quarter.

"What's the difference between the green and white roofies?" Vega asked, turning a foil pack around in her hand.

"White's the older model," said Corey. "I mean, they still work, just dissolve quicker than the green." He picked up a small baggie filled with bright blue tablets. "These are really fun," he said, handing them to Vega. "They're like regular ex but in the last hour or so instead of winding down you get a little jump. It's like, what do you call that," he said, squinting, trying to remember something. "Time-release."

Vega nodded and grinned stupidly, still pretending to be a bougie high school teacher outside her comfort zone. She studied Corey's upper body—he was fit but not blasted. Flat stomach but no six-pack, muscle tone in his arms from bench pressing in the backyard or surfing. Maybe a few too many tacos after bong hits.

Vega took the baggie from him and fumbled with it, letting it fall from her hands to the floor.

"Sorry," she said, grabbing it. "I'm just a little nervous."

"That's cool," said Corey, smiling, showing his straight white teeth.

Teeth told her everything. His meant he grew up cushy, twice a year cleanings, braces.

"Do you, uh, do you have any pot we could smoke?" she asked tentatively. "I'll pay for it, of course," she quickly added.

Corey let out a shout of laughter. Either he found her endearing or thought she was attractive or both.

"Hell yeah," he said. "You don't have to pay me, though. I'll totally smoke a bowl with you."

He stood up and headed out of the room, flip-flops slapping the parquet floor. Before leaving the room he turned back to her and said, "You're a secret party girl, Alice."

Vega shrugged and tried her best to smile awkwardly, stretching her lips up and off her teeth as far as they would go.

As soon as he was gone, Vega took her phone from her pocket and texted Cap:

"Everything is fine."

She set the phone screen-down on the table and looked at the ashtray. It wasn't big but it was glass, amber in color. JERRY'S NUGGET—LAS VEGAS printed on the bottom.

Her phone hummed with a text from Cap: "U sure?"

She texted back: "Yes."

"You get some good news?" said Corey, returning.

She put the phone back in her pocket and shook her head.

"Boyfriend?" said Corey, teasing her. "Or just a crush."

Vega did her best to giggle.

"No, nothing like that."

Corey sat on the shaggy stool. He held a pipe in one hand and a baggie of weed in the other.

"If you say so," he said as he began to pack the pipe.

"Is this stuff strong?" Vega asked.

"Not the strongest, but not the weakest either," he said. "It'll get you where you need to go. A buddy of mine works at MedMen. They give them a discount. It's like working at the damn Gap now," he said, laughing at his own joke. "Okay, little lady, try this. I'm-a light it for you."

He passed the pipe to her, and she pushed back gently on his wrist.

"Would you mind taking the first hit?" she said. "I haven't smoked for a while, and I just want to watch you. You know, like a tutorial?"

Corey laughed again. "You're funny," he announced. "I might have done better in school if I had a teacher like you. If you insist, okay."

He brought the pipe to his mouth and lit the bowl with a lighter in his other hand. He took a long drag, the herb glowing and crackling, a thin trail of smoke burning off the top. He took the pipe out of his mouth and held his breath, pointing to his face.

Vega nodded encouragingly.

"Hold it as long as you can?" she said.

He nodded, then finally exhaled, coughing once at the end. The smoke filled the air, mostly sweet, a little skunky.

"You want to hold it as far down in your lungs as you can," he said, his voice raw. "You don't want to hold it here," he said pointing to his neck. "You can really burn your throat. Ready?"

"I think so," said Vega.

He gave her the pipe and she put her lips over the mouthpiece. It was warm and a little wet. Corey reached over and lit the bowl, and she inhaled but not deeply, felt the smoke hit her throat and blew it back out. She made a big show of it too, coughing and sputtering.

Corey laughed, truly amused. "You did exactly what I told you not to do!"

"I know!" Vega said, laughing. "Could you, maybe, show me one more time?"

"Yeah, yeah, hand it over."

She gave the pipe back to him and watched him take a big drag again, watched his eyes get a little dimmer, his movements get a little slower. Then back and forth twice more, each time Vega coughing up most of the smoke and Corey laughing, taking hearty drags.

"Logan's failing my class," Vega announced, her throat coarse from catching the smoke.

Corey grinned, tapped the pipe on the ashtray, and shook out the cashed bowl.

"Yeah, he never seemed too smart," he said.

"He's not as dumb as you think," said Vega.

"Whatever you say, Miss Alice."

"He knows when to talk and when to shut up," said Vega, leaning forward.

"Yeah?" said Corey absentmindedly.

He appeared to be only half-listening, cleaning out the pipe with his pinkie, looking through it with one eye like a telescope.

"Yeah," said Vega, standing.

"Hey, you leaving?" said Corey, somewhat disappointed.

"Not yet," said Vega, walking around the barrel table.

Corey's eyes were webby with red lines. He looked at her, intrigued. "What's up?" he said, laughing, confused.

"Who'd you offer Logan's car to?"

It took Corey a full second to register what she'd said. She watched the dusty tires turn in his head, and then he shook his head quickly.

"What."

"Logan's car," said Vega again, estimating the distance between them to be about a foot. "He owed you money. You said you'd forget it if he could get you a car for a day. For a friend. Who's the friend?"

Vega said it all in one breath and watched Corey's face flip to anger, shock. He scrambled to stand.

"Sit down," said Vega, holding her empty hand out to stop him.

"Who the fuck are you, for real?" he said, still standing, arms tense. "You're not a fuckin' teacher."

"Think for a second," Vega said. "Things can happen very quickly in these situations."

Corey listened to her, thought about it. She could tell he was trying to think through his chances. He was watching her, studying the lines of her body, though not lewdly.

You dumb mutt, she thought. You're gonna make a move.

"Your reflexes are shot," said Vega plainly. She would have to spell it out for him. "You take a run at me, I will break your nose here," she said evenly, pointing to the heel of her left hand. Then she continued, pointing to her right elbow: "And I will dislocate your jaw here. If you'd like to see how that's going to work out, then give it a try."

Corey widened his stride as if he'd been pushed gently off his spot, but Vega could tell he was not totally convinced.

"Why don't you look out the front window for a second?" she said.

He looked at her quizzically.

"Go on. Tell me what you see."

Corey rushed to the window. Vega quickly removed her phone, texted one word to Cap: "Wave."

"See that guy in the car across the street? He can hear everything we're saying."

Corey whipped his head around. Vega shook her phone and set it on the barrel table.

"There's a mike in here. Anything happens to me, he's gonna come in here and bring what he has in the trunk."

"What's in the trunk?" said Corey.

"You want to find out, make a move," said Vega, tapping her chest. "One more time, Corey. Sit. Down."

Corey came back to where she stood and sat, landing on the couch with a sigh.

"You cops?" he said, sounding defeated.

"No," she said. "But we know some. They would love to meet you."

"What do you want?" he said slowly.

"Who's the friend you needed a car for?"

Corey rubbed his eyes. He was wrestling with telling her something, she knew. Shaking his head remorsefully.

"I can't tell you that."

He looked up and caught Vega's gaze. She seemed very serious.

"Look—" he continued. "Whatever you could do to me, whatever's in the trunk, it's fucking nothing compared to what these guys and their people will do to me."

"Really?" she said, perching on the edge of the barrel table. "I can't wait to meet them."

Corey continued shaking his head. Vega had no way of knowing if what he said was true, or if he believed it, but she wasn't too concerned about it.

All the time in the world was an unfamiliar concept to her; every case, every day was composed of a few minutes stacked and multiplied, reminded her of the way cable and cell companies split time into bundles. Spindly bundles of seconds, weighted sacks of hours. She glanced at her phone now while Corey took some deep, stoned breaths and knew it would be a few minutes of this back-and-forth before she got a name, which was just fine.

Cap looked at the time. It had been about forty minutes, but she had texted, and also instructed him to wave to the guy at the window, who'd looked confused and squinty. He began to text: "Still okay?" but before he could send, she emerged from the front door, her hair wilder than before, eyes on everything. She took long strides across the street, reaching her hands behind her head to tie her hair back.

She got into the car and slammed the door.

"Everything's fine," she said before he had chance to speak. "Do you have any of that coffee left?"

"No," said Cap. "What happened?"

Vega didn't respond, buckled her belt and started the car, tore out of the spot a little quick. She made a lazy wide turn at the corner.

"Everything's fine," she said again.

"Okay," Cap said slowly. "So what do we know?"

"Devin Lara," said Vega. "Corey got some pressure by a guy named Devin Lara, a bigger dealer apparently—cocaine, heroin, meth, pills. He also has a financial services business as a cover. And he strong-armed Corey, said all he needed was a car for a couple of days and it would be returned. Corey didn't want to give up his own car; Logan owed him money, so Corey said he'd forgive the debt if he got him a car."

"So is Lara a murderer and a child trafficker, or just a dealer."

Vega stopped at a light and pulled at her bottom lip. She focused on something in the distance.

"Corey didn't think so. But he thinks Lara knows some guys, some of his connections from Mexico. Corey seemed to think these guys may have a lot of resources."

She turned her head abruptly then, to something she saw out the window.

"You think we need to have a more substantial talk with Otero and the DEA guys now?" Cap asked.

"We have to tell him and McTiernan to pick up Corey. He says he'd rather go to jail for a while than wait for whatever Lara's guys might do. Maybe he can make a deal, who knows."

She muttered that last phrase, and Cap noticed something was different about her. He couldn't put a finger on it. She kept touching her lips, biting them at the corners, and she sat forward on the seat as if something were about to happen. Preoccupied.

"You okay, Vega?" he said.

"Huh?" she said, then glanced at him. "Yeah, I'm just hungry. Mind if we stop at that Jack in the Box?"

She had already put the blinker on to turn in to the drive-thru.

"No prob," said Cap.

They didn't have Jack in the Boxes on the East Coast, but Cap knew it was fast food. Burgers and fries and shakes. He had never seen Vega eat anything like that. He had rarely seen her eat at all and when she did it was purely utilitarian, and junk never seemed to make the cut. Then he watched her eyes, squinting to focus on what was directly in front of her, and noticed for the first time the woody smell coming off her clothes and hair.

"Vega!" he said loudly.

She didn't exactly jump but turned to him suddenly, like he had pinched her.

"What?"

"You're stoned," he said, then chuckled.

Vega stared at the car in front of her in the drive-thru line.

"Shit, I am."

She rubbed her eyes, while Cap laughed. He wanted to take a picture of her and post it on the Internet.

"I just need something to eat and drink, and I'll be fine," she said.

"Yeah, you will."

"Do you want anything?" she asked.

"Just coffee," he said, his laughter subsiding. "So we should call Otero, right?"

"Um, I guess," said Vega, pulling up to the menu. "To tell him about Corey. I think we hold back on Lara, see if the Bastard can find him. They have really changed the menu. I used to eat here twice a week in high school."

Cap glanced at the menu, the images of the glowing food.

"Wait, you want to find Lara, me and you?"

"Yeah," said Vega, still turned away from him, examining her options.

"These are the guys from Mexico. Like Mexican cartel guys," said Cap again, trying to make it sink in.

"Yeah," said Vega, annoyed. Then she leaned out the window and said to the box: "Large curly fries and four Dasanis." She turned to Cap quickly and said, "You sure you don't want a Dasani?"

"I'm sure."

"And one large black coffee."

Vega pulled the car ahead and tapped the wheel with her fingers. Something caught her eye through the windshield. Cap followed her gaze and saw a seagull bobbing up and down in the breeze.

"As I was saying, maybe we want to call in some bigger artillery if we're dealing with Mexican gangsters. Or any gangsters, really."

He couldn't tell if she was listening. She took her hands off the wheel and inched the car forward by easing off the brake bit by bit. She bit both lips so they disappeared between her teeth. Cap was no longer sure he was tickled by Stoned Vega. He kind of missed Shit-Together Vega.

"Vega, you hearing me?"

She didn't respond but appeared thoughtful. The car in front of them pulled out of the drive-thru line and to the street. Vega pulled up to the window, took her bags from the cashier, and paid.

"Yeah, I hear you," she said, still pensive. She pulled into a space in the lot and turned the engine off.

She handed Cap his coffee and then opened a bottle of water and drank most of it in one gulp. Then she started in on the curly fries, eating one long spring that resembled a Slinky.

"You should have one of these," she said to Cap, holding them out to him.

Cap took a crispy circle and popped it in his mouth.

"They're good," he confirmed.

Vega continued to eat silently, rapidly.

Finally she spoke: "Lara's not necessarily bunked up with a gang of *narcos*. He's just another domino in the line, like Corey. We can handle him, when the Bastard finds him, me and you."

She set the fries down in the cup holder and finished the bottle of water, tossed the empty into the paper bag with the rest of the bottles. Then she opened another and took a more moderate sip.

"You get a number? Why don't we call him, pretend we want a hookup?"

Vega swallowed and said, "Corey said we can't just text this guy. Said he doesn't work that way, only has clients he personally finds and approves."

"Any particular reason you don't want to bring in Otero on Lara yet?" asked Cap.

Vega kept popping fries into her mouth, staring straight ahead, but Cap knew she was listening. She wasn't that gone. She ate fairly daintily for someone who was high, Cap thought. He'd been around a lot of stoned kids as a cop; even he and Jules used to smoke now and again when she'd get joints as thank-yous from certain students, and he was used to druggy eating being a massacre—chicken wings, barbecue chips, Halloween-size bags of candy bars. But for Vega, it was methodical; she seemed to grow more and more pensive as she ate, as if each bite honed her focus even more.

"We're not telling Otero everything, remember?" she said. "His detective, McTiernan, is tied up with LoSanto and the cash. That's where we need him right now."

"Okay," said Cap, sensing there was more. "That the only reason?"

"No," she said. "I'd like to know exactly where Otero lands, how much information gets from him to Boyce. What's his stake? What's Boyce's? Are they the same?"

"Good questions," said Cap.

Vega stuffed a napkin into the fry cup and finished the second bottle of water, slipped it in the bag. They sat for a few minutes, the only sound Vega's short fingernails tapping out an email. Then her phone buzzed with a call.

"The Bastard?" asked Cap.

Vega shook her head, examining the screen and mouthing the numbers to herself. She swiped and answered it. Cap watched her face for changes and saw her eyes travel back and forth across a line in the distance, then stop dead and stick hard right in the center.

8

CAP COULD NOT BELIEVE THE CLEANLINESS OF THE SAN DIEGO County Medical Examiner's office. The county ME's facilities in Pennsylvania, and every one he'd seen on the East Coast, had not been significantly altered since the 1960s—massive brick structures with cattle-killing fluorescent lights and gray walls inside. This office was all bright yellow and glass, the main walkway leading from the waiting room wide with a picture window along one wall. It overlooked an office park, but Cap was still impressed at how open it was, how at ease it made him feel in a building full of dead bodies.

They were being led by a security guard to meet an ME named Mia, who'd called Vega to say she had something to show her.

The guard stopped in front of swinging doors that gleamed silver in the natural light. He rapped on one with his knuckles.

"Come in," sang a youthful voice.

The guard pushed the door open.

"Your guests, Mia," he called.

Cap wasn't sure where to look first. There was a body under a sheet on an examination table—he could see the ghostly outlines. There was a sink by the head, also a long sink across the wall opposite where they had just entered.

A plus-size young woman stood at the long sink, where the water was running. She glanced over her shoulder, her smile big and toothy, tinted goggles over her eyes.

"Thanks, Sam. Hiya, Alice!" she said, cheery.

A truly odd job for someone so bubbly, thought Cap. But then, maybe it made sense. Maybe after sawing human bones and sifting through their gummy organs it was best to be perky, optimistic, to go home and have a cocktail and stream Netflix.

Vega smiled that little smile of acknowledgment she had. It was tiny in the mouth area but big and warm around the eyes.

"This is Max Caplan," she said to Mia.

Mia waved her wet fingers and turned off the sink. Cap nodded politely.

"So," said Mia, snapping two paper towels out of a dispenser. "I just wanna wait for my brain guy before we get started, if that's cool with you."

"That's fine," said Vega.

Cap watched for signs of squeamishness in her face but saw none so far. His own stomach was fine at the moment, but he knew that even though he'd seen plenty of bodies and parts of bodies as a cop, it could still get to him, not because it made him feel philosophical, just a pure biological reaction, didn't matter if you saw it every day or not. It got to everyone sooner or later, even the toughest bulldog cops who'd seen it all ended up puking in a morgue at some point. The only people it bounced off of were doctors, MEs, paramedics, RNs, because seeing bodies every day for them was like chalkboards and shiny red apples for schoolteachers.

He could smell a lot of formalin and cleaning products. He couldn't smell the blood yet, but he eyed a tray of tools next to the body on the right, and on that tray was a buzz saw. He knew exactly what that was for too.

Mia dropped the paper towels in a flip-top garbage can and stood next to the body with the tray of tools.

"So," she said. "Are you guys like a couple or what?"

Cap laughed, not particularly nervously, mostly out of being charmed by Mia's guileless attitude. He glanced at Vega, who appeared neither nervous nor charmed.

"No, he's my partner," she said plainly. It was like she was saying, These items here on my feet, they're shoes.

"Life partner?" teased Mia, raising her goggles.

"Business partner," said Vega.

"Okay, whatever you say," said Mia, singsong again.

Cap could not believe Vega was actually allowing herself to be teased, by someone she'd just met no less.

Then the swinging doors burst open, and a guy in blue scrubs with a gray rubber wolf mask came through, howling. Cap found himself jumping a little, his hand twitching in the direction of the Sig under his arm.

The masked figure stopped short after a moment.

"Goddammit, Witton," said Mia. "I told you I was gonna have people here."

The guy pulled off the mask.

"Shit, sorry," he said.

He was a skinny Asian guy with a buzz cut, the scrubs baggy on him.

"You're such a freak, dude," said Mia, putting on a fresh pair of gloves. "This is Alice Vega, who I told you about. And this is her business partner, Max."

"Hey, hi," said the wolf-boy, and he shook their hands. "I'm sorry about this," he said, waving the mask. "It's like a joke me and her have." He shoved the mask into his pants pocket, the snout sticking out.

"This is Witton Ng. He's on staff at County and he's our neuro specialist when we need him. He's a lot more mature than he looks," said Mia, somewhat affectionately.

Witton nodded shyly and walked past Cap and Vega, muttered, "Excuse me." He washed his hands quickly in the long sink and dried them, pulled on a pair of gloves.

"So remember the mark on Jane One?" Mia said to Vega. "Weird shape on the temple?"

Vega nodded.

Mia and Witton walked to the top of the exam table, near the head, and Mia gestured for Cap and Vega to follow them. They stood on either side of the table, at about where the hips were.

"We think that the mark," said Mia slowly, "wasn't from blunt trauma. We think it's a burn."

"Hard to tell," added Witton. "They can look virtually the same."

"He was here for another thing and he saw this and said— Tell them what you said," Mia urged Witton.

"I said it looks like an ECT burn, but a pretty extreme case since the skin's scarred over."

"ECT?" asked Vega.

"Like, electroshock, right?" said Cap.

"Right," said Witton.

"People still do that?" said Vega.

"Sure," said Witton. "Still a little controversial but some people swear by it, say it's better than pills for severe depression. But that's with a max voltage of 450. A burn like this, I'd say closer to a thousand."

"At what point does a person die?" asked Vega.

"Depends on the current," said Witton. "You get a thousand volts going through your heart, you probably get arrhythmia."

"So," said Cap. "What makes us think Jane One is a victim of trigger-happy electroshock and not, say, a curling iron?"

Witton glanced at Mia, who nodded. Then Mia folded the sheet down to reveal Jane 1's head. The thing about it was that the top of her skull had been removed, sawed off, from the hairline up, and the brain was exposed, brown and wet, a white acrylic board behind it at an angle, propping it up. Cap felt all the blood travel out of his own head. He wiggled his fingers and toes and reminded himself to breathe.

"You better get him an Altoid," said Vega, who did not look much better herself, pale as flour and leaning against the doors of a freestanding steel cabinet.

Mia nodded enthusiastically and produced a tin from inside her lab coat.

"I don't think there are enough in there," said Cap, a deep tonal ringing in his ears.

Mia and Witton chuckled good-naturedly, as if he were joking. Cap took two mints and shoved them into his mouth, sucked on them aggressively with whatever saliva was available, which was not much. Mia then passed the tin to Vega.

"I'll be brief. This is the prefrontal cortex," said Witton, pointing to the front of the brain, closest to the line of the severed forehead.

Don't look at the saw on the table, Cap told himself.

"It looks pretty normal except for some discoloration here," he continued, pointing to a small whitish strip of the organ near the left side of the head, where the burn was. "Now, there's really no way to diagnostically determine this, but it could be as a result of a unilateral high-voltage current; the brain could be a little . . ."

He hesitated, glanced at Mia, seemed unsure of the protocol.

"Cooked?" said Vega.

"Maybe," said Witton, a note of relief in his voice.

"So you're telling us," said Cap, wiping sweat from his forehead with his sleeve. "That someone hooked this girl up to an energy source like a Christmas tree as a means of torture?"

"We can't say anything about the means," said Mia.

"Right," said Witton. "It was a high voltage beyond any therapeutic boundary, even in the old days."

"You tell Otero about this?" Vega said.

Mia, leaning over the brain, looked up at Vega without moving.

"Not yet," she said. "It's your case, right? I wanted to tell you first."

Vega breathed into the crook of her elbow and stared at Cap over her sleeve. Cap's eyes watered, either from the formalin or from the effort it took not to vomit or, once again, from marveling at all the shit people did to hurt each other.

They were quiet for a long time in the car. It was evening, still warm, and they were driving to meet Otero on-site at one of the tunnels. They still had the taste of mint in their mouths, their lips still wet from licking them to stave off the nausea. The windows were down, and they could not seem to get enough air. Cap tilted his head out, let the wind mess up his hair.

Vega did the same at stoplights, not just for the air but to hear the noise also—car horns, music from other open windows, engines, sirens.

Cap longed to see his daughter, to check the light in her eyes. The older she got, the more afraid he became; he had always assumed it would go the other way, that once she'd stopped stubbing her pinkie toe on every damn thing and scraping up her elbows and knees on the soccer field, it would get better; she would get stronger, and he would worry less and sleep sounder. But it seemed to be moving in the opposite direction: the older she got the more he worried. Maybe it was because someone had actually put a gun to her head, but maybe it was the natural course. Maybe the kids were just fine in their cardboard box armor and cheap acrylic Halloween costumes, and the adults were the ones who needed protecting, no matter what they had in their holsters.

"Could we stop for a minute?" he asked Vega.

She looked at him sideways, suspect.

"I just have to talk to Nell real quick."

Vega nodded and pulled off the freeway at the next exit, into the parking lot of a 7-Eleven.

"Thanks, be right back," said Cap, getting out of the car.

He shrugged his shoulders forward and back to get his shirt unstuck from his skin, pulled at the legs of his pants to do the same, and texted sloppily with his thumb: "Calling 1 min."

He didn't quite wait the whole minute and tapped Nell's name on the Recents. She picked up right away.

"Dad," she said. No question mark, all business. "What's wrong?"

"Nothing, Bug," he lied, forcing levity into his voice. "Just checking in. What're you up to?"

"Oh, just at Carrie's," she said.

Cap heard laughter in the background and what sounded like singing.

"Shut up, you guys!" Nell called.

Then more laughter and a door shutting.

"I'm going upstairs. Nick is singing," she said, laughing. "He actually sounds just like Rihanna. It's uncanny."

Cap grinned. He loved Nell happy with her friends. Good kids with reasonable parents. No binge drinking and unprotected sex, or if they did, Nell was smart enough to excuse herself.

"So what's wrong?" Nell said again, as if she hadn't asked before.

"Nothing, nothing," repeated Cap like a parrot.

"Dad, come on. You wouldn't say 'nothing' twice. The second 'nothing' is trying to convince me it's really nothing. Which means it's not nothing."

Cap sighed. He leaned against a disconnected phone box and let his eyes wander over the dimly lit parking lot.

"Just wanted to hear your voice," he said finally. "See how things are going."

"Uh-huh," said Nell skeptically. "You saw a dead kid, didn't you?"

Cap sighed once more.

"Yeah. Yeah, I did," he confessed.

"You want to tell me about it?"

To tell the truth, he did. There had never been many secrets between him and Nell, but since the Brandt case, there were next to none. So he told her everything but, in the interest of time, stuck to the highlights.

"So you think they tortured her with some crude form of electroshock?" said Nell.

"Yeah, that's what we're thinking."

"Ugh, that's horrific," said Nell. "It was only on the first girl, Jane One?"

"That's right," said Cap, grinning at the thought of Nell already working out theories.

"So maybe they didn't have time to get to Jane Two?"

"Maybe."

Nell paused, and Cap heard her breathing accelerate. Walking upstairs.

"So they turn them into sex dolls, basically? Insert birth control, fry their brains?"

"Yeah," said Cap, grasping it more and more as Nell kept talking.

"But *then* they kill them?" Nell said. "Why? Why wouldn't they keep them, you know, working? Wouldn't it be more lucrative?"

"Yeah, it would," Cap said thoughtfully.

He watched Vega get out of the car and go into the 7-Eleven. She nodded at him, stern expression. Thinking of another thing.

Nell sighed, exasperated.

"Something doesn't fit," she announced.

"Well, yeah," Cap said, laughing a little bit. "We've only been talking it out for five minutes. We still have to get all the pieces in front of us." He kicked at the foot of the phone box pillar absentmindedly, had an urge to talk about less vile things. Chitchat, like normal people. "So how's your mom?"

"Oh, she's fine. She's happy I'm there. She's, like, really into knitting now—it's weird."

"Knitting," said Cap, trying to picture Jules, the feminist-literature scholar, knitting like a pilgrim wife in a rocking chair.

"Yeah, I actually think she does it to relax, like a meditation. All she knows how to make so far is scarves, though. There are scarves everywhere."

Nell began to laugh, her lovely spontaneous rambunctious laugh, and then Cap did as well—not in a mean-spirited way, he wouldn't dare, but only at the absurdity of it, picturing the floor of Jules's sleek condo covered entirely with an ocean of dowdy scarves.

Then Nell said, "She said something nice about you the other day."

Cap perked up with an unexpected hopefulness. He had no intention of reconciling with his ex-wife but still desired her approval and care from afar, or perhaps only wished to avoid her deliberate disapproval and ill will.

"Yeah? What did she say?" he asked, fantasizing it was something along the lines of "You know, I forgive your dad for putting you in the middle of that whole hostage situation a couple of years back."

"She said you've lost weight," said Nell.

"I've lost weight?"

"Yeah."

"That's it? That's the nice thing?"

"Yeah, that's a very nice thing for her to say, Dad," said Nell. "For her to say that about you—it's like the Nobel Peace Prize level of nice."

Cap laughed and rested his forehead on his fist.

"I guess I gotta start somewhere," he said.

They spoke for a few more minutes, and then Nell had to go, beckoned by her friends, promising to call in a couple of days.

Cap hung up and stretched his arms behind him, cracked his neck from one side to the other, and went to the car to wait for his partner.

Vega browsed the brightly lit aisles of the 7-Eleven, smelling bubble gum and coffee, mustard and burnt cheese. She ended up at the register, in front of the magazine rack. Recipes, arts and crafts, cars and bikes and tech, reality show stars without makeup in parking lots.

Then, behind the register and the man working there, another rack of magazines wrapped in plastic with clear strips at the tops revealing the titles, the rest of the covers opaque white.

"Can I get a *Barely Legal*?" said Vega to the counterman.

He was Middle Eastern and older, some white hair threaded through the black. He didn't react in any particular way to Vega's request, grabbing the magazine and placing it between them on the counter.

"Can I also get *Hustler, Ruff Stuff, Club* . . ."

The counterman picked out and dropped each one with a light slap and still portrayed no reaction, not even a seen-it-all weariness.

Vega spotted a magazine behind the others; all that was visible was a woman's face next to a horse's.

"And a *Mount*."

At that, the counterman raised an eyebrow, impressed.

Vega paid and refused a bag, carried the magazines to the car and got inside.

"So Nell had a good question," said Cap, who'd been texting. Then he noticed the magazines. "Hey, what's with all the porn?"

He was a little too seasoned to be embarrassed or aroused, especially considering Vega's expression, which was all business. She tore open the plastic on the *Barely Legal* and began flipping through the glossy pages as if she were searching for something very specific.

Vega examined the photos, her eyes skimming each one briefly before turning to the next.

"We looking for something in particular?" said Cap.

"Yes and no," said Vega. "I'm just trying to get in their heads a little bit."

"Who—the killer's?" said Cap for clarity. "Vega, a guy who's into porn is not necessarily the same guy who tortures girls."

"Right," said Vega. "But the johns might, the guys who rent the girls from the guy who tortures girls. They might be into porn."

"Sure," said Cap. "That's a little more realistic."

"So I could just have the Bastard scan for men in the area with the most traffic for this particular topic," she said, holding out the *Barely Legal*.

Cap laughed.

"Are you kidding? Vega, it'll melt his server. Besides, now I don't have any stats to back this up, but I'd bet that some guys, *some* guys," he repeated to emphasize the "some." "They look at this stuff and then don't need to go any further. Privacy of their own homes, no one gets hurt."

"So really it's providing a public service, said Vega flatly.

"I didn't say that," said Cap. "For example, this," he said, picking up *Mount*. "I'm not sure this is helping anyone."

Vega turned back to her magazine. Cap unwrapped *Mount* and opened it.

"Thought so," he said, holding the page open so Vega could see. "Just naked ladies *next* to horses. Washing them, et cetera."

Cap could tell that Vega was focusing neither on what he was saying nor on what was in front of her though she continued to page through. Typically he let her be in such moments, like earlier when she'd been high, but she wasn't high now, and he thought, What if everything she isn't saying is a good theory that just needs a little water and air? She had a tendency to announce what she was thinking only when it was fully formed, the opposite of what Cap had been used to as a cop, pitching whatever waltzed into his head. Even if it didn't bear out in the end, he gave it words and a shape, and sometimes it fit.

"What are you thinking?" he said softly.

Vega turned her head toward him with her chin tucked down near her shoulder so he could only see her face at a three-quarter angle. It felt rather intimate, much as his inquiry and tone had sounded to her.

"I'm thinking about motivations," she said. "How men pretty much have a triangle. Sex, drugs, money," she said, drawing a triangle in the air with her finger. "Every man who commits a criminal act does it in service to one or more of those three things."

Then she thought about it a moment more, mentally scanning the lineup of skips and snatchers she'd come across, and added, "Most men, actually, do everything because of them."

Cap eyed her invisible triangle somewhat suspiciously.

"I don't disagree," he said. "You gonna tell me what motivates women?"

Vega thought. She watched her blanched reflection in the wind-shield for clues and remembered the anguished face of the Brandt girls' mother.

"Love," said Vega finally. "Women are motivated by love. All of them."

Cap looked at his own long reflection in the windshield, thought better of asking Vega, "You too?" and instead said, "Goddammit, you're right."

Vega handed Cap the rest of the magazines and buckled her seatbelt. It was getting too dark for her to wear sunglasses but she propped them on top of her head anyway, just in case the sun snuck back up before it was supposed to.

The air was colder in the desert. Cap felt his jaw clench with the chill and buttoned his jacket. He thought the landscape was beautiful, the sky looking like it was draped out of some rich blue fabric, the stars having been punched through with a sharp pencil point. There were cactuses around them and short, fat palm trees and brushy shrubs, and the rhythmic clicks and low chirps of hidden wildlife.

It would have been one of the most strange and peaceful places Cap had ever been were it not for the mass of thirty or so men and women in various law enforcement uniforms and their equipment gathered on one side of the two-lane road, giant spotlights on cranes and tripods casting bright white beams on a singular patch of dirt.

He and Vega walked on the blacktop, following a line of smoking orange flares. She had texted Otero, who'd called and told her to meet him at the scene.

"What a circus," said Cap under his breath as a figure approached them.

"Ms. Vega," said Otero, shaking her hand.

"Hi, Commander. This is Max Caplan, my partner."

Cap shook hands with him, both of them offering brief, pleasant smiles.

"This one, we just found," said Otero, gesturing to the scene behind him. He turned and began to walk back to it, waving Cap and Vega along with him. "We had people patrolling this stretch less than a week ago, and there was nothing there, and now . . ."

He paused as they all went from the side of the road onto the sand, which was much firmer under Cap's feet than he would have expected. Everyone was busy: a cluster of DEA agents stood around a tablet talking and pointing; cops, plainclothed and uniformed, stretched out concentric circles of crime scene string (for the life of him Cap could not conceive of what evidence they could possibly lift from sand but he held his tongue) in front of an opening three feet by three feet, coming out of the ground like a periscope. Also, most noticeably, there were six cops in full riot gear, Kevlar on their chests, AR-15s on their arms.

"We're pretty sure it's either the Perez cartel or Eduardo Montalvo," Otero said with confidence.

Cap nodded as if he knew the names but assumed Vega did.

Otero continued: "As I said, the tunnel's only been operational a week, max, so we feel we're in a good position, that not too much product's been moved."

Cap examined Vega's face for clues. She leaned her head to the side, looking over Otero's shoulder so she could see the tunnel's opening.

"So what makes you think it's definitely drugs coming through and not something else?" she asked, sounding inoffensive.

Otero showed a slight flinch in his eyes.

"Like what exactly?"

"Like people."

Otero rested his hands on his hips, seemingly impatient.

"Past experience, Ms. Vega," he said with a small note of defensiveness. "Considering the murders of the two Mexican border control officials a month ago, I think we've adapted a bit better to the situation now. These are not immigrants seeking refuge; they're criminals and they're killers, and this time, when they come through, we'll be ready for them."

Now Otero seemed energized, excited.

He continued: "If we just get one of them, we can roll him for names and locations of everyone else on his team in the county."

"You make it sound so easy," said Cap.

"On the contrary, Mr. Caplan," said Otero. "As Ms. Vega can tell you, we've been on these tunnels for the better part of a year, and this is the first real breakthrough, or chance of one, we've had. So you understand my distraction. Now, you wanted to brief me?"

"Not a brief, just a question," said Vega. "Do you know the name Devin Lara?"

Otero's face reflected a mild recognition but nothing over the top.

"Yeah," he said casually. "How'd he come up for you?"

Vega paused, but only for a moment. Cap suspected she was considering waiting another round to see what Otero knew first, but then the need for information won out. So she told him everything.

Otero took it all in, nodding cursorily.

"Yes, actually," he said. "Starters, we think he's a distributor, or at the very least a liaison, for one or more Mexican organizations and has been for a long time."

"Any reason he hasn't been arrested yet?" said Vega, not trying to be cute or rude in any way.

Otero smiled, a gold canine on the top row of teeth gleaming.

"We suspect this to be the case, never had enough evidence for a warrant."

Vega let her eyes wander to the tunnel entrance. Not over the fence, under the ground, she thought.

"Do you know where I can find him?" she said.

Otero's smile dissipated. He tilted his head forward to close the gap in space between them.

"Agent Boyce will want to know about it, about what brought you to Lara—that's all in his house."

"That's fine," said Vega.

Otero added: "He'll probably want us to strategize, get our heads together."

"Sounds good," said Vega. "But if it's all the same to you, if you could let me know what you know in terms of known associates, financials, last known address, then I can get started."

Cap noticed the action around them taking on a different energy suddenly. Louder, busier. The group of DEAs had dispersed and were now talking to cops or chattering on their Bluetooths. The yellow jumpsuits were shouting calls and responses to one another. One had begun to climb into the tunnel.

But the air between Vega and Otero was still.

"You want your work to stick, right?" said Otero slowly. Not waiting for her to answer, he said, "Better to wait for Boyce. I'll let him know one of your arrows is pointing to Lara, and we can all have a meeting."

Cap studied Vega's face and thought, If you didn't know her you might think that she was maybe a quiet type with an accommodating streak, the way her expression was so open and understanding just then.

And when she said, "Sounds good," such a clean clipping of a response but just a strand too cheery to be real, thought Cap. A little too much like a waitress who just took your order.

They wrapped it up. Said goodbye and shook hands, and then they headed back to Vega's car. As they got further from the tunnel and the activity, it got darker, and not just the sky, but to Cap, it felt as if the very air in front of them grew darker and colder too. It felt like he imagined outer space to be, the voices fading behind them.

Then he thought about the space of Vega's mind, how crowded it must be in there, swirling stars and planetary systems, but how only one path was charted through.

They got into the car, and Cap blew air into his hands.

"You have no intention of meeting with Boyce before approaching Devin Lara, do you?" he said.

Vega started the car, removed her phone from her pocket, and placed it in the tray between them. The light from the tunnel site reflected off the rearview in a strip across her eyes.

"Depends how fast the Bastard is," she said.

"Don't you think you might want to wait, since Boyce is the one paying you?" Cap asked, using the same tone he would use with Nell when she'd already decided on an answer but he wanted her to think about the other thing anyway.

Vega didn't start driving and took her hands off the wheel.

"We're not waiting for Boyce's calendar to open up before we follow our leads." She paused, then turned to Cap and added, "Do you really think that's a good use of our time?"

"Hey," he said, holding his hands up in defense. "Just a consultant doing some casual consulting."

Vega didn't laugh but she didn't glare at him either, so Cap considered it a win.

And then, her phone buzzed, rattling around in the tray, and they both stared down to see what it would do next.

9

SOMETIMES VEGA COUNTED DURING THE HANDSTAND. DOWN FROM one thousand. By the time she hit about 970 things would start to open up. Her shoulders and her thoughts. She had been up until about two in the morning, reading online about human trafficking. She'd also done some searching for Devin Lara, had found a profile on LinkedIn but no picture. The Bastard had as well, but she just wanted to check. He had, however, found two addresses—an office and a residence.

"Let's go," Vega had said to Cap, typing the home address into a map app.

Cap had been unusually quiet, the muscles near his eyes and mouth softening. Vega could tell he was trying to figure out a way to tell her something.

"This is a guy who's used to being watched," he'd said. "He probably has some security measures in place. We can't just stake him out."

Vega had watched the address load on her screen, the blue dot in the middle, the streets and blocks around it coming into focus.

"What do you think we should do?" she'd asked him.

Now she felt the sweat start, budding on her forehead near her hairline. She thought of Jane 1 with her skull removed like a batter's helmet, the brain pulsing with electrical current. Tell me something, thought Vega. Tell me where you're from.

The Jane 1 of her dream didn't speak, still dead. Or resting.

Vega came down from the stand and stretched her arms behind her head one at a time in tight triangles. She went to the bathroom and drank water from a plastic cup, then heard a quiet tapping at the door. She glanced at the clock: 6:05.

She went to the door and peered through the peephole. It was Caplan, smiling toothily, holding two cups. Vega stared at his face, distorted in the glass. She looked away for a quick second, then opened the door.

She registered him seeing her body, and she didn't look down but thought briefly about what she was wearing—a ribbed tank top with no bra and running shorts. She noticed his eyes landing on her stomach, at the exposed ribbon of skin. She didn't feel any particular way about it either, not the urge to cover up or to reveal more. It all took only a second, if that, and then she took the cup with the string and tag from him.

"Morning," he said.

"Hey."

She motioned for him to enter, and he shut the door behind him. She opened the curtains wide to get as much light as possible. The sun was just beginning to head up.

"I've been thinking," said Cap, leaning on the small table in the corner.

Vega nodded at him, signaling that he should continue.

"I'm thinking it's going to be a challenge to get at Lara through the business—what's it listed as—"

Vega grabbed her phone and scrolled to find the email from the Bastard.

"Lincoln Investments. Provides investment services to middle-market companies," she read.

"Right," said Cap, thinking. "I mean, we could fake it if we had to. I could go buy a suit, you could read up on private equity, but that's going to take time, so I say let's go known-associates route."

"Sure," said Vega, sitting on the edge of the bed. "But if you're thinking of the team at his company, you're still going to have to buy a suit."

"No, no business. And no residence either," said Cap.

Vega searched Cap's face. He looked a little amused.

"You want to impersonate a gas station attendant and catch him between the two?" she said.

Cap grinned and sipped his coffee. His grin was so big he had trouble drinking, had to dab the corners of his mouth with a napkin.

"You didn't look at the most recent Mastercard statement," he said.

"Yeah, I did," said Vega, bringing it up on her phone. "Food, gas, clothes. He's doing any other purchases with cash." She paused. "Or another currency."

"But did you see the type of food? Almost every day?"

Vega scanned the charges. Most of the names were not familiar to her, except some chains.

"Juicy Lucy," she read. "So he likes juice?"

"Yeah, he does," said Cap. "Same store number. Twenty-eight seventy, right?"

"Right," said Vega, taking it in. "He gets juice at the same place almost every day."

Cap smiled, proud of himself.

"According to the dates, looks like Mondays, Wednesdays, Fridays, Saturdays," he said. "And today is Friday. And you might not know this about me, Vega, but I don't really get enough antioxidants."

Vega understood now.

"Meet you at the car in fifteen," she said, convinced. He nodded and still stood there, grinning, not moving. "I'm going to take a shower," she added.

"And I am going to leave you alone to do that," said Cap.

He turned toward the door, and Vega began to turn in the direction of the bathroom but then stopped.

"Caplan," she said.

"Yeah?" he said, his hand on the knob.

"Did you see me through the window just now, in the handstand?"

He paused, and when he didn't respond with a firm, immediate "no," she knew the answer.

"Yeah, I did."

He didn't sound apologetic, just a touch embarrassed.

Vega crossed her arms and pressed her fingers into her biceps, the muscles still humming.

"It's a thing I do," she said. "Every morning. Helps me think."

Cap nodded and looked at the ground.

"Sure," he said sympathetically.

Vega stared at him, willing him to look her in the eye, but he didn't. She tapped her fingertips against her skin, felt the chill snake its way up and down the length of her arms.

"See you downstairs," he said quickly and then left.

Vega stood there for a minute afterward on the chance he'd knock. But he didn't. Not this time.

An hour later they sat at a Juicy Lucy two tables away from the door. Vega faced it, Cap away, both of them sipping green juices. On a screen on Vega's phone, she had a scan of Lara's driver's license. As photos went, licenses weren't the best, faces straight to the camera and stoic were never the way people actually looked. Social media pictures were generally much better, candid—barbecues, selfies, every angle of the face and unflattering, honest bodies. But Devin Lara didn't have any of those online so she made a list of everything she noticed from the license shot: dark hair, eyes, brows; egg-shaped face with weight under the chin.

Vega glanced at Cap and saw him smiling, imagined he was texting Nell. And his smile was so warm and he struck Vega as being so old, frankly, but in a comfortable way. Like a nice sweater or a robe, Vega imagined, if she had owned either one.

Then a text popped up on her phone. It was from JPat: "You leave town and don't tell me??"

Vega texted back fast, one word: "Working."

"I'd hate to be on the other end of that text," said Cap, adding, "Your face."

Vega didn't have time to consider her face because then Devin Lara walked in. He was about six foot and a little beefy in the chest, more overweight than muscle. He wore expensive jeans and sneakers with a three-button shirt. Clean-shaven, wet hair.

"On time," said Vega.

"Oh yeah?" said Cap, not turning around to confirm. "What's he up to?"

"Mobile order."

She watched Lara go the counter, pick up a large cup filled with reddish orange juice, consult the printed label on the side, and then turn to leave.

"Leaving," said Vega.

Lara wove his way toward the door, and Cap stood and crossed quickly to get there first. Then Vega stood and followed them both.

Cap held the door open for Lara, and Lara held the door open for Vega with two fingers. As soon as it closed behind her, Cap turned quickly and knocked Lara's juice out of his hands. It splashed onto his shirt in a wave, the juice viscous and pulpy, the cup falling to the ground.

"Fuck!" Lara shouted.

"I'm so sorry," said Cap, handing him a wad of napkins. "My reflexes are shitty since the transplant."

"Devin Lara," said Vega.

Lara was confused enough to not instantly become combative. Vega knew that the natural thing you did when someone walked toward you, if you weren't thinking straight, was to back up. So she moved swiftly toward him to get them all away from the front door of Juicy Lucy, and Lara backed up, disoriented, pissed, wet, and cold. He stood with his back flat against the wall.

"Do I know you?" he said, relatively calm.

"No," she said. "I'm Vega. This is Caplan. I got your name from Corey Lloyd."

"Don't know him," said Lara, patting his shirt with the napkins.

"He knows you. Says you put a thumb on him to find a car."

Lara didn't flinch, glanced up at Vega, then Cap behind her, continued to dab the mess on his shirt.

"Don't know him. Don't know anything about a car."

"I can remind you," said Vega. "You needed a car registered to a nobody so that you or someone you know could dump the body of a dead girl in it."

Lara looked at her, rolled the napkins into a ball, and tossed them into a garbage can to his right.

"What'd you say your name was again?" he said. Still calm.

"Alice Vega."

"Hi, Alice Vega. I'm Devin. And that's my driver, Richie," said Lara pointing past her.

Cap and Vega turned and saw a thick-necked thug coming at them fast. He quickly removed his black suit jacket and was unbuttoning the cuffs of his gray dress shirt.

"Caplan" was all Vega had time to say before the driver was on him.

"Hey, just leaving," Cap called to him, holding his hands out in mild surrender.

The driver didn't listen, just snapped a fist back and threw a jab to Cap's stomach. Cap didn't really have time to block, but Vega thought he must have at least tensed his abs a little bit in preparation, since he didn't fall, only doubled over, coughing.

In a second, Lara and the driver were striding away. Vega saw them get into an SUV before she placed her hand on Cap's back. Then he vomited a little bit at his feet. All green juice. He stood up, his face red.

"Tastes like aquarium," he said, before another round of coughing.

"Breathe," said Vega, watching the SUV speed out of the parking lot, turn in to traffic. She turned back to Cap. "Are you okay?"

He breathed, nodded.

"I think that guy went easy on me, all things considered," he said.

"Makes sense," said Vega. "Lara doesn't know who we are, who we work for." She watched the color in Cap's face return to its normal olive shade. "Sorry I couldn't move on him," she added.

Cap shook his head, waved off her apology.

"Not many people could've moved on that guy," he said. "What now?"

Vega looked toward the street where the SUV had gone. She thought about it. They couldn't just come at Lara with their two baby firearms and spilled juice. They would have to wait and have the Bastard keep digging. Perry would have said it best: Hurry up and wait.

Sean McTiernan, Otero's detective, was a barrel-chested guy with glasses. He greeted them in the reception of the PD and introduced himself, having only emailed with Vega, and shook their hands vigorously, a thin laptop tucked under his arm. He reminded Cap a little bit of his old friend Em, with his good-natured-frat-boy eagerness.

"Detective McTiernan?" Cap repeated, sounding more uncertain than he'd meant to.

"I know. Black guy, Irish name. Fluent in Spanish, too," said McTiernan. "Got to stay unpredictable. Follow me, okay?"

Cap and Vega followed him, and he talked as he walked.

"So the good news is we got a trace on most of the bills from LoSanto's apartment," said McTiernan, pushing through a thick steel door into a stairwell. "Bad news is they're clean. Random serials; random dates."

"They looked well worn," said Vega.

"You could say that," said McTiernan, over his shoulder. "Most've probably been through G-strings in strip clubs, you know?"

Cap felt obliged to laugh, sensing it was a joke meant for him. Vega gave him a mild side eye.

"And LoSanto?" said Cap, bringing it back to business.

McTiernan opened a door leading to the second floor. Cap was struck at the cleanliness of the hallway, the lack of characteristic locker room smells. Did the warm weather make people want to dust more, he thought.

"We're pushing for grand theft for the IUDs, but realistically his lawyer will probably get it down to misdemeanor," said McTiernan.

He opened a door to a small conference room that smelled like coffee and had a long window with a nice view of some office parks and the freeway behind it. But even that was pretty here, Cap thought. All green and blue.

McTiernan gestured for them to have a seat and asked if they wanted coffee, which Cap accepted.

"But what does he know?" said Vega.

"Nothing," said McTiernan, matter-of-fact. "Got an email offering him a chance to make some easy money and he took it. Didn't know the buyer. Was instructed to leave the items in a specific locker at the bus station downtown and return a few hours later to get the money from the same locker, which he did."

"You have any video from the bus station?" said Vega.

"Yep," said McTiernan. "But it's no great shakes. You can barely make out LoSanto and you really can't make out the cash dropper."

"Can we see it anyway?"

McTiernan nodded and opened the laptop, cued a video and played it. A block of square lockers, and people coming and going.

"There's LoSanto at ten thirty-three a.m.," McTiernan narrated.

There he was in a hooded windbreaker, opening a locker in the far right corner of the screen, placing a backpack inside and closing the door. When he turned, Vega could see LoSanto's face, or the vague shape of it anyway. If she hadn't known it was him, the chances of identifying him would have been slim.

"And then we bring it forward," said McTiernan, dragging the time dot, as the light in the bus station flickered slightly, and people came and went in high speed.

McTiernan slowed the footage down. A figure wearing a baggy sweatshirt, jeans, and a ski hat with a concentric circle target design on the top approached the locker, opened it, removed LoSanto's backpack, and shoved a gym duffel inside. Then left, face turned away from the screen.

"You use any facial recognition software?" asked Cap.

"Sure, but look at that," said McTiernan, tapping the screen with his thick finger. "We can't get anything with that kind of resolution. If this was an airport, not a bus station, maybe. Low-tech, low-fi."

"LoSanto know anything else that might be of interest?" said Vega.

"Not really," said McTiernan. "My take is that he wanted some quick cash, didn't think it would hurt anyone, actually thought maybe it was some kind of public service."

"Like a birth control Robin Hood," said Cap.

"Exactly," said McTiernan. "Had no idea where the units were actually going."

Vega stared at the screen, at the image of the cash dropper. Fuzzy face, maybe Caucasian male but she couldn't be sure.

"Did you follow this guy through the security footage?" she said. "Track him to the parking lot?"

"We lost him in the crowd. I can give you the video but nothing too meaningful came from it."

"Sure," said Vega.

McTiernan patted his breast pocket, then his pants. He pulled out a black USB drive and plugged it into the laptop, started dragging and dropping files.

"You interview the girlfriend?" said Vega.

McTiernan let a tiny wrinkle cross his brow.

"LoSanto didn't mention a girlfriend," he said. "We checked the apartment, too. No female personal items; no extra toothbrush." He smiled at Vega, curious. "Do you have reason to believe he has a girlfriend?"

Vega felt an odd warmth surge through her chest and rib cage, like the first minute or two of her handstand in the morning, an instant assurance. Clarity, as people in AA would call it; the light, as the chakra thumpers would say in yoga. Vega had no name for it, only noticed it when things started to line up and make sense.

"Nope," she said. "Thought he mentioned one. Might've heard him wrong."

McTiernan believed her, nodded quickly. "We could ask him again. Couldn't hurt."

Vega shrugged innocently. Couldn't hurt. She looked to Cap, who nodded helpfully. She had told him all about Sarita the girlfriend, but you would never know it from his face, the perfect mix of eager and oblivious. Vega was quietly thankful for his undercover skills, and she felt her fingers start to twitch in anticipation of a new email to the Bastard, as she could almost smell the cotton candy in the air.

It was close to two o'clock when they found the strip mall where Sarita Guerra worked in a nail salon, or so her paychecks from the past year had shown. The sun through the window was hot on Cap's lap; he flipped the sun guard down and to the side, but still the light burned a small parallelogram of heat on his thigh. The mall had a hacienda vibe, faux adobe and stucco, a tiled arch above each store.

Vega parked in front of a taco shop next to the nail salon, powered down the windows, and turned the engine off. Didn't make a move to get out.

"We waiting for something?" said Cap.

He could see only the very edge of her eye behind her sunglasses, a dot of light bouncing off the iris.

"I don't want to spook her in her place of business," said Vega. "Her friends might want to get involved, call 911." She shook her head, added, "Not worth it."

Cap glanced at the time on the dash.

"We're a little past average lunchtime," he said. "Could be a while before she's out."

Vega unbuckled her seatbelt and leaned forward so her head almost rested on the top of the steering wheel.

"She'll be out soon," she said. "She's a vaper. Probably tried smoking but it made her cough so now she inhales this candy-flavored stuff."

"So convenient that now you don't have to choose between candy and cigarettes," said Cap.

Vega didn't respond, kept her eyes on the door of the salon. After a few minutes a lady with cheetah-print leggings went inside. Then, two women carrying giant purses came out. It was about a half hour later that Sarita came through the door with another woman with the ends of her hair dyed pink. They huddled around the cigarette butt receptacle shaped like a genie's lamp. Sarita held and lit her vape pipe. The woman with the pink tips smoked a long, thin cigarette.

"Just stay behind me, okay?" said Vega.

"Sure thing," said Cap.

They got out. Cap leaned on the hood and watched Vega step onto the curb and quickly approach Sarita and Pink Tips.

"Sarita," said Vega.

Sarita turned and froze, eyes flaring. Pink Tips, thin with a tan face full of smoker's lines, regarded Vega quizzically.

"Friend of yours?" she said to Sarita.

Sarita didn't speak, only took one shuffling step backward, away from Vega.

"I'm her insurance representative," said Vega. "Would you mind excusing us? I'd like to speak to her confidentially about her policy."

Pink Tips stared at her blankly.

"What?" she said.

"Sarita," said Vega, coming closer to her.

Sarita backed up another small step. Cap could see the gun-shyness in her eyes, thought she was probably remembering the sound of Vega's Springfield cracking the glass picture frame. She held the vape pipe with both hands to her chest.

"Your policy," said Vega, removing her glasses so Sarita could see her eyes.

"Wait, so who are you?" said Pink Tips, her voice gaining an edge of impatience.

Cap came off the hood a second. He had no doubt Vega could handle this situation without thumbs and eyes, but he wanted to be ready, just in case.

"She's my insurance representative," said Sarita quietly. "For life insurance . . . I have to talk to her confidentially."

"Okay, cool," said Pink Tips, accepting the story. She pulled her phone from the back pocket of her jeans and said, "You do you."

Vega held her arm out, showing Sarita the way. They walked back to the car, Sarita in front of Vega. Sarita froze again when she saw Cap. Cap hadn't ever thought he was an imposing figure, even when he'd had a badge to flash, but this girl seemed jittery to begin with; any unknown thing or person would push her into panic mode.

"It's okay," said Vega. "He's my partner, Max Caplan."

"Hi," said Cap, raising his hand in a wave.

Sarita only nodded, still looking stunned.

"Are you arresting me?" she said.

"No," said Vega. "We're not cops. Remember I told you I work for the SDPD? I'm a private investigator; I don't have the authority to arrest you. I just need to ask you a couple of questions."

Sarita nodded again, turned around to look at Pink Tips, who was engrossed in texting.

"Do you understand?" said Vega. "Can you say you understand?"

"Yeah," said Sarita. "I understand."

"Are you aware that Tony told the police he didn't have a girlfriend or a spouse?"

"Yeah," said Sarita sadly.

"Do you know why he would do that?"

"He didn't want me to get in trouble."

"Why would you be in trouble?"

"I wouldn't!" Sarita said, a little too loudly. She glanced back at Pink Tips, who still wasn't paying attention. "I wouldn't," she said again, quieter. "He just didn't want me to get involved. He said we needed to spend some time apart—"

Now the corners of her mouth curled into an unstoppable frown like that of a little kid. Cap felt very sorry for her.

"So he could go away for what he did and the cops wouldn't bother me." She turned to Cap. "He knows he committed a crime; he just wanted to put away some money for us," she implored him.

Cap gave her a sympathetic smile and nod. Keep talking.

"Here's the thing, Sarita," said Vega. "I think there are two possible reasons Tony didn't tell the cops about you. Either it's exactly like you say, and he didn't want you to have to deal with it . . ."

Sarita wiped the corners of her eyes.

Vega continued: "Or you are connected to this money somehow, this crime. You might know some information that would be useful to the police, and Tony doesn't want them to know that information."

"I don't . . . I don't know anything," said Sarita desperately.

"Actually, I believe you," said Vega. "But I think you know someone or something that links you to what Tony did, and you may not realize it."

Sarita shook her head, her tight black curls bouncing off her shoulders.

"No, I swear, I don't. I swear."

"I believe you," said Vega, "but you may know something, even if you think it's nothing. Even on the off chance that it might help you, and maybe even take some pressure off Tony, wouldn't you want to at least try?"

Sarita thought about it. Her eyes welled again and again she wiped them. She nodded.

"Yeah."

"Okay," said Vega softly. "But I need you to concentrate."

Sarita nodded. Cap thought she looked a little more composed and serious now.

"Can you remember anyone—a family member, or a friend, or a co-worker," said Vega, gesturing toward the nail salon, "who expressed an interest in Tony's job?"

Sarita thought. "Um, I don't know, I'm having trouble thinking," she said, her voice shaky.

"That's okay," said Vega. "You can just say if anyone comes to mind, or if they don't, you can say that, too. How about anyone who makes a good living, has a lot of cash on hand?"

"Sure, I guess," Sarita said uneasily. "My uncle runs a car dealership up in L.A. He makes a lot of money. But we don't really see him too often."

"Great, that's a good start," said Vega. "Anyone else?"

"Lot of the girls have cash who work at the salon—tips and everything like that," said Sarita, looking back at Pink Tips.

Cap and Vega looked at Pink Tips too. Cap glanced at Vega. Slim chance anyone in the salon would be involved. Not enough money.

"I got this cousin," said Vega, leaning on the car casually, tapping her key against the roof. "Always getting into binds. Does a little jail time now and again. I think pretty much everyone has a relative like that, right?" she said to Cap.

"Definitely," said Cap. "More of a gray sheep, though, right? Because they're not bad people necessarily; bad situations just have a tendency to find them."

Sarita's face brightened up.

"Oh yeah," she said. "My brother Joe's just like that. But he's . . . he's not rich or anything."

Tension quickly coursed back into her face.

"He hasn't been in trouble in a long time," she said, plainly worried she had said too much.

"That's okay," said Vega. "Remember, we're not cops. We're not arresting anybody. We're trying to help Tony."

Sarita seemed to accept this and continued.

"We don't see him too much," she said.

"When's the last time you saw him, do you think?" said Vega.

"Probably around the holidays. Yeah, Three Kings?"

"Do you happen to remember if he talked to Tony at all?"

She shrugged.

"I don't know. Probably?" She looked from Vega to Cap, back to Vega. "But that doesn't mean he has anything to do with this."

"You're right," said Vega. "Not necessarily. What does Joe do for work now?"

Sarita pursed her lips.

"Last time I talked to him he was . . ." As she remembered she blushed pink in the cheeks. "He was working at a club. A strip club."

Cap thought Vega had the expression of a foreigner, or perhaps an alien, who had heard the words "strip club" before but was unsure of their meaning.

"What did he do there?" Vega asked. "Was he a bouncer?"

"I think he did a little of everything. What did he call it?" she said, trying to remember something. "You know, like they do in the army? What is that word?" she said, frustrated. "You know, he did some scouting for the dancers, like hiring."

"Recruitment," said Vega.

Cap watched Vega carefully. He knew what her questions would be before she asked them, but still she managed to make them seem fresh, innocent, curious. She pulled every last bit of information from Sarita Guerra like she was winding the string on a kite, drawing it in for a tight, safe landing.

The place was called Rare Strip; the sign was an animated woman holding a fork with heat lines coming off the prongs. Vega and Cap kept their guns on them, took the chance that there was no metal detector, which turned out to be the case. The bouncer was a fat, bald white guy. Not Joe Guerra, Vega knew, both from the description Sarita had provided and from the photos on Facebook and Instagram.

Inside was dim and smelled of antibacterial wipes, the music loud but not deafening. The stage was a single runway, three topless girls on poles in various states of straddle, surrounded on either side by small cocktail tables, six booths against the walls on both sides. A bar ran along the wall near the entrance, a single female bartender behind it. Vega estimated about twenty patrons, spread out, a couple of heavies sitting close to the stage.

There were two guys at the bar, one white-haired wearing a sleeveless fleece vest with a tie underneath, sipping a beer and watching the girls. The other sat at the end of the bar furthest from the front door, wearing sunglasses and a black sweatshirt with the hood up, texting, facing away from the stage. Vega thought it looked like Joe Guerra but couldn't be sure until she got a little closer.

"Why don't you get a table, wait for the waitress, get a drink," she said to Cap, nodding toward the stage.

"Got it," he said. "Let me know what you need."

She nodded again, and Cap left her, sat at a table near the edge of the stage. Vega made her way to the end of the bar. She remembered Sarita saying her brother had star tattoos on both hands. Vega sat two seats down from the guy in the black sweatshirt and could easily see the star on his right hand as he texted with his thumbs.

"Can I get you something?" asked the bartender, a beachy blonde with a tight white T-shirt and no bra.

"Club soda," said Vega.

The bartender filled a glass from the soda gun and passed it to Vega. Vega put some dollars on the bar and squeezed the lime wedge over the water, stirred it with the thin red straw. She swiveled around on her chair to face the stage, turning toward Guerra, who remained focused on his phone. She estimated him at about five eight or five nine, but his chest and shoulders looked broad under the sweatshirt, his neck thick from what she could see of it. Height was never the whole story and sometimes even made people clumsier, more likely to trip over their own feet.

Vega caught Cap's eye; he was smiling and chatting politely with a waitress. You okay? said his eye. Vega tilted her chin up to signal Yes, I am just fine, Caplan.

"You have a favorite?" she said in Guerra's direction.

Guerra didn't respond at first, then seemed to realize Vega was speaking to him.

He cast a quick glance at the girls on the stage and said, "Nah, I work here. You know, don't shit where you eat."

He smiled at Vega, had that look men got when they encountered an attractive woman in an unexpected place.

"I like the girl in the middle," said Vega. "She looks the strongest," she added, making it sound like an impartial observation.

"Yeah?" said Guerra, intrigued. He turned to look at the stage. "Her name's Phoenix, like the city. You want me to introduce you? A hundred for a ten-minute private dance."

"Maybe later," said Vega. "I'm actually looking for girls a little younger than that."

Guerra's smile shrank, and he went back to texting.

"You're outta luck. We don't hire under eighteen."

"That's too bad," said Vega. "You know anyone who does?"

Guerra pulled his sunglasses off and set them on the bar.

"I told you we don't hire under eighteen."

"Yeah, I heard that part," said Vega, moving onto the seat next to him. Then she said slowly, "And I asked *you* if you know anyone who does."

Guerra sighed through his nose and pointed to a sign behind the bar.

"You read that? Right to refuse anyone service, just 'cause we feel like it. In about a minute I'm-a feel like it with you, girl."

"Then I got a whole minute to tell you what I know and what I think, Joe Guerra," said Vega, watching him rear back in surprise. He began to stand. "Don't stand," she said. "Sarita told me where to find you. And I know how to find her."

Guerra's eyes flashed as he hovered over his chair.

"You don't know shit," he mumbled.

"Sit down," Vega said gently.

He sat.

"There you go," said Vega. "Now I'm going to tell you what I think. I think someone offered you some money to find some off-market birth control, and you hooked him up with your sister's boyfriend. I think you may have done other sorts of favors and jobs for someone. I think someone's advantage in using you is he doesn't have to show his face. But like I said, now I know your face."

Guerra returned to texting and said with a sneer, "You a cop or what?"

"Or what," said Vega. She sipped her club soda. "Oh yeah, something else I know," she said, tapping her temple. "I know I need someone's name, and I know you can give that to me. And I know if you don't, I can have some police here pretty quickly."

Guerra pushed off the bar and stood so he stared right down into Vega's eyes.

"And I *know* me and my boys can do a little damage to your man over there before any cop can get here."

Vega let her gaze shift to Cap, who drank a bottle of light beer and watched the girls distractedly. She imagined her arms being pinned back while watching Guerra and the bouncer take turns cracking his ribs and jaw with their fists.

"It won't be his first body hit today," she said, shrugging. "You do you," she added, ambivalent.

Then Guerra's phone began to ring and buzz simultaneously. He didn't look at it, kept staring Vega down.

"You better get that," said Vega, not looking at the phone either. "It's your sister."

Guerra snapped his head back to check and then grabbed it, answered.

"Rita," he said.

He kept his eyes on Vega while he listened to his sister. Vega moved the straw in her drink in circles. She watched his face change, his eyes finally breaking away from the stare and skipping scattershot around the room, which Vega thought must mean he was taking in a lot of information, fast and urgent.

"Alice Vega," he said aloud, repeating. "Yeah, I got it. Don't worry, girl. I'll talk to you later."

He hit the red button on the screen of his phone and dropped it on the bar.

"How's she doing?" said Vega, staring into her drink.

"She said you told her to call me. You're Vega?" he said.

"Yep," she said. "She say anything else?"

"That you came to see her where she works and you're helping her."

"She's right," said Vega, looking up at her reflection in the mirror behind the bar, lit from beneath with a blue LED strip. "I'm helping her avoid getting arrested as an accomplice to grand theft."

She sensed Guerra tensing up, even as he backed away from her.

"Or as an accomplice to whatever kind of mess you're into."

In the mirror she could see him sit down. She picked up her phone and waved it at him a little bit.

"So this is an email to the cop working the case for SDPD. It's all about how your sister introduced you to her boyfriend for the purpose of you all illegally moving birth control."

Vega lifted one shoulder, scratching her chin.

"Between you and me, I don't believe that. But I think I could convince some people of it," she said, placing the phone on the bar carefully. "I have a guy on the outside who's going to send it on my behalf in about . . ." She checked her watch. "Ten minutes, unless he hears from me."

Guerra clenched his jaw and looked at his own reflection in the blue light.

"What makes you think I give a shit what happens to my sister?"

"I don't," she said. "But she seems like a nice kid and genuinely doesn't know that her boyfriend and her brother could put her in a state penitentiary for eighteen months or so because of their bullshit."

Guerra flipped his phone around in his hands, appearing to consider his options.

"You got about eight minutes, Joe," said Vega. She stood up, smoothed out her pant legs.

She took a step toward him and leaned down. She was not exactly whispering in his ear but she could still feel the heat of her breath bounce back from his skin to her lips. Close enough.

"You want to be smart, you'll answer my questions. You want to keep on being dumb, you go right the fuck ahead. I'll be over there with my partner if you want to have a conversation."

She walked away, felt him watching. She couldn't help but feel a rush, not sexual necessarily, but it was usually all mixed up for her anyway—adrenaline and control and desire and knowing she had such a big tough guy in a tiny bubble between her thumb and forefinger.

"So you want to interrogate him in the back of a car like the mafia or something?" said Cap in the parking lot of Rare Strip, after Guerra had obediently gone into the backseat. "When we have a nicely appointed police station we can bring him to?"

Vega glared at him.

"He's ours right now. The second he walks through the doors he's theirs. Their questions, their strategy," she said, pausing to rub her chin. "Their rules."

"Okay, I'm not trying to be the cockblocker here, but it wouldn't be bad to have their rules with a guy like this, with whomever he's associated, if we need to elevate the level of, say, security, manpower, backup, things of that nature. And McTiernan seems to know his way around."

He gestured with his hands as he spoke, like a lawyer making a case to the judge.

"What do you think?" he said, when she hadn't said anything.

"I think it's a pretty cockblocky thing to say," she said, putting her sunglasses on. "But not untrue." She tilted her head to one side and took a fast breath in, thinking about it. "Okay. We'll try it. Can you text McTiernan, tell him we're coming?"

Cap grinned broadly, said, "Anything for you, Miss Vega."

Vega shook her head at him, rolled her eyes under her sunglasses.

McTiernan was smarter than he looked, Cap thought.

Not that he was dumb, but he looked like a cop. And not that cops were dumb, but cops had a way of thinking like doctors checking boxes off a list. Science, not art. It was a little like the old game of Clue that he used to play with Nell. Eliminating each person, each weapon, each place. Except in police work there were a hell of a lot more suspects, objects, locations, and then the thing that connected all of them or split them all apart—motive. It was murky, messy, and tangled, and rarely ended with three cards folded neatly inside a tiny brown envelope.

When Cap and Vega showed up at the impeccably clean police station with Joe Guerra following them voluntarily, McTiernan shook his hand politely and welcomed him like Guerra was someone he was expecting and was glad finally to meet. McTiernan took them all to a small conference room and told Guerra to make himself comfortable, offered him a selection of beverages—coffee, water, soda. Guerra accepted a chilled bottled water, and then McTiernan shut the door on Guerra and stood with Cap and Vega in the hallway.

"How is he connected?" he asked them, crossing his arms.

Vega told him the truth.

McTiernan took it in, pushed his glasses firmer back on the bridge of his nose.

"So LoSanto did have a girlfriend," he said, not quite like a reprimand.

"I met her before," said Vega. "She knows me. I knew I was more likely to get something out of her than if we brought her in here."

"That's fine," said McTiernan, plainly unoffended. "We got him here right now. How do you think we should do this?"

Vega hesitated, so Cap spoke up.

"We told him it's him or his sister, so I think he'll tell us—we didn't ask him anything yet. We wanted it to take place here, on the record with you."

"And I appreciate it," he said. "Comm will feel more comfortable if I'm in there. One of you want to come in with me; the other one want to watch from behind the double-side, I'm good with it."

"Wait," said Cap. "*That's* your interrogation room?"

"One of them," said McTiernan. "It's for this particular type of suspect. We want him relaxed because he's coming in willingly, but we still want to observe and get what we can get."

"There's a ficus in there," said Cap incredulously. "I'm sorry, it's just the nicest interrogation room I've ever seen."

"But there's no mirror," said Vega.

McTiernan beckoned them with his finger.

"Follow me a sec," he said.

They followed him into the room adjacent to the conference room.

It was about the same size and had no windows to the outside, with a clear glass pane about two by two feet. There was Guerra, slumped in his chair, staring at his phone screen.

"The picture," said Vega.

"Yeah," said McTiernan. "The photo of the boat on the wall—it's a double-side."

"No shit," said Cap in awe, turning to peer through the glass.

McTiernan smiled and said, "So, one of you want to come in?"

"Yeah, she will," said Cap, running his finger along the pane. "I'll watch from in here. You have a camera or some other recording device?"

"We got cameras in the light fixtures," said McTiernan, pointing toward the ceiling in the conference room. "They're voice-activated—as soon as we start talking they'll start recording."

"Come. On," said Cap.

"Truth," said McTiernan, chuckling. "Where'd you say you're from, Cap?"

"Nineteen fifty-six, apparently," said Cap.

"You ready?" Vega said to McTiernan, done listening to the banter.

"Well, yeah," he said congenially. "You have a way you like to do this?"

"I can ask what I need to ask, then you can jump in if I don't cover what you need," said Vega.

"That works," said McTiernan. "After you."

Vega headed for the door, tapping out a quick text before leaving the room. McTiernan followed her, and then Cap was alone. He watched them walk into the interrogation room, watched Joe Guerra remain seated as McTiernan did a little spiel about rights and lawyers. Guerra didn't appear to care less about his rights, Cap suspected because he knew Vega would hold his sister under the water like a runt kitten if Guerra didn't talk. Cap's phone buzzed. It was the text Vega had sent on her way out.

It read "Keep eye out for Otero."

They all set their phones aside.

Guerra's upper body was much wider than the chair. He'd removed his hoodie, revealing two full sleeves of tattoos—dragons and tigers. He sat with one arm hooked around the back of the chair. Vega could see him as a kid in junior high, throwing paper airplanes at girls.

"Could you tell us your name?" Vega said.

"Jose Ramon Guerra."

"Could you tell us how you know Antonio LoSanto?"

"He's my sister's boyfriend."

"Did you broker a deal between LoSanto and another party to exchange money for IUD birth control units?"

Guerra ran his tongue over his top row of teeth, maybe wrestling one last time with offering the confession, Vega thought.

"Yeah," he said.

Vega paused, thinking he might add something without being prompted. He rolled his shoulders back in a small stretch, didn't speak.

"Who is the other party?" said Vega.

"Guy named Coyote Ben," said Guerra.

"Last name?"

Guerra sighed. "Davis. Like the pants, you know?"

"He's Caucasian?" said Vega.

Guerra nodded.

"Could you say yes or no?"

"Yeah. How you know that?"

"Coyote's what they call white guys who bring people over the border, right?" said Vega.

Now Guerra shrugged.

"If you say so."

"How did you first meet him?"

Guerra leaned forward, glanced quickly over his shoulder, not consciously looking for someone, Vega thought, but just out of habit.

"He brought me a girl. I knew she was too young. We don't hire underage," he said to McTiernan. "He said she was his cousin who just moved from Tijuana and needed a job."

"Did you believe that?" said Vega.

"Hell nah," said Guerra. "He tried to convince me she was eighteen. Girl had, like, baby fat in her face." Guerra tapped under his chin with the top of his hand.

"So who do you think she was?" said Vega.

Guerra regarded Vega like there was something she wasn't grasping. "Some girl he got sold," said Guerra. "There's all kinds of these girls from down south; their family sends them up, they just get sold."

"Coyote Ben gifted in that area?" said Vega. "Selling girls?"

"Hey," said Joe, coming off the back of the chair. "My place is all legal.

All of it. Check the paperwork. Check the taxes. I don't got a thing to do with what Coyote Ben does for work."

"Right," said Vega. "What'd he say next?"

Joe breathed big through his nose, nostrils expanding to catch all the air he could get out of the room.

"He said if I didn't want that girl, the baby face, he had others that could bring in more cash," he said. "I told him, Shit, Flaco, you got a lotta cousins."

"But you still told him no?" said Vega.

"Yeah, no," he said, then reflecting on the confusing sound of it, added, "Correct, I said no fucking way."

"So how'd it happen he get to asking you about black-market birth control?" said Vega.

"The guy asked for it."

"He just asked for that specific thing, outright? IUDs," said Vega.

Guerra flattened his lips, straining to remember.

"Nah, we're sitting in the office, I'm telling him we don't take under-age girls. He just starts talking about ways a guy could make extra cash, says he needs a way to keep girls from getting pregnant, asks do I talk to my girls about shit like that."

"Do you?" said Vega.

"Hell, no," said Guerra, rearing his head. "I ain't their daddy. I told him I don't know shit about that."

"What did he say?"

"He asked if I knew anyone who could get prescription birth control. Equipment, not pills."

Vega didn't follow up with another question right away. Guerra glanced at McTiernan, who didn't make a move to speak either.

"Then I thought of Tony," said Guerra, filling in the space. "I knew he worked at a clinic. Thought he could use the money, buy my sister something."

Vega stared at him and thought. After she didn't speak for a minute, Guerra added, "I didn't think it was so big. Not like knocking off a gas station."

Vega stood suddenly and Guerra appeared to brace himself, hunching shoulders forward, hands not quite forming fists but fingers extended in his lap.

"Joe. Detective," Vega said to McTiernan. "I need to step out. Excuse me."

Guerra returned to the more relaxed posture, sitting back in the chair. McTiernan nodded and asked Guerra, "Did you think about why someone would request birth control for a group of teenage girls?"

Guerra started talking, his tone defensive, while Vega left the conference room and went next door.

"Hey," Cap said, leaning against the wall next to the double-side. "Why'd you leave? It's just getting good."

Vega wandered up to the glass and stood about an inch away.

"Something's not square," she said.

"With Guerra?" said Cap. "I think I believe him."

"Yeah," said Vega airily. Then she tapped the glass lightly, as if she were pointing to a fish she liked, but not trying to get its attention. "I think I do, too."

She shut her eyes briefly and saw doors. Car doors, hotel room doors, sliding glass doors, mechanical garage doors. It was not an unfamiliar image, nor was the instinctual reaction that closed doors elicited (frustration, anger), but there was a different thing here. Vega's fingers twitched, and she knew—the doors were shut but they were unlocked. Just like Dylan Duffy's car.

She opened her eyes and said, "Guerra doesn't have anything to do with it. There's someone else—someone bigger."

Vega felt her phone buzz continuously and aggressively, like it did when there was a flood or fire warning. As she pulled it from her pocket she saw McTiernan through the glass doing the same thing. Cap noticed it too, looking from one to the other, his own phone silent.

It was a series of five texts from Otero, all the same message: "STOP INVESTIGATION NOW."

Vega showed it to Cap, both of them standing back from the phone as if it would detonate. Vega looked at McTiernan, who shot a quick glance in her direction from where he sat.

"The hell," muttered Cap.

But before he could finish his thought or Vega could concur, they watched McTiernan twist around toward the door as a plainclothes officer came through it. Vega turned to their door, didn't get to a count of one before it opened.

10

CAP, VEGA, AND McTIERNAN WERE ALL BROUGHT TO ANOTHER room that Cap thought looked like a nice place for a board meeting. There was a long table in the shape of a surfboard surrounded by twenty or so wheeled ergonomic chairs. Commander Otero stood near the entrance, looking just a little anxious, Cap thought. A slightly short, slightly chunky guy with pursed lips tapped notes on his phone screen. Cap figured he was Mackey, Boyce's partner, since Vega had described Boyce as being a Ken doll type, and this man was not that.

Otero made quiet, strained introductions. The man with the phone was in fact Mackey. Otero gestured to the chairs and asked them all to sit, which they did, Vega in the middle between McTiernan and Cap. Otero was on their side of the table as well but swiveled his chair so that he faced them.

"We appreciate all of your work here, all three of you," he began. "Ms. Vega, you move even faster and with more precision than your reputation had suggested. I've had a chance to circle back with Agent Mackey about the recon you've done and what you've turned up so far. I'm pleased to let you know that we will no longer require your services on this case."

Cap felt a smile, mostly born of confusion, come to his lips, and he covered his mouth with his hand and rubbed his face to hide it. Vega didn't move. McTiernan was visibly shocked, turning to look at Vega, then Cap, then Mackey, then back to Otero.

"Detective McTiernan," said Otero. "You've also done good solid work this week. You can consider the case closed for now."

"Commander," said McTiernan. "I'm literally in the middle of an interrogation with a subject related to the case. Right now. Literally."

"I'm aware of that, and when we wrap this meeting up, you can give me a quick debrief."

"Commander—" McTiernan said again.

"Detective," said Otero sternly, holding up a fatherly hand. Not now, son, said the hand. He brought his attention back to Vega. "If you have any materials you'd like to share before you and Mr. Caplan leave, you're welcome to do so. Otherwise, we'd like to thank you for your assistance."

Cap didn't move, could see the fingers on Vega's right hand fan out, like she was about to play the piano.

"So which is it?" she said quietly. "Is the case closed or do you no longer require my services?"

Otero smiled politely.

"I can't go into detail," he said. "But some new evidence has come to light that requires us to hand the case over to Agents Mackey and Boyce," he said, gesturing to Mackey across the table. "To answer your question, it's both things—for the SDPD and for you, the case is closed, and we therefore no longer require your services."

Cap watched the tremor in Vega's fingers as she touched each tip to her thumbnail. She looked at Mackey, still intent on texting, and breathed deeply. Cap knew she was waiting them out with her silence, and he knew better than to fill up the space with chatter. McTiernan, however, was still agitated.

"I don't understand," he said plainly. "We still don't know who killed the Janes, right?" When he didn't receive a response, he continued: "And we still don't know if there are other girls out there, and where they are? Because of Vega we have a through line, Commander—Guerra gave us a name: Ben Davis. Coyote Ben. All we have to do is track this guy." When Otero didn't immediately answer, he addressed Mackey directly: "There's no point in shutting us down when we can help you, right?"

"Detective," said Mackey, finally breaking away from the phone. "Like the commander said, we appreciate it. But we need to take it from here. We're hoping we can count on you to keep all the details of the case confidential."

"Yeah, of course," said McTiernan, just missing the "duh."

"You understand how this can turn in a second," Mackey continued, speaking to all of them ostensibly, but looking in Vega's direction. "Something pops up, we need to move fast and take care of it." Then he turned back to McTiernan and smiled. "Does that address your question, Detective . . ."

Mackey let the end of the question hang, struggling to remember McTiernan's name.

"McTiernan," said Cap, pissed off now. Pissed at Otero for not standing up for his people and pissed at Mackey for being so goddamn tone-deaf. "M-C-T-I-E-R-N-A-N," he spelled. "Starts with an 'M,' like Mackey, so you should be able to remember that."

Mackey paused, a light flashing through his eyes as he regarded Cap.

"Thank you, Mr. Caplan. I think I will."

His phone lit up with an incoming text, and he glanced at it.

"Great," said Cap, feeling his heart rate rise. He could almost hear Nell telling him, Dad, calm down, think of your blood pressure. "I know I'm not from here, but I was a cop for fifteen years, and usually we wanted continuity, like a chain of custody in a case. You lose us, you're losing the connections we've established so far—" Cap counted on his fingers. "The witness relationships, evidence, game plan." He paused. "Opinions. Are you at all interested in what we think, or are you too busy staring at your fucking phone?"

Cap slapped his palm on the table, and Mackey jumped in his chair and finally looked up. Cap noticed Vega's hands were still, and that had a somewhat pacifying effect on him. He pulled his hand from the table and leaned back in his chair, tugged the bottom flaps of his jacket down to straighten them.

"Mr. Caplan," said Otero, level as the Mona Lisa, "as I've said, we remain interested in all of the intelligence you've gathered. You may feel free to fax it to me at a later time."

"To *fax* it to you?" Cap said, in a state of shock.

"Offline," said Vega to him, though he knew she was fully aware everyone could hear her. "They want to keep it offline."

"That's correct," said Otero. "To maintain confidentiality and reduce the chance the information will be compromised."

Cap was really all done. For reasons he could not identify, the mention of a fax put him right over the edge. He stood up and pointed at the commander.

"Now you want to get a fax like an out-of-date cop shop instead of all your ridiculous tech bullshit? Sure thing, Commander, I'll be sure to send you a fax, whenever the hell I come across a fax machine."

He had not planned this and wasn't a hundred percent sure Vega would just follow him out the door, but he couldn't turn back now, and was also genuinely enraged at what seemed like a bureaucratic bottleneck.

"Good luck," he said in passing to McTiernan and placed a hand on his shoulder before leaving the room.

In the hallway it took him only a second to realize Vega was right behind him, hurrying to keep up.

"Sorry, Vega."

"Don't apologize, that all worked really well," she said as she pushed through the door to the stairwell.

"What do you mean?"

"Blowing up like that," she said under her breath, as they skipped down the stairs quickly. "Now they think we're done."

They walked through the lobby and out the front door without speaking, down the front steps into the parking lot. Cap squinted at the sun off the windshields, making the air blurry in the heat.

"Aren't we?" he said. "Done?"

Vega slipped her sunglasses on, pulled her key from her pocket.

"I don't think so. Do you?"

Cap stopped walking.

"No. But we just sort of got fired. Or laid off, it felt like," he said.

Vega stopped walking now and turned to face him.

"Sort of," she said. "They're not interested in anything we found out, I don't think. I think they're just interested in Devin Lara, and as soon as he came up, they shut it down." She peered over Cap's shoulder toward the station. "I'm not really sure why, don't think I care too much. There can't be that many Ben Davises that fit the description of the cash dropper. I'll put the Bastard on it, and we go from there."

Cap felt the afternoon sun start to hit him, full assault on the back of the neck and head, sweat forming on his upper back.

"You were good in there," said Vega.

"I was merely reacting to the waves of bullshit."

"You got us out clean."

Cap couldn't see her eyes behind the glasses, but he imagined them soft and bright.

"You see, Caplan?" she added. "You're so good you don't even know how good you are."

Cap resisted the urge to reach out and hook his arm around her waist. Instead he blushed and shrugged, fifteen years old inside.

A couple of hours later they sat in Vega's hotel room, scrolling through driver's licenses on the laptop. Cap ate a sandwich, Vega a banana. It was not difficult to find him. Of the seven Ben Davises with a California zip code south of Los Angeles (five Benjamins, one Benton, one just Ben), Vega and Cap narrowed their suspects to only two viable candidates: a thirty-three-year-old and a twenty-six-year-old.

After some preliminary googling and emails exchanged with the Bastard, Vega found the thirty-three-year-old Davis all over social media, posing alternately with a wife and kid in some pictures and in a football jersey tailgating in a parking lot in others. Vega guessed this was probably not their guy, or if it was, he had a fairly comprehensive cover—multiple posts and tweets about what adorable things his kids did and how cutting-edge his job as an IT specialist was.

Though the resolution of the bus station video was poor, Vega and Cap could still tell that the IT specialist family man was likely not the cash dropper.

The twenty-six-year-old's picture showed he was light-complected, with blue eyes and short-cropped blond hair.

"Says he's five ten," said Cap, staring at the laptop screen.

Vega clicked the play button on the video app, and they watched the bus station footage again. She paused it when the cash dropper turned toward the camera, though they couldn't get a true look at his face with the poor quality.

"Could be him," said Vega.

He proved harder to find. He did not show up on social media, nor could the Bastard track any issued checks from any of the national payroll companies. Vega typed in his address on the map app.

"Looks like apartments in San Marcos," she said.

"His residence as of three years ago," Cap said, reading the issue date on the license. "He could be anywhere now."

"But he could be there," said Vega, pointing to the screen. She tossed the banana peel into the trash, said, "Feel like a drive?"

Benchmark Apartments was an unimpressive cluster of buildings surrounding a pool that looked like it hadn't been cleaned in a while, small brown leaves and grass clippings floating on the surface of the water. The apartment number listed on the license was 3-204, so Vega and Cap walked around and found Building 3 of four, then went up the external stairs to the second floor and found the door. Knocked and rang the buzzer. No answer.

"How long you want to wait?" said Cap, leaning over the railing and peering down at the pool.

"Not long," said Vega, pulling a small leather pouch from the inside pocket of her jacket.

It took Cap a second to realize what it was. Then he said, "What—no more bobby pins?"

Vega unzipped the pouch.

"This is what I carry when I don't have to go through airport security," she said.

She removed a long steel pick the size of a pencil, and another almost identical except with a small hook at the top. She zipped up the pouch and slid it back into her pocket. Then she approached the door holding both tools in one hand like chopsticks.

"Hey, Vega?" said Cap. "Could we maybe, possibly, get through a case without breaking and entering?"

Vega stuck the hooked pick into the bolt lock upside down and began to wiggle it. Cap sighed.

"There are probably security cameras somewhere," he said, looking up to the corners of the hallway.

"Maybe," said Vega, sticking the second pick into the eye of the lock. "If there are, they're probably shit." She turned to him while she spoke, like she was sensing the inner workings of the lock by feel alone.

Cap sighed again to express his general disapproval but resigned himself to the position of lookout, leaning over the railing again and scanning the area around the pool and parking lot for people. He saw a couple here and there but they didn't seem to notice him.

"Really hope this doesn't end up like it did the last time we did this," he said ruefully.

"What—with a dead guy?" said Vega.

The bolt clicked and snapped. Vega pulled the sleeve of her jacket over her hand and turned the knob. She pushed the door open and stepped into the apartment. Cap sighed again and added a bonus grumble but followed her in, then gingerly shut the door behind them.

"See? No dead guy," said Vega.

"So far," said Cap.

They both looked around the room from where they stood. It appeared to be the ordinary apartment of a basic bro. A little furniture, piles of clothes, bottles, Styrofoam take-out containers. No books. Strong, sweet scent—food-related garbage mixed with spicy incense.

"I'm going to check the other rooms," said Vega.

"Yeah," said Cap. "We know what we're looking for?" he called to her, after she'd disappeared down a hallway.

She didn't answer but he knew what it was already: anything. Anything that might be something. Notes scribbled on scraps of paper, drops of blood or saliva, clothes that didn't belong to the occupant or items that didn't belong, period. But it was hard to tell what was out of place in such a dump.

Cap took a pen from his pocket and pushed around some of the food boxes on the low table in the living room, fruit flies swirling above it. Then he went to the kitchen, which consisted basically of a counter, oven, and refrigerator. On the counter was a pair of shorts, a half-drunk bottle of Muscle Milk, and some scattered change.

Vega emerged from the hallway with a black laptop under her arm.

"Let's go," she said.

"Theft, breaking and entering," said Cap, pointing to the laptop.

Vega pointed at Cap and added, "Whining."

"We're not working with your pal Otero anymore," said Cap. "He might not be as cool with us just plowing through suspects' apartments, warrantless."

"First of all, we're not cops," she started.

Cap finished her sentence, annoyed: "So we don't need a warrant. Right. But then we're plain old citizens engaging in some criminal activity."

Vega reached into her pocket and pulled something out of it—a small article of clothing. She tossed it to Cap.

"That's us," she said. "Plain old citizens."

Cap unfolded what she'd thrown him. It was a burgundy ski hat with yellow concentric circles printed on it, the top like a target. Just like the hat the cash dropper wore in the bus station video. Cap felt the thick-knit threads in his fingers. Damn and damn.

"Coming?" said Vega at the door.

Cap sighed once more, really loud this time, then followed her to wherever was next.

11

THE WATER IN THE HOTEL SHOWER WAS CONTROLLED BY ONE chrome knob that had a thin, etched line delineating hot and cold, so Vega moved it back and forth like a tuner on an old radio until she got the right temperature, a little colder than lukewarm, and let the water fall. After five minutes or so her skin reacted with prickly bumps, the tip of her nose and ears cold. She stayed in for another few minutes until she was thoroughly chilled, and then she turned the arrow on the knob further toward the blue C. When she could no longer feel the tips of her toes and fingers, she turned the water off and got out, wrapped a towel around herself, and felt her skin start to itch with the rush of warmth. She pulled her hair back into a rope and wrung the water out.

She left the bathroom and got cold again, the air conditioner humming steadily under the window. She saw her phone lighting up on the dresser and grabbed it, saw three texts from JPat.

"WTF."

"I don't get you."

"Calling you."

She glanced at her missed calls and didn't see his name, and then the phone started vibrating and ringing. It was him. She answered.

"Vega?" he said, sounding surprised.

"Yeah, it's me," she said, sitting on the edge of the bed.

He was quiet for a second and then said, in an exasperated burst, "*Where are you?*"

"El Centro," she said. "For a job."

"Wh—" he said, unable to get a whole word out. "When? Since when?"

"A few days ago," she said, taking her Bluetooth earbuds out of the case.

"You could have told me that. I've been, like, texting you, and you missed class and two privates."

Vega stuck the buds into her ears and held the phone in her lap, started to read her emails.

"Yes, because I'm in El Centro for a job."

She heard him exhaling in a huff.

"Well, what the fuck, man. You didn't think you might want to tell me? I don't hear from you, you don't show up to class—"

"You can charge me," said Vega.

"That's not the point, Vega," he said, walking quickly, his breath uneven.

"I had to leave right away for a job," she said again.

"Okay," he said loudly, as if that were just the last straw in the stack. "I get it. I'm telling you, if I left town, I would tell you. That's it."

Vega looked up from her phone. She could hear that he was upset. It was a thing she understood. She remembered him teaching her how to use her knee to dislodge someone's abdominal organs in their one-on-ones. She pictured his stomach, and what it felt like under her hands. She did not want to hurt his feelings, but she also found no reason to lie.

"John," she said. "If you feel like this, we should not do this thing. And if you don't want to do the classes anymore, or the one-on-ones, that's fine."

He made a sound somewhere between a laugh and a sigh.

"That's it, huh? Five months and that's it."

Vega had not realized she'd been sleeping with him for five months. She'd been taking classes with him for eight months. She knew that because of her credit card statement, and also because she thought about fighting differently now than she used to, how to leverage her strength with her elbows and knees.

"John, I have to go," she said. "If you want, you can text me in a couple of weeks, when I might be back."

"If I want?" he said. He stopped breathing heavily; Vega assumed he was standing still. "You know what? Fuck you."

Then he hung up. Vega pulled the headphones out of her ears and placed them back in the case. She heard it a few more times in her head: Fuck you, Fuck you, Fuck you. She wished he didn't feel the way he did, for his sake, but also wasn't particularly sad or angry herself. This was a thing she was used to.

She scanned her emails on the phone and then realized a text had come through from McTiernan while she'd been talking to John. She read it and called him, and as they spoke she got dressed, moving quicker and quicker until she was nearly running out the door and pounding on Cap's with her fist, calling his name.

Cap picked at a fruit salad in a cup as he left a message for Nell that went on too long, a problem of his that she'd pointed out many times before.

"Hey, Bug, it's me. Just having some fruit for dinner because, you know, it's healthy eating here in California. Case is going good. Well, actually, we technically got fired this afternoon, or laid off, because, well, we don't know why. And Vega, you know, she didn't take to it, so we're just going to keep moving it forward. Which may be against some laws, not real sure about that. But I trust her, Bug. I think I trust that she knows what she's doing. Anyway, thinking about you. Give me a call or a text. Love you."

He hung up and ate a piece of pineapple so fresh it made his eyes water, and then in rapid succession, he heard the door to Vega's room open and slam shut and, before he could get out of his chair, pounding on his own door. Cap ran to open it, and Vega stood there, her hair in a wet strip over her shoulder, making an even darker spot on her black T-shirt. She held her phone in her hand and waved it at Cap.

"I just got off with McTiernan," she said, stepping inside.

"Really? So soon?"

"He got a call from a guy claiming to be the brother of Jane Two."

Cap shut the door behind her and thought about it.

"How did that happen?"

"He called the station, asked to file a missing persons report. Guess who got bumped back to missing persons after our little meeting today?"

"McTiernan," said Cap.

"He starts describing his sister to McTiernan, sends a picture."

Vega tapped on her phone and showed the screen to Cap. It was a picture of a girl so fresh and youthful it looked like she'd just taken a bath in a stream, her skin glowing, a mouth of slightly crooked teeth smiling widely. She wore a pink T-shirt and was leaning out a window, a wash-rag draped over the sill. She was alive.

Vega flipped her phone back around and then scrolled to bring up another picture and showed Cap again. It was the head shot of the body of Jane 2, lips parted, frozen about an inch apart, crooked teeth hidden. But she looked like she had once been the girl in the previous picture. Once she had laughed and leaned out a window. Long before she wrote Vega's name on a scrap of paper and clutched it in her hand as she died.

"Looks like her," Cap agreed. "So why is McTiernan calling you and not bringing it to Otero and the DEA guys?"

"I don't know. He said he'd explain it when he got here."

"He's coming here?" said Cap.

"Yeah," said Vega. "Now. With the brother."

"Shit," said Cap. "You think he's going off the grid?"

"Seems that way."

They brainstormed about questions to ask the brother, and McTiernan, Cap jotting them down in a small black notebook. Then they waited, Vega checking her phone and also going to the window and peering out through the nearly closed curtains.

Soon it was completely dark outside, and Vega's phone began to buzz. She wrote a text with her thumb and went to the window.

"That them?" said Cap.

She nodded, and a minute later they heard two sets of footsteps on the landing outside, then a knock. It was McTiernan and a young Latino guy, short and stocky, wearing a baseball hat backward and a Padres sweatshirt. He had the shadow of a goatee on his upper lip and chin. He stood behind McTiernan and glanced around the room nervously, unsure if he'd have to talk or fight.

McTiernan shook Vega's hand with both of his as if it had been a long time since he'd seen her last. Then he shook Cap's.

"This is Rodrigo Villareal," he said.

Rodrigo stepped forward, nodding at Cap and Vega furtively. He said something in Spanish to McTiernan, who answered, "*Sí, sí.*"

Vega then introduced herself and Cap in Spanish to Rodrigo, which was about the limit of Cap's understanding of the language. Rodrigo nodded again, and McTiernan presented one of the chairs at the small table to him. Rodrigo looked at the chair, then at all of them. Cap took it upon himself to sit down first, thought it might make Rodrigo more comfortable.

It worked. Rodrigo didn't smile but sat in the chair opposite Cap. Vega sat on the edge of the bed closest to them, and McTiernan stood behind Rodrigo, leaning on the air-conditioning unit.

"You speak Spanish?" McTiernan said to Cap.

"No, unfortunately," said Cap. "I can get a word here or there."

"We'll translate for you," said McTiernan, nodding to Vega.

"You want to bring us up to speed?" she asked.

"Yeah, but let me tell him first," said McTiernan. He spoke to Rodrigo, who nodded, his eyes alert. McTiernan said to Vega: "He calls, gets patched through to the junior on Missing Persons, guy doesn't speak Spanish so hands him off to me. He's not exactly here legally, wants to meet me outside the station, so I did. He shows me the picture, looks like Jane Two, right?"

"It does," said Vega. "But there are questions." Then she turned to Cap and said, "I'm going to tell him we're not police." She spoke to Rodrigo, who nodded. Cap picked up the "*policía.*" Then she asked his sister's name.

"Maricel," he said.

"Maricel," Vega repeated, just to hear it again.

Vega asked how old she was, and how old he was. Fourteen and nineteen were the answers.

"I'm going to ask him how they got here," said Vega, and then she asked.

Rodrigo lifted his hat to run his hand over his hair, flat and black, and then he began to speak in a hushed voice, almost a murmur.

McTiernan translated: "Where they're from outside Mexico City, there aren't a lot of jobs; everything's very expensive. Water comes brown out of the faucets. Schools aren't safe so he and his sister stopped going. They hear gunfire every night from the gangs. Maricel finds a bullet in one of the pots she cooks rice for the family in."

Rodrigo paused, pinched and rubbed his nose. Cap couldn't tell if he was becoming emotional, preparing or fighting off the urge to cry. Rodrigo sniffed loudly and continued, and so did McTiernan.

"Their mother was killed last year, shot, standing on the street during a gang drive-by. They get poorer and poorer. They all get thin and sick. A friend from the neighborhood says he knows someone who can get them into the U.S., but only two spots left, two spaces left," said McTiernan, stumbling over the right words. Rodrigo holds up two fingers. "He says he can get Maricel a job as a housekeeper in a motel. But their father wants him, wants Rodrigo, to go with her to protect her. Also to get a job to send money back so they can send the grandmother someday. So they decide Maricel should go, work, and maybe go to school eventually. Rodrigo goes with her."

Rodrigo took his hat off, dropped it on the table. He pressed the back of his hand to his forehead, like he was feeling his own temperature. He started speaking again, his voice growing louder.

"They rode in the trunk of a car with two girls lying on top of them. Four of them in there. They get out when they cross the border, and the guy who brings them across, a white guy, says he only has a job for Maricel and he, Rodrigo, can't come."

Rodrigo paused and pursed his lips, winced and shook his head like he'd been poked with a pin. Then he and McTiernan continued.

"I knew I shouldn't leave her. It was a mistake, and I knew it when it happened. Was happening," McTiernan said, correcting the tense.

He stopped talking for a minute.

Vega said something to him then. Cap didn't understand it, but her tone was blunt and interrogatory. Rodrigo reared his head back, and even McTiernan looked surprised.

Then Rodrigo stood and kicked his chair back with his leg. He glared at Vega.

"What the hell did you say?" said Cap to her.

"I asked what I'm supposed to ask," said Vega, keeping her eyes on Rodrigo. "I asked him why he left her. If he knew he shouldn't."

Rodrigo pointed at her, said something quick and sharp.

No one made a move.

"He says I don't know anything," Vega said.

She and Rodrigo continued to stare at each other until McTiernan broke it up.

"I'm going to firm up the time line," he said, then asked Rodrigo a question.

Rodrigo slowly sat back down and started to speak. McTiernan translated: "We came six months ago. The white guy said he would find me and let me know how she was doing once a month. I got a job as a busboy and he showed up every month around the fifteenth with a picture on his phone and a letter."

Rodrigo reached into the back pocket of his jeans and pulled out a small sheet of lined paper. He handed it to Vega, who read it aloud.

" 'Rigo—I am fine. I have enough food and am working and making money. I will come and visit you soon. Love, Mari.' "

"Ask him if that's her handwriting," said Cap eagerly.

Vega asked.

Rodrigo glanced at her sideways and said, "*Sí.*" He kept talking, and

McTiernan continued to interpret: "Every month her letter says the same thing in different ways. I ask the white guy when will she come to visit, can I go visit her. He says no, her bosses won't like it." He shook his head angrily and knocked on the table with his fist. "I know something is very wrong with all of it, but I am too scared and weak to find her. Last week is the fifteenth. White guy doesn't come. Each day I know I have to do something. I call the police two days ago but hang up. Today I wake up and say, I am nothing, not even an animal if I don't do something. So I call."

Rodrigo stopped talking. They all sat in silence. Then he pointed up to McTiernan and spoke directly to Vega.

"He says, 'This cop tells me I have to meet you. Here I am. Do you know where my sister is?'" said McTiernan.

Cap recognized Vega's answer: *"Quizás."* Maybe.

He knew she wasn't trying to be coy; just honest.

Then she pulled out her phone and tapped on a photo. Cap braced himself for Rodrigo's response to the Jane 2 photo. He'd delivered a lot of bad news as a cop and as a PI, but someone seeing the body of a dead loved one, especially when he didn't expect it, was a singular trauma.

But Rodrigo's face brightened as he rose a bit out of his chair and pointed at the phone. He spoke a phrase a couple of times to Vega but to Cap's ear it sounded like a cluster of "a"s and "s"s and "l"s.

Vega showed the phone to Cap. It was Ben Davis's driver's license photo.

"He says that's him."

Mia met them in the parking lot of the ME office. She seemed a little sleepy, her eyes narrow, as she sipped a whipped iced coffee drink out of a long green straw.

"Aw shit, Mc-T," she said when she saw McTiernan, and she hugged him. McTiernan smiled warmly but was reserved. "Hey, Alice," she said. Then to Cap, "Mr. Alice."

Cap couldn't help but laugh, mostly because it was so silly.

Mia wiggled her fingers in a wave to Rodrigo.

"Mia Paiva," she said.

Rodrigo nodded solemnly and didn't speak.

"We need to see Jane Two," said Vega.

"That's fine," said Mia. "We moved them to the coolers downstairs since we're done with the autopsies."

Mia led them into the lobby, unlocking the front door by keypad code and hand scans. Vega touched her gently on the arm and pulled ahead of the other three.

"We think we have an ID. Rodrigo might be her brother," Vega said quietly.

"No shit," Mia whispered. "Look, full disclosure, I smoked just the smidgiest amount of weed before I got here, okay?"

"Can you still do your job effectively?" said Vega, fairly certain of the answer.

"I can do my job asleep," Mia said, leading them all down the stairs. "Just wanted you to know."

Mia pressed her hand against a pad by a set of double doors, which opened with a suctioned pop. The lights came on by sensor as soon as she walked in. She pumped hand sanitizer from a dispenser on the wall and rubbed her hands together, then pulled two fresh gloves out of a box and put them on. The room was big and cold, with rows of steel drawers, each with its own small keypad, lining the walls on three sides.

"Does he know what's coming?" Mia said under her breath to Vega.

"I don't know," said Vega, because she didn't.

Mia went to the back wall, looked at her phone, and pointed her finger at the drawers and counted, looking for the right one. She stopped in front of the drawer marked B63 and punched in a four-digit code. There was a mechanical snap, and she pulled the drawer open. There was the gurney and the white polyethylene bag with Jane 2 inside.

Vega took a step back, behind Mia, to get out of the way. Cap and McTiernan stepped to the sides to do the same, and Rodrigo came forward between them.

"Next of kin?" Mia said to Rodrigo.

He shook his head, said he didn't understand.

"Relative?" Mia asked in Spanish.

Rodrigo nodded.

Mia unzipped the bag from the upper right corner, across to the upper left and down, then peeled the flap open to reveal the body to the breastplate. Vega knew that bodies looked not much like the people the way you knew them and more like well-fitted costumes.

Rodrigo got up close and leaned down to Jane 2's face. A sound came out of him, a cough and a cry combined. He brought his hand to his mouth as if it were someone else's, continued to make the sound in spite of it.

Vega never felt a lot of embarrassment—it wasn't a conscious decision she had made to avoid it; it was just something she didn't have, like not needing glasses. But the thing she felt while Rodrigo screamed into his hand tightly clasped over his own mouth as if he were taking himself hostage was part embarrassment, not for him, but for herself, for not having somehow stopped the thing that had happened. Also there was a distant, familiar chill chasing up her spine and neck, spreading to a patch on the back of her scalp, the feeling that something was horrifically wrong with a note of panic that it was too late to set it right. She and Cap looked at each other. She knew he felt the same thing.

Mia stood a few inches away from the body, her hands clasped in front of her. She watched Rodrigo with soft, empathetic eyes but Vega sensed she remained a bit removed, so that she could do her job effectively. Vega liked that.

Rodrigo eventually stopped making the noise and stood up straight. He pressed the heels of his hands to his eyes.

"Okay, that's enough," he said.

"Mr. Villareal, are you able to make a positive ID on this body?" said Mia, her voice soft and grave.

He nodded.

"It's my sister. My little sister," he said, coughing on the word "little." He continued: "Maricel Villareal."

"Okay," said Mia. Then she gestured to the bag and said, "May I close it?"

He said yes, and Mia zipped up the bag, slid the drawer in gently. They all stayed in their places, and Rodrigo made his hands into fists, bit his lips but didn't appear to be crying.

"I didn't see the whole thing," he said, forming his hands into a dome shape, what Vega thought to encompass physically the whole thing. "I was stupid to let her go. I said, 'Okay, okay, okay.'"

He said the "okay"s in English. Then he looked at Vega and said, "I was stupid." Then angrier and louder: "I *am* stupid."

Here was something Vega knew: It didn't matter if someone told you you weren't to blame, even if the person telling you was the one you'd done the thing to; if you thought it was your fault, it was always going to be your fault. Anything else was just white noise. So Vega took a sizable step closer to Rodrigo and told him the only thing she thought would cut through the mess of static in his head:

"I'll find him."

He shrugged aggressively, as if he were trying to shake off what he was feeling. He glared at Vega, unpersuaded by her conviction and unapologetic about showing it.

A couple of hours later, after McTiernan had taken Rodrigo back to the apartment he shared with six other busboys and barbacks, they returned to the hotel. McTiernan stood with Cap and Vega on the landing outside Vega's room. It was dark and a little cold. Mosquitoes buzzed around their ears and ankles; Cap could hear a wave of cricket chatter over the traffic from the freeway.

"This is some intense shit," said McTiernan. "I worked Missing Persons six years. There's something different happening here."

"We think so, too," said Vega.

She looked at Cap, and he knew what it meant. It was time to ask McTiernan how willing he was.

"Thanks for bringing us Rodrigo," said Cap. "I mean, we got an ID, right? We never thought we'd get that."

"Just happy I could help," McTiernan said, looking tired and proud.

"We are, too," said Cap. "Which is why I gotta ask you, why'd you come to us and not your boss?"

The guise of pride washed out of McTiernan's face quick.

"You know I've been a cop," Cap continued. "I ran up against the brass, and when they shitcanned me, they couldn't take my pension away fast enough."

McTiernan shook his head and seemed beat down. He opened his mouth a couple of times to start speaking but then stopped. Finally he was able to put some words together.

"Otero's always been straight up," he said. "But the DEA comes in swinging their dicks and he backs off."

Vega interjected: "Is it any DEA, or Boyce and Mackey?"

McTiernan thought.

"He's worked with them before. But that meeting today was jacked. I've never seen him take the backseat like that in his house."

"So you'd say that behavior was uncharacteristic of him?" said Cap. "You have to understand, we just met him. Maybe this is what he does."

"No," said McTiernan emphatically. "Otero's a baller. He covers his team, hundred percent transparency."

Cap shrugged, said, "This is not the guy we've seen."

"I wanted to follow you guys out of there today. So when Rodrigo came through, I don't know, I didn't think about it too much. Just called you," he said to Vega. "I knew Otero would pass it to Boyce and Mackey. Something's . . ." He shook his head. "Something ain't right."

"How far do you want to go?" said Vega. "You can step out now. We can cover for you if anyone ever asks, say Rodrigo got to us on his own."

"I don't know," said McTiernan. Again, quieter: "I don't know." He pinched at his forehead.

"Why don't you let us know tomorrow?" said Vega. "No hard feelings if it's not your thing."

Cap believed her when she said this. To her, they had already gotten the biggest get McTiernan could offer, and he could now be jettisoned. Cap, however, thought McTiernan seemed like more than a good soldier, and more than a little resourceful.

"It's not that it's not my thing," said McTiernan quickly, as if he didn't want to offend her. "I did this all on the fly . . ."

"And anything else is planned," Vega continued. "With intent, yes?"

McTiernan appeared to absorb everything Vega had said all at once, the rules he'd already broken and the ones he was considering breaking, porous crab shells under his feet on a beach.

"Yes," he said.

They agreed to speak tomorrow. They said good night and good-bye, and he left. Vega leaned over the railing of the hotel walkway and watched McTiernan get into his car, while Cap hung back against Vega's room door as if he were guarding it.

Vega turned around to face him and hiked her elbows on the railing, stared at Cap intently.

"What about you, A. Vega?" said Cap.

"What do you mean?" she said, knowing what he meant.

Cap shrugged. "We could get out, too. You thought about it. What do you owe anyone now?"

He wasn't exactly teasing her, but he was a little unclear himself. Breaking into Ben Davis's apartment was an afterthought to Vega, a why-not. Now it was something else.

Vega threw her glance over her shoulder, into the air.

"Jane is a Maricel" was all she said.

"That didn't slow you down before, the anonymity," said Cap.

Vega pushed off the railing and looked at Cap like he was missing something, said, "She was a Maricel yesterday, too."

Vega set up her laptop next to Ben Davis's on the table in her hotel room. She sent the Bastard an IM and waited for a response, glancing between screens, a password prompt on Davis's. Cap stood behind her with his arms folded.

"How long will it take to get in there?" he said.

"Getting in isn't the problem," Vega said, clicking around Ben Davis's screen. "The Bastard can cut through most of that stuff in five minutes. It might take us a little longer to find anything worth finding."

A chat window from the Bastard popped up in the corner of Vega's PC screen. Vega typed: "Need to get into a non-network laptop. Right in front of me, prompting for password." Vega paused while the Bastard wrote back. "The Bastard is typing" read the screen. Then came the response: "Press these keys together and I'll walk U thru." Vega did as she was instructed and the screen on Ben Davis's machine went dark with just a blinking cursor at the top.

"You know what you're doing there?" said Cap.

"Nope," said Vega. "But he does."

The Bastard sent through lines of code, and Vega began to type them, letter for letter, onto Davis's laptop.

"I think we're just overriding the password right now."

Finally the Bastard sent through "Hit Return," and Vega did. Lines of code burst onto the screen, one after another like busy centipedes. Then the screen went black again, and then brightened up to a screen saver image of a galaxy, purple and blue.

"We're in?" said Cap, still unsure, bending his neck down to see the screen.

"Yeah," said Vega, her eyes scanning the desktop.

There wasn't much on the desktop, and the usual apps on the dock below. Vega double-clicked on the Internet and looked at the history. Yahoo! Mail log-in page. Vega clicked. Ben Davis had clicked the Remember Me box, leaving his email address intact on the page. Davis93129. Now all they needed was the password.

"Should we try the same as his general log-in?" suggested Cap.

"Probably not," said Vega. "I don't think he's dumb enough to make all his passwords the same word with a different number or exclamation point at the end."

Cap was silent and scratched his head. Vega stopped typing for a second and looked up at him.

"Caplan, tell me your passwords aren't the same word with a different number or exclamation point at the end."

Cap smiled sheepishly.

She continued: "And please don't tell me it's some variation of Nell's name."

Cap rested his hands on his hips.

"That bad, huh?" he said.

"Terrible," said Vega. "You're just asking someone like the Bastard to hack your bank account to pieces and trash your credit score. And buy a bunch of game consoles on your Amazon Prime."

Cap nodded to the laptops.

"So how're we going to find Davis's?"

"Let's see," said Vega.

She typed to the Bastard, "We need a password to a Yahoo account from the laptop. Can we bring up everything typed in the last 12 hours?"

"Better do twenty-four," said Cap, reading over her shoulder. "The food in his apartment had been there awhile."

"Good, Caplan, good," said Vega, deleting the 12.

The Bastard sent more instructions. Vega held down the three keys and brought the screen to black again, the cursor blinking at the top like a hazard light. The Bastard sent more code, and Vega typed it in, hitting Return at the end.

About twenty lines of text popped up. Vega scanned them all quickly, read a phrase: "too late for pickup." Then a message came through on the dialogue box from the Bastard: "Look for a single word w/ letters/ numbers/punc. Something that looks like a pword."

Vega scrolled down the screen and saw a word by itself on a line: "FResno49." She pressed Esc, and the screen reverted. Then she typed "FResno49" into the Password line and clicked Next.

Davis's in-box opened up.

"Are we in?" said Cap.

"We're in," said Vega, skimming the subject lines.

Another message popped up from the Bastard: "U need help?"

Vega typed: "I'll take a look around first. Will let you know. Thx."

The chat box closed.

"Here," said Vega, handing Davis's laptop to Cap. "Start fishing in his hard drive, Word documents, PDFs, anything that could be anything. I'll log on to his email on my laptop."

"Yes, ma'am, Ms. Vega," said Cap. "Mind if I make some of that crappy hotel coffee in the pot over here?"

"All yours."

Cap made the coffee, and soon the smell filled the room. He sat in the chair opposite from Vega and put his feet on the table, the laptop on his lap.

"Okay, now don't laugh," he said, pulling a slim case from his jacket hanging over the back of the chair.

Vega shook her head, indicating she would not. Cap opened the case and took out a pair of reading glasses, put them on his face. Vega thought he looked like a high school science teacher.

She opened up Davis's email and began to sift. There was a lot of spam. She skimmed the senders' names and found one from Becky Davis which read "Party starts at noon on Sunday! Can you bring beer of your choice and ice?? Thanks! Love, Mom." Everyone has a mom, thought Vega.

She continued to comb through, making occasional notes. Cap finished his coffee and also made notes. Around eleven Cap began to yawn, and Vega stretched her arms up, linking her fingers.

"You find anything?" Cap asked.

"I don't know," said Vega. "Nothing on fire, but it feels like I'm not very far in."

"Me, too," said Cap, rolling his head side to side. "He's got a lot of random documents, lists of frequent flyer miles and stuff like that—"

"Most people do," Vega added.

"Music, photos . . ." Cap listed.

"Anyone you recognize in the pictures?"

"You mean Maricel Villareal or Jane One with the burn mark? No," he said. "A lot of bros. High school, maybe? At the beach, at a football game. Maybe he was the yearbook editor, who knows."

"Keep looking," said Vega.

"Yeah."

They went back to work. About an hour later, Cap got up to use the bathroom and, when he returned, picked up Davis's laptop and sat on the bed closest to the door. Vega looked sideways at him.

"I have to get out of that chair," he said. "Old folks like me need to rest the bones."

"If you sit on the bed you're going to fall asleep," said Vega.

"I won't," he assured her. "Seriously, that chair is made of toothpicks. I'm going to need an osteopath in the morning."

Vega shrugged. You do you. Cap sat on the bed and kept the laptop on his lap, went back to work. She saw a familiar name embedded in an email address in the From line: SMiller. She clicked on the message.

"The doctor from the clinic," she said to Cap. "His name was Scott Miller, right?"

"Yeah, I think so. Why?"

"An S. Miller sent an email to Davis, about six months ago."

"What's it say?"

" 'Have you thought about what we discussed?' " she read.

"That's it?"

Vega read it again silently.

"That's it," she said.

Cap scratched the back of his head and yawned.

"If that's the doctor, what do we think that means?" he said.

"Not sure yet," she said. "Stack it up and save it for later."

Vega kept scrolling and skimming. She became aware of muscles in her back tightening, a result of so much driving and sitting in the chair for so long. She felt the left side of her neck, the trapezius muscle, throb and realized she'd been tilting her head at a strange angle for some hours. Also a knot beneath her shoulder blade, the tightness running through to her right pec above her breast from leaning over and writing on the pad. She stretched her arms across her body one by one in front of her and glanced back at Cap. He was lying on his side.

"I'm a hundred percent awake," he said, his voice hoarse.

"Sure," said Vega. "Anything?"

"Odds and ends," he said, looking over what he'd written down.

"Me, too."

Back to the screen, further into Davis's emails. A girlfriend, an ex-girlfriend, fratty buddies, mom. Vega's eyes began to sting around 1:00 a.m. She shut them hard and blinked rapidly. She kept clicking, reading, scratching down notes that had no link except for their apparent truncated writing styles. Then, around two, she saw a familiar name in the From line. She clicked on it and read, "Thank you for registering with Lincoln Investments! Please use this code to set your password . . ."

"Caplan," she said, her tongue sticking a little to her teeth, mouth dry.

When he didn't respond, she turned and saw that he was a hundred percent asleep, head resting on his arm, his glasses crooked, the laptop still open. She stood and went over to him, closed the laptop quietly and moved it to the table between the two beds.

Then, gently pinching each of the earpieces with her thumbs and forefingers, she pulled the glasses off his face, folded them, and placed them on top of the laptop. She watched him for a minute. A thought came and went about lying down next to him.

Instead she turned off the lights, brushed her teeth, changed into a tank top and shorts, and got into the bed across from Cap. She knew she wouldn't sleep much but thought her muscles needed to go through the motions anyway. She was not restless but felt awake. She lay on her back and turned her head. Seeing Cap sleeping there cast a calm over her. She tried to match his breathing, slow and even.

Then she wasn't exactly dreaming, which made sense because she had no recollection of falling asleep. But Maricel and Jane 1, the burn victim, sat on the edge of the bed where Vega slept, alive. They whispered to each other in Spanish, and Vega could just make out what they were saying.

"My head still hurts," said Jane 1, pointing to the incision just below her hairline.

"Take this," said Maricel, handing her something small and white.

Jane 1 examined it—it was a white ball.

"Open it," ordered Maricel.

Jane 1 opened it. It was the note that read "ALICE VEGA."

"Now swallow it," said Maricel. "I did."

Jane 1 looked skeptically at her friend. But then she crumpled the paper back into a ball and popped it in her mouth anyway and swallowed.

Vega could feel the edges of the paper cutting her throat and woke up, coughing.

12

THE FIRST THING CAP HEARD WAS A FAN BLOWING IN BURSTS, AS IF someone were toggling the switch between levels—1, 2, 1, 2. Before he opened his eyes he remembered where he was. Hotel. California. Like the song. But some things were off. He wasn't under the bedspread or the sheet, and he was fully clothed, his jacket next to him. He cocked his head around, putting pieces together. Then he saw her: Vega standing on her hands in the middle of the room.

It was the same as when he'd seen her through the window, except now he was right here. The intermittent fan sounds were actually her breaths—loud, then soft, through her nose. He did his best to not make any noise, partially so he wouldn't disturb her morning ritual, and also so he could keep watching her.

Cap didn't think he was aroused; it was more observational, nearly scientific, witnessing Alice Vega in her natural state, previously unseen by human eyes. He thought of the few times he'd tried yoga, only because Jules loved it, that and Pilates, the latter of which always seemed to him like a particularly Zero Dark Thirty way of working out with all the equipment and everything. He'd never gotten very far with any of it, could never stretch or balance enough and always felt more drained afterward than invigorated.

And though he'd never imagined Vega as the yoga type, she didn't seem to have a problem with stretch or balance. Or strength. She wore a tank top and shorts, just like when he'd glimpsed her before, and he could not spot a bite of fat on her, nothing gathered around the waist or thighs.

He propped himself up on his elbows and watched her for ten minutes or so, and she showed no signs of coming down. Until about three more minutes passed and then she did. One leg at a time; then the way she moved her back, Cap didn't really understand it—it really did look as if her spine were partitioned, vertebra by vertebra, each rolling up, ending with her neck and finally her head.

Cap quickly lay back down again and closed his eyes, playing possum.

Vega's pronounced breathing had stopped. Cap focused on staying still, tried to prevent his eyes from moving around underneath his lids.

"Good, Caplan, you're awake," said Vega. Her voice sounded scratchy and really impossibly sexy, Cap thought.

He opened one eye.

"Morning, Vega," he said, figuring that pretending in front of her was useless. "Sorry I fell asleep here."

She stretched her arms behind her head. Her face glowed with a light sweat, just the start of dark semicircles under the arms of the tank top.

"It's okay," she said. "I found an email from about eighteen months ago to Ben Davis from Lincoln Investments.

"Lincoln Investments," Cap repeated. "Is that . . ."

"Devin Lara's company," said Vega.

"Well, how about that," said Cap. "What do we think that connection's all about?"

"Not sure," said Vega, drinking from a bottle of water. "Let's ask him."

"Davis?"

"Lara," said Vega, heading toward the bathroom.

Cap stood up from the bed and said after her: "Vega, we go near Lara, you're asking for Otero and Mackey and Boyce and whoever else is interested to come down on us. Including Lara's driver."

She stopped walking and turned around, said, "I'm okay with that."

"For whatever reason, like you said, Lara is a hot spot for them. I thought we were staying away from him for now. To avoid the attention. One fight at a time and all that."

She tilted her head.

"Is that what you think we should do?" she asked.

Cap scratched the back of his head and paused.

"Yeah," he said. "Why muddy this up? Why not just keep on the track for Ben Davis?" he added, holding his hands out parallel, to show what a track might look like.

"Right, but we have no efficient way to find Davis yet, besides staking out his apartment, which he seemed to leave in a hurry and doesn't get back to often. And we do know how to find Lara. And today is Saturday," she said. "So it is a juice day."

"I—" Cap began, then considered how to present the information in the most attractive light. "We go the Ben Davis route, we might have to wait a day or two, but we will get him. And we can move completely under the radar. No PD, no DEA."

Vega's face fell; she suddenly looked away from him.

Cap added, in an effort to make her laugh: "Just traditional Cap and Vega Justice. Trademarked."

Vega did not laugh, only rubbed her eyes, appeared worn out.

"Can I ask you something?" she said.

Cap squinted his eyes since he was physiologically unable to squint with his ears. He'd been asked this question many times before, usually by women and usually preceding a discussion about capital "E" emotions.

He'd never expected it from Vega.

"Yeah, of course," he said.

She crossed her arms and hugged them against her chest, still not looking him in the eyes.

"Do you ever see the Brandt girls?" she said, almost inaudibly.

Cap thought a second. It wasn't that he had a tough time recalling the details—he knew exactly when and where he'd seen the Brandt girls. His being taken aback grew solely from the act of Vega asking. He always had the impression that she shook off the dust of past cases as soon as they were closed. But perhaps the Brandt case had been different; it certainly was for him.

"Just once if you can believe that," he said. "It was a couple of months ago, actually. I was in a mall with Nell. She was making me buy new running shoes because one of mine had a hole but they still had plenty of support—anyway, different story," he said, sweeping the air with his hand. "And I saw them, the girls with the mom, walking around."

Vega looked up at him now, her eyes wide with expectation.

"How did they look?" she said.

"You know, older," said Cap. "Jamie's lost a lot of weight. A little too much, if you ask me. And she looked . . ."

Cap paused, unable to put his finger on it at the time but remembering it now, he could finally identify her expression.

"Confused," he said. "She seemed confused. Bailey was next to her talking a mile a minute." Cap smiled at the memory, continued: "I passed them, and they didn't see me, or maybe didn't recognize me— I was out of context there, and Nell didn't see them. Bailey was going through a list or something—"we have to go here, here, and here.""

"What about Kylie?" said Vega urgently.

Cap took a hearty breath in.

"She was behind them. Texting on her phone. She was dressed . . . well, let me say as a father I strongly disapproved of the way she was dressed. These short shorts and almost like a bathing suit top. A ton of makeup. I'd never let Nell out of the house looking like that as a seventeen-year-old, much less as an eleven-, twelve-year-old, and I fully embrace that I'm a cliché right now."

"Nell would never want to leave the house looking like that," added Vega.

"True. Point is, they were fine, Vega. Normal."

Vega shook her head, her hair loose around her shoulders.

"Whatever they are, they would have been better if we'd gotten to them sooner, and you know it," she said.

"Hypothetical," said Cap sternly. "We got them as soon as we could get them."

Vega's expression remained the same, filled with disappointment, regret.

"You can't play what-if in our line of work, Vega. That is what I know," he said.

She looked away sadly, and it pissed him off.

"You listen to me, goddammit," he said, taking a step closer to her, his voice cracking. "We saved their lives, and just in time. One more day could have been too late. And it's better they're alive and broken than dead and perfect, you know?"

Vega dropped her hands to her sides, the whites of her eyes gleaming in the dim room.

"You're right, Caplan. One more day could have been too late. And that brings us to today."

Cap rubbed his chin. She wasn't sad at all. She'd pulled him right into admitting that they had to go full-court press. No waiting.

"I see what happened there," he said.

She raised an eyebrow. Oh do you?

"I suppose you think you're pretty clever," he added.

She ignored the comment, said, "Meet at the car in a half hour, okay?"

She didn't wait for him to respond, instead turned and removed her tank top, dropped it on the floor at her feet before stepping into the bathroom. Cap shot his line of vision up to the corner of the room and shut his eyes simultaneously but there they were stamped on his eyelids, the translucent stepping-stones that made up the bones of her spine.

They sat in Vega's car, parked at the entrance of the lot. Cap drank coffee. Vega drank nothing and kept her hands on the wheel, peering ahead through her sunglasses.

"So the plan is to convince him to get in the car and talk to us?" he said.

"Sure."

"So I should just be prepared to get cleaned again?"

Vega shook her head.

"When Lara comes out with the juice, you talk to him. I'll take care of Richie."

Cap combed his teeth over his bottom lip.

"And we're not drawing firearms here on this nice sunny morning, right?"

"I don't plan to," said Vega.

"You want to share with me what you do plan to do?"

"You talk to Lara first," Vega said calmly. "I'll get what I have in the trunk and take care of Richie."

Cap's face blanched; he looked as if he'd lost a packed wallet.

"Vega, I didn't tell you—I tried to open the trunk," he said, pointing to it. "It doesn't work. It's jammed."

Vega turned to him.

"I rigged it so it'll only open with the key," she said. "Just wanted to see if you'd look."

"Huh," said Cap. "I see. A little test. Did I pass or no?"

Vega's mouth curled at the edges, but then opened, her eyes peering over the glasses at something past Cap. He turned around, and there was a black sedan entering the lot with Richie driving. Vega could see the shape of Lara in the backseat through the darkened window. She started the car and slowly pulled out of the space.

"Keep your eye on it," she said.

"He's parking. Why don't we get as close as we can to the juice place?" said Cap.

Vega nodded and accelerated.

"Slide down," she said. "Just in case he's got eyes in the back of his head."

Cap didn't question, slid down in his seat. Vega leaned her head back next to the headrest to hide as best she could. She parked in a spot close to the storefronts, and they both watched as Lara got out of the sedan and ambled toward the juice shop, focused on the phone in his hand, texting with his thumbs.

"He's got a mobile order," said Vega. "You should go."

"All right," said Cap, taking a steely breath.

He got out of the car and shut the door behind him, removed his jacket and dropped it through the window onto his seat.

"Caplan," said Vega.

He leaned down.

"Yeah?"

"I got you. You know that, right?"

"I sure hope so, girl," said Cap with a tiny laugh.

Then he left, heading toward Juicy Lucy with big strides. Vega spotted Lara's sedan in the opposite row, three or four rows in front of hers. Richie was looking down, also on his phone, she figured.

Vega opened the door and got out of the car. She went to the trunk and unlocked it with her key. And there they were: twenty-four-inch, steel-jawed bolt cutters. She picked them up, clasping the padded grips tightly in one hand, slammed the trunk closed. Counted in her head. This was when time made long jumps; it was useful to count the beats. She estimated twenty real seconds before contact.

She started walking toward Cap (one-two-three-four); Cap moved quickly toward the door of the Juicy Lucy (five-six-seven); she paused and hid behind an SUV, heard Lara's sedan door slam shut (eight-nine-ten); Lara emerged from the shop, juice in one hand, phone in the other, and Cap called, "Hey, Devin!" (eleven-twelve-thirteen); Lara shook his head like, some people never learn, and Richie walked with purpose down the middle of the parking lot aisle (fourteen-fifteen-sixteen).

Vega took off from her position, holding the bolt cutters up over her left shoulder, feeling the weight of the jaws at the top. She took a swing in front of her and heard the catch of the air splitting (seventeen-eighteen-nineteen-twenty).

Time was up.

"You must be one dumb sonofabitch," said Richie to Cap as he unbuttoned the cuffs of his sleeves.

"Yeah," said Cap congenially, keeping his eyes on Vega.

Devin Lara watched Richie approach and had a gloriously self-righteous expression like he was about to say, "That's what you get when you break the rules." But then his gaze shifted as he recognized Vega. The smirk dropped from his face as he opened his mouth to shout, "What," pointing to her over Richie's head.

Richie turned around, and Vega was two feet away from him. Twenty-four inches. The jaws of the bolt cutters up in the air. She swung hard, feeling her triceps and traps stretch and strain. Richie brought up one of his meaty hands to block, and she swung and knocked it out of the way, hearing a brittle crack of bone.

Richie screamed and groaned, held his hand, which sprayed blood, but didn't fall, so Vega swung again from the other side and brought the jaws down just above the knee on the left side, hoping to snap his IT band, a ligament running from the hip to the shin, which could be excruciating if not stretched properly after a jog, so if it were severed at the knee, Vega could only imagine the pain. Not to mention a kneecap fracture.

She definitely hit one or both because Richie crumpled and screamed haltingly, too shocked with agony to make a continuous sound. Devin Lara was stunned, trying to type something with his thumbs on his phone but shaking too much.

"You should come with us, Devin," said Cap. "We have a few questions to ask you, and then you'll be free to enjoy the rest of your day."

Lara appeared to regain the power of speech, his eyes glistening wildly.

"Fuck you, I'm not going anywhere with you," he whispered.

Vega rested the clipper end of the bolt cutters on her shoulder as if it were an ax and she were taking a break from chopping a cord of wood.

Cap pointed to her and said, "Now I'm not saying my partner will definitely smash your ankles with those bolt cutters, but she can be a little unpredictable."

Vega stared Lara down while Richie vomited at her feet.

Just then a couple fresh from morning spin class emerged from Juicy Lucy; the woman gasped when she saw Richie. The man's gaze bounced from Vega to Cap then Lara and didn't seem to compute the events that had come before.

"I'll call an ambulance!" he announced bravely, fumbling for his phone.

"You should," said Cap. "Police, too. Devin?" he said, gesturing in the direction of Vega's car. "You want to wait for the police or come with us?"

Lara considered it, chest pumping up and down quickly.

"Decide quicker," said Vega, taking a step closer to him.

"Oh God," the spin class woman said, finally stringing the beads together, looking from Vega to Richie while her boyfriend chattered on the phone.

"Let's go," said Vega definitively, and Lara started walking, Cap next to him, Vega right behind.

As they approached the car, Vega stuck the keys into Cap's hand, feeling the warmth of his palm, the fingertips cool.

"You drive," she said.

Cap unlocked the car and opened the backseat door for Lara. Lara turned and faced Vega, looked her over once more. She held the bolt cutters with both hands, the jaws resting on the ground between her feet.

"Police any minute now, Devin," said Cap, standing at the driver's side door.

The adrenaline in Lara's eyes had tempered just a little bit but still, the wave of resignation crossed his face.

"I'm not afraid of the police," he said, a little patronizing, like Cap was a real rube for worrying about it.

"Good, neither am I," Vega said, stepping forward to close the distance between them, smelling the fruit of the red juice on Lara's breath. "Now get in the fucking car."

Lara didn't think about it anymore, just recoiled, falling into the backseat. Vega followed him and pulled the door shut behind her. She held the bolt cutters across her lap and faced him, pitching her legs at a sideways angle in the well, her back leaning against the door. Cap started the car, and Vega heard sirens.

"How do you know Ben Davis?" she asked.

Lara blinked, glanced at the bolt cutters.

"Don't recognize the name."

"You sure?" said Vega. "Coyote Ben knows you."

Lara paused, and Vega guessed which way he would go.

"What about Antonio LoSanto?"

Lara shook his head.

"What about Joe Guerra?"

"No," said Lara.

"What about Corey Lloyd?"

"You asked me that before," said Lara, now a little more confident in his denials. "I never heard of him." He paused. "Sorry, you got the wrong guy."

Vega studied his face. Still breathing rapidly, dilated pupils. Scared enough to get in the car but not enough to talk. Okay, then.

"So Corey Lloyd's got it wrong, just arbitrarily named you as the guy who told him he needed a car where a girl ended up dead, and your company arbitrarily sent an email to one of the prime suspects in that girl's murder eighteen months ago. These things are not connected at all."

"People know my name," said Lara, shrugging. "And my company sends information to hundreds of prospective clients each month."

"So you're saying it's a coincidence," said Vega.

"Yeah, I guess," said Lara.

"You know what they say about coincidences," said Vega.

"What—that there are none?" said Lara.

"Is that what they say," said Vega, meeting Cap's eye in the rearview. "I thought they said something else."

Though Vega wasn't sure of San Diego geography by sight, she thought they must be getting close to the college, the streets looking like they belonged in a little village, the way all college towns looked, cafés and bars, restaurants and shops peddling knickknacks.

"Cap, why don't we pull over up ahead," said Vega.

He pulled over into a metered spot in front of a bagel shop. California kids came in and out dressed like surfers and stoners and punks. Vega watched the relief flood Lara's eyes when he saw how many people were around. He looked to Vega, defensive but hopeful, wondering what was going to come next.

"Our mistake," she said finally.

"Whatever," said Lara, shrugging.

"You can press charges against me if you want. I'd totally understand," said Vega. "For aggravated assault of your man back there."

"And kidnapping, too, I think," Cap chimed in.

"Sure," said Vega. "Kidnapping, too."

"No, that's okay," Lara was quick to add. "Don't worry about it."

"You could, though. That would be fair. After all, you're just a private citizen and everything."

Lara pulled at the door handle, and it snapped back into place.

"Could you unlock the door, please?" he said, both trepidatious and annoyed.

"Oh, yeah, sure. Cap, could you unlock that child lock?"

Cap pressed a button, and they heard the lock click.

Devin took another look at her and Cap, opened the door wide, and jumped out.

The smile vanished from Vega's face.

"Vega?" said Cap.

"Just giving him ten seconds."

She watched him get onto the sidewalk and tap his phone, lift it to his ear.

"Ten," said Vega, getting out of the car.

She left the bolt cutters behind.

On the sidewalk, students milled around her holding coffee cups and yoga mats. Lara was still speaking on the phone, the red juice in his left hand at his side. Vega could not make out the words he was saying.

She came up fast behind him and slapped the juice out of his hand. It splattered onto the ground in the shape of a beam cast from a lighthouse.

Lara whipped around and saw her for less than a second before she took two quick jabs, one to each side of his face, right, then left hand, and then as he started to fall backward she jumped and got him once more, the right elbow under his chin, jamming the jaw.

He screamed, fell to the ground, blood bursting from his mouth and nose. Vega squatted and grabbed his phone, which had fallen facedown next to him.

"I bith my tongue," he cried, sitting up somewhat, spitting blood into his hands. Then he reached into the pool in his palm and picked out a small spongy bit. "Thith ith the tip of my tongue," he said in shock.

"Would you look at that," said Vega, indifferent.

She grabbed the collar of his shirt and yanked him toward her.

"Where is Ben Davis right now?"

Lara's face twitched and roiled with pain and nausea.

Vega said, "Tell me right now before you pass out or I will take the rest of your fucking tongue out of your mouth."

"He'th at the houth . . ." Lara said.

"What house? Where?"

"Thalton."

Salton, she thought. She'd never been but had seen pictures. A man-made lake, surrounded by double-wides.

Lara shook his head, eyes fluttering, losing consciousness.

"Address," she said, shaking him vigorously.

"Hey, stop it, you can't do that," one of the bros watching remarked.

Vega didn't turn her head fully but angled it toward the voice and said, "Shut up. He fucks little girls." Then, back to Lara: "What's the address?"

Lara passed out. His head was loose on his neck. Vega let go of his collar, and his upper body dropped to the concrete.

She stood up, her shirt and hands damp with blood. College kids stood around, stunned, filming her, texting, speaking quietly. But none taking a run at her. Vega turned and walked past them all, and they didn't try to stop her. The college kids chattered; she vaguely heard them say, "stop," "police," "tongue," "fucks little girls."

She tapped Lara's phone, which hadn't yet locked, and scrolled through the recents. Then she scrolled through the contacts and found Davis. She pressed her thumb on the name and began to write a text, got into the car, the engine still running.

"Ready?" said Cap.

"Go."

He peeled out of the spot with a tight scream off the rear wheels.

Again, they heard sirens.

"Where to?" said Cap.

"Salton City," said Vega. "It's east."

Two police cars passed them heading the opposite direction. Cap drove for a minute.

"That's what was in the trunk—bolt cutters?"

"Yeah—why?"

Cap shrugged. "Didn't think it would be so low-tech."

"They're superuseful," said Vega somewhat defensively. "Get on the freeway in half a mile."

She continued her text to Davis.

"Is that Lara's phone?" Cap asked.

"Yes, I'm sending Davis a text."

"Pretending to be Lara," said Cap, beginning to understand.

Vega nodded. Her thumb hovered over the Send button. She checked her map app. Two hours twenty-nine minutes to Salton. She sent the text: "VIP on the way. Text him with directions. Number attached. Will pay triple for youngest we have."

. . .

Later they sat in the car on a street that looked recently paved, the smell of tar pushing through the vents along with the faint scent of decaying plant life. Here and there were houses but they were spread far apart, two or three to each sprawling block but not because they were upmarket properties, because there seemed to be no one or nothing out here. Cap noted that he hadn't seen another car or human for at least a couple of miles.

"You think I can pass for a VIP?" he said, examining his face in the rearview.

"I didn't ask you to come here just because you're good at your job," Vega said.

"You needed a guy."

"I needed a guy," she repeated.

Cap gazed at the house down the block.

"Wish we had some time for recon," he said.

"We only have until Lara regains consciousness and gets to a phone," said Vega. "Maybe more if he doesn't know Davis's number from memory, which is possible."

Cap unbuckled his seatbelt and touched the Sig under his jacket.

"You think they'll pat down?"

"They have no reason to," said Vega. She tilted her head against the window and raised her eyebrows, looking at the house. "You get in there, let me know. If it feels like we have a shot, we take it."

Cap breathed hard and hot through his nose.

"What am I there for?" he said.

"The youngest."

He began to shake his head, almost like he couldn't believe it but of course he could. Of course there were more Janes, alive right now. For now.

"Vega—" he began, and he knew it sounded like he was about to launch into a protest.

"You have to move quickly," she said.

He paused.

"Caplan?"

"Vega, don't mistake my hesitation for lack of enthusiasm," he said. "I just think I should enter engaging the purpose of recon, and the possibility of rescue."

Vega faced forward, considering it.

He continued: "What if they're armed?"

"They might be but it won't be an arsenal."

"You sure? They do have a habit of stabbing people in the kidneys and forcibly administering electroshock. These are those guys."

Vega shut her eyes. Cap shifted his weight in his seat, rubbed the stubble on his cheeks and chin.

"Okay," she conceded. "Get in a room with a girl and text me. That's it. Head count, firearms, whatever you want." She paused, then added, "If you're in danger, get out. No questions."

Cap nodded, aware of the blood pumping in and around his heart.

"You should go," said Vega, when she saw he wasn't moving.

"Yeah, I'm going," he said, staring at her, still not moving.

"Don't worry, I'm not going to kiss you," said Vega.

Cap broke into a laugh. Vega looked out the window.

"Well, shit," said Cap. "The hell I'm sticking around here for?"

He got out of the car then and walked away quickly without looking back, right up to the long blue house with the rose pink doorframe.

He knocked and waited, then knocked once more. Someone came quickly. It was Davis.

"Caplan, right?" he said.

Cap nodded, looked him over. His hair was about an inch long, blond at the tips, light silvery color in the eyes, narrow but alert.

"You Davis?"

"Yeah. Come in."

He leaned against the door, and Cap stepped past him, into the house.

It smelled like air freshener, the cardboard pine trees that dangled from rearviews, or aftershave. The carpet was tan and stained here and there with bleach spots. Did Davis dye his hair and then walk down the hall, spilling and dripping, Cap thought as he followed him.

Davis led him into a room full of girls. There were nine, Cap counted quickly, all in bras and underwear or skimpy slips. All barefoot. Some looked up at him as he entered, and some watched a game show on a TV in the corner. Two girls lay on their stomachs in front of the screen. Cap flashed briefly to Jaylin Duffy and her sensory deprivation project, and he smiled thinking of her.

"It's good, right?" said Davis, assuming Cap was happy with the options.

Cap played along.

"Yeah."

There were drawn blinds on a long picture window in the middle of one wall, an L-shaped counter on the opposite side of the room covered with bottles of rum, tequila, red Solo cups. A nearly obese guy with a black goatee sat on a stool at the counter, a Glock 42 on a belt on his hip. Dammit, Vega, thought Cap. Of course they're armed.

"Lara said you wanted the youngest?"

Cap felt his stomach churning, smelled synthetic strawberry and vanilla perfume and lotion. He nodded, his eyes covering the room once more.

"Missy's twelve."

One of the girls lying on the floor turned her head and looked at Davis.

"That's her," said Davis, pointing. "Missy, *levántate*," he called to her.

Missy stood. She was maybe four feet tall. She met Cap's eyes and turned all the way around, 360, so he could see her body from every angle prior to purchase. She wore a skimpy black teddy.

Cap nodded again.

"So that's six hundred for the hour. We take it up front," Davis said.

Cap pulled his wallet from his pants and pulled out the hundreds, folded them in the middle, and handed them to Davis, who counted them again.

"Anything you want, just show her," said Davis. "You can hit but not the face."

Cap stayed silent and nodded again, almost said, "How much can I pay to hit you in the face?"

Missy came forward and stood in front of Cap. Davis gripped her arm and whispered something in her ear. She looked at the floor.

"Hour starts now," said Davis.

Missy took Cap's hand with both of hers and smiled. Cap guessed she was attempting to be alluring but it just looked like a little girl wearing her mom's makeup in the bathroom mirror. And scared to death underneath.

She led Cap out of the girl room and down the stairs, where there was a hallway with closed doors on either side. She stopped in front of a door near the end of the hall and opened it. She held her arm out, presenting the room to Cap. He stepped inside. The room was about the size of a storage locker. There was a twin bed with only a fitted sheet on it, a folded towel at the foot, and a single-drawer filing cabinet, which Cap registered as odd, even though he was not certain he was processing everything exactly as it was, feeling somewhat in shock.

Missy pressed a button in the doorknob after shutting the door. She stood in front of Cap and smiled again at him, the same pretend-smile. Then she removed the teddy and dropped it on the floor. Her breasts were small and Cap stared at her face so he would not have to look at her body. She took his hand and began to bring it to her breast, and Cap yanked it away. Her eyes lit up with fear and confusion.

"No," he said, a little too loudly. Then he whispered, calmer, "No." He reached down and picked up the teddy, handed it back to her. "Please," he said. *"Por favor."*

He mimed putting the teddy back on. Missy stared at him. He pressed the teddy against her.

"Please," he whispered again.

Missy suddenly became shy and put the teddy on quickly, folded her arms in front of her to cover up even more. She said some words quietly in Spanish; Cap didn't know much, almost nothing in fact, but he thought he heard a word that sounded like "other," and he assumed she was asking him if he wanted someone else, some other girl.

He shook his head vigorously and then held up his finger. Wait, one second.

From the inside pocket of his jacket, he pulled out the picture of Maricel Villareal at the window. He showed it to Missy.

"Do you know her?" he whispered in English. "Do you know this girl? Maricel?"

Missy's eyes flashed with panic. Her mouth opened slightly as she took the picture from him.

"Maricel," she said.

"Yes, *sí,*" said Cap. Then he pointed to himself and said, "I'm here to help you. *Ayuda,*" he added, pointing at her.

Missy seemed stunned, still staring at the picture in her hand.

Then, because he thought it would be impossible to explain how even though he was a private investigator and not technically a police officer, he and his partner were working with the police until very recently when they'd been let go, he placed his open palm on his chest and said, *"Policía."*

Missy shook her head and began to chatter in Spanish, too fast for Cap to pick anything out. She pushed the picture back at him and backed away, talking fast and anxious, and kept pointing to the door.

"Rafa," she said. Then more urgently quiet, as if she were being choked: *"Rafa . . ."*

Cap looked toward the door. What was rafa?

"Rafa?" he repeated.

She kept talking, shaking her head no, her small hands and fingers trembling. Cap held up his finger again to indicate one minute more, and he pulled out his phone and texted Vega, "One big guy with Glock in living room with 8 girls. In bedroom with 9th girl. Recognizes Maricel."

He hit Send. Missy had backed up to the bed now, was curled against the wall, making her body so small and flat it reminded Cap of a pressed flower.

"Hey, it's okay," he said in his kindest, calmest voice possible. "I'm not going to hurt you. *Ayuda,*" he said again.

Vega's text came back: "Any other guys/guns?"

Cap wrote: "No. Only fat man and Davis."

He tapped Send and then quickly added a separate text: "What does rafa mean?"

Missy was crying, covering her mouth with both hands, the breath from her nostrils audible.

"Come on now, I'm going to get you out of here," said Cap. He took a small step closer to her, and then his phone buzzed.

He glanced down, saw Vega's response.

"On my way. Don't know rafa. Name maybe?"

Just as he felt that land in his head, the door burst open. Missy screamed now, full volume, and Cap saw why: there was a third guy, at least two heads taller than him, built not like a linebacker but maybe like the guy who bullies linebackers in grade school, black hair to his shoulders and pierces in his cheeks, ears, eyebrows, neck. Dead dark eyes.

Rafa.

He was holding something in his right hand but Cap didn't stop to identify it. Cap reached for the Sig but wasn't quick enough. Rafa thrust his hand forward and shot him with a standard two-probe Taser, like the kind Cap had been trained to use as a cop. Then Cap fell to the ground but didn't feel the hit, didn't feel anything, not asleep and not awake, thinking few thoughts as his eyes remained open and body paralyzed, like he was in an elevator the size of a coffin going down, down, down.

. . .

Vega wasn't getting anything back.

"Respond," she wrote.

He didn't.

"Goddammit, Caplan," she said out loud.

She got out of the car, picked up the bolt cutters with her left hand, and set the jaws on her shoulder. She shut the car door, and then she drew the Springfield with her right hand.

She had practiced something like this with John Patrick, as a method of arm strengthening, twenty-pound weights in each hand, swinging each in front of her in windmills. It built the shoulders especially, and she felt the control she had now of the things in both hands.

She came to the door of the house with big strides and swung the bolt cutters up and then down, cracking them into the door near the handle. The wood splintered and buckled but didn't break so Vega wound it up again and slammed the clips in the same place. The handle broke clean off, and Vega put her hand through the hole she'd made and felt around for other locks. She felt a bolt above and unlocked it. Then she opened the door.

A house with no air and screaming girls. She ran toward the screams into an arched doorway on her right, and right away she took in the girls but didn't dwell on them (later, later, scuttled through her head). There was a fat guy on the other side of the room, and as soon as he saw Vega, he grabbed a girl standing next to a counter covered with liquor bottles and cut limes. He fastened his arm around the girl's neck, pinning her in front of him, and put a gun to her head.

"I'll put her down like a dog you come any closer," he said.

Vega did a quick diagnostic of the truth and possibility of that statement. Even though there were the two dead Janes, here were nine more in this house, and they were all money in the bank. Whatever the reason was for killing the other two, would collateral against a stranger make the cut?

Vega didn't think so. She locked eyes with the girl, who didn't seem particularly alarmed. Shock, thought Vega. The other girls in the room screamed and cried and clung to the walls.

Even though Vega's right arm was steady, she held the bolt cutters underneath her forearm, crossing just below the elbow to get a flat surface.

"Here's the thing about the human shield," said Vega, shutting her left eye. "You have to find someone bigger than your fat ass."

She fired twice, one after the other, got him in the elbow of his firing hand, then the knee. He cried out and crumpled, fell hard to the floor, and Vega felt the floor shake under the weight. The gun dropped; the girl stayed standing, her bare skin sprayed with blood.

Vega walked in a direct path to the fat guy and kneeled down. He was moaning, writhing as best he could with his various rolls of flesh. Vega got in his face and positioned the bolt cutters in his groin. Hit 'em where it hurts, Perry would have said.

"How many guys here beside you and Davis?" she said.

The fat guy groaned, saliva leaking from his mouth. Vega scissored the bolt cutters tighter.

He shouted.

"How many?" she said again.

"Just one, just Rafa," he uttered, and then he began to pass out.

Vega unclasped the jaws from his testicles, and he gasped, his head rolling back onto the carpet. She eyed his bullet wounds. They were bleeding steadily but she hadn't hit any organs or arteries. Just some bones and fat but enough to keep him down so she could get to work. She took his Glock and stuck it between her pants and the small of her back. Then she stood up.

Vega addressed the girl that the fat guy had grabbed.

"Are you hurt?" Vega said in Spanish.

The girl shook her head. The right side of her face was sprayed with blood. She appeared to be on the older side of the group. She wore a spaghetti strap tank top with no bra and pink underwear. Bare feet. They all had bare feet.

"My name is Vega. I'm here to help you."

The girl didn't respond, so Vega continued.

"I need to find my partner first, the white man who just came in. Do you know where he is?"

"Rafa took him to the garage," she said.

"Where's the garage?"

The girl pointed toward the door. Outside. Vega remembered seeing a shed next to the house, figured that was it.

"Any other men here besides Coyote Ben and Rafa?"

The girl shook her head.

"Any other girls besides who's right here?" Vega said, gesturing gently to the others.

"Two," said the girl. "Missy and Chicago."

She pronounced the "Ch" hard, like in "chitchat."

"There's a man with Chicago downstairs. No gun. Bald," said the girl, pointing to her head.

Vega glanced around at the other girls. They pressed themselves against the walls and in the corners like they were trying to camouflage their bodies into the paper-white paint.

"Does Coyote Ben have a gun?" asked Vega.

The girl shrugged. Unsure.

"He has a knife," she said. Then she held her fingers out, about six inches apart. "This long."

Vega nodded, assumed this girl must have seen it at least a couple of times to remember it so well.

"Does Rafa have a gun?" Vega asked.

"Rafa has everything."

"I'll take care of him," said Vega.

She knew she was saying it wrong. She'd learned Spanish from her father and from high school and spoke it well, had picked up slang and idioms working in fugitive recovery but had to concentrate sometimes to find the right verb. She knew she was using the wrong one, *cuidar a,* like to be a caretaker of a baby or a patient in the hospital. The girl squinted at her. Vega wasn't sure she understood but she didn't need to. Vega was going to do it anyway.

She peered over at the fat guy; he had passed out for good but was definitely still alive, the gelatinous mass of his stomach rising and falling steadily.

"Will you stay here while I find my partner?" asked Vega.

The girl nodded with a puzzled look in her eye. Like, where else would she go? Vega scanned the room, looked around at the girls. They all seemed scared, but they had stopped screaming. There was a distance there, a separation; it was like they were wearing masks of scared faces. Vega wondered if they'd been sedated.

Vega nodded back at the girl and left, found the stairs and went down, to the rooms. She stepped as lightly as she could, her right arm extended with the Springfield aimed straight ahead, the jaws of the bolt cutters resting on her left shoulder. She stuck close to the wall and listened, thought she heard movement—feet shuffling, fabric rustling, the scrape of denim. She froze and waited, gritted her teeth and thought, C'mon, you sonofabitch, come see all the damage I got for you right here.

. . .

Cap was aware that he was being dragged outdoors, could feel the gravel on his back, could see the sun above him glaring into his unblinking eyes, tears leaking out of the corners.

Rafa was pulling him, his thick hand clasping the collars of Cap's jacket and shirt. Cap could feel the second button pressing on his neck, garroting him, but he couldn't move any muscle in particular, was unable even to summon a cough. Had he and Nell once talked about autoerotic asphyxiation? The memory of a conversation floated past.

Then he was yanked inside again, a new room, a smell like an old electric train set when the cars run off the tracks. Burnt batteries.

He could see toothpicks of sunlight shooting through panels on the wall. Wood, siding, he wasn't sure. He was dropped, felt the back of his head hit the concrete, stinging flashes of pain crowding his vision. A sound came from his throat unwittingly, halfway between a gurgle and a cry.

Rafa moved above him, walking back and forth. Cap followed him with his eyes as far as they would roll to the corner of the room where the door was. Cap heard the door shut, then a series of locks.

Rafa returned, leaned down into Cap's face, and examined him like he was a specimen in a jar. Scrutinizing. Cap could smell the sweat on his skin. Rafa stuck his hands in Cap's underarms and heaved him up, threw him over his shoulder in a fireman's carry, then dropped him on a narrow table.

Cap's eyes shot to the walls. Tools hung there—a saw, hammers, screwdrivers. A vise, prongs, tongs. All of them dotted and splattered with odd patterns of rust.

Cap's knowledge as a handyman was limited to basic carpentry and the contents of a set of Time Life how-to books his parents had purchased in the eighties. But he only had to think about it for a second, that rust didn't form and dry like a liquid on tools.

Only blood could do that.

Vega made a sharp turn at the bottom of the stairs. There was another smaller hallway and a little girl in a lacy top and underwear crouching in a doorway to a room. The fear on her face was the opposite of the distant fear on the faces of the girls upstairs. This girl's fear was immediate and alive. It appeared to be gobbling her up right there, her teeth chattering, words spilling out fast and slurry, her eyes darting to different points on the ceiling like there was a connect-the-dots up there.

"It's okay," said Vega quietly, in Spanish. "I'm here to help you."

The girl shook her head desperately.

"Rafa," she whispered.

"He took the white guy to the garage," said Vega.

The girl stopped shaking her head.

"Where is Coyote Ben?" asked Vega.

"I don't know."

"Are you Missy?"

She nodded.

"What about Chicago—the girl, Chicago?"

Missy pointed down the hall and held up three fingers—the third room.

For the first time Vega looked at the layout: there were four doors on each side, the rooms like makeshift cubicles, small and clearly not part of the original architecture of the house, constructed out of white fiberboard, divided by thin strips of sheet metal.

Vega walked down the narrow hallway and counted the rooms on her right. One-two-three. She pointed at the door in front of her and looked at Missy. Vega knocked with the nose of her gun lightly. There was no answer so she pounded on the door three times with the jaws of the bolt cutters.

The door opened about a foot wide, and a chunky bald guy leaned his head into the opening to speak.

"I have twelve more minutes," he said to Vega. He seemed almost on the verge of tears.

Vega kicked the door all the way open and aimed the Springfield at his face. He stumbled backward, naked except for a white T-shirt. Vega chased him to the floor, and he scrambled on his hands and ass into the wall. Vega kept the gun in his face.

"Where are your car keys?" she said.

She pressed the nose of the gun against his forehead, felt it slide with the sweat.

"In the pants," he said, a tiny drop of spittle escaping the corner of his mouth with the "p."

Vega took a step back and pulled the gun away from his skin.

"Get them," she said.

He crawled to his pants and frantically searched the pockets, pulled out a small ring of keys.

Vega let her eyes jump briefly to Chicago, who lay on the bed naked. She hadn't made a move to cover herself. She looked about sixteen and had a circular red burn mark on her temple just like Jane 1. Was she on something? Had her brain been cooked? Or was it the fog of trauma, multiple rapes and beatings? Vega knew fear could punch deeper holes with longer-lasting damage in neural pathways than ice picks could.

The bald man started to wriggle his stocky legs into his pants, fussing with the belt in his shaking hands.

"Leave the fucking clothes, you dumb motherfucker!" Vega yelled at him, her voice reverberating off the flimsy walls, stinging her own eardrums.

He stood up, cowering, holding his keys in front of his crotch as if they would cover his rapidly shrinking dick.

"Get the fuck out," she said.

He ran out the door, past her, his keys jingling.

Vega lowered her gun and looked to Chicago, who watched her like a deer.

"Do you know where Coyote Ben is?" Vega said.

The girl just stared at Vega, the words not getting through.

"You should go upstairs. With the other girls," said Vega.

Chicago got off the bed and stood. Vega realized Chicago was actually taller than she was. She could see the girl's ribs underneath the perfect semicircles of her breasts. Chicago left the room, taking no clothes with her.

Vega stepped out of the room. Chicago had joined Missy at the bottom of the stairs, and the two headed up. Vega could hear Missy whispering to Chicago urgently, but Chicago didn't react.

Vega moved down the hallway and kicked open the doors to the rest of the rooms. They were empty and identical—twin beds, filing cabinets. No Davis.

She turned and ran, thinking about how narrow it was—the hallway, the stairway, no visibility around the corners, and she really hated that. She took the stairs two at a time, not worrying about the sound because now Davis could only be upstairs if he was anywhere in the house, if he hadn't skipped totally and was well on his way to Tijuana.

Vega came to the top and headed to the right, the direction of the girls, but then Davis appeared, lunging at her abdomen with a knife in his hand.

Vega heard her jacket and shirt rip at the side and dropped her gun, fell back against the wall, away from Davis. She knew he'd gotten her but didn't feel the pain, just the warmth of her blood like a broth spilling through her clothes, but she also knew she was upright, not falling, not fainting, so realized it was just a swipe, nothing punctured, might not even need stitches.

It was not even a full second—not a one-Mississippi, and then Davis came at her again, this time the blade pointed right at her, gripping it from below with one hand, his left outstretched heading for the wall or her shoulder. Vega was familiar with the stance; the slice had been meant to stun. Now he wasn't looking to stab; he was aiming to gut.

Fortunately she still had the bolt cutters.

She swung them with whatever momentum she could gather with both hands, and the jaws met Davis's hip before he got near her, knocking him down. He dropped the knife and screamed, grabbed his smashed hip with both hands and yelled, "Shit, shit, shit."

Vega knew she wanted to get information from him at some point soon. But at the moment she wanted to knock all of his teeth out more. She swung at his mouth, not with her full weight, not hard enough to bury the alloy steel into his skull, but enough to unhinge his jaws, destroy his sinuses, splinter his nice suburban teeth. He screamed and cried and whined when she pulled the bolt cutters from his mouth, his hands slapped over his lips, waterfalls of blood and spit pouring over his fingers, real genuine tears leaking from his eyes.

Vega picked up her gun and pressed her elbow tight to the incision in her side. She stepped over Davis and headed for the front door, not looking back, thinking, Good boy, down you go.

Cap could hear the hum. He remembered rock shows from his youth and Nell's fall band concerts—the sound of the amps as the musicians plugged in and tuned up. Early MTV heavy metal videos, the single victorious drumstick twirling.

This wasn't that. Rafa stood next to him, shifting things around on a table near Cap's head. Then he sat in a wheeled chair. He leaned down and pulled Cap's eyelids up with his thumb, peered into one eye and then the other.

"All right, boss," he said, like he was about to serve him a drink. "You should wear a better costume next time, hey?"

He opened Cap's mouth and pushed his rows of teeth open with two fingers, shoved in a mouth guard, like the kind boxers used. Cap could feel it pressing on his gums, stretching the frenulum of his upper lip.

"You bite your tongue off, more cleanup for me, boss," Rafa said.

Cap's breathing sped up. He huffed through his nose.

"Yeah, I know, the first time's a bitch."

Rafa leaned over and flipped a switch. The humming grew louder, and Rafa pressed a silicon patch onto Cap's left temple. Cap felt one tiny twitch in his right pinkie. He concentrated on his toes and fingertips and willed them to wiggle. But then Rafa flipped another switch, and the humming got louder still, a gargantuan alien mosquito in his ears, and then the very last switch flipped.

The volts shot through Cap, and there was no more thinking, just all the meat of his muscles snapping into spasms, his brain off the clock.

Vega went out to the garage. It was a rickety shed, made of cheap siding. There was a single door with a handle and Vega pulled it, then pushed, but it was locked. She shoved her shoulder into the door and felt something solid and immovable behind it. Not as weak as it looked.

She lifted the bolt cutters with both hands and swung full force into the door. The jaws made a dent, and the whole wall shook but didn't break, didn't open.

"You can't open it like that," said a voice in Spanish from behind Vega.

Vega turned to see the older girl, still with the spray of blood from the fat guy on her face. The other girls stood behind her, blinking into the sunlight. Some sat on the dirt. None appeared to be trying to run.

"There is . . ." the girl said and paused, trying to find the right words. "Metal behind the door."

Vega's mind raced. Steel, aluminum, acrylic. Only if it were specifically ballistic resistant would it kick back a bullet.

"You should stand over there," she said to the girl, pointing to the others.

The girl backed up and regarded Vega with curiosity.

Vega pulled the Springfield from her holster and flipped the safety with her thumb. She took a step back and aimed down, at about a forty-five-degree angle, and fired. The bullet hit the door with a tinny crash and the casing dropped to the dirt. The door was dented. There was something bulletproof behind it.

Vega walked back a few paces, thought briefly about walking around the shed and firing along the perimeter but two things gave her pause:

she couldn't be sure where they were inside and it would give Rafa time. She could sacrifice one but not the other. She needed something faster, bigger.

She ran to her car, the entire right side of her shirt, the right leg of her pants soaked with her blood now. But she knew she couldn't be losing that much; she was still thinking, processing, taking deep breaths, and not feeling faint, not yet.

She got into the driver's seat and threw the bolt cutters on the seat next to her, stuck her gun back into the holster. Buckled the seatbelt and winced at the pressure on the cut but ignored it, yanked on the belt twice to make it as tight as possible across her. Then she pushed the driver's side door open.

Time to go.

She started the car and kept her left foot on the brake while she tapped the gas gently with her right, felt the engine rev. Forty should do it, she thought. She put her hands at 3 and 9 and pressed the back of her head into the headrest. She took her foot off the brake, and the car lurched at first, not the best pickup anymore. The tires screeched, and she pushed on the gas, watched the speedometer climb like it had a fever, right up to forty, the street blurring by.

Then she was on the curb and the second before making contact she slammed the brake and turned her head, crashed into the side of the shed, tearing through the wall.

The airbag inflated and Vega felt it sock her in the cheek with the weight of a packed boxing glove, smelled the smoke and the powder. She held her breath and shut her eyes and with her right hand followed the seatbelt down to the buckle and snapped it open. The right side of her stomach and thigh had gone numb now, but she didn't feel the pain of the cut anymore. The crash had pumped more adrenaline into her heart than a hypodermic.

She slid to the left of the airbag near the door, which had been blown back toward the car on impact but had not shut. She pushed it open with her shoulder and squatted behind it, on the floor of the shed, pulled the Springfield out of the holster with her right hand, then the fat guy's Glock from her waistband with her left.

She looked up to the ceiling. The car had ripped one of the walls off a corner, smashed the bottom half of it open so it looked like a half-open garage door. The room smelled like smoke, but Vega couldn't tell what was burning.

She poked her head up and peered through the glass of the car door. Caplan was on a table, but she couldn't see his face. He wasn't moving. Rafa had a gun out and fired into the windshield. He was a big boy—six four without shoes—and looked like he'd lifted pretty regularly.

She held the Springfield just above the window of the car door and fired, aimed for his legs, got a thigh. He screamed and fell to the floor with a crash. Then she stood up and walked quickly toward him. Fired with the Glock into his other leg. He screamed again and moved his hands instinctually to the newer wound.

The Glock was bigger than Vega's gun and kicked back in her hand a little but she held it steady and then fired once more with the Springfield into his foot. He convulsed with the pain and tried to reach for the injured foot but couldn't seem to make it, cried out as his hands curled in front of his stomach, his head twisting on his neck.

Vega put her guns away and ran to Cap. His eyes were open and blinking rapidly. He had an electrode patch on his head and his mouth was open an inch. Vega could see a solid bulk of white against his teeth.

"Caplan," she said, reaching her fingers into his mouth.

She pulled out a mouth guard and tossed it to the floor. Then she carefully unpeeled the patch and dropped it, let it swing from a wire attached to a box the size and shape of an old VCR. There was a pink burn on Cap's left temple where the patch had been.

"Caplan," she said again, quieter.

She held his face in her hands. He was looking at her, his eyes searching her face, but he didn't speak. Muscles were twitching, his lips, arms and fingers, feet. His head shook toward his shoulder.

"Can you hear me?" she said.

He tilted his chin up in a sharp nod. She took his hand and bent his arm at the elbow, as if they were about to arm-wrestle.

"Can you squeeze my hand?"

He squeezed. It wasn't strong but it was there.

"Move your feet," said Vega.

He moved them, pointing the toes. One, two.

"Now your whole leg. This one," she said, patting his left thigh. "Just lift it off the table a little."

Cap blinked heavily at her, as if he didn't understand the command at first, but then he did it, hovering his leg over the table about an inch.

"How about the other one?"

He lifted the other one. Hokeypokey.

"Okay," said Vega. "I'm going to pull you up."

She leaned close to him and kept her hand tightly clasped around his, then put her other arm around his back and pulled him upright. She could feel his biceps and flexors working. She let go of his hand. Without her telling him to, he swiveled his whole body to the side so his legs hung off the table, like he was at his annual physical.

Vega stood next to him, took his hand, and pulled his arm around her shoulders so they were side by side.

"On three," she said.

He nodded.

"One. Two. Three."

She lifted him, and he stood at the same time. They began to walk, Cap's feet not stepping too far off the ground. Vega's side began to ache again. They walked around Rafa's twitching body, past the wreckage of Vega's car, through the hole in the wall of the shed, out into the light.

13

VEGA HAD STAYED WITH HIM AS LONG AS SHE COULD.

Now she was in a hospital room on a bed wearing a gown, saline fluid and a bag of blood dripping down into a spike in her hand while a doctor, sitting on a stool next to her, stitched her up. She'd taken the shots of lidocaine in the cut, so she didn't exactly feel the point of the needle now, just the dull pressure from the threading back and forth through her skin.

Her phone had no reception either.

She shut her eyes and saw it all—the girls, the ambulance, Otero, Cap leaning most of his weight on her, cobbling together words like a foreigner. Head, feels funny, girls, Otero, Nell, Vega. Vega.

We'll speak later, Otero had said kindly as he shuffled her and Cap into the back of the ambulance. At that point, Vega had begun to feel faint. Smudgy, was how she thought of it, as if someone had pressed his thumb on her and blurred out her senses, thought processes. She'd tried to argue with Otero, what about the girls, where are they going, where's the girl sprayed with blood. She watched them file into a small bus. It didn't say DEPT OF CORRECTIONS anywhere but there were crisscross bars on the windows. Then the doors of the ambulance closed, and she sat next to Cap, who lay on the gurney while the paramedic took his vitals, his speech still sounding like clipped ransom note words.

"He's been electrocuted," Vega said. "A thousand volts. He needs a CT scan."

She'd been pressing her hand against the cut in her side, hadn't realized she'd begun to shiver so hard she was sporadically biting the insides of her cheeks.

Now the doctor took his time, threading in and out. He had orange hair with a baby face, his skin pale and freckled; it seemed to Vega like he should have been licking an ice cream cone instead of providing any medical service.

When they'd arrived at the ER, they were separated, Cap pushed away on the gurney and Vega in a wheelchair. She'd tried to stand but felt her head go cold and her eyes cloud over the second her knees locked, so she sat back down and let them take her to Triage. She struggled to keep her eyes open, losing feeling in her toes and fingertips, and finally let her lids fall as the nurses moved her to a bed.

She had no idea if Cap was still in the ER, getting an MRI, if they'd let him go, or if he was in bed in the room right next to her, unconscious.

"Hey, are you almost done?" she asked the doctor.

"Just about," he said. Then, with some amusement, "Is there somewhere you need to be?"

"Yeah, there is."

"You'll have to wait until you get the full pint," he said, pointing up to the blood. "Your screens haven't come back yet so it's hard to tell how much you've lost."

He continued to stitch slowly, tugging the thread after each pull like a grandma with a needlepoint canvas.

"You don't want to get light-headed again," he added.

Vega propped herself up on her elbows.

"Not light-headed anymore," she said.

"It's tricky," the doctor said, not looking up. "You might feel okay now, but then, an hour or two passes, you're more confident . . ." A mild cast of derision crossed his face, as if he disapproved of the behavior he was describing.

Vega glanced at the bag of blood, almost half-empty.

"How much longer will that take?" she said.

"Between thirty and sixty minutes," he said, not looking at it.

Vega picked up her phone once more from the tray table attached to the bed. No new messages, texts. Still no reception.

"Okay," said the doctor with an air of finality. "Come back to us or your personal physician in two weeks to take these out," he said, snipping the edges of the black thread with scissors.

He pressed a strip of gauze over the wound and sealed it with medical tape, then held up a roll of each to show Vega.

"I'm going to give you these," he said. "Change the bandage tomorrow, then every day for a week. Bleeding seems to be under control but if that changes, call us or your doctor."

"Thanks," said Vega, sitting straight up, feeling only the slightest burn from the wound.

The doctor stood.

"Take it easy," he said, holding his hand out as if to stop her, his tone a little too dictatorial for Vega's taste, especially since he looked about nineteen. He might have also realized it because then he broke into a smile. "You don't want to pass out again, do you?"

"I'm feeling better," she said. "I'll get dressed while I wait." She nodded up to the blood.

The doctor smiled.

"Okay, then. Take care."

He turned to leave. Vega swung her legs over the side of the bed and stared at the empty hanger and hook on the door. She glanced at the yogurt-colored chair in the corner, the air-conditioning unit under the window. The doctor opened the door.

"Where are my clothes?" she said.

The doctor stopped for a moment and looked back at her. His eyebrows were so fair Vega couldn't immediately tell their position on his face; it neutralized his expression. She didn't know if he was surprised, confused, something else.

"They're not here?" he said, peering around the room. "Huh. They must have been left in Triage. I'll have someone go take a look."

He gave her one more curt smile before leaving. Vega stared at the door after it closed. She waited a full minute, then stood up and went to the door, pulling the IV stand with her, the toes of her socks slipping on the floor a little with each step.

She opened the door. There, in the hallway, was what she expected. Two cops, uniformed officers in the hall, one black, one white, both young.

"Can we help you, ma'am?" said the white one.

"Just looking for my clothes," said Vega, her volume low.

"Someone's gone to find them," said the black cop. "You should sit tight while you wait. You're probably really wiped out." He smiled broadly.

All they were missing were open-plain twangs and cowboy hats to tip in her direction. You sit tight now, little lady.

She paused a moment before smiling back along with a nod of acknowledgment. Then she retreated into the room and shut the door. She tapped her fingers on the surface, too light for the cops to hear. And for once the voice in her head wasn't Perry's. It was actually McTiernan's, a direct quote from the day before: Something. Ain't. Right.

.   .   .

Cap didn't exactly come to; it was more a gradual process of awakening. He thought he'd been conscious the whole time, from the house in Salton to the shed to the ambulance to the ER, to the booming cracks of the MRI machine. But a series of black tape redactions spread through his memory. Was it Vega in the ambulance with him, or Nell, or Jules? Was there actually a car with the hood smoking inside of the shed when he left it? Was it day or night? Did he sit on the lawn with the girls, and did Missy, the girl he'd gone downstairs with, hold his hand and lean her head against his shoulder while Vega talked on the phone next to him? Was Vega bleeding?

All results of shock, he knew. Foggy memory of the events immediately surrounding the trauma was normal and expected. It would all come back, he told himself hopefully.

Muscles in his body twitched one by one—feet, legs, arms, and he began to feel more awake. He took a brief inventory of his surroundings: standard hospital room, socks on his feet, gown and boxer shorts on his body. IV dripping clear fluid into his hand.

The door to the room was open but Cap didn't hear anything. No chatter, no nurses' intercom, no oxygen canister gasps, no bells, no beeps. California, he thought in an attempt to convince himself this was normal—apparently they produced even fewer sick people.

He examined his hands, which looked fine. He knew there was something he should be holding but couldn't quite identify what that should be. A gun, another hand, a phone. Phone, he thought definitively. He needed to call Nell. Maybe he wouldn't tell her everything this time. Could he get away with that, he thought, withholding being the same as lying—hadn't they had that conversation?

He saw his phone lying on a tray table next to his bed, alongside a plastic pitcher of water. He picked it up and swiped and saw there were no messages, no texts, no voice mails. Then he saw why. No service.

"No reception, Mr. Caplan?"

Cap looked up. There was a dark-haired Latino man in the doorway.

"Nope," said Cap.

"Me neither," said the man, holding up his phone as if Cap could see the lack of bars from ten feet away.

The man stepped inside the room and approached Cap's bed. He extended his hand and said, "Deputy Chief Armando Posada."

"Max Caplan," said Cap, shaking Posada's hand, noticing one bulky gold ring on his middle finger.

Posada pulled up one of the visitor's chairs and sat next to the bed. He had a deep triangular scar right above his chin.

"How are you feeling, Mr. Caplan?" he said, a slight accent in his voice.

His face was earnest and weathered. He looked to Cap like he'd spent a lot of time in the sun and may at one point have been a smoker though Cap could not smell it on him now. His clothes were impeccable and seemed too pressed and creased for a cop, even a deputy chief. Gray suit pants and a white collared shirt. Gold cuff links, no tie.

"Strange," said Cap. "But okay."

"Are you hungry?" asked Posada. "We can find some food for you."

"No thanks, not quite yet," said Cap. "Deputy Chief, do you know where my partner is? Or Commander Otero. I'd like us all to talk, give a statement and whatever you need so we can move this forward."

Though he hadn't discussed it with Vega, Cap thought the best course now was to assume they would all work together, since they had found the girls, after all.

Posada held his hand out gently. Cap had the feeling he would have patted Cap on the head if it weren't totally weird and unprofessional.

"There'll be plenty of time for that," said Posada. "Ms. Vega has actually lost quite a bit of blood, so she's receiving a transfusion." He paused, then added: "In another ward."

Cap flipped through the patchy images in his mind. Blood on her arms, on the hand in which she gripped her phone. Dripping from her side, just above her belt, onto the strands of dry grass where she sat.

"She got hurt," said Cap, remembering. "What happened?"

"She was stabbed," said Posada evenly. "But they tell me no organs were harmed, so that's a good thing."

Cap stared at Posada while he tried to absorb the information. She was hurt.

"Is she awake? Is she conscious?" said Cap, connecting the words quicker than before.

"Yes, yes, don't be concerned," said Posada. He seemed close to chuckling. "She'll be fine."

"I need to speak with her," said Cap, a little more forcefully.

He pushed the nurse call button, which buzzed. There was no response, so he pressed it again, for longer.

"Mr. Caplan, I was hoping we could speak first, you and I."

"Shoot," Cap said, finally releasing the button.

The news of Vega getting hurt had pulled him out of the last of the fog. He sat up straight in the bed.

"I wanted to thank you personally for your part in solving this case."

Then Posada just smiled kindly, generously, and didn't say anything else.

"You're welcome?" Cap said, a little unsure that was the response he was looking for.

"I'm sure you're eager to get back to your life. Where was it, Philadelphia?"

"Yeah, more or less," said Cap. "Once we get those girls back to their families and find out who's behind the whole operation. Devin Lara, Ben Davis, someone else—where's all the money going, right?"

Posada sat up and back in the chair. Less conversational, Cap noticed. More like an interview. Or an interrogation. He didn't speak right away.

"Right, Deputy Chief?" said Cap.

"Maybe these girls don't have families anymore," Posada finally said.

He seemed a little sad about it but mostly resigned.

"Maybe," said Cap, growing impatient. "But they have been trafficked—that's pretty clear."

"We don't have much to go on," said Posada, his eyes wandering up the walls. "So we will keep investigating until we know."

"Uh-huh," said Cap.

He could detect the scent of being purposefully misled, a little sleight-of-hand action. And he knew for certain Posada wasn't telling him the whole truth. Or possibly no truth at all.

"I've spoken to Commander Otero and Agent Mackey. We've agreed no charges should be brought against you or Ms. Vega for interfering in a police investigation."

Cap coughed out a laugh, unable to contain it.

"What a relief," he said.

Posada continued, as if Cap hadn't said anything: "Impersonating a police officer, multiple counts of aggravated assault and battery, disturbing the peace."

He flicked all of his fingernails against the tips of his thumbs, like a magician presenting the big finish. Poof.

"Gone," he said.

"That's really something, Deputy Chief," Cap said, struggling to control the edge in his voice. "For you all to be so magnanimous, seeing that *you* asked *us* to work the case in the first place. And seeing we located ten missing minors and, possibly, probably, found the killers of your two Janes."

Cap heard his voice rise and was heartened by it—it felt familiar and sharp; if he could grab it, it would slice up his hands like a broken bottle. Posada remained narrow-eyed and unruffled by Cap's anger, which made Cap want to shock him into responding.

"We're so thorough my partner got herself stabbed with your goddamn murder weapon," he uttered through clenched teeth. "So again, appreciate you letting us slide."

Cap reached over and pressed the nurse call button again, tugged at the IV tube.

"Are you in a hurry, Mr. Caplan?" said Posada.

"Just ready to leave. As much as I love hospitals."

"You're still waiting for the result of the MRI, I believe."

"They can email it to me," Cap said, swinging his legs off the bed.

"Don't stand up too quickly now," said Posada, scooting his chair out of the way. "Don't want you going down. Are you understanding me, Mr. Caplan?"

Cap felt a cool cover of sweat spread on his forehead and held on to the bed rail for support. Slowly he stood, took some breaths. He glanced around the room, figured he seemed confused because Posada asked, "Everything okay?"

"Yeah," said Cap. "Just can't find my clothes."

Posada frowned slightly.

"That's strange. Maybe they didn't make it up from the ER. I'll have a girl bring them up," he said, standing.

"Okay, thanks," said Cap, feeling a little less sure of his physical stability. "Could you see if there's a nurse out there to take out the IV?"

"Of course," said Posada, extending his hand once more. "Pleasure to meet you, Mr. Caplan. Please remember what I said about standing up too quickly."

Cap shook his hand, and then Posada was gone, shutting the door behind him. Cap walked around the room, pulling the IV stand with him, examining every surface where his clothes might have been left, checked behind the drapes. He squatted down and looked under the bed.

He touched his head where the burn was, felt the slick of whatever antibiotic ointment had been applied. The image of Rafa came to him in a jolt, and he sat on the bed, remembering the feeling of the electricity in his bones. He examined his hands again, turned his head to the closed door, thought, Vega, where are you?

Try the thing that makes the most sense first.

That was Vega's line of thinking. Why treat the situation hostilely until she knew it was hostile? Maybe Otero was just worried about her and wanted her to have extra security. Maybe the staff really did just leave her clothes in Triage. Maybe.

She opened the door.

"Can we help you, ma'am?" said the white cop again.

"Hope so," she said, smiling amiably. "I have to leave, but I need my clothes first."

She added a little laugh to that, like losing her clothes was something she did regularly.

Both cops smiled back, friendly as they could be. They looked at each other to decide who would speak first.

"Yeah, the nurse hasn't come up yet," said the black cop. "We'll be right here with you until she's back."

"I appreciate the company," said Vega. "But I'd like to walk around the floor if you don't mind."

The white cop opened his mouth to speak, and Vega cut him off.

"See, my mom died in a hospital, and up until about a week before that she liked to walk around the floor, do a lap, you know? It helped her muscles not ache, and I think it might help my injury," Vega said, gesturing to her side. "I'm not a fall risk, so I don't think it will be any kind of liability issue."

She stepped out into the hall, and the black cop moved to the side so he was directly in front of her, the white cop right behind him.

"Ma'am, I'm sorry, we have some orders," said the black cop. Polite but firm.

Vega leaned her face closer to his. He was young, him and the white cop, not a wrinkle, not a gray hair.

"And what are those orders," she said in a hushed voice, not smiling anymore.

"To keep you safe."

Vega cast her glance down the hall in both directions. There was no one. No nurses, no doctors, no cleaning staff, no candy stripers. Just closed doors, all the color of Pepto.

"Any way you could call a nurse to take this out?" she said, pulling on the IV tube, the empty bags dangling.

"Yes, ma'am, right away," said the black cop. "If you'll just wait in the room, someone will be right here soon to assist you with that."

"And my clothes, too, right?" she said in the white cop's direction.

"Right," he said.

Vega stepped back across the threshold, dragging the IV stand with her.

"Appreciate it," she said.

They smiled and nodded. Happy to be of service. Vega shut the door, and this time turned around and leaned against it with all her weight, running through her options considering the situation, which, on the Hostile Scale, she identified as Hostile as Fuck.

Cap watched his phone for signs of life. He walked around the room again, holding the phone up in corners and near the windows, thinking maybe he could get some service, but still, nothing. Then he felt out of air, nauseous suddenly, so he sat, drank some cups of water from the plastic pitcher. He began to feel better but regretted not telling Posada that he needed some food, because now he felt a surge of hunger in every muscle, his head aching.

He pressed the call button once more, stayed on it for at least thirty seconds, and then decided to find a nurse face-to-face. He stood, pulling the IV stand toward the door, which he opened.

There was a uniformed cop there, right next to the door, a young guy with tanned, tattooed arms. Cap felt a degree of relief seeing the blue.

"You need anything, sir?" the cop said.

"Hi, Officer . . ." Cap said, reading the nameplate on his chest. "Calderon. The nurse button doesn't seem to be working. I'm ready to have this taken out," he said, gesturing to the IV.

"Sure, sir," Calderon said eagerly. "Please wait in the room, and I'll get a nurse for you."

Cap quickly glanced down the hallway and didn't see any nurses. No one at all, in fact. And that turned a few knobs in his old cop brain. The conversation with Posada had been odd enough, and now, an empty hospital floor. And an armed guard.

"Actually," said Cap, moving into the hallway, "I don't have any reception in there. I think . . ." He paused, pretended he was just casually spitballing about ways to spend the afternoon. "I think I might take a spin around the floor, see if I can get some service, make some calls to my loved ones."

He watched Calderon's eyes grow as Cap took a step toward him.

"Sir, I have to ask you to stay in the room for now," he said, the tone in his voice just a little strained. "It's for your own safety."

Cap thought about that. He allowed himself to smirk.

"So, you're keeping me safe, right?"

"Yes, sir, those are my orders."

"And, uh," Cap said, leaning forward. "Who are you keeping me safe from?" he asked with genuine interest.

Alarm crossed the young man's face, gave him some wrinkles.

"Because there doesn't appear to be any immediate threat here," said Cap, gesturing to the empty hallway.

"I don't know the details, sir," Calderon said. "I've been told to guard you in your room."

"You take this order from the deputy chief?"

A confused expression danced over the young cop's face but then passed.

"No, I'm not at liberty to say," he said. "I have to ask you, please back up, into your room."

Cap didn't back up. He wasn't trying to be aggressive, just wanted to get a feel for what was what.

"Sir," said Calderon, rooting his feet firmly where he stood. "I have to ask you to back up."

Cap waited a moment and then backed up.

"No prob, Officer."

He smiled, and Calderon smiled back, a little nervously.

Cap closed the door and stared at it. He had a feeling that Calderon was a nice kid, an inside-the-lines cop, probably had Sunday dinner with his mom every week.

Not that it made a difference. Cap had to get past him, no matter what kind of kid or cop or son he was. All that mattered was that he was in Cap's way.

Vega pressed a square of toilet tissue over the top of her hand and removed the IV needle, let it dangle next to the stand. She washed her hands in the sink next to the bathroom with a lot of foaming soap and then sat on the bed. She removed her socks and let them fall to the floor. She lifted up the side of her gown and pressed the skin around the bandage that covered her wound. The lidocaine had worn off, which was what she had expected but still hoped against.

If only there were one, not two out there, she would have been more confident. But not two. And not just two, but also armed and trained. Not sloppy under the haze of drugs or drink. Play the damn cards, she thought.

She peeled off the bandage, strands of the medical tape sticking and fraying on her skin. She dropped the gauze to the ground, next to her socks. Her skin surrounding the injury felt wet, the incision itself still throbbing. Davis had cut as deep as he could in that one swipe, probably had a lot of practice. Vega flicked her finger against the end of the nylon black string stitched so thoroughly by the redheaded doctor.

Vega wiggled her toes and thought the thing she always thought when she knew pain was coming: This is not your body.

She took a breath in, gripped the ends of the string as firmly as she could, and pulled. She managed to loosen the first knot and stitch, and the whole top half of her body convulsed with the pain. She bit the insides of her cheeks to keep from screaming. Band-Aid, she thought. Rip it off.

She kept pulling, using both hands, the string unraveling, popping out of her skin, blood dripping in big steady drops onto the white floor. Breathe, she told herself, and she began gulping air in shallow breaths, blowing it out with her lips pursed in a diamond like she was about to whistle.

Similar to other times she'd been injured, the pain reached a certain level and then didn't surpass it. Once she realized that, the task and what followed became easier. She wound the black thread around two fingers and yanked one last time to pull out the final knot and stitch.

She gasped and chuffed through her nose like a horse but kept breathing and shook the thread off her fingers, now coated with blood. Then she leaned to her right, the side where the wound was, and let the blood continue to drip onto the floor in a steadily expanding puddle.

She moved to the floor then and thought about her position. On her side, she decided. She hovered over the puddle, made sure the blood coated her hands and at least one side of her gown. It was wet and cool, and she shivered for a moment but told herself, You've had a pint of blood and a pint of saline and you're fine.

She was ready. She took the deepest breath she could, filled her lungs and her diaphragm and her stomach full of air until she felt like she'd pop if pricked with a pin, and then she screamed. It was more of a howl, really, with all the volume available, sustained and dry in her throat.

The cops burst in, their faces reflecting what they saw with shock and fear. Vega knew cops see a lot, even if they're young, even in a nice neighborhood in San Diego, but almost anyone would be disturbed by a half-naked woman covered in blood, screaming. And these guys were no exception.

"My stitches came out! My stitches!" Vega screamed. "Get a doctor! Now!"

The black cop, nearest the door, nodded quickly and took off. The white cop ran and kneeled in front of her but didn't seem to know what to do with his hands.

"Someone will be here soon, ma'am," he said, tentatively sliding his arms underneath her.

Vega screamed again, and he pulled his arms away like he'd been burned.

"Don't touch me!" Vega yelled. "Please get a doctor, please!"

"Ma'am," the cop said, struggling to keep his voice steady. "My partner will get a doctor for you right away."

Vega reached out and gripped his shirt.

"Listen to me—I'm a hemophiliac, and they don't know that. I didn't tell the doctor because I wanted to get out of here and didn't want to wait for another transfusion. But I am losing blood at a rapid rate and . . ."

She tried to prop herself up but then let herself fall.

"I'm losing consciousness quick . . ."

"Ma'am, you just have to hold on," the white cop said. "Let me move you up to the bed."

He reached forward to touch her again, and she recoiled.

"Don't touch me, please," she said, her voice faint. "Please . . . go look for someone, I don't need a babysitter, I need a doctor." Vega lay down completely on the floor and turned her head to face the white cop. She said, as weakly as she could manage, "If I bleed out I could die. And you're supposed to keep me safe, right?"

She watched the reality of what she'd said land on the cop. His eyes became frantic. Whoever it was who'd given him the order to watch her might be a little upset if she died on his watch.

He pulled his walkie from his belt and spoke into it: "Young, what's your status, over?"

There was no immediate response. Vega closed her eyes.

"I'm just going to rest for a second," she said dreamily.

"No, ma'am, please don't fall asleep," the white cop said.

Then the black cop's voice came back, between heaves and gasps, sounded like he was going down the stairs: "Still looking for friendly doctor."

Vega could hear the leather on the white cop's belt squeaking; she sensed he was standing up.

"Ma'am, I'll be right back. I'm going to find some help for you."

Vega opened one eye.

"Please hurry," she said.

The white cop ran.

Vega counted to thirty.

She got to her feet and rinsed her hands in the sink. Glanced in the mirror, saw that half of her face was covered with blood. She splashed water on it but then knew she had to go. She grabbed her phone, picked up the gauze and medical tape that the redheaded doctor had given her, and left. Ideally, she knew, she should have bandaged up before leaving the room but she didn't have much time.

She ran hard on bare feet down the hall, stopping only to pull down the T-shaped switches on the fire alarms.

Cap heard an alarm. A small square light flashed on the ceiling in the corner. The sounds he heard were not the musical beeps of an inquiry tone but the intrusive honks of a real fire alarm. A drill, he guessed. But seeing that he seemed to be the only one on this floor, it seemed a little silly to have a drill just for him.

He opened the door and saw Calderon there, at his phone and holding his walkie to his ear.

"Hey," said Cap loudly. "Is this a drill?"

"I don't know," shouted Calderon. "Trying to find out."

The lights flashed in the hall, the alarm louder than in Cap's room. Calderon looked at the face of his phone and stuck his walkie in his belt. He shook his head in frustration.

"No service?" yelled Cap.

Calderon shook his head.

"We can't stay here, man," said Cap. "We gotta go!"

Cap pointed toward the end of the hallway, in case Calderon had not heard him. Calderon nodded, gestured for Cap to follow him. Calderon walked briskly, seeming to gain urgency with each step. Cap tried to catch up, still dragging the IV stand along, the needle still firmly stuck in the vein on the surface of his hand.

The alarm continued to blare, and Cap continued to notice that no one else was emerging from the rooms, the whiteboards next to the doors blank and wrapped in plastic.

"Officer!" Cap yelled. "Stairs!"

He pointed to a door marked STAIRWELL B.

Calderon shook his head and shouted, "No entry there. Only one on the floor—come on!"

Cap couldn't move as fast with the IV stand but sped up to try to match Calderon's pace. He was a good yard behind, though, as Calderon began to turn the corner, but Cap jumped back when someone swung a wheeled office chair at Calderon's face, and he flew back and down at Cap's feet, hands to his nose with blood spurting out like it was a public park water fountain.

Vega dropped the chair.

She panted, her mouth and throat dry from screaming. Her side ached and she was freezing but she ignored it all and allowed herself to soak in the relief of finding Cap, even though he seemed to be suffering a kind of input overload between the alarm and the cop on the floor with the busted nose.

She took his hand, the one with the IV needle still stuck in it.

"We have to go," she said.

"We can't just leave him here. What if it's not a drill?"

"It's a drill. I did it," she said.

She pressed the roll of gauze on top of Cap's hand and pulled the needle out roughly. He winced and looked back at the cop on the floor. Vega could see he was torn but she had no time for him to weigh the pros and cons.

"We have to leave now," she said, pulling him by the wrist.

Finally his feet seemed to come loose from their spots and he began to walk, then run with her, around the corner away from the cop, past the nurses' station with the chairs and desktop computers and filing cabinets covered with stretched plastic wrap.

"Only one stairwell works," Cap said to her.

"Yeah, it's C," Vega said, pointing straight ahead.

They ran and pushed through the door into the stairwell. The alarm wasn't sounding here, and all Vega could hear was her and Cap breathing heavily as they started down. She glanced over her shoulder to see the sign posted on the door, FLOOR 16 UNDER RENOVATION, AUTHORIZED PERSONNEL ONLY.

"Is that your blood on you?" Cap said.

Vega nodded.

"Davis cut me. They stitched me but I had to pull them out to get rid of the cops outside my door."

"Wait," said Cap, stopping her on a landing.

He took hold of her shoulders and turned her to face him.

"You're freezing cold, and bleeding. And you just assaulted a police officer, which is up to ten in Pennsylvania."

"It's only three here if they get you on the felony," Vega said, losing feeling in her lips. "Fucking East Coast," she added.

"Vega," said Cap, shaking her gently. "We can't escape from this hospital while you're bleeding out, and they're looking for us. We have no clothes and no ID. We have to just start this process over, find Otero and talk to him."

"Caplan, Otero must have fucking put us here," Vega said, pulling away from his grasp. "He needed to stash us somewhere while the Janes got sent somewhere else."

Cap's face froze as he considered it. He set his phone on the stairs and grabbed the gauze and medical tape from her, which was not difficult, her hold loose and getting weaker.

"Let me tape you, please, quickly," he said.

She lifted the right side of her gown and he tore a strip of gauze with his teeth, then worked fast and lined strips of the tape along the sides.

"What you say makes sense," he said. "But we're not going to get far. Not with this particular set of constraints."

They heard a door open in the stairwell a few floors above them, and then voices. Vega curled her lips against her teeth and made some fierce eye contact with Cap. Move.

Cap threaded his arm through hers and then really examined the extent of her blood soaking the gown, dripping down her right side in a sheet. They started again down the stairs, faster now.

Vega couldn't tell if the voices were closing in, if the people they belonged to were coming down the stairs. The air in the stairwell was hot and stagnant; Vega got nauseous if she inhaled too deeply so she kept her breaths shallow and only through her nose.

When they reached the fifth floor, Cap pointed to the door and pulled Vega gently to him, so he could whisper in her ear.

"We have to try one of them."

She nodded. Cap pointed to himself. Him first. She nodded again. He pulled the handle and went through. Vega leaned against the door and listened to the murmur of the voices above her. They weren't coming yet but they might soon. She wanted to wait for Cap's all clear, but she would go through the door if she had to. It would not be the first time.

Cap came out onto a floor identical to the one he and Vega were being kept on except this one had people, equipment, noise. He kept his head down, tried his best not to be noticed, and walked straight down the hall like he belonged there.

He glanced to the rooms on his right, heard the sounds of televisions and music, water in sinks and toilets flushing. He peered to the side out of the corner of his eye, looking for the first closed room door, knowing that the chances of a patient being asleep there would be better. He found one and went in, pushed the door closed quietly behind him.

He quickly looked to the bed and saw a man asleep there. Cap exhaled in silent gratitude to someone or something and took in the basics: around sixty; copper gray hair surrounding a wide bald strip in the middle; tanned face with mouth slack, open just a bit; hooked up to half a dozen machines. From the outline of his body under the sheet, Cap thought he and the man would perhaps wear similar clothing sizes if Cap could in fact lose the gown, if he could find said clothes, assuming they were somewhere in the room. Which was a lot of luck to count on. If Cap believed in luck.

Cap padded around the bed toward a standing wardrobe in the corner. He opened it and saw no clothes, but resting on top of a drawer inside was an extra gown. Good enough. He grabbed it and held his breath, slowly walked around the bed, his own gown stuck to his back with sweat.

He got to the door and opened it a sliver, peered through to the hallway. He knew he just had to go through, get to Vega so she could switch out her gown, and then, and then—he didn't know. Not a lot made sense so he had to follow the instinct, and the instinct was to run.

Vega slumped against the door but held on to the handle, keeping her arm stiff so she wouldn't slide down to the floor. Above her a door had slammed, and the voices had stopped after some shuffling of footsteps, but Vega knew they'd be back, and if it wasn't them it would be others.

She held her phone in front of her, saw she had a couple of bars, and saw some texts from McTiernan ("Pls call when you can" and "Anything new?"). Also messages from Sarita Guerra and Mia, both of which she scrolled past. Nothing from Cap yet. But at least she had service. She tapped her map app and let it load, the roads and streets populating around the blue dot that was her. Southland Gate Hospital. You are here.

She pressed McTiernan's name and held the phone to her ear, heard a spotty ringtone. Then, his voice mail picked up.

"McT," she said weakly, cupping her hand over the phone.

She hadn't planned to use the nickname she'd heard Mia call McTiernan, but she found herself low on air so that was how it came out.

"It's Vega," she continued. "I'm in a hospital called Southland General. What we talked about last night, about this being your thing . . ." She paused, let the lids fall over her eyes for a second. "If it turns out that it is, I would need your, uh, your skills any time now."

She heard the door a few floors up open and close again, the slam echoing off the walls. Vega's eyes shot open, and she tapped the red disconnect button with her thumb. There were no more voices this time, just feet. She tried to identify exactly how many pairs but had trouble with it. More than two, fewer than five.

So she went through the door, almost ran right into Cap. He said nothing, shuffled her into a bathroom a few feet away, closed and locked the door.

Lights fluttered on. Vega backed up and sat on the edge of the toilet seat.

"I got a gown," said Cap, shaking it out. "Let's get this one off."

He untied the string around her neck, and Vega held her arms out straight so he could pull the gown off. She watched him stuff the bloody gown in the garbage and then look her over, taking inventory of the situation. Then he yanked a handful of paper towels from the dispenser and wet them in the sink. He handed her a wad.

"I'll get your hip and leg, okay?" he said.

He began to wipe the blood off as best he could. He'd had blood on him a lot in his life. He knew only a hot shower at maximum pressure with a lot of tough-guy soap, the kind that felt like gravel, would clean it off the skin completely. Otherwise there was the pink or light brown tint, which, in this case, would be fine. The goal was to escape, and the only way they had a chance was if they didn't look like slasher movie extras.

Vega wiped her neck roughly, glanced down to see blood seeping fast through the bandage. Cap saw it too and pressed another layer of gauze on top of the existing strip, retaped the rectangle, and reinforced the whole thing with more tape in the shape of an X over the center.

Vega tapped the blue dot on her phone.

"Hospital's Southland Gate, eastern outskirts of San Diego," she narrated to Cap.

She tried to scroll through the hospital's website, which slogged along, the service present but not great. She clicked the icon of the hospital's internal map but the wheel spun and spun.

"There's got to be at least two exits on the ground floor," said Cap. "ER and visitor entrance."

He wiped the last of the blood away from the edges of Vega's bandage.

"If we can get there, maybe we can just run and get an Uber," he said, thinking out loud. "Why not, right? We'll probably get better service the closer we get to the street."

"There are people in the stairwell," said Vega. "They were coming down when I came out."

"We gotta wait, then," said Cap. "We can't exactly take the elevator."

Vega held her arms out again, and Cap put the new gown on her, tied the string in the back.

"Ready?" he said.

Vega nodded and stood. She threw the remaining gauze and tape in the sink and held only her phone. Cap opened the door about an inch wide and peered through. He saw a woman in scrubs go into a room. He closed the door quickly.

"Busy?"

"A nurse," he said. "Doing rounds."

Then he held up a finger. One second. He opened the door once more. All clear.

"Let's go. Quick."

He slipped out the door into the hallway and Vega followed, pressing her elbow tightly at her side, over the wound, which throbbed. They went into the stairwell, which was empty and quiet, and started down again, not speaking. When they got to the second floor, Vega tapped open the Uber app and hit Request Car Now. She found the street address of the hospital on the map and dropped a pin two blocks away. Then they made it to the first floor and paused at the door.

"Here we go," said Cap, sweat trickling down his forehead into his eyes.

Vega hunched over and rested her hands on her knees.

"Uber's coming in seven minutes. Two blocks away . . ." She checked her phone screen. "East."

She turned the phone around in her hands to gauge the direction.

"That way," she said, holding her left hand out at a forty-five-degree angle away from her body.

Cap followed the line of her arm with his eyes and reviewed the wall she pointed to as if it were transparent.

"Now all we need is a door," he said.

He turned away from her then and went to the door, opened it a couple of inches, then shut it right away.

"There are people everywhere, and security," he said, then added, with a sad little laugh, "I don't know how we're going to do this."

Vega moved her tongue around in her mouth; it felt like it weighed a few pounds.

"We just have to walk through it," she said. "Shoot for both of us getting out but if just one of us does, then one of us does."

Cap opened his mouth to speak but then didn't. Instead he moved his head from side to side like he was deciding between two things.

"I agree with that except for one thing."

Vega stared at him, in no mood for riddles.

"We don't walk through it," he said, allowing himself half a grin. "We run at it."

Cap burst through the door into the lobby, which was divided into three separate sections with a receptionist at each sitting behind a semicircle of a desk. People milled around and waited on couches and cushioned chairs. There was a gift shop in front of the receptionist furthest from him. And there were security guards, at least six, standing at various posts.

Cap stumbled to the nearest one, a tall black guy, graying hair at the temples, who moved toward him as soon as he came into his view.

"There's a fire alarm going off on sixteen," Cap said, adding enough urgency to his voice to seem agitated but not enough to cause a scene.

Not many people seemed to notice him. Only a few turned their heads away from their phones and crinkled magazines and stale coffee for a moment and then went back to their business. It was, after all, a hospital, and he was wearing a hospital gown, not a cocktail dress.

"Sir, it's all right," said the security guard calmly. "There was a false alarm on the sixteenth floor."

His voice was low and throaty, and also somewhat soothing. Cap thought he could probably do justice to a variety of Johnny Cash numbers. His nameplate read H. WILLIAMS, SECURITY OFFICER.

"Nothing to worry about," the guard continued. "Let's get you back to fifteen now. What's your last name?"

"Are you sure?" said Cap. "I could still hear it on my way down the stairs."

"They turned it off, trust me. There's no one on sixteen through eighteen—those floors are all under construction right now. Still working out the kinks," the guard said.

He held out his hand as if he were about to place it on Cap's back but didn't, guiding him toward the reception desk just by suggestion. Cap recognized it as something a cop would do.

"You retired PD?" he said congenially.

The guard looked surprised but then smiled.

"That obvious? How'd you guess?"

"You know how they say dogs of the same breed can recognize each other?" said Cap, thinking, It can't be as easy as just distracting this guy with old shoptalk.

"Guess that makes us dogs," the guard said, not appearing offended and not wishing to extend the conversation. He held out his hand toward the reception desk.

"Shit," said Cap, scratching the back of his head, feigning concern. "Look, I gotta tell you, I'm a little embarrassed. I heard the alarm, and you know, I just had a fight or flight kind of reaction."

Cap glanced over his shoulders. The other security guards were not looking, one chitchatting with a receptionist, the other watching a news program on the TV in the corner of the ceiling nearest him.

"Nothing wrong with that," said the guard.

Cap heard the stairwell door opening and closing, peripherally saw Vega moving toward the revolving glass doors to the street.

"Look," said Cap. "If it's all the same to you, could I just show myself to the elevator? I know where I'm going, and I'd rather not, you know, make any more of a fool of myself."

A gently pained expression swept across the guard's face.

"I'd like to do that, sir, but now that we're talking here, see, you're on my watch. I've got to make sure you get back to your room all right."

Cap lifted his gaze just an inch or so above the guard's right shoulder. Vega had tied the gown in a knot above her knees and to the side—Cap knew she'd thought about it, knew that people just glancing at her out of the corners of their eyes, like he'd done, wouldn't notice she was in a hospital gown or barefoot. They would know only if they looked right at her. And she'd kept her head down and walked straight with a degree of purpose. Sometimes it was a good thing most people wished to avoid confrontation. Vega was through the door, outside now, and walked with purpose and head down to the left, out of Cap's line of vision.

Cap looked back to the guard and saw the next few minutes in front of him in his mind's crystal ball. Would he have to try to knock the guard down in the elevator? Would he try a straight kick to the knee? He was not totally confident he could take the guard; even though the guy had twenty years or so on Cap, he looked to be in decent shape and was almost a whole head taller. Cap forced the images away. That wasn't how he wanted this to go. There had to be another way.

"Wait, what time is it?" Cap said.

The guard looked at his watch and said, "About five fifteen."

"This is perfect," Cap said, doing his best to look like someone who found his keys. "My girlfriend, she's visiting today, she's supposed to be here at five thirty. Could we just wait a few minutes for her, and then maybe she could walk me upstairs?"

Cap let it hang. The guard didn't give anything away in his face, which way he was leaning, so Cap just jumped.

"Please, it's only a few minutes."

The guard gave him a sad-eyed smile and said, "Five minutes, sir, how's that. You want, you can sit down and wait," he said.

"Thanks," said Cap, genuinely grateful.

Cap turned around and saw Vega running by, this time in the opposite direction, on the sidewalk in front of the hospital, toward the adjacent parking structure, a smear of blood seeping through her gown. He walked to the glass and put his hands on it.

"What the hell was that," said the guard behind him.

The other guards stepped forward when they saw Vega run by, one of them pulling his phone from his belt.

"Sir," said the guard behind him, still kind but stern this time.

And then two uniformed cops emerged from the stairwell exit, one black and one white, both out of breath.

Cap didn't wait for their eyes to land on him. He shoved the push bar on the disabled-access door and just ran.

Vega had minimal feeling in her feet, but she ran toward the parking structure at full speed anyway and hoped Cap was behind her. She tore up the ramp and squatted to get under the entrance barrier, barely slowing down.

She kept running, veered right looking for the ramp to the lower levels, and when she saw it surged even more. Her side no longer hurt, but her head was light, and all her extremities tingled. She ignored everything and just continued to pound her feet down the ramp, the echo reverberating off the concrete walls.

She slipped behind a van and leaned against the fender. She peered around the corner, pressing her face to the van's rear door. She heard more fast steps and then some yelling.

Then she saw Caplan come down the ramp, picking up speed, but the black and white cops from the sixteenth floor were behind him; they were picking up speed too and yelling at him to stop. Neither had his gun drawn, which Vega thought was a good sign.

With all variables as they were, she did not have many options, but she ran through them anyway. All of them involved leaving Cap behind. She bent over her knees and was aware of the sweat and blood coming off her body, watching both drip on and around her dirty feet, feeling useless.

Cap had to stop. Vega was out of sight, and the cops were on him, fifty feet and closing. He felt like so many shoplifters and petty thugs he'd busted when he was a cop, their faces fallen and rueful, having missed their escapes by an inch or a hair or a mile. He remembered that moment when they realized they were cooked, how they'd stop running or driving, sometimes literally throw their hands up, angrier at themselves than they were at him.

Although plenty had been angry at him too.

Cap slowed his pace and then stopped, in the middle of the floor, and turned around to face them. They continued to run at him, and he thought he would make it easy for them so he put his hands behind his head and laced his fingers, not that he had anywhere to hide a weapon at the moment.

"Where's Alice Vega?" the white one said as they approached.

Cap looked over both shoulders.

"Don't see her," he said.

The white cop pulled a phone from his belt, and the black cop took his cuffs off his and walked quickly to Cap, who kept his hands on his head to wait for the order. Best to do what the guys with the guns say when they say it.

But before the black cop unlocked the strands on the cuffs, a blue midsize car bounded down the ramp, screeched, and halted in front of them. The cops whirled around, and Cap's anxiety spiked with the thought, What we don't need now are any more surprises. But when Cap saw the driver, he had to bite his tongue to keep from smiling.

Vega heard tires screech and peered around the corner of the van. There was the blue Camry. She was relieved but not entirely. They weren't out yet.

But she couldn't help feeling better when she actually watched McTiernan get out of the car and stride up to the cops. She also heard sirens in the distance. Police, not ambulance.

"Officers," McTiernan said, sounding authoritative. "Young and Kernan, right?"

He flipped his wallet, which was already in hand, and flashed his badge.

"Detective McTiernan," he said. "Thanks for your help here. I have orders from Commander Roland Otero to bring this suspect in for questioning."

Vega kept her face pressed to the van as she watched Young and Kernan stare at McTiernan.

"We have pretty specific instructions as well from our commanding officer," said the white cop, his chest still heaving from sprinting in full uniform. "And we haven't had any order for a change."

"Understood," said McTiernan, not backing down. "But unless you've received your orders from the Deputy Chief or Chief of Police of San Diego County, my order outranks yours, and even so . . ." McTiernan paused, allowing it all to burrow into the cops' psyches. "I outrank you. So for this minute right here, that's as specific as you need."

McTiernan pulled a nylon cuff strip from his pocket and walked to Cap, who obediently brought his hands behind his back.

"You'd best get in touch with your commanding officer," said McTiernan. "Your orders may have changed."

The sirens from the street grew louder. The cops stood there, still, as McTiernan fastened the cuff onto Cap's wrists, cinching the strap through the bridge to tighten it.

"Let's go, gentlemen!" McTiernan said, raising his voice. "Don't wait for a goddamn letter in the mail."

The cops said, "Yes, sir," and left. As they jogged back up the ramp, McTiernan pulled Cap by the arm to his car. When the sound of their footsteps dissipated completely, Vega crept out from the behind the van and ran to them.

"I got your message," McTiernan said to her, his eyes lighting up with recognition. "We have to go right now. You should see the shit they're spinning about you two."

"Vega needs a medic," said Cap, offering his wrists to McTiernan, who snapped them apart with a pocketknife.

McTiernan looked her over, saw the blood on Vega's side and dripping down her leg, her face washed clean of color.

"Okay, first we need to get out of the five-block radius," he said, and then, aiming his thumb behind him, "You two got to get in the trunk."

Vega nodded and couldn't control the weak smile that sprang to her face when she realized she'd be able to lie down.

McTiernan popped the trunk, and Cap got in first, bending his body into a spoon. McTiernan held his arm out to Vega to steady herself, and she climbed in, turning her cut side up in an effort to ease the blood flow.

"We're not going far. I'll drive quick as I can," said McTiernan, looking down at them.

"Thanks," said Cap, extending his hand.

McTiernan shook it.

"Don't thank me yet."

He slammed the trunk shut, and it was all black in front of Vega's eyes except for the thin line of light along the edge of the lid. She could feel Cap breathing, his chest pressed against her back, his arm draped across her upper abdomen away from the cut. She tried to keep her eyes open but couldn't fight anymore; they came down heavy, old movie theater curtains hitting a dusty stage.

Cap didn't think Vega should sleep. He felt her body go limp in front of him, her head dropping away from right under his neck, lolling forward.

"Vega," he said, tensing the arm that he had wrapped around her slightly. "Try to stay awake."

"I can't," she said dreamily, into the dark, hot air of the trunk.

The car lurched uphill, onto the ramp and out of the garage, Cap figured. Vega rolled against him with gravity, and he tightened his grip on her body so she wouldn't flop around when the car got level again. She stirred a little at the pressure but seemed to remain in her dozing state.

Shit, thought Cap, I have to let her sleep. He angled his face toward her so his nose was in her hair and he smelled it, thought this would be a different sort of experience if she didn't have a severe body wound. It was in a movie, wasn't it, he thought. Wasn't it the same one he'd thought of recently where George Clooney or Brad Pitt threw the tie down? He, the male lead, is in a trunk with the curvy female lead, Cap remembered, but as usual, he recalled no details. Nell would have made fun of him if she could hear him talk it out. Probably Clark Gable and Claudette Colbert, Dad.

The car was moving at a steady speed now, and Cap tried to take short breaths in an attempt to leave as much oxygen for Vega as possible. He heard sirens grow loud and then shrink into silence.

He loosened his arm around her, didn't pull it back in case there were sudden stops, but wanted to take any force out of it so as not to agitate her injury. She wasn't snoring but breathing loudly through her nose, slowly and evenly. He kissed the top of her head lightly—he didn't even really think about doing it, about whether she was half-asleep or what, pros and cons and whether it was a smart move. Everything seemed to be speeding up just then, the whole damn world a blur, Cap sensing a sickness in his throat, the unnerving, unreal feeling of things quickly spinning out of control.

14

VEGA OPENED HER EYES TO A BRIGHT ROOM, AND McTIERNAN AND Cap standing over her, Cap still in the hospital gown.

"You think you can walk?" said Cap.

Vega nodded, realized she was still in the trunk of McTiernan's car. She sat up, wincing at the pain in her side, her head buzzing.

"Watch it now," said McTiernan, holding both his arms out so she could take them.

"You should get on your knees first," said Cap, placing his hand on her back.

Vega kneeled, hunching over so she wouldn't hit her head on the lid. She glanced around and saw they were in a garage, plastic storage containers on pegboard shelves, twin bare lightbulbs on the ceiling.

They helped her step out of the trunk, and she stood on wobbly legs, one hand in Cap's, the other on McTiernan's forearm.

"This your place?" she asked.

"My girlfriend's. She's out of town for work. Flight attendant," said McTiernan. "Come on in this way."

He led them to a door in the corner of the garage and went inside. Cap followed first, then held the door open for Vega, and she walked under his arm into a kitchen with a brown tile floor, wooden cabinets with brass-plated handles. There were three brown leather stools next to a counter, and McTiernan waved toward them.

"Have a seat up there. I'm going to see what supplies we have in the bathroom."

McTiernan hurried out of the room, and Cap offered his arm for Vega to hold. She shook her head and hiked herself up on the stool. Cap opened and closed cabinets and found a glass, filled it with water from the sink, and brought it back to Vega. Vega drank it but found she couldn't take big gulps; if she sipped too much her throat seemed to push the liquid back up.

"Easy," said Cap as he filled another glass for himself.

He drank it down quickly, streams spilling on either side of his mouth. Then another.

McTiernan rushed back in, carrying a red and blue beach towel and a smaller washcloth.

"Here, do you want to . . ." he said, handing Vega the washcloth.

McTiernan averted his eyes while Vega lifted the gown and wiped off the excess blood from her side. His shyness only highlighted Cap's lack of it, both in the bathroom at the hospital and now, as Cap watched Vega clean herself, his brow deeply creased with concern. While Vega cleaned up, McTiernan talked.

"I have someone who can come over and sew you up," he said.

"Is it soon?" said Cap. "The blood's not stopping."

"I'm fine," said Vega, placing the washcloth on the counter.

She held her hand out for the towel, and McTiernan passed it to her.

"Soon," said McTiernan.

He and Cap watched as Vega pressed the towel over the bandage and held it tightly there with her elbow. McTiernan ran his hands over his head and sighed.

"There's some shit going on, you guys," he said, taking his phone from his pocket and tapping it repeatedly with his index finger. "Listen to this."

He held his phone in front of Vega, and Cap crossed the kitchen to look over her shoulder.

"A few hours ago I get this from Otero," McTiernan said, retrieving a voice mail. He held the phone out and clicked up the volume: "Detective, this is Commander Otero—should you hear from Alice Vega or Max Caplan, please do *not* respond to them and please notify me immediately by phone. Thanks very much."

"All caps on the 'not,'" said Cap.

"Then two hours ago I get this," McTiernan said, scrolling again. "We get email blasts grouped by rank when there are bulletins of prioritized, urgent assignments, orders. This was department-wide, as in whole of San Diego department from Otero to everyone, detective and above."

McTiernan tapped on a message and read aloud: "'Two suspects wanted for questioning w/r to homicides of two Jane Does. Suspects' names are Alice Vega, Maxwell Caplan.'"

"You are fucking kidding me," said Cap in disbelief. "Those girls died before I booked my plane ticket out here."

"That is what I would categorize as information we know," said McTiernan, spinning his finger around in a circle to indicate the three of them. "That is not what anyone else knows."

"Except Otero and Boyce and Mackey," said Vega.

"No way," said Cap, correcting her. He counted on his fingers, "McT, the nice people at the hotel, the rental car lady. We have over a dozen witnesses who know we just got here, not to mention a hundred back in our respective hometowns to vouch for us before this week."

"It would take a while for all that to come to light," said Vega calmly. "And they'd find a way to keep you quiet," she said to McTiernan. "They're planning to move quickly enough to bypass the details. They just want us contained."

"You were hired to find the rest of the Janes. That is what Otero told me to my face," said McTiernan.

"We did find them," said Vega wearily.

"What?" McTiernan said, genuinely shocked.

"That's how we ended up like this," said Cap, presenting himself. "We found them at a house in Salton. Ben Davis sliced up Vega, and some Frankenstein motherfucker electrocuted me," he said, tapping his temple, still sore.

"Where are they, though—the girls?" said McTiernan.

Vega clenched the beach towel to her side while her mind raced.

"So no one knows we found them?" she said.

"Somebody knows," said Cap, ranting. "Otero was there, in Salton. I remember his goddamn face."

"I do, too," said Vega thoughtfully.

"Who else?" said McTiernan, eager now to fill in the rest of the story. "Were Boyce and Mackey there? Any other cops?"

Vega shook her head.

"We weren't in the best condition," she said. "But all I remember is Otero, and paramedics. And they . . ." She paused, trying to bring back the picture of the last time she saw the girls. "They put the girls in a bus, like an inmate-transport bus."

"Wait," said McTiernan, confused. "The paramedics did?"

"I don't know," Vega said. "I can't remember."

"Then what?"

Cap hit his forehead lightly with the palm of his hand.

"Then I was out for a while," he said.

Vega picked it up: "They brought us to the ER and split us up."

"Then we ended up in separate rooms on an abandoned floor in that hospital," said Cap, rubbing his face. "And your deputy chief came to have a chat."

Vega and McTiernan both looked at Cap with interest.

"Posada?" said McTiernan.

"Yeah," said Cap. "I thought it was a strange conversation at the time, but now . . ." He paused. "Now it seems like he was just there to threaten me."

"Armando Posada?" said McTiernan, clarifying. "He threatened you?"

"Sure felt like it," said Cap. "I mean, he did it nicely, but I think he was telling me to get out of town."

This appeared to shake McTiernan up. He leaned against the counter, deep in thought.

"I take it this was out of character for him," said Cap.

"Yeah, you could say that. The guy's by the book," said McTiernan. "*All* the books."

Cap thought of his former boss, Chief Traynor, how his near-obsessive attention to detail was what subjected him to endless ribbing but was also the thing that made him good at what he did. Cap never balked at Traynor's spotless office or exhaustive list making; he thought that's what you want in police brass, for them to remember every line of law, everything airtight.

Cap scratched the back of his head.

"He kind of had a change of heart," he said, matter-of-fact.

"So how far up does this go?" McTiernan asked the room plaintively.

Vega recognized the emotion in his eyes. She'd actually seen it a lot, usually in parents of missing children. It was despair: sadness and worry with the water rising steadily. She imagined McTiernan had just felt a sizable surge in the sea level.

"Wrong question," said Vega, channeling Perry, although he would have added a game show buzzer *Enh!*

Her arm began to ache from pressing the beach towel against her side, so she lifted it and leaned hard on the counter to keep up the pressure. Cap and McTiernan looked at her expectantly.

"It's why," she said. "We know why, we just plug in the names like a . . ." she said, hesitating, trying to recall the name of the word game from childhood. Finally she remembered: "Mad Libs."

"Well, sure," said Cap. "Why bring you in just to pin you down later for the crime?" he said to her.

The doorbell rang; McTiernan and Cap jumped a bit.

"That'll be the medic," McTiernan said. Then to Cap, "Go down the hall to your right. Trina's got some of my clothes in the dresser, bottom drawer. They should fit you okay."

Cap nodded and hurried out of the room.

"You sure he's safe?" said Vega.

McTiernan nodded and went to the front door, opened it and let the medic in.

Vega managed a tired wave when she saw who it was.

Cap found McTiernan's clothes and put them on: a short-sleeved plaid button-down, khaki pants, socks. The shoes might be tougher. He examined himself in the mirror on the door. McTiernan was a little taller than Cap and also a little heavier around the waist, but the pants were not too loose and only a little baggier at the bottom.

He nodded at his reflection, went back out, down the hall, where he saw Vega walking slowly, flanked by McTiernan and Mia the patholo-gist, holding a slim black zippered case under her arm.

"Hey," Mia said to Cap, grinning.

"Hi," said Cap. "Where are we going?"

"Bathroom," said McTiernan.

"Might be some blood," said Mia.

Cap waited in the doorway of the bathroom while the other three went in. Mia stood by the tub while McTiernan unfolded a white towel onto the floor.

"Is this going to be enough room?" he asked Mia.

"Should be," she said, washing her hands in the sink. "I can't get to her in the bathtub."

Cap watched Vega, who stood against the wall, holding on to a towel rack.

"You need help getting down?" he said to her.

She nodded, her breath choppy.

McTiernan quickly left the bathroom to make room for Cap. Vega came off the wall, and Cap gripped her hand and held her arm steady as she kneeled and then lay down on the towel. Then Cap went back to the doorway to watch. He stuck his hands in his pockets to keep from touching his face and realized he was nervous.

"You got a couple washcloths with a little antibacterial soap for me?" said Mia to McTiernan, who nodded and ran back to the kitchen.

Mia removed her jacket, a key-lime-pie-colored windbreaker, and draped it over the bathtub. She kneeled with some effort because of her girth, but appeared completely comfortable with the conditions. McTiernan returned and handed her the washcloths, and she lifted Vega's gown and gently pulled off the bandage and all the tape Cap had applied. She dabbed the area directly surrounding the cut.

Vega inhaled sharply with the pain.

"Hang in there," said Mia. "Lucky for you I got some lidocaine."

Mia finished wiping the cut clean and tossed one of the washcloths behind her into the bathtub. She unzipped her case and removed a syringe and a small glass vial, stuck the needle in the top and pulled the plunger back. She pulled the needle from the bottle and squirted a drop out.

"Ready?" she said to Vega.

Vega nodded.

Mia gave her five small shots, right under the bottom flap of skin. Vega stared at the crimped light fixture on the ceiling. Cap looked away but only for a second.

"So," said Mia, putting the vial and the needle back in the case. "So this," she said, removing a gray circle of thread, "is from my office. It's thicker than what you're used to because it's usually used to hold together dead people skin."

She unspooled the thread and attached it to an inch-long needle.

"You might have some scarring, might be more difficult to remove, et cetera. It's usually not removed is all."

"I'm okay with it," said Vega.

"Great."

Mia went to work. Cap watched for a few seconds and then averted his gaze. It actually wasn't the puncturing of the skin that bothered him, but the blood swelling and dripping down every time Mia cinched the thread. In most situations he wasn't skittish, but he felt it getting to him. Best to leave, he thought, instead of pretend to be a tough guy and end up passing out.

"Could we borrow some of your girlfriend's clothes?" said Cap, to McTiernan.

"Yeah, downstairs in the basement she's got her gym stuff—that'll probably fit Vega."

Cap jogged downstairs, saw an elliptical and a rack with hand weights next to a small dresser. He opened the drawers and sorted through stacks of spandex clothes, picked out a pair of gray leggings and a dark blue racer-back tank top that appeared loose around the abdominal area. He also found a thin gray hoodie to match the leggings, a balled-up pair of socks, and neon green sneakers, then headed upstairs.

Back in the bathroom, Mia was finishing up, tying a knot at the end of the thread. She snipped the end with a pair of scissors from her kit, then patted the cut with the fresh washcloth.

"So just take it easy today, okay? No strenuous activity," Mia said in a doctorly voice.

Vega lifted her head off the floor to stare at her. Cap and McTiernan gaped.

"JK," said Mia, holding her hands up in surrender. "You need to stay in that position for at least thirty minutes, though, let it clot up."

Vega gave a nod, leaned her head back down on the tile.

"Okay," announced Mia, wrinkling up her squirrel nose. "Does somebody wanna tell me what the fuck is going on?"

Forty-five minutes later Vega emerged from the bathroom in McTiernan's girlfriend's activewear, having taken the Cipro tablet Mia had brought. The lidocaine was wearing off but Mia had rebandaged the cut tightly and securely, so now all Vega felt was a dull ache and the occasional twinge of pain when it throbbed.

She went into the kitchen, where Cap and McTiernan gulped coffee and Mia tapped and scrolled the screen of her phone.

"Fit okay?" McTiernan said to Vega.

She looked down to the bottom of the leggings.

"Just had to roll them up a little," she said, wiggling her toes inside the slightly oversize sneakers.

"How do you feel?" said Cap.

"Better," said Vega. Then to Mia, "Thanks."

"Any time," said Mia, tapping one last letter on her phone and then lifting her gaze.

"So," said McTiernan. "Word's probably gotten back to Otero that Cap went with me. They'll head to my place first."

"They know you have a girlfriend?" said Cap.

McTiernan shrugged.

"A few people. But that will slow them down. I give them," he said, pausing to check his watch, "an hour, maybe."

"There's two ways to do this," said Vega, gingerly perching on one of the counter stools. "We avoid them or we run at them."

"Didn't we just try running at them?" said Cap. "Didn't turn out so good."

"Running at one of them," said Vega. "Otero's the one who doesn't fit. Up to this point, he's been solid." Vega then addressed Mia: "Rowlie, right? Police commanders up to their necks in crooked shit don't get nicknames."

"Truth," said Mia. "He's a good guy. And he's got, like, a hot grandpa thing going on. But that's neither here nor there."

"But what about Posada?" McTiernan said. "That makes no sense either."

"Okay," said Cap, talking it through. "Their story was they didn't have the resources to investigate the deaths and the potential missing Janes, so they pay you, us, under the table."

"Shit, they wouldn't even know about the missing Janes if it wasn't for me," scoffed Mia, back to her phone.

"That's right," said Vega, realizing something. "Back it up. Mia—you said Otero told you not to wait for him if you've got a lead."

"Yeah," said Mia, remembering. "So when I saw the thing with the IUDs, you know, the sequential numbers, I sent him an email, and he didn't get back to me right away, which was weird. He usually gets back within an hour or something."

"What did he write when he got back to you?" said Vega.

"He didn't. I mean, he didn't write."

"He called," said Cap.

Mia nodded.

"Do you remember if you talked to him right away?" asked Vega.

"No, I think he left me a voice mail," said Mia, squinting, trying to recall.

"You still have it?" said Vega.

"Think so," said Mia, tapping and scrolling. "Yeah, this is it."

She held her phone out so they could all listen. Tapped the speaker button and clicked up the volume.

"Hi, Miss Mia, it's Commander Otero," said Otero, sounding congenial and like he was walking up stairs. "Thanks for the email, that's a find. I'm bringing on a potential consultant for this, so please keep your work with the Janes confidential for now, and if I can ask, hold off on the log until you hear from me."

The voice mail ended and Mia said, "I forgot about that—he didn't want me to log it in the system."

"Did you eventually?"

Mia tilted her head, thinking about it.

"Well, all bodies get logged coming in, but I never put the IUD in the notes. And bodies get logged when they go out, but Jane One and Maricel Villareal are still in the coolers downstairs."

"So what happens in the hours between Mia sending the email and Otero leaving the voice mail?" said McTiernan, capping and recapping a pen in his hands.

"You cc anyone?" said Vega. "On the email."

"Shit, yeah, I did," she said, looking back to her phone. "Any time we get any deceased, any remains of anyone that might be connected to anything tunnel-related, we're supposed to cc DEA."

"How long has that been enforced?" asked Cap.

"A few months," said Mia, still scrolling. "Since they found the big tunnel. See, here, this is the contact," she said, holding up her phone again for them to see the screen. "Michael Mackey."

"Boyce's partner slash toadie," said Cap. "So in the time between the email and the voice mail, Mackey and Boyce go to Otero."

"Say what, let's keep this off the books?" McTiernan asked.

"But the bodies are already logged in," said Mia.

Vega found that the cut had begun to pulse with a little more frequency than before. She carefully crossed her right leg over the left, and the pain abated a bit.

"So he says, 'Going forward, the IUDs, off the books,'" she added.

"Why?" said Mia, exasperated. "What do Mackey and Boyce have to gain from hiding it?"

"Wrong why," Vega said, shifting on her stool.

Cap crossed his arms and stared his partner in the eyes. Although, Vega thought, he seemed to be deep in his own head, gazing way past where she sat.

"Why does Otero say yes," Cap said. A statement, not a question.

"We'll get to Boyce and Mackey," said Vega.

"First we got to get to Otero," said McTiernan, with an air of resignation. He capped his pen one last time and stuck it in his breast pocket, got a quizzical look. "So when they called you in originally," he said to Vega. "How'd they say they found you?"

"The note in Maricel's hand," said Vega. "With my name on it."

"Didn't they admit that was their reason for hiring you?" said Cap.

Vega nodded. "They needed a freelancer, why not pick the one preferred by the victim."

Cap appeared lost in a cloud of thought again.

"Not just any freelancer. An ex–bounty hunter, mercenary type," he said, pointing at Vega.

"The note wasn't a plant," said Vega. Then to Mia, for confirmation: "Right?"

"I took it out of Maricel's rigored fingers myself," she said. "It was tight in there, too. Even the killer might not have seen it."

"Okay," agreed Cap. "All I'm saying is that they had the idea and then got lucky with the note. The perfect person handed to them—you don't get any more off-the-books than Alice Vega."

Vega raised her eyebrows in concession.

"But why does Otero do it," said McTiernan, his face genuinely pained with dilemma. "Why does he say, 'sure'?"

"Why does it take Boyce and Mackey less than an hour to convince him?" said Cap.

"Got something on him," Vega suggested.

"Yeah, but what?" said McTiernan, still not convinced. "Not his job—DEA doesn't have authority over PD."

"Not in chain of command, maybe, but federal always outplays police," Cap said to him. "Same all over."

"Then it's not professional," said Vega. "So it's the other thing."

McTiernan opened his mouth to speak but was interrupted by the phone buzzing in his pocket, radar beeps for a ringtone. He took it out and examined the screen, then flipped it so they could all read the name of the caller: "COMM. OTERO."

"Y'all are burnt," said Mia after the phone stopped ringing.

"We have to leave," said McT.

"I have to get to work," said Mia, digging around a tote bag she'd left on the counter. "But you can go to my place."

She produced a ring of keys and threw them to McTiernan.

"They won't look for you there," she added. "Not yet anyway."

"Where do you live again?" asked McTiernan. "By the beach?"

Mia nodded.

"How long's the drive?" said Vega.

"Half hour, no traffic."

They all thought about that. Vega envisioned her face on a Wanted poster from the Old West.

"You have a garage?" said Vega.

"No, carport."

McTiernan aggressively tapped the voice mail button on his phone but the message was taking its time.

"You'll draw more attention getting in and out of the trunk," said McTiernan. "Besides, you're not wearing a bloody hospital gown anymore, and there's no APB as of yet. Just emails."

Vega picked up her own phone and started writing an email to the Bastard.

"That's because he thinks it's contained. That voice mail is him being nice and easy. Giving you an out," she said, pointing to McTiernan's phone. "Another hour, you're going to get a meaner one."

McTiernan tapped his phone, the voice mail finally delivered, and clicked up the volume on the speaker. Otero's voice filled the room and reverberated off the cabinets.

"Detective McTiernan, this is Commander Otero. Please call in when you get this message, to me directly. I realize you may be acting on former orders, but we have a lot of new information that I'd like to discuss with you. Please call."

That was it. McTiernan tapped his phone, puffed his cheeks a little, blew some air out.

Cap tilted his head to one side and shut his eyes.

"Anyone else hear something in that, 'Please call'?" he asked the room. "Just that last part."

"Always professional," McTiernan suggested, shrugging.

"Sure," said Cap, smiling like he had a secret, showing his teeth. "But he's desperate, too."

McTiernan shook his head quickly, like he was trying to knock something out of it.

"Why?" said McTiernan. Then, as an afterthought: "What do Boyce and Mackey have on him?"

"Maybe Otero's wife knows," said Vega. "I say we ask her," she added, her voice taking on a guise of innocence.

McTiernan and Cap stared at her. Mia began to laugh.

"This bitch is crazy," she said.

Vega smiled at her, then shifted her eyes to Cap. He leaned against the sink and rubbed his chin and cheeks. Vega imagined what it felt like, the short wiry hair, two days without a shave.

He had worry in his eyes, though. Skepticism.

Vega nodded at him quickly, almost imperceptibly, tried to tell him without saying the words. Keep going. Right up to the front door.

15

THE AIR WAS COOLER BY THE BEACH. CAP COULD SEE THE OCEAN in the short distance as he leaned his head out the window in McTiernan's backseat. The sun was heading down but wasn't there yet, which he couldn't quite believe. He tabbed the day as one of the longest he'd had in a while.

McTiernan took a left, and Cap could no longer see the water or beach, just sun-bleached condo complexes and apartment buildings, three or four stories with balconies cluttered with tropical plants and pool chairs.

Vega and McTiernan had been talking but Cap had missed the last bit.

"You sure she's coming this late," McTiernan asked, glancing at the sun in his rearview. "It's late."

"She's coming," said Vega. "She just confirmed. Says she has a lot of clients in the evening to accommodate their work schedules."

McTiernan parked the car across from Mia's building and turned off the engine.

"Police commander's wife," said Cap. "Probably has a lot of lonely nights to herself."

"You guys should stay out here," said Vega, getting out of the car.

"Come on," said Cap, getting out of the car. "We can hide in the bedroom."

"That's real weird," said Vega. "And the more normal this seems the better."

Cap shrugged. Suit yourself.

"Text us," McTiernan said, handing her Mia's keys through the window. "Unit 3G."

Vega glanced across the street and nodded. She zipped up the hoodie and pulled the hood over her head.

"Watch yourself," Cap said under his breath, before getting into the front seat.

He wasn't sure she'd heard him but didn't want to say it again, didn't want to embarrass either himself or her.

She turned and jogged across the street, and Cap moved the passenger seat back and shut the door. He and McTiernan watched Vega find the key to the front door of the complex and go inside. Cap leaned back in the seat, found himself feeling relieved.

McTiernan started the engine and said, "We got to circle."

"Wait, no," said Cap emphatically. "We have to stay here and wait for her. In case she needs backup."

McTiernan started to say something and then stopped. Then he started again.

"She's not going to need backup against Otero's wife."

"Probably not," said Cap. "But it's a thing we do. She goes in, I wait. I go in, she waits."

McTiernan let out a little sigh and turned to face him.

"Look at all the windows," he said.

Cap glanced across the street at the windows, not knowing what he was searching for.

McTiernan continued: "I know you're not from here. I don't know how it is in on the East Coast. This particular neighborhood is not necessarily the whitest, but it's definitely not a black part of town, which means, it'll take about ten minutes for one or more white people to look out their windows and see a black guy in a car parked on their block. Not going through garbage cans or putting flyers under their wipers or selling hippie incense. Just sitting. That's fifteen, twenty minutes until a cop taps his knuckles on my window to ask if I'm lost and if I need an escort off the block."

Cap felt like an asshole.

"Yeah, it's the same on the East Coast," he said. "So we circle."

McTiernan nodded, pulled out of the spot, repeated, "So we circle."

Cap watched Mia's condo get smaller in the side mirror. He looked at his own face, the fresh burn on his temple, the gulfs under his eyes almost blue with exhaustion. But sleep and rest and exhaling full breaths from robust pink lungs were not close. In fact, they were looking more and more like animals swiftly moving from the endangered column to the extinct.

Vega stepped through the door of Mia's condo and flipped on the light. There was a small kitchenette to her left with some dishes in the sink and a sleek silver fridge. Ahead of her was a large living room with a sliding glass door onto a balcony facing the street. Gray carpet with a fuzzy white rug thrown over it. Nothing on the walls except a dream catcher and two small photos of birds. Also a plush white couch; in front of it a square tiled table with a purple bong the size of a desk lamp on top.

Vega walked around the space quickly, picking up some stray socks and books from the floor, then grabbed the bong and headed into the bedroom. There was a king bed, white sheets and a leopard-print blanket bunched up in a roll, and a short dresser the width of one wall with a variety of marijuana paraphernalia on the surface: another bong, a few pipes, baggies, some full, some empty. Vega hurriedly set the purple bong down next to the other one and left.

She went to the fridge in the small kitchen, saw some kids' drawings scrawled with crayons and school photos of the artists, Vega assumed, a boy and a girl with Mia's round cheeks. Vega left them where they were. She opened the door, counted ten or so filled Tupperwares, a Domino's pizza box, three boxes of Entenmann's donuts, a twelve-pack of cherry Coke, and on the door bottles of coconut water and Gatorade. On top of the fridge full bags of kettle corn and Doritos.

Everyone has a thing, she thought, and Mia's was food. And maybe also weed. Vega found her affection for Mia unfettered by knowing this. You can't order a person like you order a sandwich, Perry would have said. Take this, hold that.

Vega took two bottles of coconut water and shut the fridge. She went to the living room and sat on the couch, set the waters down on the square table. She checked her phone, saw a text from Cap: "Circling. Text for backup." She opened her email to see if the Bastard had written her back with anything else, and there was nothing yet. She placed the phone in her lap and looked out the glass doors to the sun setting, the sky blurry and melting with color.

Cap sat in the car while McTiernan went in the taco shop. After they'd left Mia's block, Cap realized he hadn't eaten since the morning and had been running on the fumes of fumes for some hours now. McTiernan pulled over at the first opportunity.

Cap's phone buzzed with a text from Vega: "OK."

Cap shut his eyes and opened his mouth, just to hear the sound of his own breath. He found himself squeezing his eyes closed and tried to relax the lids, but it wasn't working, so he opened them again. He picked his phone up from his lap and started typing a text to Nell: "Hey just checking in. Everything cool here." He hit Send with his thumb and waited, saw the three flickering dots.

Then came Nell's response: "I'm fine. What's happening with case???"

Cap looked away from the phone, toward his reflection in the side mirror, and angled his face so he could see the burn on his temple. He shook his head at himself and wrote back to Nell: "Crawling along. Might have break soon." He tapped Send and thought as long as he didn't talk to her on the phone, she wouldn't hear his voice and know something was wrong. Really very wrong.

She sent back: 👍

Cap looked up and saw McTiernan walking toward the car holding two paper trays of food stacked and a paper bag under his arm. Cap flipped his phone over on his leg and reached across to open McTiernan's door.

"Thanks," said McTiernan, getting in.

He handed Cap the bag and one of the trays and pulled the door shut.

"Two shrimp a la diablas," he said.

"Thanks, man," said Cap, picking up a taco.

It appeared to have two shells—one crispy, and one soft inside of that, and the shrimp was glossy and grilled, a zigzag of red sauce down the middle. Cap held it with both hands and took a bite. The hot sauce woke him up and suddenly he felt possessed—he couldn't get the taco into his mouth fast enough. He paused for only a second before swallowing the other one.

"My goodness," said McTiernan, only halfway through his first.

Cap wiped sauce from the side of his mouth and then felt the burn, a few seconds delayed. It was everywhere in his mouth at once—tongue, cheeks, gums. Cap fumbled for the paper bag and pulled out a bottle of water.

"Yeah, that's habanero sauce, you need to pace yourself," said McTiernan kindly.

Cap drained the bottle.

"I didn't realize how hungry I was," he said, gasping.

"It's been a motherfucker of a day," said McTiernan, staring straight ahead. "You hear from Vega?"

Cap glanced at the phone and shook his head.

McTiernan swallowed a bite and said, "If we don't get the jump . . ."

He didn't finish.

"Look," said Cap. "If there is a thing to find out from Otero's wife, Vega's gonna find it out."

"We can't keep rolling with no lead," said McTiernan.

"Give her an hour," said Cap, hitting his chest lightly with his fist to speed the digestion. "She'll make that room smaller and smaller like a magic trick."

Then the digital radar beeps returned, and Cap twitched. McTiernan took his phone from his breast pocket.

"She better," he said, showing it to Cap.

"COMM. OTERO" read the screen.

The second call.

Vega waited on the other side of the door. She'd just removed her thumb from the buzzer, letting her guest through the front door of the building, and now was waiting for her to come up in the elevator. She leaned her head back and caught sight of herself in the mirror over the bathroom sink. She smiled, a perky exclamation point of a smile.

Then there was the knock, three in a row, light, hesitant. Vega kept the smile pasted on and opened the door and took her in: blond hair, blue eyes, teeth as white as they come. Designer jeans with a couture tear above the knee. Ballet flats, a small white rolling suitcase at her side, leather tote purse over her shoulder.

"Hi? Alice?" she said.

"Yeah, Palmer, right?"

Palmer Otero appeared beside herself with relief that she was in the right place. She pumped Vega's hand.

"So nice to meet you," she said.

Vega nodded and showed her in.

"Thanks for coming so late and last minute," she said, attempting to sound flustered. "It's sort of an emergency."

"No worries," Palmer said, wheeling her suitcase into the living room. "Literally happens all the time. I see most of my clients weeknights. May I?" she asked, gesturing to the table.

"Please do."

Palmer pushed the handle of the rolling suitcase down and unzipped it, removed two soft leather cosmetics bags, one black and one tan. She set them on the table in front of the couch, and then they both sat, side by side.

"You said in your email you were looking for a hydrating foundation?" said Palmer.

"That's right."

Palmer unzipped the tan bag and opened it, brought out four small tubes of cream.

"So," she said, "these are all tinting foundations and we can do a small skin test to see which matches your tone. Now, you said you run fair to tan depending on the season, right?"

Vega nodded.

Palmer continued: "And you said you've never used BeautyMark products before?"

"Nope," said Vega, rolling her shoulders up and down in a quick shrug.

"Then you get to hear my intro," Palmer said, touching Vega's arm playfully.

She reached into the black bag and pulled out a small bottle of lotion.

"All of BeautyMark's products are made from all-natural ingredients. No dyes, no harsh chemicals, and absolutely *no* animal testing."

Vega nodded solemnly to match Palmer's dedicated tone, as though animal testing were the deal breaker.

"Natural cosmetics for natural beauty," said Palmer. Then she smiled earnestly. "That's BeautyMark. So I highly, highly recommend moisturizing with our twelve-hour day cream before applying any foundation to your face."

She handed Vega the small bottle.

"That's a tester," she said, leaning forward to pull a mirror from the tan bag. "You can try some on your cheeks or your whole face if you like. Whatever you're comfortable with."

Palmer turned her body to face Vega and held the mirror in her lap, angled up at Vega's face. Vega flipped the top on the bottle and squeezed a drop of lotion onto her finger. She rubbed it on her cheek in circles.

"Do you have an event tomorrow?" asked Palmer.

"No," Vega said, a little forlornly. "Just a work thing."

"Boo, that doesn't sound fun," said Palmer, adding a cute frown of commiseration.

"It's not all bad," said Vega, applying another drop of lotion to her fingers and rubbing it around her forehead.

"Well, that's good. What is it you do?"

"It's complicated," said Vega, then said, "Not trying to offend you, I'm sure you would understand, but it just might be boring for you to hear the whole thing. TMI."

"We've got some time," Palmer said, grinning. "Our experts recommend letting the moisturizer settle in for at least ten minutes before applying foundation."

Vega handed the bottle back and leaned down to look at herself in the mirror. She placed a hand on her cheek.

"Now that's soft," she said.

"Trust me, you use this every day," said Palmer, holding up the bottle, "your skin will get even softer. It's made from naturally sourced oils and plants. You can see on me, I've been using these products for two years. Right now I'm wearing just the minimum amount of foundation, because my complexion is just that clear."

She held her hand next to her face but didn't touch it.

"Amazing," said Vega.

"Isn't it," said Palmer. Then she got a look like she suddenly remembered something. "Let's look at lip color while we're waiting for the cream to set."

She went back into the black bag and pulled out three lipstick tubes.

"These are all lipsticks, but we also do a gloss and a liner. Just no lip stain because—"

"It's not natural," Vega said, finishing her sentence.

"You got it," said Palmer, smiling, proud of her student. "I think, for work, a slightly darker nude than yours would work best for you."

She handed the lipstick to Vega and tilted the mirror up again. Vega pulled the cap off the tube and twisted the base. She brought it to her bottom lip first, back and forth, watching her reflection.

"So go on, about your work," Palmer said gamely.

"Okay," said Vega, applying the lipstick to her upper lip. "I find missing persons. Children mostly. Missing children."

"Oh my God," said Palmer in awe, placing her hand to her chest. "That's . . . incredible. I had no idea. That must be such a hard job."

"It is," said Vega, pressing her lips together. "Do you have a tissue?"

Palmer grabbed one from the tan bag and handed it to Vega.

"So do you have, like, a presentation or something for tomorrow?" Palmer asked, genuinely interested.

"No," said Vega, folding the tissue in half and flattening it on her leg. "Not really. But I'm in the middle of a case, and I need all the help I can get."

Palmer laughed nervously.

"Of course. Look, I totally get it if you can't tell me anything else. My husband's in law enforcement—I understand the sensitivity of these things."

"I'm sure you do," said Vega. "I can't tell you everything, but I can tell you that I was hired to find a group of girls who are being trafficked for sex work."

"Oh my God," Palmer uttered, stunned.

"Yes. And I found them this morning."

Palmer's mouth dropped open.

"You did? That's wonderful."

"It was," said Vega slowly. "But then I lost them again."

Palmer's lineless face grew confused. She didn't speak.

"Well, I didn't exactly lose them," Vega said, correcting herself. "Your husband put them on a bus and sent them somewhere."

Vega blotted her lips on the tissue.

Now Palmer's eyes turned wild with the terror of ambush.

"Who *are* you?" she asked, her voice hoarse.

"Alice Vega," said Vega. "Same as before."

Palmer's chest rose and fell a little quicker. She glanced toward the floor where she'd set her purse down. Vega admonished her in her head: You never look at the thing you're about to grab.

"Don't," said Vega, holding her hand out. "Just don't."

Palmer clutched the mirror in her lap, her fingers white. Vega straightened her back and squared her hips the best she could in a seated position, ready to cross-jab if she had to but all she had to do was look at Palmer's face to know she was too freaked to fight.

"Are you going to hurt me?" Palmer asked, her breath choppy.

"I don't think so," Vega answered honestly.

"Then what do you want?"

"You ever met a guy named either Christian Boyce or Mike Mackey? Work for the DEA?" said Vega.

Palmer shook her head. Vega could tell by the rapid response it was the truth.

Vega began: "Your husband and those two paid me cash off the books to find these girls. Like I said, I found the girls. Now the girls are gone. Everything I've heard about your husband is that he's honest, clean, knows exactly which tie he's wearing when he wakes up in the morning. That's the impression I got when I met him. That sound right to you?"

Palmer nodded emphatically, still holding the mirror. Vega could see herself speaking.

"So why would he get involved in something like this?" she asked.

Palmer quickly blinked a few times.

"He wouldn't," she said indignantly. Then a little more confident, added, "You're lying."

She seemed to realize just then she was still holding the mirror and pushed it off her lap to the corner of the couch.

"I'm not," said Vega calmly. "I can prove it. Would you like me to do that?"

Palmer stared at her, unable to speak.

Vega pulled her phone from the pocket of the hoodie and found the voice mail. She pressed the arrow and played it on speaker. Here was Otero's voice:

"Hi, Ms. Vega. I just wanted to thank you again for taking this job, and for your discretion." There was a pause; Vega had figured he was searching for the precise word. "I believe this is important work, helping these girls. And I appreciate your . . . flexibility with the unconventional circumstance. That's all I wanted to say. Thank you."

Palmer bit her lips, her eyes batting back and forth in distress.

"That could mean a lot of things," she said breathlessly.

"Maybe," said Vega, feeling an urge to give her the benefit of the doubt. "But probably not."

Palmer shook her head rhythmically and didn't stop. It was slow, though, the pendulum in a grandfather clock.

"He didn't tell me anything," she said.

"Does he usually tell you about his work?" Vega asked.

"When it's important."

Palmer pressed her hands together and lifted them to her lips.

"I don't understand," she said. "Why did you have me come here?"

"I think Boyce and Mackey have something on your husband. Something personal."

Vega let those words hang for a few seconds.

"Do you know what that might be?"

Palmer shook her head.

"I don't. I swear, I don't know."

"I believe you," said Vega. "But you may know something and not know that you know it."

Palmer wrinkled up her nose in bewilderment. She peered past Vega's shoulder toward the door.

"I'm not going to trap you," said Vega. "You can walk out of here and call your husband and tell him all about me, and maybe you'll get a straight answer from him and maybe you won't."

Palmer's face changed. The lines flattened out. Her expression became steely.

"How do I know I can trust you?"

"You don't," said Vega. "And you don't have to. But I think your husband's in trouble, and you might be able to help him, you see?"

Palmer thought about it. Vega didn't think she was dumb, but she also wasn't bleeding all her cards just yet.

"I think he's in trouble, too," Palmer said finally.

"What makes you say that?"

"My husband doesn't get nervous," Palmer said, smiling a little. "He's the steady hand; I'm the high-strung one. When our kids were little, I was the helicopter mom. He was the one who suggested I start doing this," she said, gesturing to the bags. "The BeautyMark stuff, so I could keep myself busy and not micromanage the kids' lives and clean the house constantly."

Vega smiled agreeably, felt a familiar painful twinge; she thought of her mother and the incapacitating anxiety that made a meal of her neural pathways for most of her life.

"But recently I noticed, he's missing a step. He just seems preoccupied."

Vega didn't nod or speak, thought she'd let Palmer get to the bones of it on her own.

"You know, we've been married twenty years and he's been a cop longer than that, so I'm used to him working a lot of hours, but he usually leaves it at the office. But the last few days he hasn't been around a lot but when he has, he's been, well, a nervous wreck."

"How so?" asked Vega.

"Spilling every glass he's holding, taking a lot of work calls, more than usual. I honestly don't think he's been to bed in a week or so. I caught him dozing on the couch downstairs the other night. He just said he's working on a case and it's intense."

"But he's worked on intense cases before."

"All the time," said Palmer. "He keeps it distant. He's very good at that, but not lately."

"And you'd say this has been the past week?"

"I think so."

"Why didn't you ask him about it?" Vega said, being sure to clear any note of judgment from her voice.

Palmer shrugged and let out a tense sigh.

"I don't know. I didn't want to make it worse. Also, our son is starting his senior year of high school next week, and I didn't want to introduce any more tension in the house than necessary."

Vega thought this was interesting but didn't let on. It allowed her to slide Palmer into the category of conflict avoider.

"Is your son . . ." Vega paused. "Sensitive?"

Then Palmer broke into a nervous laugh.

"I didn't mean to make it sound like that. He's a great kid, gets good grades, plays football. He can just be a little shy."

"Is he nervous?" said Vega.

Palmer cast her eyes down. Vega knew she had something to say, on the fence if she should say it.

"He's been in therapy and on medication for anxiety since he was fourteen," she said. "But there's no shame in it," she added defensively. "His sister, my daughter, who's in the eighth grade now, is the opposite— outgoing and has a ton of friends, but RJ's had a harder time of it."

Palmer looked away for a moment and then appeared to gain some steam.

"He's done amazingly well. He has some good friends now, but you know, we're all getting ready for him to start applying to colleges and I just didn't want to rock the boat upsetting Roland any more than he already was."

"What colleges are you thinking of?" said Vega.

"Oh, we have a big list," Palmer said, her face relaxing, smiling a little. "UCSD, of course, and some other UCs . . ."

She kept talking but Vega wasn't listening and didn't care. She just needed a minute to think.

"Has your son ever gotten into trouble at school?" Vega asked, interrupting Palmer.

"No," she said. "Never."

Vega thought of Nell, the same age as Otero's son.

"He ever get pulled over or get a traffic ticket?" asked Vega.

"Oh, no," said Palmer. "He's like his dad in that way, plays by the rules."

"What about your daughter?"

"Elsie?" Palmer said, as if she were asking Vega. "She's great. And she's very pretty but in a little girl sort of way. She still likes unicorns and glitter and all that."

"Did she ever get in any kind of trouble at school?" Vega asked, unable to help the feeling that she was getting closer to something. It was like playing Marco Polo in a pool, sensing where people were by the movement of the water.

"No," said Palmer, but held on to the word a little bit, which made Vega think there was more coming.

"But?" said Vega.

"But, this is really nothing, just a bit of teen drama," said Palmer. "We didn't even tell Roland about it. Earlier in the summer a friend of RJ's from the football team, they come to the house a lot and, you know, clean us out of all the snacks we buy at Costco." She rolled her eyes then. These kids. "And he, Graham, he flirted with her a little bit, and she flirted back but I don't know if she even knew she was flirting. She's just . . ."

"Outgoing," Vega added.

"Right. And he just got a little carried away, that's all."

Palmer paused again and smoothed out her jean legs. Then Vega realized she wasn't pausing; she was done with the story.

"What does that mean exactly, carried away?" said Vega.

Palmer sighed, seemed annoyed at the memory of it.

"He kissed her. He grabbed her and kissed her in the kitchen. I wasn't there, but she told me about it later and said it scared her. So I said just never be alone in a room with him again and it would be fine. And it was."

Vega cocked her head, as if she had missed something.

"What did Graham's parents say?"

"I never spoke to them," Palmer said, shocked, like she'd never considered it. "I didn't want to—"

"Rock the boat," they said at the same time.

"Exactly," said Palmer, giggling at the coincidence.

"You ever tell your husband about it?"

"No," she said, growing agitated now. "It wasn't necessary."

"Does Graham still come to your house?"

"Sure, he's one of RJ's best friends."

"So," said Vega, feeling a little agitated herself. "A teenage boy assaulted your daughter, and you allow him back into your house on a regular basis."

Palmer's nostrils flared, her lips growing tight.

"It was not an assault. It was a kiss, one kiss. And I took care of it."

"Because he's one of your son's best friends," said Vega.

"That's right."

Palmer seemed to reach the end of her patience. She stood.

"I don't have to listen to this," she said with a burst of self-righteous energy. "I don't even know what I'm doing here."

"You are helping your husband," said Vega, remaining seated.

That shut her up for a second but then she continued: "I've made a huge mistake telling you all this. I don't know you. You could be making all of this up."

"It would be a pretty elaborate thing to make up," said Vega, standing.

The cut began to pulse again. She pressed her elbow against it, chicken-wing style. Vega watched as Palmer registered this information, then shook her head to push it away.

"I'm leaving now," she said bravely, her voice quavering.

She gathered the makeup bags and mirrors and shoved them into the suitcase.

"I'm calling my husband," she said, gaining some defiance.

"You do you," said Vega. "You leave here, call him, tell him where you saw me and what I told you, and you watch his face fall apart; you listen to his voice crack. And you tell him I can help him, because no one else will. I know he's stuck, and the waves are getting faster and stronger and they're coming so fast he can't get a breath in his lungs or a foot in the sand. But I can. So you have him call me."

Palmer's gently moisturized face buckled into a frown, tears crowning from her eyes and smearing the hypoallergenic mascara. Vega stepped aside, and Palmer rushed past her, out the door.

Vega waited before emailing the Bastard and texting Cap. She stood in the middle of the darkening room, hearing only the hum of Mia's refrigerator and the screech and whine of a seagull outside.

16

CAP PERKED UP IN HIS SEAT WHEN HE SAW VEGA APPROACHING the corner of Mia's block. McTiernan saw her too, slowed the car and pulled over so Vega could get into the backseat. Cap could sense the chemistry in the car change when she sat down and shut the door: like a hit of adrenaline had been added, or a B12 shot. It shook him awake from the taco fugue.

McTiernan sped around the corner and away from the beach. Cap turned toward the backseat and handed Vega a taco in a white paper tray.

"It's shrimp. It's hot," he warned her.

"Thanks," she said.

She ate it almost as quickly as Cap had but managed not to get any of the sauce on her face. Practice, thought Cap. There are more tacos in California. He passed her a bottle of water.

"We getting on the freeway?" asked McTiernan.

"Yeah," said Vega. "Escondido."

She cracked open the water and took a healthy sip. McTiernan watched her from the rearview.

"At least you made it out of there," he said.

"I did," said Vega, pinching the corners of her mouth to siphon the excess water off. "She wanted to talk. Otero's been acting weird around the house for the last week or so."

"Weird how?" said Cap.

"Nervous. On edge. Not sleeping. Which is so unlike him that she's noticed. She, herself, doesn't know why, but I think it has to do with their kids."

McTiernan glanced at her in the mirror and said, "Teenagers, right?"

Vega nodded and continued: "Daughter's twelve or thirteen. Son's a senior in high school. I think he's at the middle of this somehow, but the girl's involved secondarily."

"Isn't the kid a football star?" said McTiernan.

"I wouldn't say star. Looks like he's made the local paper a few times along with the rest of the team," said Vega, skimming the email the Bastard had just shot back to her. "He, Roland Junior, RJ, according to Palmer, has some emotional issues. Been on medication for a few years to manage it."

Vega paused to quickly read the rest of the email.

"How's the son involved?" Cap asked.

"Not sure yet," said Vega. "But he's the weakness." She thought about it for a minute. "He's Otero's weakness."

"How did you leave it with the wife?" said Cap.

"I told her to have Otero call me."

"He called again but didn't leave a voice mail," said McTiernan.

"What now?" said Cap.

"Whatever Boyce and Mackey are holding over him is enough that Otero's willing to trash his career and reputation over it. He needs help," said Vega, as if all of this were obvious.

"Us, Vega," said Cap, tapping his chest with his fingers. "*We* need help. We escaped from the goddamn *Twilight Zone* hospital."

"I need help as well," said McTiernan, raising his hand like he wanted a hall pass.

"Don't just look at this one thing," said Vega. "Look at all of it stacked up. Otero doesn't want to do what he's doing. We neutralize the threat to him, we can pull him over to our side and take on Boyce and Mackey together."

Cap pressed his hands together and held them to his lips.

"Okay," he said, unable to disagree. "How do we start?"

"What's in Escondido?" McTiernan added.

"That's where Otero lives, right?"

"You want to talk to the son?" Cap said. "That's a high-risk situation for us, don't you think?"

Vega actually agreed with him. Her instinct was important; sometimes it was all she had, but she could not guarantee that Palmer wouldn't completely spin out and call every cop she knew to chase them down. And if they showed up at Otero's house to interrogate his son, they could very well be driving into an ambush with no guns or even a white flag to wave.

"Yeah, I do," Vega said thoughtfully.

She read the email from the Bastard once more, looked over the

Facebook and Instagram links for RJ Otero, the articles pulled from the paper about the team. Black-and-white action shots of field goals, touchdowns, the lines of scrimmage. A caption under one: "Quarterback Graham Miller calls the winning play."

A window popped up on her screen alerting her to a new email. It was sex spam—"Hot Young Girls" read the subject. Vega intuitively thumbed the "x" in the corner, then zoomed in on the pictures of Graham Miller. She swiped into his Facebook page. He seemed to be a standard level of good-looking—clean-cut and straight teeth. Holding footballs, throwing footballs, at football games.

Vega scrolled back to her deleted items and brought up the Hot Young Girls email again and opened it, examined the pictures. The girls didn't look particularly young, just dressed that way. Pleated skirts and kneesocks, blowing big pink gum bubbles.

Vega sat forward in her seat.

"We're not going to talk to RJ Otero yet. We need Graham Miller first," she said.

"Still in Escondido?" confirmed McTiernan.

"Think so. I'll check," she said, typing fast to the Bastard.

"Who's Graham Miller?" said Cap.

"RJ Otero's good friend. So good in fact, Palmer was totally complicit when he forced his tongue in her daughter's mouth."

"What?" Cap said, enraged. "What the hell's wrong with her?"

"Unclear," said Vega. "I think she's so worried about the son having a normal life she's willing to sacrifice anything."

"Even her daughter?" said McTiernan.

Cap tightened his lips and shook his head angrily.

"I don't think she sees it like that," said Vega.

"So what do you think the friend has to do with us?" asked McTiernan.

"I'm not sure," said Vega, meeting his eye in the rearview. "But the underage girl connection—it's too much of a good fit, you know?"

Cap faced forward, squinting through the windshield. His fatherly fury appeared to dissipate, and he grew pensive.

"Vega, the doctor I staked out when I first got here, the guy who might have sent an email to Ben Davis—Dr. Scott Miller."

Vega hit Send on the email to the Bastard and remembered.

"Yeah. From the clinic."

"In Escondido," Cap said.

"You want to put a chip down on them being related?" said Vega.

Cap turned to face her again and smiled with exactly one half of his mouth.

The Bastard fired back the address of Graham Miller, and Vega knew it was the same as Dr. Scott Miller, didn't even have to open the email before telling McTiernan where to go. The pain from the cut in her side had reduced to intermittent thumps against the bandage, and she felt a familiar twitch in her fingertips, ready for the next thing.

Cap couldn't say he recognized the block or the house since it was in a subdivision where all the blocks and houses looked the same. Tan and white upscale townhomes, two or three cars in the driveways, palm-tree-lined streets. The sun had sunk completely now, but the sky retained a faint, almost celestial golden glow in its memory.

McTiernan pulled over down the block from the Millers' house. They all unsnapped their seatbelts and examined themselves. Vega looked at the selfie-mode camera app and thought the lotion and lipstick from Palmer had actually done her skin quite a bit of good. She didn't look as tired as she felt, and she'd even gained some of her natural color back.

"You two start, front door?" Vega said.

"Where are you gonna be?" said Cap.

Vega looked up from her phone and said, "I'm just going to take a look around back."

"You sure that's a good idea?" said McTiernan, patting the sides of his hair with his hands. "Trespassing could bring some attention on you pretty quick."

"Look at me," she said. Waving her hand, presenting her outfit. "Just going for a jog, right? Joggers get lost all the time."

Cap shot her a reproachful glance and then went back to his reflection in the sun guard mirror. The bags under his eyes remained, and there was no way to cover up the Kennedy-dollar-size burn on his temple. Add the unshaved cheeks, he thought he could be a good stand-in for the hobo in a Norman Rockwell painting.

"Christ, I look like shit," he said.

"Yeah, you do," said Vega.

A laugh burst out from McTiernan, and he said, "Damn."

"Yeah, damn, Vega," said Cap.

She shrugged one shoulder.

"I got the badge," said McTiernan. Then, to Cap: "You're the consultant. Cover could be, I don't know, string of burglaries?"

"Sure," said Cap. "We just have to keep them talking. Mom, Dad, son. Whoever's home. There's got to be some connection between the kid being best friends with Otero's boy, and the dad having something to do with the missing IUDs and Ben Davis."

"Yeah, think about the lineup here," said McTiernan, counting on his fingers. "LoSanto, who we got. From the people you all described as being suspects at the Salton house: Ben Davis; Fat Guard, and the big guy, the guy who hooked you up," he said to Cap, unable to remember the name, pointing to Cap's burn.

"Rafa," Cap said, his mouth very dry.

"Rafa," McTiernan repeated. "I don't see any of these guys able, I'm saying trained to insert IUDs in those girls. LoSanto comes the closest but he's an X-ray tech. And Rafa, I have a feeling he's not trained in the medical profession to do what he does."

"Safe to say," Cap said, flipping the sun guard up with a snap.

"So someone had to do it," said Vega, picking up McTiernan's thread.

"That's what I'm saying," he said. "And we got a doctor right here used to work at a clinic primarily serving women."

"Start with burglaries and see what lands," said Cap.

"Yes," agreed McTiernan. He turned to Vega. "You want to walk with us or wait?"

"I'll wait," said Vega. "Give you guys a chance to settle in with them."

"Answer your texts, please," Cap said, sounding like a dad.

Vega showed him her phone.

"Eighty percent battery," she said in her defense.

Cap shook out his shoulders with nervous energy.

"Ready?" said McTiernan.

"Yeah."

They got out of the car, and Vega watched them go. Cap began to recognize the street a little bit as they got closer to the house, saw the space across the street where he'd parked the other night, right next to a palm tree with a NO DOG POOP sign stuck in the dirt at its base.

"You lead?" he said to McTiernan.

McTiernan nodded, and they crossed the street, walked up the driveway to the door. McTiernan pressed the bell, and they heard it ringing hollow inside.

Mrs. Miller opened the door a few seconds later, and though she wasn't in an evening gown, Cap recognized her right away. She appeared sober now, and her brunette hair was long, past her shoulders in gently coiling waves, as opposed to the other night, when her hair had been up in a twist. She still looked thin, wearing an off-the-shoulder white ruffled blouse, exposing her upper arms and clavicle. Her face was cleanly made up; Cap could see the shine of a gloss on her lips. She was attractive close-up, he thought, probably in her early forties like him, though from the stones on her ears and fingers, he also gathered she had expensive tastes.

"Mrs. Miller?" said McTiernan softly but with a coppish air of authority.

"Yes?"

McTiernan flipped open his badge like a pro and said, "Detective Sean McTiernan, SDPD. This is Max Caplan, security consultant."

Her eyes goggled at the badge, and then she looked up at both of them confusedly.

"How can I help you?" she said, her voice raspy.

"We're wondering if we could perhaps ask you some questions about a series of burglaries in the neighborhood recently."

"Burglaries?" said Mrs. Miller, as if she had never heard the word pronounced quite that way.

"Yes," said McTiernan. "One over on Cypress, and one on Pine. Within the past week."

If Mrs. Miller was alarmed at the news, she was pretty good at hiding it, Cap thought.

"I don't know anything about it," she said plainly.

"Of course not," said McTiernan. "You wouldn't have yet."

McTiernan tilted his body slightly forward to say something more intimate. Cap did the same.

McTiernan continued: "Without going into too much detail, ma'am, we have reason to believe your house is the next target."

Now Mrs. Miller reacted—she reared back in surprise, looking back and forth between the two of them.

"What?" she said, her voice louder. "What kind of reason?"

"May we come in, Mrs. Miller?" said McTiernan gently. "So we can explain."

She scrutinized them for a moment more and then nodded hastily and stood aside. She led them to the left of a staircase into a two-story, open living room with large picture windows and a wall-mounted fireplace.

"Please," she said, gesturing to a brown leather couch and chair.

McTiernan sat on the couch, so Cap chose the chair. Mrs. Miller sat on the couch, on the opposite end from McTiernan. She did not offer them drinks. Cap also noticed there was no smell of food drifting in from the kitchen, which he could see from where he sat, a curved, spotted marble counter. It stood out as strange to him—it was now past eight, and most families either would have eaten dinner or would be preparing to eat.

"You were saying?" she said. "You have reason to believe my house is a target?"

"Yes," said McTiernan. He coughed one small, humble cough before continuing. "As I said, both burglaries have happened within the past week so we're watching this area very closely. Our suspects are targeting people who collect art, sculptures mainly." McTiernan gestured to a large piece next to the fireplace, three smoothed wooden blocks on a plank.

He said it with such plausibility that Cap almost said, Really, they are? Instead he nodded sagely.

"We only have this, and a piece in the master bedroom," said Mrs. Miller. "And you can't see either from the street, so how would they know they were here?"

"My associate, Mr. Caplan, is a securities expert, and can elaborate a little on the suspects' MO and what you can do to protect your home."

"We have an alarm system," said Mrs. Miller, turning to Cap. "We turn it on whenever we leave the house."

"That's good," said Cap. "But these guys are surprisingly sophisticated. They've been able to disarm quite a few home security systems. And they're in it for the long game, meaning they may have been monitoring your house for quite some time. Could I ask you what your schedules are like, generally, yours and your family's?"

A crease crossed Mrs. Miller's copper eyebrows as she thought about it.

"My husband works in medical research so generally eight- or nine-hour days during the week and a little bit on the weekend. He leaves the house around seven and comes back around six. Tonight he's at an event. He has a lot of fundraising-type events. I work three days a week at a marketing firm for nonprofits, and our son, he's seventeen, so between school and football practice and social activities he's not home very much. So I'm home the most, you could say." She paused and regarded Cap inquisitively. "Are they breaking into the houses during the day or at night?"

"At night," Cap added definitively. "Both have taken place at night but before midnight. Do you ever attend evening events with your husband?"

"Yes, sometimes," she said, bringing her arms slowly across her abdomen, crossing them.

Cap noticed her body language changing the more she talked about her husband: the crossed arms, the features on her face freezing up.

McTiernan must have noticed it too; he picked up the line where Cap had dropped it: "May we ask, when was the last time you and your husband were at an evening event together?"

She thought about it, eyes searching the high angled ceiling.

"That would've been Wednesday," she said, adjusting a silver bracelet on her wrist.

Her mouth and jaw were clenched shut after she spoke. Cap remembered her stumbling, angry, drunk. He struggled to recall her exact words to her husband, but couldn't forget her face in the dim streetlight and warm air. She'd had the same expression she wore now, like there was so much to be angry about if only she had a big enough frown to express it.

"What type of event was it?" McTiernan said, trying to sound matter-of-fact and doing well enough, but Cap knew he shouldn't push it.

"A fundraiser for a friend—Green Streets, or Green City, something like that. Environmental," she said, appearing not too interested in remembering the details.

"Sounds like you had a great time," Cap said, trying to be cute, adding a grin.

The start of a smile loosened up Mrs. Miller's lips but didn't get very far.

"It was fine," she said. "Just not my thing."

"What time did you return home after that event?" said McTiernan, still all business.

"I don't know," she said, trying to remember. "Probably eleven."

"Did you see anyone or anything strange when you got here? Anything on the street? People or cars out of place?" asked McTiernan.

Cap felt a flutter of anxiety in his chest, hoping Mrs. Miller didn't have some kind of latent photographic memory, and she would suddenly remember seeing someone who looked just like him parked in a rental car across the street.

"No," she said immediately. "We parked the car in the driveway and came inside. I didn't see anything unusual. Do you think they're watching houses?" she asked, looking at Cap.

"Possibly," he said. "Now, you said your husband's at an event tonight. Might your son be available—is he at home?"

"He's home, but he wasn't that night. Out with friends," she offered.

"Do you mind if we ask him what we've asked you?" said McTiernan. "If he saw anything unusual?"

Mrs. Miller paused, and Cap could sense a retreat, even though she didn't move a hair or alter her expression. He thought two things: that she was practiced in concealing which way she leaned, and also that she was used to being in a position where she had to.

"I'm sure he would have told me if he'd seen anything strange," she said, measured.

"Absolutely," said McTiernan. "But please understand, we all see a lot of things in plain sight and we don't realize we're seeing them. They may not have seemed strange at the time, but in hindsight, they may prove helpful to us."

Cap admired how genuine McTiernan sounded, but Mrs. Miller didn't seem moved. In fact she sat up a little straighter.

"I think I'd like to have my husband here, or counsel, if you want to ask my son any questions," she said, stern but polite. "Him being a minor."

Cap was impressed by her savvy, even though it temporarily wrenched their strategy. He couldn't blame her; he'd never let any cop or reporter or lawyer near Nell unless they had a subpoena or a warrant or both, but since most people learned their rights from TV shows, he'd hoped he and McTiernan might have gotten a little more leeway here.

Cap's phone buzzed and he pulled it from his pocket. He read the text while McTiernan attempted to finesse Mrs. Miller.

From Vega: "Status?"

Cap typed back: "Kid's in house but mom blocking. She's smart. Dr not home."

"I understand your hesitation," McTiernan was saying.

He was doing his best, a great job, thought Cap, running lap after lap without dropping the relay baton, but at this moment right here, it didn't matter. Mrs. Miller nodded politely and didn't say a damn word.

· · ·

Vega ran around the block once at a slow trot. She actually didn't think anyone was watching her but wanted to be prepared should she be stopped. She passed the Miller house, noticed some lights on inside, but didn't linger.

The cut under the bandage ached mildly, so Vega tried her best to run using only her leg muscles, raising the quads evenly and keeping her hips steady so they wouldn't swing back and forth.

She stopped at the corner, checked her watch, jogged in place and stretched her arms out over her head. Then she jogged up a dimly lit path next to a dark house with a real estate broker sign on a white post stuck in the lawn, a strip of stubby cactuses planted in pebbles to her left.

The path led to a deck overlooking a backyard. Vega lightly stepped up the stairs like she belonged there and onto the deck, walking heel to toe. A motion light shone on her, but there was no alarm; Vega stayed clear of the sliding doors just in case. She took a quick look inside; the place was scarcely decorated, like an open house: a white dining table with fake fruit. But she didn't care too much about what was in the house; all she wanted was the view from the deck.

Her phone buzzed with an email from the Bastard.

"Punk's set the party posts to private" was all it read, with a link to Facebook.

Vega clicked and scrolled through a dozen photos: Graham Miller and jock friends with Solo cups and cigarettes or girls; their eyes were narrow and bloodshot, their grins sloppy and stupid. RJ Otero was in a couple, smiling sheepishly. One caught Vega's eye: a blond girl asleep on a couch, Graham sitting on the arm, pointing down at her, laughing. RJ Otero stood behind the couch, his smile forced, the strain in his jaw visible. The caption read "Aw big boy's growing up."

She could see the back of the Miller house and backyard four lots away. All of the houses were separated by cedar wooden fences, about four or five feet high, more for delineation than security, she thought. The lawns were all the same size and square shape, laid out like a checkerboard, some with decks like the one she stood on, some with vinyl playground sets, others with aboveground swimming pools or trampolines, but no people in any of the backyards between Vega and the Miller house.

She came down the steps of the deck and backed up about ten feet. She rubbed her hands together and pulled the sleeves of the hoodie over the heels of her hands, trying to give herself a little cushion.

She started slow, then sped up, remembered not to look at her left leg hitting the wall but keep her eyes up to the top of the fence, where she hooked her hands, felt the wood splinter her a little but it was treated and sanded so not so bad. Then she hiked her right leg up and hoisted her butt on the fence, brought the left leg over and jumped into the next yard.

She pulled the hood of the hoodie, which had fallen back, over her head and scurried along the back wall. Her cut throbbed a little from landing, and her fingers itched from the wood, but she kept going. She was absolutely in plain sight; anyone looking out the back window to check for raccoons or search for the sideways dome of the moon might see her if he paused for just one extra second.

So she kept moving over each fence and into each yard, the injury and her fingers moaning a little more with each jump. Vega ignored the discomfort.

Her feet touched down into the Millers' yard, and she stuck close to the back fence, stepping onto a strip of smooth rocks laid out in geometric flower patterns. She examined the house: there was a well-lit square deck, a dim light on the first floor somewhere inside, near the front of the house; no lights on upstairs.

Vega squatted and peered under the deck, saw three small rectangular windows along the ground. A basement or a rec room, she thought. She came up into a crouch and scurried under the deck into the darkness, the grass smelling mossier here. She approached the window furthest to her left and kneeled.

It was a basement, and there was Graham Miller, playing a video game. First-person shooter. He sat on a couch, and Vega could see only the back of his head but knew it was him: the gingerbread brown hair, his long legs extended, feet resting on a beanbag. She estimated he was about six feet tall, couldn't tell from the shoulders how strong he was, only that he had shitty posture.

She could hear the sounds of the video game, muffled through the glass, gunshots and grenades. She could see Graham working the switches and buttons with his thumbs, tilting his head from one side to the other. Vega could count on her fingers how many times she'd played a video game; they didn't hold her interest for more than a minute and she usually found that the people who played them regularly were lazy.

Or maybe that's just what she thought of Graham Miller.

She squatted next to the window and leaned against the house, examined Cap's text on her phone.

Vega typed: "Do you think you can swing her?"

She waited a moment, and then came his response: "Possible. Not likely."

Cap placed his phone screen-down on his leg while McTiernan continued to navigate the questioning of Mrs. Miller, such as it was. She didn't appear agitated, nor did she seem to be in a hurry for them to leave necessarily, but it was becoming clear that she would continue to say no politely until they wore themselves out from asking.

"We're not here to trick anyone," McTiernan said. "We just need to make sure he didn't see anything."

Mrs. Miller gathered her hair and brought it over one shoulder. Cap thought she looked lovely.

"I think it's a little strange," she said, matter-of-fact. "We're close to the Oteros—you must know Roland Otero?"

If McTiernan was spooked, he didn't show it.

"Of course, he's my commanding officer," he said, like he was pleased to have discovered a mutual friend.

"I talk to Palmer Otero almost every day. She hasn't said anything about burglaries in the neighborhood."

McTiernan didn't miss a drop, knocked the ball right back: "This is all somewhat sensitive, Mrs. Miller. It's quite possible that Commander Otero hasn't shared the information with his wife."

Cap couldn't tell if she believed him, but still, she seemed calm. Then McTiernan's phone began to ring. He pulled it from his pocket and glanced at the screen while he continued to make his case.

"We don't want to scare people here, just get as much intel as we can."

McTiernan turned the sound off on his ringer and passed the phone to Cap. It buzzed in his hand and the caller ID flashed across the top of the screen: "DEA MACKEY." Cap picked up his own phone and texted Vega:

"How sure are u the kid knows something?"

McTiernan's phone finally stopped buzzing.

Mrs. Miller gave a shrug.

"I wish I could be more help to you, but you're not talking to my son, I'm sorry," she said, her voice light, eyes averted to the side.

Cap saw that Vega had written back: "Not sure." He clenched his jaw.

"Do you gentlemen need to leave?" Mrs. Miller asked earnestly. "You seem to be very busy," she said, nodding to the phones in Cap's lap.

McTiernan fixed a smile on his face and stared at Cap. What now?

And just then another text came back from Vega: "Gut is sure. One way to find out. Any chance she'll break?"

"Just five more minutes of your time, Mrs. Miller," said Cap. "Then we'll be on our way."

McTiernan picked it up, kept stalling like a kid on Christmas Eve, and Cap wrote back as fast as he could to Vega:

"No. U do u."

Vega powered down her phone and rapped on the small rectangular window with her knuckles. Graham Miller didn't turn around, couldn't hear over the video game war, Vega figured. She knocked again with her whole fist, and he turned, his face a mix of surprise and irritation. Vega smiled and gestured with her hand to come closer.

Graham stood up from the couch and approached the window slowly, watching her suspiciously.

"Hi!" Vega called through the glass. "Could you, uh, open this?"

His head was directly at the level of the window; Vega guessed he was not quite six feet tall. Slender athletic build. Light tannish fuzz on his cheeks matching his hair color, hazel eyes with not much space between them and the bridge of his nose. Vega imagined to girls at school this might make him look like a rugged royal type, the result of generations of moneyed inbreeding. To her, it looked like he'd originally had one giant eye that had been split into two at a later time.

He flipped the window open. It was awning style, the glass tilting inward so that it lay flat in the middle of the frame. Vega figured that it was about twelve inches wide by six tall, nowhere near wide enough for her to wriggle through.

"Hi, I'm so sorry to bother you," she said, speaking quickly and in the highest register she could reach without sounding like an animated bunny. "My name's Alice, and I just bought the place on the corner— thirty-one hundred? And I was out running, and I locked myself out. No battery," she said, waving her phone. "I can't believe I did this," she said, shaking her head.

Graham stared at her and appeared sort of disgusted, not like he didn't believe her but like he thought locking oneself out was untoward, next to picking your nose in public.

"You can, uh, come around front, and my mom can let you in."

"Oh, that's okay," said Vega. "I don't need to bother your mom. If I could just use your phone to call my husband. Then I'll get out of here."

The best lies are the simplest, she thought. When asking for something, just make it sound like the most natural thing in the world and talk fast. This story that I'm selling to you is the only story that makes sense.

Lucky for her, Graham wasn't smart enough to think too much about it. His face looked blank, and he turned and jogged over to the couch, where his phone was sitting, then came back, opened the phone app for her, and handed it to her through the open window. She took it and felt his fingers, warm and damp from gripping a game console all day.

"Oh, this is different from mine," she said. "Is this a ten?"

"Yeah, it's old," he said, barely interested.

She clicked out of the keypad and went to his texts, swiped her thumb down and took in the names as quickly as she could: RJ, Thalia, Rea, Nix, Mom, DrFuckface (Vega assumed that was his father).

"Hey, all you have to do is dial," he said, letting his arms rest on the sill, his hands in the grass.

She kept scrolling. Searching.

"Yeah, it's just a different look and feel from mine, sorry," she said.

She bounced out of the texts and went to Recents on the phone app. A lot of RJ. Home, Mom. She saw about two weeks previous, quite a few numbers without contact names, and below the numbers, locations: San Diego, CA; Escondido, CA. And then three in a row: Salton City, CA.

"Hey, could you just give me my phone back and go talk to my mom? She's upstairs like I said."

Vega looked straight at him, at his slack jaw and chapped lips, dull heavy-lidded eyes, row of pimples sprouting near the hairline. She found all of his physical features in service to his spoiled, entitled core and had the urge to knock them off his face one by one. She rooted her knees in the grass and leaned forward.

"You really want me to talk to your mom, Graham? You want me to tell her about Elsie Otero, or just the girls in the house in Salton?"

That gave him a jolt. His face opened up like someone had lit a pilot light behind his eyes.

"The fuck are you?" he said, his voice raised but not yelling, still in a sort of shock, his social-media-stoned teenager brain trying to fit the jig around the wood.

Vega didn't answer him. She could see him shift from figuring out she wasn't a lost jogger to realizing he had to stop her. She was hoping he'd do that.

Graham reached for her Frankenstein-style through the window opening, stiff and without any range of motion from his position. Vega guessed he was on his tiptoes. But the way the house was built and the basement windows were set, she was actually above him.

He kept swiping his hands at her and managed to grab her hoodie but couldn't gain any leverage to pull her. Vega tossed both their phones over her shoulder onto the grass and hunched forward. She grabbed the ribbed collar of his T-shirt with one hand and his oily hair with the other and yanked with her whole body like she was in a tug-of-war.

Graham's forehead hit the bottom of the tilted window so hard a two-inch gash split open right away, and his hands flew to it. Vega didn't let him go.

"The house in Salton," she said. "How many times did you go?"

"Once," he said, the color washing out of his face.

Then he seemed to gain some balance and tried again to pull Vega, but he couldn't get a grip on any part of her, the hoodie slipping through his fingers.

Vega released his hair and clutched his T-shirt with both hands, pulling him under the window glass now, almost through the opening. Seeing him like that, his head sinking down through the neck of his shirt, stunned by the pain, coming to the immediate terms of his own helplessness, Vega understood something. She could hear McTiernan's voice on replay like he was standing right behind her: What do Boyce and Mackey have over Otero? How are they holding Otero up by the neck of his shirt, she thought.

"How did you find out about it? Your daddy tell you? Huh?"

She yanked at his collar as if it were a choke chain.

"No," he wheezed. "I saw texts on his phone. He didn't know I went until after."

"You took RJ Otero with you, didn't you," she said, gripping even tighter. "Didn't you."

Graham didn't say yes or no, just reacted to each sensation as it hit him, right now the threat of suffocation paramount as he brought his hands to Vega's wrists, trying to pry them off.

But before Vega had the chance to tighten her grip, a woman emerged from a staircase on the opposite side of the room, Cap and McTiernan right behind her.

Vega opened both hands wide, and Graham began to fall. The woman rushed to him, shouting his name as if her volume and intensity would prevent him from hitting the floor. He landed in a clump, and Vega didn't wait to see what would happen. She sprang to her feet, grabbed both phones, and was gone.

Cap caught just a flash of the white glow of Vega's face before she disappeared into the dark on the other side of the window. He watched the teenage boy he assumed to be Graham Miller crumple to the floor, and Mrs. Miller running to him.

"Graham? Your head, oh my God, are you okay? Graham?" she said, upset but calm. Not crying.

Graham sat up in a daze, a long bleeding cut in the middle of his forehead.

"This girl stole my phone," he said, sounding unconvinced, perhaps thinking he'd imagined it.

"What girl?" said Mrs. Miller, sitting on the floor with him, placing her hands on either side of his face to examine it. "What happened?"

"The girl came to the window," Graham said, and that was all. It seemed to be all he could put together at the moment.

"I'm calling the police," Mrs. Miller said, looking to Cap and McTiernan, suddenly suspicious, adding, "Other police."

"We can get someone here for you," said McTiernan, still playing the part.

Graham grabbed his mother's arm.

"She knew about Dad. She knew about everything," he said, too stunned to worry about who was listening.

Mrs. Miller stood and looked at Cap and McTiernan, guilty but still incensed.

"What's 'everything,' Mrs. Miller?" said Cap, even though he already knew.

"My husband is the one you want," she said coldly. "Not my son."

"That's really not what it sounds like," said Cap.

She fixed her eyes on him, and Cap recognized her expression—it was exactly how she'd looked at her husband the other night in the driveway: disgusted, the stitches of composure just starting to break along the seam.

"How it sounds to you is of no interest to me," she said. "Dr. Miller was the one who did those procedures. My son and I had nothing to do with it."

"You know that for certain, ma'am?" said McTiernan, not daring to even glance at Cap for fear of interrupting the confession.

Mrs. Miller glared at him like he was dumb or crazy.

"Yes, Detective. This was all his idea."

"Why would he put his whole family at risk?" asked McTiernan.

"You'd have to ask him but it likely has something to do with money," she said glibly. "Not this money," she said, her hand flitting around in the air, gesturing to her finely appointed house. "Bigger, darker money."

"You realize that we can use everything you're saying to us right now—" began McTiernan.

"In a court of law," said Mrs. Miller, unconcerned. "Yes, I watch TV."

"And I guess your boy's just a victim, right?" said Cap spitefully.

Mrs. Miller didn't answer, returned to the floor and held her son's head in her hands.

"Not another word, Graham," she said. Then she looked up to Cap and McTiernan and said, "I'd like you both to leave now."

"Thanks for your time, ma'am," said McTiernan as if he were wrapping up a standard interview.

Mrs. Miller didn't answer, just took out her phone from the back pocket of her jeans and began to dial, still staring at them. Cap felt his own phone buzz as he and McTiernan backed away. They turned to run up the stairs and out the door as Cap read Vega's text:

"Meet at car. Got what we came for."

Vega jumped her last fence and ran up a driveway, out into the street. She had correctly estimated where McTiernan's car was parked and now rushed and crouched next to it.

About a minute later she heard the sounds of two sets of feet coming toward her, distant then loud, and she stood up halfway and saw them running full speed, McTiernan beeping the doors unlocked as he approached.

Vega got into the backseat, and the men got into the front, McTiernan gasping a little. He didn't seem to be in the best shape, thought Vega, but he was young, which made up the difference.

McTiernan started the car and pulled a U so as not to pass the Miller house on the way to the freeway.

Vega placed both phones on her lap and said, "I know what it is. What Boyce and Mackey have on Otero." She tapped qwertys on repeat into the Notes on Graham's phone to keep it unlocked and continued: "It's the son. Graham saw texts on his dad's phone about the Salton house and brought RJ there for a frat boy birthday gift."

"That's the everything," said McTiernan.

"What's the everything?" asked Vega.

"Graham said you knew about Dr. Miller, about 'everything,'" said Cap. "And the wife knows, too, and just threw her husband under a sizable Greyhound coach."

"Yeah?" said Vega.

"Yeah," said Cap. "Turns out she only cares about her son and thinks he's still a golden boy even though he dabbles in statutory."

"The wife also implied that the doctor did it for cash but not just some bills in a picture frame," said McTiernan.

"'Bigger, darker money' were her exact words," said Cap, wiping his forehead with his hand, sweating aggressively.

"Good to know," said Vega. "So Boyce and Mackey find out, somehow, that RJ went to the Salton house and they have some kind of proof, so a week, two weeks ago, they go to Otero and say, we need to run a case on the DL by our rules only and if you don't come along—"

"We'll turn out your boy," McTiernan finished the thought.

They all sat with that for a moment and let the streetlights pass over them as they neared the on-ramp.

"You got one big narrative problem," said Cap. "If Boyce and Mackey know RJ went to Salton, it means they know about Salton, full stop. So then why do they hire you?" Cap said to Vega.

McTiernan drove onto the freeway and immediately hit a patch of stalled traffic.

"Here," he said, passing Cap his phone. "Are we lucky enough to think Mackey left me a voice mail telling me?"

Cap tapped the message, pressed Speaker, and held the phone out so they could all hear.

Then came Mackey's voice, full of false friendly professionalism: "Hello, Detective McTiernan. This is Agent Mackey with the DEA. Just wanted to give you a heads-up, one enforcement official to another: Alice Vega and Max Caplan are about to become fugitives under California state law, and if you are harboring or aiding them in any way, you could be pressed with equal or greater charges, being a police officer, and if found guilty, I can make sure you'll get fast-tracked to Stockton South Penitentiary, where there's a nice community of white nationalists who'd love to get to know you. I could even talk to a friend about getting you placed in the right block inside.

"That said, feel free to shoot me or Commander Otero a text any time now. Looking forward to it."

The message ended. Cap rubbed his eyebrows and temples, and Vega knew that meant he had a headache. She watched the strip of McTiernan's face in the rearview; he was not looking back at her or over at Cap, just straight ahead at the car in front of them.

"McT," Cap began.

McTiernan raised his hand, signaling that Cap should shut up. Then he shook his head, lamenting something silently.

"They don't have anything on us," said Vega. "That's why he's saying we're 'about' to be fugitives. Right now we're just wanted for questioning. He won't be able to pin you for a thing."

Cap shot her a look that said, Pull back. Easy on the consolation.

Vega didn't want to pull back.

"They have nothing," she said again, spitting the words out, leaning forward so much the seatbelt sliced across the bandage on her side.

"But we both think you need to look out for yourself first," said Cap, raising his voice, staring at Vega.

"*We* don't think that," said Vega. "*We* want your help."

"I hate it when you guys fight," said McTiernan, seemingly genuinely sad. "It makes me feel bad about myself."

Cap laughed, and Vega leaned back in the seat. The traffic began to crawl.

"Vega's right. Until they charge you, they can't charge me," McTiernan added, hunching close to the wheel.

"But they can fire you," said Cap.

McTiernan's gaze turned toward the shoulder as they slowly passed an accident, two cars with busted fenders, one ambulance, one highway patrol car.

"Anyone else think it's weird that Mackey left me that message instead of Boyce?" said McTiernan.

"Yes," said Vega. "Boyce is the alpha in that relationship."

"When I met Mackey the first time he came off as like a paper pusher," added Cap. "Desk guy."

"He didn't sound like that just now," Vega said, reflective.

"Why's he got to threaten me anyway?" asked McTiernan, to no one specifically. "I'm nobody."

"Maybe he's just as desperate as Otero," said Vega, watching a woman, one of the owners of the cars with the busted fenders, shaking her head and texting. She looked frazzled and tired and like this was the last thing she needed.

"It's because we're close to something, and he knows it," said McTiernan, now meeting Vega's eye in the mirror.

Cap gave McTiernan a confused glance.

"So if Boyce and Mackey have the drop on Otero, who's got the drop on Boyce and Mackey?" he said.

"Don't know. We should get a beer though," said McTiernan, sighing, his shoulders falling. "And probably swap out this car, just in case."

Vega let Cap answer and turned to watch the accident out the rear window, the red lights from the emergency vehicles still flashing, the woman no longer texting and now perched on the crushed metal of her car, face buried in her hands.

17

CAP COULDN'T TELL IF THE BAR McTIERNAN BROUGHT THEM TO was genuinely retro or forcibly retro, with its dark cherrywood interior and red leather booths. He couldn't put a finger on the clientele either; it seemed to be composed of well-heeled young women in clusters and a man here or there, but no one sloppy, no one appearing to be on the move or make.

They sat in an L-shape around one of the corners of the bar facing the TV, drinking bottled beers. It was after ten now, and the local nightly news was on with no sound.

"You got an idea where you can get another car?" said Cap.

McTiernan nodded. "My girlfriend's is parked at the airport. I got a key."

"Your girlfriend's a good person to know."

"Who're you telling," said McTiernan. "She's the only reason I know about this place. It's a flight attendant bar. Figured we couldn't go to a cop bar."

Cap glanced around again, everything making sense now.

Vega had her hood up, taking small sips of beer. Cap could see the light from the TV screen bouncing off her eyes.

"We get the car, then, what, we contact Otero?" Cap said.

"With what?" said McTiernan. "We have to keep moving until we have a theory at least of who has what on Boyce and/or Mackey."

McTiernan brought a fist to his mouth to cover a yawn. He excused himself to go to the restroom, and Cap scooted to the edge of his stool to get a little closer to Vega.

"I wasn't trying to hurt our argument before. I just wanted McT to know he has options," he said, his eyes wandering to the TV too.

"He's a grown-ass man, Caplan," said Vega. "And we need him."

"I got that. It's not terrible to think for a minute before we take down a guy's career, though."

Vega kept staring at the screen but shook her head impatiently.

"You worry too much about other people's bullshit," she said. "We're not all Nell."

"Okay, let's watch it," he said, turning to her, setting his beer down loudly on the bar. "I'm not getting off on being father of the year here. I am expressing concern about a guy who has our back and could stand to lose a lot."

Cap realized he was getting louder, glanced over his shoulder and saw McTiernan chatting with two women in blue suits at a table. He leaned his head over to Vega and said quietly, "And were we to ever be charged with anything, he'd be screwed, just like Mackey said."

Vega looked at him for a second and then back to the TV. She wriggled her nose and tightened her lips in frustration.

Her phone began to buzz and she whipped it out of her pocket and looked at the screen.

"Goddammit," she said under her breath and then slapped her phone on the bar, screen down.

"Who is that?" said Cap.

Vega took a swig of beer and said, "It's this guy I slept with a few times. He thinks we're married or something."

Cap took in the information, batted away the first impulse of jealousy. He thought maybe he should just let it drop but then figured there was really nothing to lose by doing a little more fact-finding. He could count on one hand the times Vega had offered up personal intel about herself, and the temptation to find out what kinds of guys she liked was too great to pass up.

"How many times did you sleep with him?" Cap asked casually, as if they'd discussed this sort of thing all the time.

Vega shrugged, unfazed by the question.

"I don't know, thirty, forty?" she said.

Cap did his best not to let his jaw swing open.

"That's a lot," he said.

"Is it?" she asked. "It's been the past few months. He's my Muay Thai instructor."

Cap pictured all sorts of jacked-up types now, guys chugging Muscle Milk while doing box jumps. It wasn't what he'd ever imagined when he thought of Vega having a boyfriend, but he wasn't sure what guy would make sense in that role instead.

"Did you," Cap said, looking back up at the TV, "break it off with him?"

"There's nothing to break off," Vega said, getting agitated. "It was sex. He didn't seem to mind any of the thirty or forty times when we never . . ." She paused, searching for words, then waving toward the TV. "Watched the news together afterward."

Cap laughed at her.

"Vega, are you under the impression that's what couples do? Watch the news together?"

She shrugged again, and Cap realized she truly had no idea. He continued to laugh.

"The fuck are you laughing at?" she said, her tone serious but a lightness appearing in her eyes.

"Nothing. Nothing at all," he said. "All I'll say is that if a man tried to pull what you're pulling," he continued, pointing the beer bottle at her, "he'd be branded an asshole immediately."

Vega rolled her eyes, looking weary.

"So start a blog, Caplan," she said, which made Cap laugh even harder.

She began to smile then, her lips curling at the edges like a single sheet of paper starting to burn. Cap finished his beer and asked Vega if she wanted another. She shook her head and showed him hers half-full. Cap signaled to the bartender for one more.

He took a sip of his second beer, and they both watched the news without a great deal of focus, Cap feeling the diminutive alcohol content from one-point-five beers start to have an effect. Normally it would have taken more than that, but he was so physically reduced that it was hitting him instantly, causing him to feel a pleasant numbness of the extremities, a soporific haze of the mind.

There were cops on the TV, looked to Cap to be suits with badges at a press conference. Brass. He squinted to see the caption. "Deputy Chief of Police Armando Posada." Cap couldn't see it perfectly but the man on the screen was overweight with light skin, a white guy. Looked more Irish than Latino.

"Those are Trina's friends," said McTiernan, reclaiming his seat. "Safe bet they won't burn us."

"McT, who is that?" Cap said, pointing to the screen above.

"That's your friend Posada," said McTiernan.

"He's talking about the tunnels," said Vega.

Then the cops were gone, replaced with footage of a wildfire up north. Cap didn't know if it was exhaustion, his eyes, or the beer that was tripping him up. He took out his phone and went to the Internet, searched for Deputy Chief Armando Posada. He tapped the images, scrolled and scrolled.

"This guy," said Cap, showing the screen to McTiernan. "This is Posada?"

McTiernan glanced and nodded. "Yeah, from the hospital, right? I'm at a loss to say how the hell he fits into this."

"This is not who I met in the hospital," Cap said emphatically. "The guy I met is Latino."

"Posada's half-Mexican, I think," said McTiernan, not understanding. "Looks white."

"No, I'm saying it was a different guy," said Cap. "Not him."

"What'd he look like?" said Vega. "The guy who said he was Posada."

Cap sifted through all the activity and stress of his memory of the day and did his best to remember the man from the hospital.

"Definitely darker-skinned than this guy," he said, tapping the phone screen. "Nicely dressed. Not just nice, though, sharp. Gold cuff links." Cap tried to remember the face. "A scar, a big one, right here," he said, bringing his finger to his chin.

"And he threatened you?' said McTiernan. "This other guy with the scar?"

"Sure seemed like it," said Cap.

"Ring anything anywhere for you?" Vega said to McTiernan. "Scar on the chin, Mexican, sharp dresser?"

McTiernan thought, shook his head.

"I don't know. No one pops."

"We can't afford to spend time on it now," said Vega. "We know it wasn't Posada in the hospital but we have to keep moving."

She took a last small sip of beer and set the bottle on the bar, stood up to leave. McTiernan did the same, and Cap did too, somewhat reluctant to give up the gloriously ordinary feeling of having a drink in a bar, but he knew it was time to go, and he knew Vega was right, to stack that question on top of all the others and keep pushing until every last one of them cracked open.

They headed to the airport. McTiernan approached the parking entrance, powered down his window, grabbed the ticket from the machine, and took the ramp for long-term parking. As they pulled into an open-air lot, Vega watched a security camera near the elevators spin and follow them.

"She usually parks in the K section, near the walkway," he said.

Vega saw an armed guard standing on an island between A–K and L–Z. She leaned back in her seat, staring into her lap as they passed him. She saw McTiernan watching him in the side mirror.

"Normal for parking security to carry an AR-15 here?" she asked.

"Depends on the day, I guess," McTiernan said.

He pulled into a spot at the end of a row of cars in Section J. The three got out, McTiernan locked up, and they started to walk, weaving through cars, McTiernan studying the signs on the posts above. When they reached K, McTiernan held the fob above his head and pressed the horn button twice. They heard the honking to their left and went toward it, McTiernan pressing the button a few more times until they saw the lights of his girlfriend's car flashing.

Vega winced every time. It seemed noticeably loud in the empty lot, even under the steady whoosh of planes landing and taking off nearby. She and Cap followed McTiernan until he stopped in front of the car, a tiny red hatchback that reminded Vega of a candy apple.

McTiernan pressed the Unlock button and tugged at the driver's side door, but it didn't open.

"I didn't hear a click," said Cap, leaning his head down to the window. "Try it again."

McTiernan pressed it again, also leaning his head down. Vega hung back, crossing her arms, glancing over her shoulders. McTiernan tried the door again, and still, it didn't open.

"I didn't hear it either," he said.

Cap tried the passenger side, then the backseat.

"Fuck," said McTiernan, hushed.

"When's the last time you used her key?" said Cap.

McTiernan shook his head.

"Year ago, maybe."

"Battery might be dead," said Cap.

"Let's go back to your car," Vega said. "Now."

"I'm giving it another minute," said McTiernan, continuing to press the button.

"Yeah, when mine's going dead it works sporadically," said Cap, as if this were a tested method.

Neither of them seemed too concerned, both pulling on the handles.

Vega turned all the way around, watching out for any movement. She saw a couple of cars in different directions, parking and circling.

"You click, I'll yank," said Cap, troubleshooting.

McTiernan clicked. Still locked.

"Horn still works," said McTiernan.

He pressed it, and the horn honked loudly, lights flashing.

"Stop it," Vega hissed. "Let's go back to your car."

"Vega, we got a chance to get a new vehicle, we need to take it," said Cap.

Then she heard the sound of jet engines, and a plane roared directly over their heads, the sound shredding any remaining quiet around them. When it had finally passed, Vega's eardrums buzzed and hummed.

"Enough tries. Let's go," she said, her voice sounding like it was coming through a foam mattress.

McTiernan nodded and looked about to say something, but then stopped, just as Vega heard a sound she knew well, even muffled. It was the unmistakable click of a safety on an assault rifle. Looking at McTiernan's and Cap's faces, she knew she was right as they gazed past her, watching their hands rise slowly into the air above their heads.

18

VERY CIVILIZED HERE ON THE WEST COAST, THOUGHT CAP AS THEY pulled into the SDPD lot. No cuffs, plenty of please-and-thank-you; they even got to hold on to their phones, and no one made a move to take McTiernan's firearm. The worst thing he could say about the experience of not quite being arrested but brought in for questioning here was that the three of them were crammed into the backseat of an undercover cop car, which did not allow for a lot of free movement among them.

Even the guy with the AR-15 had been polite, saying they could lower their hands as long as he could see them, and that they would have to wait only a few minutes before someone would take them to see Commander Otero, who would explain things.

Great, Cap had thought. I would love to have things explained.

Vega sat in the middle, McTiernan on the other side. He had kept asking the detectives in the front seat, whom he knew somewhat, for details and they either didn't know anything or were pretending not to. After they'd parked, Cap unbuckled his seatbelt but stayed put, knew better than to get out of the car before the undercovers. Then once McTiernan and Vega slid out, Cap followed.

They were brought through a side door, up the stairs to a hallway. The undercovers were ahead of them, but McTiernan hustled to keep up, continuing to pepper them with questions or, more specifically, different iterations of the same question.

"You get the orders from Otero personally, though?" McTiernan asked one of them, a stout black guy.

"Nah, it came from Rebeuto," he said.

Cap realized they were heading to the interrogation room with the ficus, where they had questioned Joe Guerra.

"Yeah, but did Rebeuto get it from Otero?" said McTiernan, stopping in front of the door.

"We do A to B," said the other guy, wiry and white, bald head. "No C. Rebeuto says pick you up, drop you in the room. All friendly."

Cap believed them. He was tired but could usually tell when a cop was lying. Right now these two were passing the test; no feathers tickling the back of Cap's neck signaling otherwise.

It seemed like McTiernan believed the undercovers too. They shook hands with him and said nice to meet you to Cap and Vega, then left. Cap saw in that moment the exhaustion in McTiernan's face, his eyes bloodshot, his shoulders hunched in defeat.

McTiernan opened the door to the interrogation room, and there was a man sitting at the round table who looked like a cop but a little older than the average, Cap thought. A white guy but tan with silver hair clipped short and gelled to stay in place, spiky on the top. He stood when he saw them, and McTiernan sighed and groaned simultaneously.

"Dammit, Wayne," he said.

Wayne held his arms out, like he was presenting himself. He snapped gum between his back teeth.

"Hi, Detective. You gonna introduce me to your friends?"

McTiernan rubbed his eyes and let out a small, sad laugh.

"Alice Vega, Max Caplan. This is Mickey Wayne, IA."

"Pleasure," said Wayne, pulling his suit jacket off the back of the chair. "Sorry we can't stay."

Wayne walked to the door, and Cap and Vega moved out of his way. McTiernan didn't move. He stood there, letting his hands fall to his sides. Cap had the feeling he would've sat down on the floor, fatigued from running and reconciled himself to getting caught.

"Detective, you coming?" said Wayne, standing in the doorway.

"Yep," said McTiernan.

He followed Wayne but stopped and turned to look at Cap and Vega one more time.

"I'll text you," said Vega, sounding much more certain than Cap felt or McTiernan looked.

McTiernan gave a slight nod, and Wayne's gum cracked once more as he opened his mouth to speak.

"Let's get moving," he said, not particularly aggressively.

McTiernan left, and Wayne began to close the door but stuck his head in to say, "Someone will be right here."

Then the door shut.

Cap stared at it and put his hands behind his neck, trying in vain to massage the muscles, hard and tight as extension cords.

"Dammit," he said, angry and tired.

He turned to glance at Vega, who was sitting at the round table, scrolling through pictures on her phone. She didn't seem concerned about anything.

"We just got McT shitcanned," he said, trying to bring the moment home to her.

"Maybe," said Vega.

She seemed distracted, an absentmindedness cast over her face as she swiped right with two fingers.

Cap paced and continued to talk: "Someone calls Internal Affairs, it's never a good sign. It doesn't end well even when it ends well."

He stopped pacing, gripped the back of a chair, and leaned forward on it.

"They don't have enough to arrest us, but they can do whatever they want to McT," he added.

Vega set her phone down on the table and unzipped and removed her hoodie.

"We've been over this," she said, standing.

"Sorry I'm boring you," said Cap, getting pissed. "Just grabbing for a handle here."

Vega didn't respond, lifted the right side of her shirt and began to peel one corner of the bandage.

"What are you doing?" said Cap.

"Take a picture of the cut, would you," she said, handing him her phone.

She peeled the gauze back, only a hint of discomfort visible in the pursing of her lips. The cut was glossy but not bleeding, the dead thread holding the skin together tight, looked to Cap to be as thick as barbed wire.

"Why am I doing this?" he said, coming around the table.

He bent down and zoomed in to the cut.

"Don't worry about it," she said. "You were saying, about the handle."

Cap pressed the red button five or six times and said, "I'm thinking maybe we offer a deal for McT. Like we do whatever they want us to do, within reason. A trial or information . . ." He placed the phone on the table, and Vega began to carefully reapply the bandage, smoothing out the tape against her skin in a rectangle.

"We say okay, take us instead," Cap said, dropping into a chair.

"They might be hearing everything you say," Vega said, nodding to the painting.

"I don't give a shit, girl," he said. "I'm not sending a cop up. I'm not going to do it."

Vega readjusted her shirt and sat back down, picked up her phone and began typing a text.

"So you're doing a rerun of exactly what you did to get yourself fired from the Denville PD. Throw yourself on the tracks again."

Strangely, Cap had not directly made the connection until Vega pointed it out.

"Yeah, I am," he said, feeling slightly liberated. "And the same thing tomorrow."

Vega put down her phone and met his eye.

"Because that is who you are," she said.

"Yes," said Cap.

"You know who I am?" she said, leaning forward, hands folded, a smile lurking somewhere around her lips.

"Who?" Cap said, playing along.

She cupped her hand next to her mouth and started to whisper. Cap couldn't quite hear the first word, and was about to tell her to speak up, when the door opened, and there was Otero.

Vega sat back in her chair, and Cap stood up and stuck his hand out. Otero shook it but barely looked at him, focused on Vega.

"Mr. Caplan," he said. Then, "Ms. Vega."

Vega stayed seated and didn't say anything. Cap attempted to read her expression but it wasn't easy. There was a humor in it, amusement. He knew she wasn't the type to put her nerves on display, but her default was the steel, the frost in her eyes. This wasn't that. She looked about to laugh.

Otero sat in the chair opposite her, and Cap sat between them, watching them regard each other like dogs off the leash in the street. A minute passed, and then another. No one looked at a phone. One more minute dragged by, and then Otero spoke.

"I talked to my wife," he said, his tone flat.

Vega let another thirty seconds pass before answering: "Yeah, I talked to her, too."

Otero slung one arm behind the chair and crossed his legs, getting comfortable.

"Usually we don't like to involve families in this department," he said calmly.

Cap thought of Nell, flashed on coming through the door in the morning after third shift when she was little, his heart still clattering around in his chest after a night of breaking up bar fights and answering domestic violence calls. He would pick her up off the floor and pat her hair, knotted from sleep, smell toothpaste and Froot Loops on her breath.

Vega leaned forward and folded her hands.

"The Janes have families, too," she said.

Otero smiled briefly.

"I have good news for both of you," he said. "You're not under arrest, and we see no need to recommend to the DA to bring charges against you."

"What a relief," Cap said, recalling the similar exchange with the Posada impersonator in the hospital. "What about Detective McTiernan?"

"That's a little more complicated," said Otero. "There's a process he has to go through. He disobeyed direct orders from his commanding officer."

Cap gnashed his teeth against his tongue so he wouldn't talk.

"So," said Vega, sighing. "Do you have our clothes?"

Otero chuckled.

"Sure, I have your clothes. I'll have someone get them for you."

"We've heard that a lot today," snapped Cap.

"You get them bagged and tagged?" said Vega. "In that nice clean evidence room you showed me?"

"Bagged, not tagged yet," said Otero.

Vega angled her head toward the painting, threw her line of vision at it for a quick second.

"You have a chance to get any other items from the Salton house yet?" she added. "Run any matches for prints or blood?"

Now Cap saw she was heading toward a target. He noticed Otero shifting his weight in the chair, still casual but concerned. Otero knew she was getting close too.

Vega's phone buzzed on the table, and she picked it up, glanced at a text. The sound seemed to break Otero out of his disorientation.

"You know I can't tell you about any evidence we may or may not have seized from the premises," he said.

"Because we're not on the case anymore, Alice," Cap said, snotty as hell, suddenly confident.

He could afford to be an asshole; if Vega was sure, he'd bet his house, and whatever she had, she seemed sure. She set her phone back down and jerked her head toward the painting.

"Anyone watching us, Commander?" she said.

"No," he answered straightaway.

"What about Boyce and Mackey?"

That gave Otero pause for a second, but then he answered, "They're not here. We're not being recorded either."

Vega shrugged.

"I hope you're telling the truth, but I don't really care either way. I'm still going to tell you what I have to tell you."

She leaned back in her chair, sat straight up.

"The knife that cut me, Ben Davis's knife, is not the knife that was used to kill the Janes. That knife was a sixteenth of an inch—most knives are. Ben Davis's knife is most likely an eighth of an inch thick. You can tell because my wound, even though it's a straight-across slash, went a lot deeper than it would have with a sixteenth knife, even though he didn't stab me.

"Also, the knife used to kill the Janes was serrated. The skin around their entry wounds shows a pattern of hash-mark-shaped abrasions. Ben Davis would have had to slice me open with precision without my resisting to get a clean cut if he'd had a serrated blade. That wasn't the way it happened."

She stopped talking, let all of it land. Cap didn't try to analyze it yet, just kept watching Otero, who was remaining calm but was clearly trying to get in front of it, breathing accelerated, eyes narrowed.

"That's interesting, but I'm not sure what it brings us," he said.

"Ultimately I'm not either," said Vega. "But I have some ideas."

She paused.

"Care to hear them?"

Otero was quiet. Cap grinned like a fool, looking back and forth between them.

"I would," Cap said, giddy.

Vega tapped two fingers hard into the table and leaned in again toward Otero.

"I believe Agents Boyce and Mackey told you they had some incriminating evidence that your boy had solicited and engaged in sexual activity with an underage undocumented girl," she said.

Otero's mouth twitched only once at the mention of his son. Other than that, straight flush poker face.

Vega continued: "And then you did whatever they wanted. Kept us prisoner in the hospital, put out a baby APB on us, let their people put the girls in Salton on a bus somewhere, put your own detective through the IA relay."

Otero's eyes scanned the room as he bit his upper lip. Cap expected that a bunch of little land mines were detonating in his head.

"I don't know what their endgame is. But they have you right here," said Vega, squeezing the tips of her thumb and index finger together. "And maybe they'd be interested to know that Davis didn't kill the Janes. That is a piece of information we have that they may not."

Cap made a tight fist and pressed it into his palm. He'd grown serious after the initial spark of joy he'd gotten from realizing Vega had a path forward. Looking at the profiles of Vega and Otero, both stalwart, he knew this was no longer a dogfight—it was a proposition.

Otero spoke first: "There's really no one on the other side of that," he said, nodding to the painting.

"That's good," said Vega.

She sat back in her chair again and folded her arms.

"It's up to you which way this goes," she said to Otero.

Cap didn't dare breathe. Otero blew out some air and hunched forward, swept his hand along the side of his head.

"He's got tape on my son," he said.

"Who?" said Vega.

"Mackey," answered Otero.

"What about Boyce?"

"He's not involved. It's all Mackey."

Cap relaxed a little bit more, now trusting Otero that there really wasn't anyone watching them from the other room or recording them from the fixtures.

"Is the tape from the Salton house?" said Vega.

Otero nodded slowly.

"There's CCTV at the Salton house?" said Cap, finding it hard to believe.

"At least one camera in one hallway, clear enough audio to hear my son say his name and what he was looking for." Then Otero became self-conscious. He spoke quickly and addressed Cap also, defending himself. "I didn't know it was in Salton when I saw it, didn't know where it was. Just knew it was my son."

"What did Mackey say he's going to do with it?" said Vega.

Otero flipped his palms up, like a magician showing nothing up his sleeves before the trick.

"Anything he wants. Right to local media. Take me and my son down in one hit. You were a cop, right?" he said to Cap, who nodded. "You know you're a commander, a chief, a DC, you have mostly friends but you got a couple of enemies with grudges. You just can't get up the line without pissing at least one guy off. Mackey knows who my guys are and they'd help him any way they could."

Cap nodded again. He got it.

Vega paused before speaking, giving Otero a chance to say whatever else he wanted to say, but he was done. That had been the core of why he'd done what he'd done, the eye at the center of the cyclone.

"I can't tell you what to do about your kid. You can talk to Caplan about it; it's above my pay grade," she said. "But you want your whole life, yours and your kid's, to be in service to Mackey?" She didn't wait for a response before she continued: "Like I said, it's up to you. You keep letting Mackey run your shit, or you come with us, we come clean with Boyce, and we find out who runs Mackey."

"How would we go about that?" Otero asked.

"Not sure," she said. "But if I were conducting my own investigation, I'd have a good person to start with."

Cap tried to read Otero but it was tough, partially because he didn't know him, but also because Cap guessed Otero truly didn't know what to do. He seemed smart, like he had lists of lists available in his memory bank at all times and right now he was thumbing through all of them, trying to predict the outcome if he made one choice or the other.

It made Cap think of Nell's first day of high school, how he said, "Just be yourself" to calm her nerves, and she'd looked at him like he had peanut vines growing out of his head. What he'd meant, of course, was follow your gut, but he knew then, and was reminded daily as a cop and a PI, what an impossible task that was. What if your gut was not a natural leader? And what if it was not to be trusted?

Cap saw that Otero was trying to get quiet and sort it through. Cap knew he shouldn't speak but more than anything he wanted to communicate via ESP or brain waves and tell Otero what he himself had learned in the middle of the woods sixteen months before, that usually nothing ends clean but if he trusted Vega, he might have a shot at it.

19

OTERO TOLD THEM NO NEED TO RUSH. THEY DIDN'T TAKE THE stairs down to the evidence room slowly, but they didn't hustle either, acting like they belonged there. Otero did, of course, and he kept up a patter of professional chitchat to make their presence seem natural as other cops passed them.

They reached the vestibule at the bottom of the stairs and Otero kept talking to them, taking the tablet from the officer guarding the evidence room. Otero punched in his code and took six fresh gloves from the box beneath the transaction window. The officer pressed the button and buzzed them in, and Otero held the armored door open for Vega and Cap as they filed in.

Otero let the door close and dropped the gloves on the steel table nearest him.

He gestured for them to follow him, walking to the left-most set of shelves. There were four boxes on the floor without lids. Bagged, not tagged, thought Vega. Otero squatted and flipped through the contents.

"You worried about your surveillance in here?" Cap said, his eyes floating up to a camera in the corner.

"No one's monitoring the feed unless the officer's not there, which is third shift only. And only then as need be. These yours?" said Otero, holding up a transparent plastic bag of clothes, including shoes, to Cap.

Cap nodded, and Otero tossed him the bag.

"Yours is the Sig or the Springfield?"

"Sig," Cap answered.

Otero handed him a baggie sized and shaped specifically for firearms, about ten inches in length, Cap's gun inside. Otero handed Vega the bag with her Springfield and sorted through more bags until he came to a larger bag full of black clothes and boots.

"You?" he said to Vega.

She nodded, and he handed her the bag. She examined the contents for a second, saw specks and streaks of the dirt from the ground outside the Salton house, and even though she couldn't see it with the shirt folded the way it was, she knew there'd be a dark, stiff patch with her dried blood directly over where Ben Davis had cut her.

"This is it," said Otero, holding up a bag with Davis's knife inside. "Looks like a handmade hunting knife, eighth inch thick." He glanced up at Vega. "Not serrated."

He offered it to her, in case she wanted to see for herself. She shook her head. Otero placed the knife back in the box and stood.

"There's men's and women's restrooms off the lobby," he said. "You can change there; I'll meet you in the lot in ten, fifteen."

"We don't need to change," said Vega. "I just want to put my boots on and holster up."

"Commander," said Cap. "What about McT?"

Otero pinched his bottom lip.

"We have to let him go through IA for now. He's on our books, in our system. We can get him out later. You two," said Otero. "You're off the grid to begin with."

"We're not going to have any problem walking out of here?" said Vega.

"I could conceivably still be in the process of questioning you," said Otero, who appeared to have thought it through. "Anyone asks, I'll cover. The way it looks now, if Mackey asks around, anyone will tell him you're in informal custody."

"Informal custody," repeated Cap. "To go along with the not-quite APB."

"Mackey wants us invisible," said Vega, her eyes wandering to the Salton boxes. "We'll stay invisible. Did you reach Boyce?"

"Not yet. I'll keep trying him but have to keep it a little discreet in case Mackey's with him."

Otero stood up and rubbed his chin with his palm, looked at the bags he'd given Cap and Vega.

"You have everything you need?" he asked them.

Vega's eyes fixed on the handles of the bolt cutters, sticking up from a box next to the wall, behind the others. She smiled at them fondly, like she'd just opened her mailbox and found a letter from an old friend.

. . .

Rodrigo Villareal worked in a diner called Athena's on the corner lot of a mall between San Diego and El Centro. Otero drove, Vega in the passenger seat, and Cap in the back. It was closing in on midnight, and Rodrigo was almost off for the night.

As they sat in the parking lot, Cap wrote and rewrote a text to McTiernan. He knew he had to be careful in the wording, not wanting to jeopardize McTiernan any more than he already was with IA, but he also wanted to run a flag up, let him know he wasn't alone.

"Text when you can" was all he could come up with, and it would have to do.

He tapped Send and picked up on Vega and Otero's conversation—she was asking about the events leading to the bust at the Salton house.

"So why the shield around Devin Lara?" she asked.

"Mackey's story is that Lara's under another investigation involving some big names down south. He didn't want to spook him," said Otero, watching the parking lot through the mirrors.

"So I level him out, he calls Mackey," said Vega.

"That tracks," Otero agreed.

"My memory after Salton's patchy," said Vega. "But before you shut the ambulance doors, I saw the girls. I saw them all get in a bus, like an inmate bus."

"Mackey sent one of his guys and said he would move them to a safe house," said Otero.

"What kind of safe house?"

Otero shook his head.

"I don't know," he admitted, sounding reflective, regretful.

Pull back, Cap thought, wishing Vega could hear him. We just got the guy on our side; let's give him a chance at redemption before we beat him up. Cap watched Vega shoot Otero a brief, not necessarily withering glance and return her gaze to straight ahead.

"What about the hospital though, right?" Cap said in his best stand-up comic voice. "That was a few kinds of fucked up."

Otero took a deep breath.

"All Mackey said was he needed to keep you two sequestered for questioning, and he needed some officers to stand guard until he could get there. We'd kept another high-profile injured suspect at the hospital a couple of months back, so we knew those floors were still technically under renovation, even though they're functional."

"Mackey never got there," said Vega. "He never came to question us."

"I think you probably broke that officer's nose and escaped before he had the chance," said Otero.

"But someone impersonating your deputy chief talked to Caplan," said Vega.

Otero's usually straight face shifted, a series of creases developing on his forehead as he turned in his seat to look at Cap.

"Posada?"

"That's who he said he was, but I've seen the real Posada on TV since. It was not him," said Cap. "And he told me to leave town."

Otero clicked his tongue against the roof of his mouth as he thought.

Vega offered her theory: "I'm thinking it was someone else who works for Mackey's boss. Maybe giving us one more chance before he tried another tactic."

Otero turned to say another thing, and Cap saw a group of young Latino guys coming out of the diner. He recognized Rodrigo in the back of the group, standing apart.

"There he is," said Cap.

Vega got out of the car and jogged over to him. Cap watched as she and Rodrigo exchanged some words, Rodrigo glancing toward the car. Finally it appeared as if Vega managed to convince him—he and Vega crossed the lot and got into the car, Rodrigo in the backseat next to Cap and Vega sitting shotgun.

Rodrigo looked from Cap to Otero and back to Vega and said, *"Dónde está McTiernan?"*

Vega answered him, and Rodrigo shook his head vehemently and placed his hand on the door handle.

"Please . . . wait, Rodrigo," said Cap.

Cap thought the kid looked thinner than the day before, his eyes narrow and pinched at the edges. His shirt had grease and ketchup stains.

Then Otero cut in. He spoke for a minute or two, keeping his voice calm and quiet, and Cap gathered from his tone that he was trying to console Rodrigo and convince him of something at the same time. Rodrigo took a breath and nodded. Cap looked to Otero for the translation.

"I said it could help other girls like his sister if he tells us what he knows. That I'm not going to arrest him or turn him in to Immigration," Otero said steadily.

Rodrigo appeared at least somewhat convinced. His fingers dropped from the handle.

"If you have something to ask, I would do it before he changes his mind," said Otero to Vega.

Vega began speaking in Spanish quickly, trying to pass as much information as possible before Rodrigo's patience ran out. Cap didn't know many words, but he picked out "hermana" and "madre."

"I asked about his mother," Vega said to Cap. "The one who was shot on the street. I said if he knows anything about it not being an accident, now's the time to say."

Rodrigo looked at Cap, and Cap wished he spoke Spanish so he could tell him this was the right thing, that he wouldn't regret it.

This seemed to be a problem for Cap lately. Restrained by various barriers, unable to say the thing he really meant, so his message had to be truncated, simplified, rolled out plainly with no extra explanation. But maybe, he thought, that wasn't always bad. So now, all he said to Rodrigo's young, pained face was "It's okay."

The kid started talking. His left leg vibrated up and down, and he rubbed his hands on his dirty jeans. His Spanish was so fast and familiar and had traces of dialects Vega didn't recognize offhand, so she had a little bit of a hard time following, but she knew she could get details later from Otero, who seemed to understand.

"We weren't always poor," Rodrigo said. "Until a couple of years ago we had a little house with food and a washing machine that worked. Microwave."

He paused and then shook his head and swiped his hand through the air like a director calling "Cut" on a set.

"We weren't rich," he said, clarifying. "We lived outside the city, where everyone is poor, but we had extra for a long time. I didn't know what my father did for a job until I was thirteen. I thought he was a driver for a lawyer in the city. Then one day I'm looking around the back room where my father kept his papers, like his office, because it was my birthday soon and I wanted to see if they were hiding a skateboard.

"In his room there's a cooler I never saw before. I thought maybe there's some beers in there I can share with my friends. So I opened it."

He paused again and bit both of his lips so that they disappeared. He moved around in his seat like he was suddenly cramped.

"Go on," said Vega.

"It was full of hands," he said, holding up his own and drawing a line along the wrist with the finger of the opposite hand. "Men's hands that were cut off. They were mostly blue," he added.

"I didn't tell anyone. When my father came home from work, I told him I had found the cooler. He wasn't angry." Rodrigo's face softened at the memory. He continued: "He said his boss wasn't a lawyer but a very important man, a man who could help us for a long time. He said we had to keep it a secret from the women, that I was a man now and had to protect them, too. He said all I had to do was never tell anyone, so I didn't."

He looked away from them now, out the window and up at the parking lot floodlight, then kept talking.

"Two years ago my father starts working more and more but there isn't as much money coming in. Then my mother is killed. My father tells me it isn't safe for me and Maricel anymore, that we should come to America and get jobs. He and my grandmother will stay behind."

Rodrigo stopped speaking. He returned his gaze to them.

"The rest is like I told you. I promise you."

He didn't seem desperate for them to believe him. He looked tired, and like he had nothing left to lose or gain by lying.

"Can I ask you," said Otero. "Do you know the name of the man your father works for?"

"Only a nickname—Lalo."

Otero leaned back on his seat like he'd been pushed in the chest.

"Who is it?" Vega said in English.

"Eduardo Montalvo," said Otero. "He's the *jefe* of one of the top two cartels out of Mexico City."

"And Rodrigo's father worked for him," said Cap, putting it together from the Spanish he knew and Otero's reaction.

"Yep," said Vega, quickly recalling the rest of Rodrigo's story. She switched back to Spanish and asked him: "Did you know the other people in the car, in the trunk with you when you crossed the border? The other girls or the driver?"

"I didn't know the driver. Not even his name. We knew the girls," said Rodrigo. "They were from families we knew."

"Do you remember their names?" asked Vega.

"Dulce Díaz and Catalina Checado," he said right away.

"Checado," Vega repeated. Then to Otero and Cap, "There was a girl in the house they called Chicago. She had a burn mark on her head from Rafa. I found her in one of the downstairs rooms with a john."

"To Davis's ear," said Otero, "Chicago would be an easy nickname for Checado."

"How old was Catalina Checado?" said Vega to Rodrigo.

He shrugged, said sixteen or seventeen.

"And Dulce Díaz?" Vega asked.

"Twelve or thirteen."

Vega paused, reached for her phone, and searched for a picture.

Otero continued: "Did the fathers of these girls work for Lalo, too?"

Rodrigo answered immediately: "Yes, that's how we knew them. Our families were all friends."

"The other families sent the other girls for the same reason, because there was no money?"

"I think so," said Rodrigo. "All the money had stopped coming."

Otero caught Vega's eye at that; he seemed to be trying to tell her something. Vega nodded at him.

"Is this Dulce Díaz?" Vega said, handing him her phone.

It was the head shot of Jane 1, after the brain had been removed. It was clear the scalp was a separate piece; it appeared to balance on the frame of the face somewhat loosely.

Rodrigo winced briefly, then thrust Vega's phone back at her.

"Yes," he said, turning toward the window. "That's her. I've known her since her first communion."

"So she, and Maricel and Catalina Checado—all three of them went with Coyote Ben when you got here?" Vega said.

Rodrigo nodded and hit his forehead with his palm twice.

"It doesn't matter to me anymore," he said, angry. "If I go back home, if I stay here. I don't care if I wash dishes or clean the toilet. I did that one thing. I let her go. I let them all go."

He poked at his own chest and sighed irritably, then looked up to Vega and said, "Can you take me to my shitty house now, please? I have nothing left."

They dropped Rodrigo off at his house, and Otero did not wait for him to get inside before driving away. He also didn't wait a full second after Rodrigo got out before he started talking.

"If the money ran out for his family two years ago, that tracks with the time line of Lalo Montalvo's cartel," he began. "Perez started to edge them out about two years ago—that's when we started to see more tunnels, but Montalvo couldn't keep up. He's still in business but hanging on by a string."

"So all the girls, or these three at least—all their fathers worked for Montalvo. So we think Mackey has something to do with the trafficking of these particular girls?" said Cap.

"Who wants him to do that?" Otero posed.

No one answered right away.

Then Cap said, "Maybe it's Montalvo."

Otero's eyes batted back and forth as he thought about it.

"He sends his employees' daughters here to Mackey to protect them so he traps them as sex workers?" he said, disbelieving. "There's a lot not fitting there."

"Lara might know. I'm thinking he's the link between Mackey and the Salton house. Any idea where we can find him?" Vega asked Otero.

"I heard he was released against the advice of medical personnel from the ER of UCSD Med earlier today," said Otero. Then in defense, "They couldn't make him stay, and we didn't have a thing to hold him on."

"Recuperating at home?" said Cap hopefully.

"Or headed to the airport. Let's not waste time looking for him," said Otero, tapping on his phone. "I'll have someone survey his residence, try to confirm if he's there."

"Meantime?" said Cap.

"Let's go back to the guys in the house," said Vega, as she typed an email to the Bastard.

"Davis," said Cap.

"Do you know where he is?" Vega asked Otero.

"He was at Southland Gate, where you two were, but then he was moved to County General, near the station, so he can be charged and arraigned after he's released."

"He may know who the real boss is, or have some ideas," said Vega.

"Unless all he knows is he works for Mackey and/or Lara," said Otero, watching the traffic ahead.

"Worth an ask," said Vega.

"I'd like to join you with Davis," said Otero, stern and courteous.

"I'm fine with that," she said. "And we're still not going to have any problem moving around?"

"Not with me you won't," Otero said. "I don't expect Mackey to be there."

"Has he contacted you since we came in?"

"No," said Otero. "I texted him that the situation was controlled. Far as he knows, I have you both."

Vega glanced at Cap in the side mirror. He was looking at his phone, the glow from the screen reflected on his face. She could see the circular burn mark on his temple.

"The fat guy with the Glock who I clipped in the elbow and the knee?" she asked Otero. "Is he there, too?"

"Yes, he's conscious. I think the wounds were messy but fairly superficial," said Otero. "The other one's there, too, the really big guy. I can't imagine he's awake and coherent yet. You got him in both legs."

Cap finally met her eye in the mirror, and she saw it all right there. Gun-shyness, hesitation, fear, all ringing out in concentric circles from the trauma.

"Good," said Vega.

Otero raised an eyebrow.

"Cap can take the fat man if that's okay with you," she said to Otero, who nodded.

It was after midnight now, the cars sporadic, the sky deep and dark. Vega spread out the fingers of her right hand and then made a fist, skin stretched tight over the knuckles so she could see every vein and bone in the passing freeway lights.

Second hospital in one day.

Cap felt his shoulders tense up around his neck as they entered the main lobby, Otero not needing to flash a badge as most people seemed to know who he was: the women at the front desk, security guards, and when they reached the fourth floor, the uniformed officers placed in the hallway and at the nurses' station.

Otero stepped away from them to speak to an officer guarding a room. Cap heard the hospital noises: the phones, the machinery, the low chatter of the nurses. He winced at the lights.

"You okay?" said Vega.

He nodded quickly.

"You can take this guy, Fat Mitch?"

"That's his name?" said Cap.

Vega made a face, eye roll plus lip contraction. Cap thought that if someone could shrug with her face, it would be what she was doing right then.

"What about you and Davis?" he asked.

Vega straightened out her features, and now her expression was calm and cold, reminded Cap of a time right after he'd first met her, when she'd caught a skip lowlife Cap had been looking for and shoved him in her trunk. She'd brought him to Cap as an offering and an example of exactly what she was capable of. That day on the street outside his house in Denville, he felt like he saw the first flash of who she really was and that was someone to avoid fucking with.

"Hopefully they gave him a mouth guard or something," she said, tapping her top row of teeth. "So he can talk."

"You guys will have a lot to catch up on," said Cap. "So much has happened since you saw each other last."

Vega smirked at Cap's joke, and he didn't know if she actually thought it was funny or was just trying to make him feel good. He didn't care much. At this moment, he knew he'd take a smirk from Alice Vega over a full-face all-teeth smile from almost anyone on or off the planet.

Ben Davis had his eyes closed when Vega and Otero came into the room. He was in a gown, and his ankle was in a sling with a cast over his entire leg running up to his hip where Vega had hit him with the bolt cutters. He was wearing some kind of headgear on his face, a blue chin guard and a brace on his forehead connected by a thin metal rod, four thin wires running into the corners of his mouth. Other than the wires, his lips were sealed shut, a brown line of dried blood between them, the half of his face from the nose down mottled with purple and blue bruising.

Otero advanced to one side of the bed and looked Davis up and down. Vega didn't know him very well, so it was impossible to be sure, but it seemed to her he was impressed.

"Mr. Davis," Otero said quietly.

Davis's eyes opened immediately; he had not been asleep. He turned his head to Otero and flinched at the pain. He slowly returned his head to its previous centered position and then caught sight of Vega standing by the open door. He began to scoot his body upward onto the bed, like he was trying to get away from her, pushing with his arms off the mattress, and then screamed through his closed mouth.

Vega waved and called, "Hey, bro."

Davis made another sound, his head coming off the pillow like he was trying to point at her with it. Tears budded from his eyes.

"Relax, Mr. Davis. Ms. Vega can stay over by the door if it makes you more comfortable. Does it make you more comfortable?" said Otero.

Davis looked back and forth between the two of them and nodded.

"Okay. We met this morning, though you may not remember me," said Otero, crossing his arms. "I'm Commander Otero of the SDPD, and we'd like to ask you a few preliminary questions, before you're charged."

Davis shrugged and pointed to his mouth, glared at Otero like he was a dummy.

"I see you have some unusual challenges, but I've done a lot of inter-rogations in my career," he said as he glanced around the room. "I've learned to get creative."

Otero picked up a small whiteboard with a black marker attached on a cord from one of the bedside trays. On it was written "TOILET WATER FOOD."

"Here we go," said Otero, taking a tissue from a box, also on the tray.

He wiped the whiteboard clean and handed it to Davis.

"Good thing your hands are okay," joked Otero.

Vega was genuinely beginning to grow fond of him.

Davis wrote something quickly on the whiteboard and flipped it so Vega and Otero could see.

"HER. OUT."

Otero shook his head and said, "I'm sorry, Mr. Davis, Ms. Vega and I are working together now, so I need her here, I'm afraid."

He didn't give Davis a chance to write down an objection before launching into the first question.

"Can you please write down the name or names of who was paying you to run the Salton house?"

Davis nodded and scrawled something, flipped the whiteboard again.

"1. FUCK. 2. OFF."

Otero smiled politely and turned to Vega.

Vega kicked up the doorstop with her foot, and slowly the door closed, making a sound like air getting pumped into a bike tire. She walked toward the bed, taking her time.

"Mr. Davis, I've known Ms. Vega only a short time," said Otero. "I don't mind telling you, it doesn't appear she suffers fools."

Vega pulled up a wheeled stool and sat on it near the foot of the bed, right next to Davis's leg in the cast, but a bit too far for him to grab her if he lunged forward.

Vega reached her arm out toward his leg, and his eyes grew. Again he pushed up on the bed with his arms but didn't have a lot of range of motion. Otero watched her intently, didn't seem about to stop her but had a look in his eye like he might intervene at some point soon.

She extended her index finger, tapped three times on Davis's cast, like she was testing the quality. She pulled her arm back and said nothing, didn't need to, enjoyed knowing that all that was between them, at most, was a little plaster.

Cap stepped into the room and recognized the fat man from the waiting room at the Salton house. He had no shirt on, just white boxer briefs and a thick tan bandage wrapped around his right elbow multiple times, his right leg propped up on pillows with another bandage around the knee, his left ankle chained to the bed rail by leg irons.

"Who the fuck are you?" he said to Cap, his voice low and phlegmy.

"Max Caplan," said Cap. "I'm working with the police. You're Mitch, right?"

"That's what white people call me, yeah," he said. "You got any candy?"

"No."

"I'm not answering any questions unless I get some chocolate or something with a little peanut butter in it. Even chips, okay? I'm hungry, and the food here is shit."

Cap approached the bed but didn't sit.

"I'll see what we can do for you," he said. "But I need to know you have information that's a little useful first."

Mitch sighed and shifted his body to the right. He had a layer of sweat glossing his skin, his breasts resting on his stomach like sacks of rice.

"And, Mitch—Fat Mitch, right?" said Cap, not waiting for confirmation of the nickname. "I hate to break it to you, but you don't really have much of a choice here."

Mitch sneered and grabbed a washcloth from the tray attached to his bed, mopped his forehead.

"You know a guy named Devin Lara?" said Cap.

"Yeah, sure."

"Was he your boss?"

Mitch shrugged, grabbed an empty plastic Jell-O cup from the tray next to him.

"He gave us the money, made sure we had everything we need."

"So just to be clear," said Cap. "Devin Lara paid Ben Davis to run the house in Salton, and Davis hired you."

Mitch laughed, swept his finger inside of the Jell-O cup.

"Yeah, man, you want me to sign something, I'll sign whatever you want," he said, licking his finger.

"Something funny?" said Cap.

Mitch shrugged, tossed the Jell-O cup on the floor.

"You think going to jail for homicide for the rest of your life will be funny, too?" said Cap.

Mitch lifted up one breast and wiped the sweat under it with a washcloth, then let it drop and lifted the other.

"I didn't kill anyone," he said, not sounding too concerned. "I found them girls in the bathroom. Rafa, he's my boy but he's a little crazy. Gets carried away. It's not the first time. *You* know what I'm saying, *vato*," he said, tapping his temple right where Rafa had hooked Cap up to the machine.

Cap resisted the temptation to touch the burn, determined to keep pressing.

"Did you know Maricel Villareal and Dulce Díaz?"

Mitch shrugged lazily.

"I'm not so good with names," he said.

"Those are the girls Rafa murdered," Cap said slowly.

"Oh yeah," Mitch said, as if he were remembering an old friend. "The first one he found a spot for, but the second one, I guess he didn't have too much time to think about it so he said he just dropped her in the middle of the night." Mitch shrugged again. "I don't know, man—it was his mess, I told him he had to clean it."

Cap gritted his teeth again. He had the distinct feeling that Mitch wasn't taking any of this very seriously, and as he stared at the empty Jell-O cup on the floor, he realized he could change that.

Vega lifted up her shirt on the side and showed the bandage to Davis.

"You got me pretty good, you know," she said.

Davis stared at her, his eyes big and wet, as he breathed heavily through his nose. Vega dropped her shirt, rolled her stool to the left, closer to his head. She pulled out her phone and swiped around with her thumb.

"I'm going to say things, and you can nod or shake your head. How about if you nod right now to show us you understand," said Vega, still looking at her phone.

Davis didn't nod, made a quick mark on the whiteboard and turned it around so Vega could see. He had drawn a circle around the "1. FUCK. 2. OFF."

Vega glanced at the whiteboard and then held up her phone to him.

"So you want me to tell your mom you can't make it to the barbecue?"

Davis's eyes bugged, and he huffed through his nose, blowing mucus onto his upper lip.

"She's got a lot of cute stuff on her Facebook feed," said Vega, tapping the screen. "Kittens playing with grapes and things like that."

Now Davis's eyes grew small as he seethed. He furiously erased what was on the whiteboard with his palm, scrawled new words, and showed it to Vega.

She read it aloud: "DON'T GO NEAR HER."

Vega glanced over at Otero, who took a step back and leaned against the wall. Though he kept a straight face, Vega took his lack of concern as an implicit approval.

Davis turned the whiteboard around again to erase it and write something else. He flipped the board around, the surface ashy with the smeared marks of previous messages with the new words scrawled, thick and messy.

"STAY AWAY BITCH" it read.

"Huh," said Vega, like she'd just learned an interesting nature fact, smiling at him, impressed. Then she continued: "I'll make you a deal," she said, pointing to the whiteboard. "Wait, I'm the bitch, right?" she said, purely for clarification. "You don't have to answer that one. But my other questions, you can answer by nodding or shaking your head no, and then if you answer them I will stay away from your mommy and not fuck her teeth up with my bolt cutters, okay?"

Davis gripped the whiteboard and glared at Vega.

"That door is closed," she said, pointing behind her. Then she pointed to Otero: "He's a police commander, and he's good with whatever I do here. Nod to show me you understand now."

Slowly, he nodded.

Vega continued; now it was easy.

"You've been a coyote for a while, right, helping people cross the border illegally for money?"

Davis nodded.

"When did you start the business in Salton? Was it more than a year ago?"

Nod. He pinched his fingers together.

"A little longer than a year ago?"

Nod.

"Did anyone give you any financial assistance with regards to starting the business?"

Nod.

Vega paused, thought she'd take a swipe.

"Was it Devin Lara?"

Nod.

"You staffed the house with undocumented underage girls?"

Nod.

"Did Devin Lara bring you the girls named Maricel Villareal, Catalina Checado, Dulce Díaz, and one more?"

Davis shook his head emphatically.

Vega glanced at Otero.

Then she asked, "Was it a guy that Devin Lara introduced you to?"

Nod.

"Was it Michael Mackey?"

Nod.

"Mackey brought you four girls."

Davis shook his head. Held up six fingers.

"Six girls," she said.

Davis nodded.

"You got IUDs from Antonio LoSanto and then hired Scott Miller to do the procedures."

Nod.

"You gave LoSanto a few thousand but offered Miller more."

Davis didn't nod or shake his head. He held his hand out flat and tipped it side to side. So-so.

"You didn't offer Miller more. He demanded it," said Vega, the realization setting in as she spoke.

Davis nodded.

"He found out you had a resource for bigger money, maybe threatened to call the authorities unless you gave him a cut."

Nod.

Vega paused, rewound. Then she continued: "So Mackey brought you six girls. Two of them turned up dead. How'd that happen?"

Davis wiped the whiteboard with the corner of his sheet and wrote down some letters. He was eager to flip the board and show them his response: "RAFA."

Vega glanced briefly at Otero. Davis hadn't seemed to wrestle a lot with that one.

"Do you know who Mackey's working for?" she said.

Davis didn't nod. He looked from Vega to Otero and back again. Now he was wrestling.

Otero paused, then said, "I want you to listen carefully to the question I'm going to ask you, and I want you to think about your answer. It doesn't do you any good to lie to us right now. You're looking at a respectable turn in a state prison no matter what you do or say, but if you tell us the truth now, it will go a ways with our DA in softening the sentence request."

Davis blinked his eyes a few times, snorting through his nose. He tilted his head down in a subtle nod.

"Is Mackey's boss Lalo Montalvo?" said Otero.

It was hard for Vega to discern Davis's exact expression with the apparatus over his face, his cheeks and jaw and chin swollen like a water balloon, but he continued to blink frantically, and then pressed his fists into the bed and brought his head off the pillow, lifted his torso off the mattress, and swiveled side to side in a full upper-body shake to tell them no.

Cap fed dollars into the vending machine in the waiting room, one after another. He pressed a few sets of buttons, numbers and letters, and watched the packages fall into the well—Lay's Classic, Ruffles cheddar & sour cream, Hot Cheetos, Reese's, M&M's, Snickers, the Kit Kat that was one big bar as opposed to the four little perforated sticks.

Cap stuffed the candy into his pants pockets and held the chips in his hands, pinning a bag of Doritos under his chin. He walked back to Mitch's room, blinked at the officer, who smirked at him and opened the door to let him in. Cap thanked him and went inside.

Mitch was still awake, eating a cup of cold oatmeal. Cap sat in a chair next to the door.

"Aw fucking right," said Mitch. "Bring that shit over here, yo."

Cap set all of the bags down on his lap, candy bars falling out of his pockets to the floor; he did not reach to pick them up.

"Uh, no," said Cap, tearing open the bag of M&M's. He poured them into his mouth. "I'm going to eat every motherfucking one of these snacks in front of you unless you tell me what I need to know."

Mitch threw his oatmeal cup toward Cap and it landed about a foot away from him with a sad thud.

"Give me the fucking chocolate, *puto,* or—"

"What, Mitch," said Cap, his mouth full. "You gonna do a magic trick and get out of that leg iron?"

Cap dropped the empty M&M's bag to the ground and opened the Reese's cups.

"These are the kind that have the Reese's pieces inside," he said, then shoved a whole disk into his mouth.

Mitch pulled at his hair and let out a shriek of frustration. Cap had of course heard of people addicted to sugar and that it could be as bad as drugs but had never seen the evidence before now. Mitch looked crazy, his eyes manic, jostling from side to side in the bed, his rolls of flesh undulating. He batted at his cheeks like he was trying to wake himself up from a nightmare.

"Who sent Maricel Villareal, Catalina Checado, and Dulce Díaz to the Salton house?" said Cap, swallowing the second peanut butter cup.

"Fuck you, man. You gonna find out soon enough."

Cap shrugged, dropped the Reese's wrapper at his feet, and opened the giant Kit Kat.

"Never had one of these before," he said, pointing it at Mitch.

He took a huge bite and briefly wished he'd stopped at the soda machine as well but pushed through it, the chocolate and the wafers grainy on his tongue and throat.

"It's really good," said Cap. "Tastes like the regular Kit Kats. Just bigger is all."

"Come on," said Mitch, his desperation molding the anger into pure begging. "It doesn't matter if I tell you shit or not."

Cap forced the rest of the Kit Kat down and then tore open the Snickers.

"This is the last candy," Cap said, holding it up in the air. "Was it Lalo Montalvo who sent those girls?"

Mitch's eyes followed the Snickers but then he registered what Cap had said and shook his head.

"Montalvo?" he said, bewildered. "You crazy?"

"Why do you ask if I'm crazy? Why do you say that?" said Cap, lowering the Snickers.

"'Cause you say you with the cops, you don't know Montalvo's good as gone," said Mitch, sitting up, trying to scoot his upper body forward, perhaps hoping to inch the whole bed closer to Cap and the candy.

"Okay," said Cap. "Not Montalvo, who?"

"The one guy left, man. Last man standing."

Then Cap pulled the name from the wreckage that had accrued in his memory from the past few days.

"Perez," he said.

"Shit, yeah, Perez," echoed Mitch, as if he'd given Cap the name a hundred times.

"The last man standing," said Cap.

"Yeah, I will tell you this, I'm glad I got these leg cuffs and that cop outside, and I might get a lawyer and go to a nice California state prison because if I wasn't, Perro Perez would kill me and do all kind of shit to my body before and after."

Cap was only half-listening to him, realizing they'd had the story all wrong.

"So it's all good that nasty bitch shot me," said Mitch. "Now give me the fucking chocolate!"

Cap stood up, all of the bags of chips dropping to the floor. He knew he had to find Vega.

"Give it to me, man!" yelled Mitch, shaking the rails of the bed.

Cap stripped the wrapper off the Snickers in one piece like it was a banana peel.

"This is for calling my girl a nasty bitch," he said, and he crammed as much of the Snickers as could fit into his mouth, trying to mash it with his molars as it barreled toward his throat.

Mitch screamed unnaturally high for a man, Cap thought as he ran from the room. He labored to chew the candy bar, debated spitting it out but thought it would be less messy just to swallow it now.

Vega rushed around the corner of the hallway toward him, followed by Otero on his phone. Mitch continued to yell in his room, and the officer on watch seemed undisturbed by it, swiping around on his phone screen with his thumb.

Cap continued to aggressively chew and swallow the Snickers, his mouth still full.

"It's Perez," he tried to say, but it came out garbled. There was just too much nougat.

"What are you eating?" Vega said, more fascinated than disgusted.

Cap could only point to his mouth, trying to indicate he'd be done soon.

"They don't work for Montalvo," said Vega.

"I know," said Cap, finally swallowing. "It's Perez. Mitch says he's relieved to go to an American prison so Perez won't get a chance to kill him." Cap nodded back to Otero. "Who's he talking to?"

"Boyce. Otero thinks maybe we should meet up."

Vega and Cap began heading toward the end of the hall, where the elevators were. Otero trailed behind them, still on the phone, his voice low.

Cap stopped at the open door and peered into the room. A female officer was guarding it, sipping an iced coffee drink through a straw. She put her arm out to block Cap from entering but then saw Otero, who pointed to Cap and gave a thumbs-up. The guard lowered her arm, and Cap took a step into the room.

It was Rafa in the bed, asleep, an oxygen mask over his mouth and nose. He wore a hospital gown, both of his legs bandaged and elevated in slings. He was so tall and broad his body seemed to cover every inch of the bed, his head well above the pillow, lolling backward.

Cap didn't realize he'd shut his eyes, but quickly he flashed on Rafa standing over him in the shed, felt the adhesive of the electrode patch on his temple.

"Caplan," said Vega.

Cap's eyes shot open.

"It's okay," said Vega. "He's not conscious. Let's go."

Cap didn't move, so Vega placed her hand on his arm and gently pulled him toward the door. He let her direct him for a second, then seemed to wake up when they stepped out of the room.

Otero approached them and was hanging up on his call.

"Boyce says he's open to meeting," he said, heading to the elevators.

"What if he's in on it?" said Cap, pressing the Down button.

"He's not," said Otero. "He's skeptical of us as it is. Whatever he might think of Mackey, he's still his partner."

The doors opened, and they all went inside.

"He thinks we're making this up?" said Cap, getting huffy.

"Not exactly," said Otero. "I can appreciate this is a lot for him to take in."

"You didn't seem to have a problem with it," Cap said, hitting the P button for the parking level. "And we have two corroborating accomplices—Davis and Mitch."

"We'll lay out every piece of evidence we have," said Otero.

"Mackey still thinks you have us contained?" said Vega, checking her phone for new messages.

"That's right," said Otero.

"He still thinks he has you contained," said Cap as the elevator doors opened.

Otero nodded solemnly, said, "Yes."

"He's mistaken," said Cap.

"Very much," said Otero, starting to head toward his car.

"What if we bring Boyce another witness?" said Vega, standing still.

Cap and Otero turned to her.

"If you're talking about Lara, we may be out of luck there," said Otero, holding up his phone. "My officer said residence appears dark, no car in the driveway."

"Okay then," said Vega. "How do you feel about dropping us off at our hotel, starting with Boyce solo, and then Caplan and I will catch up with both of you in an hour or two?"

Otero stared at her, a little mystified.

"I have mixed feelings about it," he said. "Why do we think it's a good tactic to split up?"

"Devin Lara took an Uber from the hospital at five twelve p.m. to an address in La Jolla," said Vega, waving her phone back at Otero. "I say Cap and I drive out there and see if we might convince him to turn himself in. Might be better if you're not there."

Vega added an unexpectedly girlish shrug, and Cap laughed under his breath.

Cap replaced his laughter with a cough and said, "She can be pretty convincing."

20

THE ADDRESS IN LA JOLLA BELONGED TO A NARROW TWO-STORY townhome with a shingled wood exterior—an effort meant to evoke a tree house, Cap thought. He began to pull the rental into a space across the street when Vega interrupted him.

"You can park right in front," she said, unbuckling her seatbelt.

It had not taken them long to get there, and they hadn't had time to discuss an exact plan, or any plan, really. Still, Cap was surprised at Vega's lack of concern about being seen.

"Should I come with you?" he said, as he made a U-turn.

"No, stay here."

Vega opened the door as Cap pulled closer to the curb.

"Wait, let me stop the car," he said.

"I'm good," she said, sticking her foot out. "Keep the engine running."

"Well," he said, sincerely trying to figure out how to be useful. "I'm coming in after fifteen if I don't hear from you."

"I'll be back in five," Vega said, getting out of the car.

"Then I'm coming in after five."

"Don't come in," said Vega through the window, over her shoulder.

Cap watched her go up the path, press her thumb against the buzzer and leave it there, then knock on the door with her fist. The door opened, and a tall, tan woman appeared, her hair long and wavy as if she'd just come from the beach. She wore a satin kimono and appeared very upset. Vega pushed right past her and disappeared from Cap's sight.

Cap felt something between a hunch and a premonition scrabbling toward the surface of his chest. He couldn't have explained why if someone had asked him, but he just knew he should pop the trunk. So he did.

A minute passed, and he stretched his neck and squinted, trying to discern any movement of shadows inside the house, but saw only closed tan shutters. He caught a glimpse of his reflection in the rearview and brushed the C-shaped curls right above his forehead with his fingers. His hair was still mostly dark with some streaks of gray, but sometimes he wondered what he would do when it flipped, when it turned more gray than black, would he be a man who dyed his hair? He'd never planned on it, but it was shocking to see the gray spread like blight on tree bark day by day, and in the past few days, considerably.

He glanced back at the clock on the dashboard. It had been four minutes. One more, and he would go.

Lara wasn't as solid as he looked, Vega thought as she pulled him by his moussed hair. It was helpful because he was still walking, though he was bent over sideways almost at a perfect right angle, shuddering from the pain of where she had kneed him in the kidney. He coughed and hacked, bloody saliva spraying from his mouth around his bandage-wrapped tongue.

Cap stood next to the car, the driver's side door open.

"Everything okay?" he said.

"Pop the trunk," said Vega.

"It's open," said Cap.

Vega yanked Lara with one hand toward the back of the car and lifted the lid with her other. Lara screamed, the sound garbled, as he tried feebly to pull away from the trunk. Vega grabbed his chin.

"You want double-kidney contusions?" she said.

Lara's eyes batted back and forth as he thought about it.

"Then get in the motherfucking trunk, French Kiss."

Vega heaved him by the shoulders into the trunk, and his body began to collapse against the fender as he screamed again. She lifted his legs and tossed them in like they were sacks of flour. Then she slammed the lid shut.

She walked around the car and got into the passenger seat, the cut on her side giving off a tiny pulse.

"Where's the woman?" said Cap, buckling his seatbelt.

"Inside," said Vega. "She's got other things on her mind."

"Is he going to expire from a kidney injury in there?" said Cap, glancing back toward the sounds of Lara thrashing around.

"Not likely. I really didn't knee him that hard," said Vega, snapping in her belt. "Hey," she said, realizing something. "Thanks for getting the trunk."

Cap nodded and sped away from the curb. Vega stared at his profile and listened to Lara's sporadic muffled thumps, just like the pounding of her twisted-up heart.

Vega walked into the sushi restaurant with the sign in the window glowing, OPEN 24 HRS. The place looked like a diner from the outside, and inside there was a long buffet in the middle of the room filled with ice, with platters of jewel-toned fish on top. It turned out there weren't many people eating sushi in San Diego at two in the morning, and Vega spotted Boyce and Otero right away, sitting at a booth in the back.

They stood up as she approached, and Boyce shook her hand and sat back down. He had a plate in front of him with the remnants of a meal—half a rice ball and a smear of wasabi.

Vega thought he looked wearier than when she'd met him, the clean-cut sheen rubbed off, stubble on his cheeks, hair mussed by stress and not style.

"Ms. Vega," said Boyce. "Please sit."

"I'm good," she said, still standing.

"Suit yourself," said Boyce.

Otero searched Vega's eyes for clues, but she gave him none.

"So," said Boyce with an air of false cheer. "Commander Otero has provided quite a report on my partner."

He might appear tired, thought Vega, but he still exuded arrogance.

"I take it you don't believe him," said Vega.

"I didn't say that," said Boyce. "I haven't been able to reach Agent Mackey in over twenty-four hours. I was cc'd on an email today from ISC, saying delivery of six girls to a detention facility was complete."

"ISC," said Vega. "Immigration?"

"Yes," said Boyce. "Now I can't tell you exactly what Mackey's into, but I can tell you I am rubbed the wrong way he did it in plain sight right in front of me. That said, all of . . ." he said, waving a chopstick toward Otero like a magic wand. "Please understand it's a lot to swallow."

"Even though we have Ben Davis and the fat man corroborating what the commander's telling you?"

"I have to think about it in terms of what I can prove, and the word of two lowlife pimps won't go far against an agent's," he said, matter-of-fact.

"Because Mackey's so reliable?" said Vega.

Boyce coughed into his fist.

"Look, he's reliable but has never been a standout. He gets promoted because he puts in the hours, not because of any exceptional performance."

"Unlike you," Vega piped in, without a whiff of sarcasm.

"That's correct," said Boyce. "Unlike me. I've worked with him eight years, and last year, I got promoted to senior supervisory agent even though he and I are about the same age and worked for the shop the same number of years."

Otero folded his arms patiently and didn't speak. Now Vega tried to catch his eye but he stared straight ahead, focused on Boyce.

"That's fine," said Vega, moving on. "I have a question for you though, if you don't mind."

"Of course," Boyce said, borderline chivalrous.

"Whose idea was it to pay me off the books?" said Vega. "To hire a consultant to do what would normally be a police case or a federal investigation?"

Boyce answered right away and didn't flinch.

"About a year and a half ago, we were told by brass to delegate and prioritize, which is code for spread yourselves as thin as plastic wrap and dump cases whenever you can."

He spun the chopstick around slowly with his fingers.

"They've bound us, see, because they want us involved in any narcotic-substance-related business but they don't want to pay for all of it. So as a result—"

"You end up hiring consultants," Vega finished.

"Yes," he said. "It's not unusual."

"And the cash?" said Vega.

Boyce looked at her as if he were surprised by the question.

"You said your people didn't want to pay for this kind of case, so who did?" said Vega.

"I did, Ms. Vega," he said. "When Commander Otero contacted us, I knew that two dead Mexican girls would be near permanently parked on the back burner. My supervisor didn't want us spending real time on it, so I outsourced. It's not the first time I've spent my own money."

He continued to spin the chopstick around with his index, middle, and ring fingers, slower now than before. He stared at the center of the stick, making its way over his knuckles.

"I don't do it to be noble," he said plainly. "The more cases that get wrapped up, the easier my work is."

They were all silent for a moment, and then Vega reached out and swiped the chopstick out of Boyce's hand.

"That's a lot to swallow, too," she said. "No offense."

Boyce sat back against the seat of the booth and shrugged.

"It's the only truth there is."

"I like that," Vega said, pointing the chopstick at him. "So what if we can get you the guy who links Mackey to Davis?"

Otero stood up and turned his head to look out the restaurant window.

"Who are we talking about?" said Boyce, grabbing his jacket and standing.

"You convinced him?" Otero said in disbelief.

"I did," said Vega. "He's in my partner's car. Waiting."

Cap leaned against the rental and saw Vega, Otero, and a man he assumed to be Boyce emerge from the restaurant. They hurried toward him, the men in more of a rush than Vega, who hung back.

"Evening," Cap said, chipper. "Agent Boyce, right? Max Caplan."

Boyce shook his hand distractedly, as he and Otero paced alongside the car.

"So where is he?" said Boyce.

Cap glanced at Vega, who nodded. Then he clicked the button on the fob, and the trunk popped open. They heard a hoarse, stifled scream.

"What in the hell," said Boyce, going to the trunk.

Otero followed him, whispering at Vega and Cap as he passed: "*This is convincing?*"

Lara waved his arms and struggled to sit up. Otero hooked one of Lara's arms around his shoulders and pulled him out of the trunk. Lara, still slightly hunched to the side, pointed at Vega angrily.

"Do you need medical attention, Mr. Lara?" asked Otero.

Lara nodded vehemently.

"Ms. Vega," said Boyce, slipping on the patronizing tone like a pair of socks. "I know you and Mr. Caplan aren't police and probably don't have a background in criminal law, but any confession you received from Mr. Lara under duress won't be admissible in any investigation, much less a court."

"Shoot, yeah, I thought that might be the case," said Vega, pulling out her phone. She found a photo and flipped the phone around so Boyce and Otero could see.

She and Cap watched their faces open up with insight.

"So these are the pounds of cocaine on Lara's girlfriend's kitchen table. She was pretty accommodating when I was there and said she gets all of her drugs from him," Vega said, gesturing to Lara.

He grunted and reached for the phone. Vega held it over her shoulder, reminded her of playing Keep-Away as a kid.

"She forwarded me some emails and texts to prove it, too," said Vega. "I told her you'd let her off the hook if she stayed out of my way."

Boyce and Otero took it in.

"You're in no position to coordinate a plea deal, Ms. Vega," Boyce said.

"It was all pretty informal," she said, tapping on her phone. "But I figure, you go easy on her, then you can roll this sack of shit, and he can roll Mackey. That's how this works, right?"

Cap leaned on the hood and watched the tension wash out of Otero's face. They looked to Boyce. Even Lara, stooped and shivering, seemed to know it was all over.

After Boyce left with Lara cuffed in the backseat, Otero stayed with Cap and Vega by the rental car and began to talk out logistics.

"After Boyce talks to his superior, Deputy Radkin, we can find out where Mackey dropped the six girls," Otero said as he checked his phone.

"Commander," said Vega, over the roof of the car before she got into the passenger seat. "You sure you're ready for whatever's coming after that, for your son?"

Otero paused for only a second, then nodded.

"There is a message that keeps coming back in my life," he said to them. "Take the hit now. Stay on your feet later."

Cap and Vega nodded in approval, and Otero knocked twice on the roof.

"Time to go home," he said.

"Commander," said Cap. "We can keep going, if you need us to make calls or sort through paperwork. I'm really good with paperwork."

"All due respect, Mr. Caplan, you've both undergone fairly severe physical trauma today. You need some sleep or neither of you will be much use to me tomorrow."

Cap geared up to argue but then looked at Vega, her face still pale from losing and regaining blood a couple of times, her lips looking drawn and her eyes, usually huge and glassy in her face, now small with the skin above her lids wilting.

"I guess we might be able to shut our eyes awhile," said Cap.

They said goodbye to Otero and watched him drive away.

"Give me the keys, okay?" said Vega.

"Come on," he said weakly. "You're barely recovering from a near-fatal knife wound."

"Brain injury beats knife wound," said Vega, pointing at his head.

Cap didn't have the energy to argue. He handed her the fob and slid into the passenger seat. He closed his eyes as she started the car.

He felt his body sink into the seat and leaned his head against the cool window as Vega drove them over empty freeways. He'd been awake at the hospital, rejuvenated after the blast of caffeine and sugar from the candy, but now, after giving himself permission to rest, it seemed to drape over his body like a wool blanket that covered his eyes first, then all the way down to his toes until he was out.

Vega tried the handstand.

She flattened her hands on the nubby hotel carpet and straightened her arms, kicked her legs up and hung there, but she knew she could hold it for only about ten seconds just with the strength of her arms alone, without using her stomach muscles. She held her breath and tightened all her abs. The cut throbbed, but not severely. She stayed put for a minute, sweat beginning to drip down her chin, over her lips, and into her nose.

Then the cut really started to sing, the pain shooting all the way around Vega's torso, feeling like a belt cinching tighter and tighter, and after another minute, her arms shaking, fingernails digging into the carpet, she brought her legs down one at a time and gasped as her butt hit the floor.

She sat there, breathed through it, and gradually the pain lessened. She stood and went to the bathroom, took a shower and kept her right side out of the direct stream. Afterward, she gently toweled off and changed her bandage, trying to replicate Mia's method of taping. She got dressed in clean black clothes—underwear, bra, fitted T-shirt, pants, boots. Brushed her hair and pulled it back in a short ponytail. Holster, gun, jacket.

She picked up her phone from the bedside table and pulled out the charging cord. 100 percent.

She stepped outside, and the sun was up already, cars on the freeway. It was past seven, and she'd slept in two hours longer than usual. She thought about going to get tea and coffee, some messy egg sandwich for Cap and a bar for herself, but then she thought she'd just wait for him outside his room so she could be right there when he woke up.

Cap woke up after a hard sleep, showered, shaved, and got dressed. He texted Nell that everything continued to be fine and he'd be home soon, figuring there was no need to get into the whole story of the day before since he would be there, maybe within the week, to explain it in person. She texted him back, "OK! Call if you can."

Cap sent a thumbs-up and a heart, knew he would not call.

He had a headache, both inside and out, where the burn was, and he knew coffee and a little Advil would help, so he holstered his gun, picked up his wallet and his phone, and left the room. And there was Vega on the landing, leaning over the railing, surveying the parking lot.

"Hey," said Cap.

Vega turned around. Cap was happy to see her back in her standard uniform even though he didn't love that she was wearing sunglasses because he wanted to see her eyes.

"Cue up the AC/DC," he said, gesturing to her and her clothes.

"What?" she said, looking confused.

"Never mind," said Cap, chuckling.

He shut the door to his room and flipped the DO NOT DISTURB sign on the knob, took a couple of steps, and stood next to her at the railing.

"Sorry I took so long," he said. "I slept like a dead person."

"It's okay," said Vega. "I slept in, too."

"You hear from Otero?"

Vega nodded.

"Boyce is meeting with Radkin in . . ." She paused and checked her phone. "In ten minutes to lay it out for him."

"Mackey around?"

"Nope. As far as we know he still thinks everything's jake."

"Everything's 'jake'?" said Cap, not sure he'd heard her correctly.

"Yeah, you know, he thinks everything's all right."

"I know what it means, Vega," said Cap, amused. "It's just an old-fashioned turn of phrase."

"Oh," said Vega, thinking about it. "Perry used to say it."

Cap squinted into the sun. He found it pleasant, ultimately, but it was intense and directly on them, the cool air of the early morning almost completely burned away.

"We have to wait, see where the facility is," she said, lazily kicking the base of the railing. "You want to get some coffee and a messy egg sandwich in the meantime?"

Cap was overwhelmed with relief just hearing her talk about breakfast.

"Yes, my God, please," he said.

Vega smiled a little at his eagerness, and they walked toward the stairway.

"So six girls at the facility," said Cap, as they headed down. "Where are the other four?"

"Davis seemed to be the point man for the Salton house, and he's not in play anymore," said Vega. "And they can't be at Mackey's house, like actually where he lives."

"So they could be anywhere," said Cap, unlocking the doors to the rental car. "And how do we find them, absent Mackey telling us himself."

They got in, and Cap turned on the engine immediately, powered down the windows, and cranked the A/C.

"Jesus, it's hot," he said.

Vega didn't respond in any way to the heat. She buckled her seatbelt, distracted, thinking about what Cap had said. Anywhere.

"I think we should go back to Lara," she said.

"Yeah?" said Cap. "Why him?"

"He knows Perez. He knows Mackey. Maybe he got paid on both sides."

Cap pulled out of the lot, headed to the corner.

"You're thinking Lara's got an extra residence?" he said.

"Doesn't have to be a residence," said Vega. "Could just be a room."

"Yeah, but it's got to be secluded," said Cap. "Maybe not a ghost town like Salton, but most citizens would call their local authorities if they saw a bunch of young girls in their underwear being marched into a condo."

Vega examined her reflection in the side mirror. The shape of the glass made her sunglasses look as if they were a mask, reminded her of a zoom lens photo of a fly.

"You're overestimating most citizens," she said. "People generally don't care unless it directly affects them."

"Aw, Vega, what about the power of the human spirit?" said Cap, teasing her.

Vega sighed, annoyed, and said, "I'm not saying it doesn't happen. I'm saying we shouldn't wait by the phone."

"I don't disagree. First, breakfast, then we definitely do not wait by the phone," Cap said. "You want to find a place with better drink options than 7-Eleven, though?"

"There's a Dunkin' Donuts a few blocks away," said Vega.

"You can't get a protein bar there, though," said Cap, stopping at a light.

"I'll find something."

"What—a donut?" said Cap, unable to imagine Vega eating such a thing. "Is there a Reno's somewhere? They have egg sandwiches, and nut bars, and coffee that doesn't taste like burnt shoes."

"Probably," said Vega, searching on her phone for the nearest Reno's. "I think you go straight two or three blocks and it'll be in the mall on the left."

She looked up from her phone and lowered her sunglasses, strained to see the street sign on the next block. From the corner of her eye she saw the side mirror darken slightly, thought it was cloud cover until she looked straight on and saw a black Suburban right behind them. The license plate had three 9s in it.

"This guy's a little close to you," she said, pointing to the mirror.

"He is, right?" said Cap.

The light turned green, and Cap sped up through the intersection.

"So what's the name of the street we're looking for?"

Vega turned to answer him, noticed the Suburban had not moved from its spot in front of the crosswalk, cars behind it honking. Then she saw another SUV, also big and black speeding through the cross street of the intersection, right behind Cap's head, coming straight for them.

She tried to tell Cap to reverse but didn't have time before the SUV slammed into the rear half of Cap's rental, and they began to spin.

· · ·

Cap planted his foot on the brake, and the car went around two, three, four times. He'd never been in a real accident, gotten rear-ended twice (once in a police cruiser), sideswiped in the Valley Diss parking lot, but never flipped, crashed, or spun. He steered left because the car was spinning to the right but wasn't thinking about it, couldn't remember any practical instruction for the circumstances.

The car slowed in the fifth or sixth rotation, then ran into a phone pole on the right side of the vehicle, the hood, but not very hard because the airbags didn't pop.

He heard his own breath coming out of his mouth in bursts, then Vega's, then noticed her hand was on his leg, nails dug in, and he squeezed it.

"Okay?" he said.

Her eyes were alert, her right hand gripping the grab handle above the window.

"Nothing broken?"

She shook her head, stunned. They both watched white smoke rise from the hood.

Then Cap's door opened, and there was a man with a thick semi-automatic pistol pointed right in Cap's face.

"Come on out," said the man, Latino with Mexican accent, wearing a black T-shirt with a white cross and Japanese characters printed on the front.

Cap followed orders, didn't seem to have a lot of wiggle room either way. He got out of the car, his legs wobbly. The man with the gun stood behind Cap and angled it up so the tip of the barrel was at his chin. Cap kept his hands at his sides.

"You, too," the man said to Vega.

Vega scooted over the gearshift into the driver's seat and then out.

"You go in front," said the man.

The SUV that had been behind them, the one with the 9s, was parked in the middle of the intersection. Cars were stopped, people out, honking, yelling.

A woman dressed in yoga clothes ran up to them.

"Are you all right? Oh my God, the same thing happened to my husband last year."

"Get in your car," said the man, and he waved the gun in her direction.

She screamed and backed away, yelled, "Gun! There's a gun!"

Then the man with the gun shot her in the foot, and she collapsed to the ground, screaming. People began to either swarm around her or drop to the pavement to avoid getting shot, and the man with the gun pressed the barrel into Cap's back.

"Go," he said.

The driver got out of the SUV. He wore suit pants and a white dress shirt and he walked around the front of the vehicle to them and quickly patted down Cap, removed the Sig from his holster, then Vega and took her Springfield. Then he opened the back door of the SUV.

"Get in," said the man with the gun.

Cap and Vega got in.

It was set up like a limo inside with seats facing each other. Cap and Vega sat on the side furthest from the driver. Across from them was a man Cap recognized as the Posada Double. The man with the gun slid into the seat next to his boss, and rapped his knuckles on the ceiling. He kept his pistol pointed in Cap and Vega's direction.

They sped away, and Cap watched the chaos out the window pass by: the crowd around the woman who'd been shot, people screaming, cars stopped at every angle in the intersection. Cap twisted his body around so he could watch it, but then they were gone, down another street.

"Mr. Caplan," said the Posada Double congenially. "I don't say this often, but you looked a bit better in the hospital."

He was as well dressed as yesterday, wore a gray suit with a white shirt unbuttoned at the top, no tie. Cap put him in his fifties, though his hair was solid black and full.

"You are Miss Vega," he said to her. "You are prettier than you look on TV."

Vega moved her eyes from him to the man with the gun, to the back of the driver's head.

"You look a lot different than you do on TV, Mr. Posada," she said. "Almost like a whole other person."

The Double chuckled.

"I apologize for the accident. You understand, I need some information from you, and I find that people are more willing to speak to me if I catch them off guard," said the Double.

He leaned back in his seat and smiled at them, but his eyes remained static—it was like only his mouth was committed but the rest of his face wasn't on board yet.

"Did you find out who killed the two girls?" he said to Vega.

"I think so," she answered. "But this isn't a charity operation. I'll give you the name if you tell me yours first."

The Double laughed once, then held up his hands as if he were playing cops and robbers with a child.

"Okay, Miss Vega, okay. I give up. My name is Javier."

"What about a last name?" said Vega.

"Not yet," he said, shaking a finger at her. "Nothing for free. Now you tell me who killed the two girls."

Vega paused, calculating her words.

"I'm fairly certain it's a guy named Rafa. He's in police custody."

"And do you have a last name for him?" said Javier.

"No, but I can find out."

"Good," said Javier. "No last names for anyone then. And you say you are fairly certain?"

"Yes."

Javier nodded, brushed an invisible speck of dust off his pant leg.

"My boss would very much like to know. I know there are ten girls in total, but we are only interested in four of them. The two who were killed were my partner's property, you understand. So we would like to find out who has damaged his property," he said to Vega.

Cap stared at the gun. Though this wasn't the first time he'd had one aimed at him, it was hard to look away. He reminded himself to breathe, felt the sweat pasting his shirt to his back. He watched Vega out of the corner of his eye. She was still, her hands resting on her legs, fingers gently curled. If she was scared for her life, she did a good impression of someone who was not.

"I don't know where Mr. Mackey is right now. I think he has decided to play a game with me," said Javier, waving his hand in the air. "All he had to do was keep six girls alive and contained. I'm not sure what he thinks he will win by losing them and keeping my money. I have friends at Immigration and at the border police, also some politicians, but they can't help me with my problem."

He leaned forward and folded his hands, rested his elbows on his knees.

"So yes, I would appreciate it if you found him and the four girls who belong to my partner. And if you can confirm the man who killed the other two girls, that would be nice as well," he added, as if he were reading his desired dishes off a menu. "Now that you are both out of the hospital, I think this will not be a problem for you."

"You seemed to want us out of town pretty bad yesterday," said Cap, wiping his palms on his pants. "Now you want us to stay."

This made Javier thoughtful. He gazed out the window, almost wistful.

"I asked Mr. Mackey if I could see you. The doctor was still with Miss Vega, but I preferred to talk to you in any case, because I thought I might be able to persuade you better than I could her."

"Why'd you think that?" said Vega, her throat dry and hot. "You never met either of us."

Now Javier laughed, his face brightening in an effortless good-natured way.

"Because Mr. Caplan is the one with the daughter. Near Philadelphia. People who have children are more easily persuaded to do things they might not otherwise do. And I thought he would be able to persuade you at a later time, Miss Vega."

Cap knew rationally Javier might be bluffing, but the mention of Nell, even in the abstract, was enough to enrage him.

"You might want to tell me who you are next time, instead of pretending to be a cop. So at least I know who's threatening my family," Cap said, leaning forward.

The man with the gun leaned forward as well, kept his aiming arm steady.

"It's the message that was important, Mr. Caplan, not the method of delivery," said Javier. "But next time I will do that," he added, happy to take the advice.

"Now that we have the message, we're done here, right?" said Vega. "How do we get in touch with you?"

"You can call me," said Javier, still smiling. "My phone has very good global service. I could be in France, and you could still call me." He turned to the man with the gun and said, "Memo—give them a card."

Memo kept aiming the gun at Cap and reached into an elastic-rimmed pouch on the door. He removed a white card and handed it to Cap. All it said was JAVIER, and then an international number beneath it.

"So you can do these things for me and my partner quickly?" said Javier. "Mr. Mackey has been disappointing for us."

"Let's just say we can't," said Cap. "Not that we won't. If we can't, what then?"

Javier's lips became a straight line.

"I don't expect that to happen," he said. "I have the greatest confidence in you both."

"That's a real shot in the arm," said Cap. He asked again, slower: "But what if we can't?"

Javier nodded in Memo's direction, and Memo knocked on the ceiling once more.

"I will have to keep looking, then, for new people who make me feel confident," said Javier, seeming a little downtrodden.

This made Cap furious. The initial shock from the crash had worn off a bit, but the adrenaline was still rushing in his blood, making him blind angry. He wanted to rip the card in half and shove it down Javier's throat.

"Is that the best you can do," Cap said, leaning forward. "Aren't you going to threaten our loved ones or describe how you're going to cut us into pieces if we don't do exactly what you say?"

Javier laughed, surprised.

"You watch too much Netflix, Mr. Caplan," he said. "Amazon Prime," he added, as an afterthought, still chuckling. "Real *narcos* will not warn you. They'll just kill you. Burn up your wife's body parts while they are still on her living body—is that more like it?"

Cap didn't answer, though that was more like it.

Then the driver pulled the car over, and Memo got out.

"This has been very nice," said Javier, genuine. "Speak with you soon, then."

The door on Vega's side opened, Memo standing aside, holding the top of the door.

Vega stepped out, and Cap after her. They were next to a chain-link fence, a field of blond grass on the other side. Across the street was a Best Buy, a big parking lot. Not many cars parked, no people.

Memo got back in, and the car sped off. It stopped about a hundred feet away from where Cap and Vega stood; the passenger door opened, and Memo leaned out and placed the Sig and the Springfield on the sidewalk.

Cap and Vega walked, then jogged to their guns and picked them up. They didn't speak for a minute.

Cap felt like hugging her, wasn't sure if it would be more for her or for himself, just wanted to feel her skin and hair and heartbeat. But she was distant at the moment, thinking, all the neural pathways firing.

He knew better than to interrupt that with any display of emotion, so he just said, "I thought we were dead twice already today."

"Yeah," said Vega, distracted. "And it's only ten thirty."

21

OTERO HURRIED TO THE CURB WHEN THE CAB PULLED UP IN FRONT of the station. Vega and Cap had not said much to each other on the ride over, Vega busy texting Otero the details, and both of them coasting down from the shock of the accident.

"You're okay," Otero said as they got out of the cab, more of a confirmation than a question.

"It appears that way," said Cap.

"As soon as I read all your texts, I put it together," he said to Vega, then held up his phone for them to see. "This is the guy, right?"

Cap and Vega looked at the screen as they walked into the station waiting room. It was a photo of Javier from the news. He was in a group, behind another man with sunglasses, all of them in suits.

"That's him," said Cap. "Javier, formerly Deputy Chief Posada."

"It's Javier Castán," said Otero, pushing open the door to the giant main room with the wraparound window. "*El Desratizador* is what he goes by or El D. It means rat exterminator," he said to Cap.

"Who is he?" asked Vega, noticing the room was much emptier than the first time she'd been there.

"He's Perro Perez's number two," said Otero, leading them to his desk in the back. "He made news last year for killing one of Montalvo's informants. Cut out the eyes and put them in the mouth," Otero rattled off like well-known lore. "I'm actually pretty surprised you're both alive."

"Us, too," said Cap. "His guy shot a woman on the street, in the intersection."

"I'm aware," said Otero, sitting at his desk, nodding to the front of the room. "That's where half my people are."

"Is she okay?" asked Cap. "She was a bystander."

"I don't know the status but she's at County receiving treatment," said Otero. "Javier Castán doesn't have any use for bystanders. And he told you outright he doesn't know where Mackey is?"

"That's right," said Vega, sitting in a chair opposite him. "I think it went like this: Montalvo told his guys to send their kids away, that Perez was coming for them, so they sent them here.

"Perez, somehow, figures it out and hooks up with Mackey, who hires Davis to set up the Salton house. They intercept six girls, and Mackey sends them to the Salton house. Davis fills out the blank spaces with six other girls. Not sure where he gets them but clearly he has a little business on the side, offers to loan some to Joe Guerra, for example, to work in his club, et cetera."

Vega tapped her fingernail on the edge of Otero's desk.

"Rafa kills two of the Montalvo girls, Maricel Villareal and Dulce Díaz. Dulce's body is dumped in Dylan Duffy's car through arrangement with his son, probably by Rafa, according to the Can Man's description, and then Rafa drops Maricel's body in a ditch." Vega paused then looked to Otero and continued: "Mackey brings you in to run the case on his terms and then us to make it look good for Boyce, thinking we'll spin our wheels for a couple of weeks and maybe that will be enough time for him to figure out how to tell Javier two of his girls got killed on his watch. We find the house way too quickly, though, and now he panics."

"Thinks Javier Castán won't take the news well that not only are the two girls dead, the whole cover of the Salton house is blown, because of you two," said Otero.

"Luckily he thinks he has you pinned," said Vega.

"Lucky thing," said Otero.

"So how far's Mackey think he's gonna get?" said Cap, amused.

"He's operating from a different place," said Otero. "He has this affect. Tough to put my finger on it."

Otero took a moment to whittle down what he was trying to say.

"It's like he's earned all of this and how dare I not be nicer about him blackmailing me."

"He's earned points with a Mexican cartel?" said Cap, skeptical. "Guy's got some priority issues."

"We don't have a whole lot of time, and we don't know where the four Montalvo girls are," said Vega. "Do we know who drove them all away in the bus yet?" she asked Otero.

"Boyce is getting back to me on it, and the location of the facility as well where the six girls are," he answered.

"Good," said Vega. Then she remembered something. "Oh, we need McTiernan back," she added.

"I told you he has to go through the motions of IA," said Otero, holding his hands up in surrender. "I started the process, totally my fault, but I can't pull him now without raising more flags."

"You've got to free him up," said Vega. "We need him."

"What do you need him for, specifically, that I can't help you with? Or another detective?" Otero said, still patient, just interested.

"Rodrigo trusts him," said Vega. "And we need one more favor from Rodrigo."

Otero sat back in his chair and turned his face to the side as if the new angle of Vega's face would reveal her intention.

"You want to tell me what the plan is here?" he said quietly.

"Not yet," said Vega.

Otero nodded rhythmically, like he was tilting back and forth on a rocking chair.

"You want to tell me why that is?" he asked.

"Not yet," Vega said again. "It's me and Cap who are dead if we don't straighten this out. So if it's all the same, I'd like to let you know the best way to move forward after we talk to Rodrigo."

"If you're suggesting that I'm not personally invested, I can remind you that my son will most probably be spending some time in a juvenile detention center instead of playing the homecoming game," said Otero, calm.

"Yeah, but it's our eyes getting cut out, and so forth," said Vega.

"Hey, don't forget the part where he puts them in our mouths," said Cap.

"That as well," said Vega. "I know I'm asking a lot, but you just have to trust me here, Commander. We trust you. Let us off the leash a little bit and let McTiernan come with us for an hour. Confirm the bus driver, and then we circle up."

Otero glanced at Cap, as if to ask him to explain. Cap responded with a firm nod, crossed his arms to show his resolve.

In truth, Cap didn't know Vega's exact plan, but like Otero, he had a message that kept coming back to him again and again in his life. It was always, without question: Trust the girl.

Cap and Vega stood next to a silver food truck parked down the block from the station and ate and drank like starved farm animals. They ate breakfast burritos with scrambled eggs, cheese, and chorizo. The food truck sold bars made with dates and nuts and soy protein isolate, but Vega found herself wanting the carbs, the salt, the substance of the eggs after the accident, the adrenaline washed from her system and replaced with weariness. Cap drank a large iced coffee with the lid off, gulping it down like Gatorade after a game. Vega drank hot tea, bottled water on the side.

They didn't speak for a good five minutes. Cap went back for seconds, another coffee and another burrito, and Vega waited on the curb for him, feeling steadier in the legs as the moments passed, the calories and caffeine making their way through her bloodstream. Cap came back to her and peeled the foil off the burrito, held it out to her, offering the first bite. She shook her head.

It was something close to ecstasy she felt. She knew it was the recovery from trauma, the elation of coming close to death and escaping. She recognized it because she had just slid by in other similar situations, like the day before, for example, but she'd been distracted by the physical injury. But something about Cap offering her the first bite of his burrito made all the joy she had in her emotional reserves well up.

Tears began to sprout in her eyes beyond her control. She turned to Cap, to attempt to explain. He was not looking her way, eating his second burrito like it was his job.

Then they heard someone calling their names.

It was McTiernan, jogging toward them.

"McT!" Cap shouted, mouth full.

They ran toward each other like in an old movie and hugged. Vega followed, and McTiernan shook her hand, gripped it hard.

"Hey, Vega," he said.

"How're you doing?" said Vega.

"Fine. Told everything to IA. No big thing. We got nothing to hide, right?" he said, excited.

"Right," said Cap. "Did Otero bring you up to speed?"

"A little," said McTiernan. "He just said we're all working together now and you guys needed me."

McTiernan blew out air, a relieved exhale.

"He didn't tell you anything else?" said Cap. "About what's happened since we saw you last?"

"No. It's only been, what, twelve hours?" he said, laughing. "Haven't y'all been asleep?"

"Where's your car?" said Cap. "We'll tell you on the way."

They walked to the station lot and got into McTiernan's car while Cap filled him in. Vega sat in the backseat, watching McTiernan's face as he listened intently. He sat still in the driver's seat, didn't start the car.

When Cap finished, McTiernan turned to him.

"So now we're up against Mackey and also the Perez cartel?"

"Yeah, I think that's all right now," said Cap.

McTiernan turned around to look at Vega, who nodded.

"Sweet," said McTiernan, a little dazed. "Just wanted to make sure I had an accurate head count. So what's next?"

"Back to Rodrigo's diner," said Cap.

"Yeah?" said McTiernan, putting on his seatbelt. "What else do we need from him?"

"We'll tell you when we get there," said Cap, looking at Vega. "Right?"

"Right," she said.

Vega shut her eyes, and McTiernan started to drive. She was vaguely aware of them talking. McTiernan asking questions and then describing his experience with Internal Affairs. She wasn't asleep, just trying to maintain a soft focus on what was about to happen, pull apart the knot of thread that was the case of the Janes and lay it flat in one long, straight line.

Rodrigo was not happy to see Vega. She stood outside the car, the door open, with Cap in the backseat now and McTiernan waving from behind the wheel. Rodrigo broke into a restrained smile when he saw McTiernan and sat in the front on the passenger side, Vega sliding into the backseat.

"*Hola*," said McTiernan warmly, patting him on the shoulder.

Rodrigo said "*Hola*" back to him and appeared self-conscious, glancing at Cap and Vega behind him like chaperones.

"We are very sorry to bother you again," said McTiernan. "We know you've been through a lot. But we have one more favor to ask of you," he said, holding up one finger.

Rodrigo stared as if the favor was spelled out on McTiernan's fingerprint. He nodded, not in agreement, but only to hear more. McTiernan gestured to Vega, who leaned forward between them.

She had Rodrigo's attention but knew he was still skeptical of her.

"We need you to call your father," she said, figuring it would do no good to put off the first punch.

"No," said Rodrigo immediately, nearly shouting. "No, I can't do that. He made me promise not to call him."

"Why?" said McTiernan.

"It's not safe," said Rodrigo. "He said he never knew who was listening."

"Do you mean someone listening on the phones, or someone listening to him speak, like in the room with him?" said Vega.

"Either," said Rodrigo. "But more like people who are around him. When I left he didn't know if there were spies for Perez working for Lalo."

"We need you to take that chance now," said Vega cautiously.

"No," said Rodrigo, pointing at her. "Fuck this. I'm not risking the life of my father for your job."

"Hey," said McTiernan. "We could find out who exactly is responsible for everything, all of this. Not just who killed your sister, but where the other girls are. All the other Maricels and Dulces."

Vega watched Rodrigo's face as McTiernan spoke his sister's name. Just a wrinkle of the nose, like an allergy had come and gone.

"It's more than that," said Vega. "We could take them all down. We already have Coyote Ben. But we could get the rest, too. Mackey, Javier Castán, Perez himself," she said, addressing Cap and McTiernan too. "But we have to talk to your father."

"Why?" said Rodrigo, plaintive. "My father's a pawn like the rest. Like Maricel," he said, the name catching in his throat.

"He's not," said Vega, sounding assured. "Neither are his friends."

Then Rodrigo's expression changed—he regarded Vega quizzically and suddenly he grasped it, even as he, and Cap and McTiernan, didn't know how all the parts were connected, he knew it was all that was left to do.

Cap carried the paper-pulp cup tray from the Reno's back to the car. Coffee for him, black tea for Vega, Diet Coke for McTiernan. McTiernan was talking animatedly in the driver's seat. They had just said goodbye to Rodrigo once again after he'd gotten off the phone with his father, whom he'd hadn't spoken with in eight months. Now the three of them were stopping briefly, waiting for Otero to call them back.

Cap got back in the car and handed out the drinks. McTiernan was in the middle of something.

"Logistically how're you going to work this?" he said to Vega, somewhat exasperated.

"I need to talk to Otero and Boyce," she said, blowing on her tea.

McTiernan laughed.

"Yeah, I'm not sure they're going to go for it," he said.

"You mean, you're not sure your old straight-arrow boss, Otero, would go for it," said Cap. "Your new recently blackmailed and liberated boss, Otero, is probably up for anything."

McTiernan cracked open his soda and chugged it like a beer.

"Maybe," he said. "But Boyce—"

"Boyce seems like the type who'll go far to make things right," said Vega, with a degree of authority, as if she were intimately familiar with such a type.

"How big are what?" Otero asked again, as if he hadn't heard her.

They were back in the station, in the large conference room where Vega had originally met them all for the first time. Cap stood against the wall behind her, and McTiernan paced and texted. Boyce was on the speakerphone console in the middle of the table. Cap thought Vega's plan was in the upper digits on the one-to-ten insanity scale, but also that everything about being alive within the past twenty-four hours had taken on a certifiably surreal quality, so Vega's idea fit squarely alongside.

"The tunnels," Vega repeated. "Are any of them big enough for a car to drive through?"

Boyce answered: "Not a standard-size car but conceivably a golf cart or a Smart car, something like that."

"The most recent one we found, the one you two saw the other day, it's built like a mine," Otero added.

"You know who built it?" asked Cap.

"Money's on Perez," said Boyce from the speakerphone. "We don't know who else would have the resources."

"You got one that's a little smaller?" asked Vega, like she was ordering steaks at a butcher counter. "Like smaller than the tricked-out one by Perez, but bigger than the ones that just fit one or two people army-crawling."

Otero nodded.

"Sure, there's one we found about three months ago. Narrow, relatively, but someone could stand almost to full height and walk through, if they were under five ten or so."

"Perez build that one, too?" said Cap.

"We don't think so," said Boyce. "From the entrance and exit points, we think it's a straight-up immigration railroad."

"You think another vehicle might fit, like a bike? Or a motorcycle?" Vega asked.

McTiernan stopped texting to see what Otero would say.

"Maybe," said Otero. Then he changed his answer: "Sure. Let's say, sure." Otero gripped the back of a chair and leaned on it. "You want to tell me what you're thinking?"

Now everyone watched Vega, and it was quiet except for desk phones ringing in another room.

"Javier said he's got people in Immigration and border police. He's got someone at the DEA, obviously. He's got politicians. He may have other people in your PD. But he doesn't have you," she said to Otero. "And he doesn't have us. He knows about his tunnels, but he doesn't know about all of them."

Otero took it in, trying to sort what she was getting at. Boyce remained silent on the other end of the line.

"What do you want to bring through the tunnel without Perez knowing?" he asked.

"Not what. Who," said Vega, glancing to Cap. "Me and Caplan, we got nothing here. Not a card. Javier knows who we are and where to find us. And our families. I want to bring the only people through the tunnel who might make Javier think twice about all of it."

"Montalvo," Boyce said, his astonishment audible.

"Not him, per se," said Vega. "Just five or six of his friends. Guys who might have a bone to pick with Perez's number two."

Otero pushed off the back of the chair and put a hand to his head.

"So you want to stage an ambush of Javier Castán before he can kill you," he said.

"Not necessarily," said Vega. "I could tell Javier where to meet us, and we're pretty busy, me and Cap, we might not make it in time. Other people might get there before us."

Otero was silent, stunned. He stared at the speakerphone as if Boyce were in the room.

"Seems we could all end up with a net gain at the end of the day," Vega added. Then she shrugged. "Something to think about."

Win-win all over, thought Cap.

Then Vega said, "Agent Boyce, do you have a location for us for the ISC facility where the six girls from the bus were dropped?"

"Not exactly," said Boyce, measured. "I called a guy I know over there who was forthcoming about it. Said an agent of theirs, the bus driver, was called in by Mackey to pick up some suspected illegals but he couldn't tell me what facility they're at."

"You call that forthcoming?" said Cap. "He wouldn't tell you where they are?"

Otero and McTiernan looked at each other, shared something specific in their glance that Cap and Vega had no idea about.

"Lately, the past year, ISC has worked a little differently in the border states," Otero explained. "Anything spills into PD jurisdiction or DEA they step back, but it's become its own animal."

"They don't keep a lot of records," added McTiernan. "A few months ago I had a case: old man, Latino, legally immigrated in the seventies. One day he goes missing—his adult kids are worried because he has bouts of dementia. Very long story short: I track him to an IS facility up near Riverside, middle of nowhere. They'd picked him up and just"— McTiernan sliced his hand through the air—"took him away. Like a, you know, a truant officer or a . . ." McTiernan said, pausing.

"Dogcatcher," said Vega.

"Right," said McTiernan. Then he continued: "They released him to me as soon as I got there, no questions asked. I was pissed, boy, but I just wanted to get him back to his family, and I told his kids, you all have got to sue ISC." McTiernan looked at Otero when he said this. "I told them, Comm, I said, 'You got a good case, sue the shit outta the state of California and ISC and whoever else.'" McTiernan paused again and shook his head. "They didn't do it. They were just grateful. And scared."

"The takeaway here," said Boyce on speakerphone, "is that we can get a district court order to have those six girls released, but before we do that I suggest you speak to the bus driver face-to-face to get more intel and the possible location of the four Montalvo girls, as well as Agent Mackey. Commander Otero?" he said.

"Still here," said Otero.

"After Ms. Vega and Mr. Caplan leave the station, let's speak about our options privately."

"Agreed," said Otero.

"I'll be in touch with Rodrigo," said McTiernan. "We can get his father and his people to the entry point."

"Let's talk to the bus driver," Cap said to Vega.

He felt some of the tension in his neck from the morning dissipate at the thought of a good old-fashioned witness interview with Vega at his side. He couldn't tell for certain from her expression, but it looked like she was also a little pleased, her eyes soft and tired, the corners of her mouth beginning to turn up. For a brief wild moment he thought she might wink at him.

Instead she stood up and said to Otero, "Can we borrow another car? Both of ours are in the shop."

22

CAP HADN'T DRIVEN AN UNDERCOVER COP CAR IN A WHILE. HE'D expected the West Coast version to be some kind of NASA-level space bullet, but it turned out undercover cars were the same everywhere— decent pickup but crappy shocks; absolutely no Bluetooth or GPS hookup. Vega read him directions to the ISC office off her phone.

ISC was in an office building not far from the police station, still downtown. Cap parked the car at a meter down the block, about to head into the main lobby when Vega pointed to a set of frosted glass double doors to the left of the main entrance. U.S. IMMIGRATION SER-VICES CONTROL read the vinyl lettering on the right door. Cap opened it, and they went inside.

There was a small empty waiting room. Cap gave their names to the woman at the reception desk and asked for Jeff Collins, the bus driver. Then he and Vega stood by the door and waited for something to happen. The woman behind the desk was texting, her long nails clicking on the screen. Ten minutes passed, and Cap went back to the reception desk.

"Hi. Me again," he said, holding up his hand in a wave. "Does Jeff Collins know we're waiting? Because we've got some time-sensitive material to discuss with him."

"He's wrapping something up, sir," she said tersely.

She had straw-colored hair and wore such thick mascara Cap won-dered if her eyelashes were false. She seemed too young to be so terse, as if she'd worked this desk for twenty years and was sick to death of people claiming they had time-sensitive material.

Cap smiled at her and leaned on the counter that separated them.

"I was in a car accident earlier today," he said.

The receptionist gaped.

"My car went like this," he said, twirling a pen on the counter so it spun like a pinwheel. "So I have to tell you I am acutely aware of time and how slow or fast it's passing. You feel me?"

"Sir—" she said, and Cap expected she would continue by adding that she most certainly did not feel him.

Then a young, pudgy man emerged from the doorway behind the receptionist's desk.

"You sent by DEA?" he said by way of greeting.

"That's right," said Cap. "You Jeff Collins?"

"Yeah," he said, reaching his hand over the counter to shake Cap's.

His palm was wet and warm.

"Max Caplan," said Cap. He turned his head toward Vega behind him. "This is Alice Vega. We have a few questions we need to ask you, Mr. Collins."

"It's Agent Collins," he said, a little embarrassed to insist that Cap respect his title.

"Agent Collins, sure," said Cap.

"Follow me, okay?"

They followed him through the doorway, where there was a cluster of cubicles surrounded by glass-doored offices along the walls. Collins led them to a cubicle and sat at the desk inside, gestured to the chair opposite him. There was only one; Cap nodded to Vega to take it. He knew she wasn't the type to be offended but would accept to move things along. She sat.

Cap stood against the cubicle wall, his head and shoulders well above the top edge. The whole cubicle seemed made for dwarves, which made Collins look even bloatier than he was, balancing on a too-small ergonomic office chair at a tiny desk overflowing with wrinkled manila folders.

"So Agent Mackey didn't keep anyone in the loop?" said Collins, adopting a teasing tone.

"Doesn't look like it, no," said Cap.

Collins laughed and took a sip of coffee from a mug in the shape of the president's head.

"Typical, right?" he said.

"We wouldn't really be able to say," said Cap.

"What—you guys aren't cops?" said Collins.

"No, we're private investigators. Consultants."

Collins found this funny. He grinned knowingly.

"Like mercenaries," he said.

"Sort of," said Cap, playing along. "Agent Collins, we know that Agent Mackey sent you an email yesterday morning, telling you he needed your assistance in transporting some girls out of a house in Salton City. Can you tell us about that?"

"Well, just what you said," said Collins. "I've known Mackey awhile. DEA and ISC overlap, as you can imagine. He knows I run a lot of transportation for illegals, and he said he needed a pickup for ten girls, that he couldn't be there so I was supposed to meet Otero and take the girls."

"Where did you bring them?" said Cap.

"Some of them I brought to one of our facilities, the rest I delivered to him."

Collins offered this information as if it was anything but urgent. Cap met Vega's eyes while Collins took another sip of coffee and unearthed a bear claw pastry from under the files on his desk.

"Sorry, never got around to breakfast," he said, taking a moist bite.

"You brought six to the facility, is that correct?" said Cap.

"Mmm," said Collins, chewing, considering it. "I think so."

"What were their names and ages?" said Cap, taking out his phone.

"I don't know," said Collins unapologetically. "Mackey texted me the names of the girls he wanted brought to him, so I brought the rest to Oren North."

Cap took a deep breath through his nose, fighting the impulse to knock the coffee out of Collins's chubby hand.

"Could we see the text, please?" asked Cap. "The names."

Collins shrugged, said, "Sure." Didn't seem to care either way.

He picked his phone up off his desk and wiped crumbs on his pant leg before tapping on the screen.

"Where are they?" said Cap slowly. "Where did you meet Mackey and drop off those four girls to him?"

"So he's really gone rogue, huh?" said Collins, still gently amused. He swallowed the chunk of the bear claw still in his mouth and said, "Just a parking lot near Holtville, east of El Centro. He packed them up in a van."

"Did he say where he was going?"

Collins chuckled again. "No, sorry. He said he had to question them. I didn't ask, you know. Not my business."

"Do you recall exactly what he said to you when you dropped off the girls?" said Cap.

"Not his exact words," said Collins. "He thanked me and said he'd be in touch. That's it."

Cap was quiet, stunned by Collins's complacency.

"Any other questions?" said Collins, chipper, taking another bite of the bear claw.

He swiped his hands together, dusting off his fingers.

"I have one," said Vega.

"She talks," Collins said to Cap, pleasantly surprised.

He laughed with his mouth open, full of pulp.

"I talk," said Vega.

She leaned forward, shifted her weight to the front of the seat.

"Was one of the girls on your bus covered in blood?" she asked.

"Uh," said Collins, squinting, trying to remember. "Yeah, I think so."

"And that didn't raise a flag for you to maybe ask some more questions?" she added.

Collins's mouth turned down in a scornful frown.

"Hey, I did my job, like I do every day, honey," he said, defensive now. "You don't like it, you can lodge a complaint with Compliance."

Vega sat back again. A small, deferent smile crossed her face.

"My bad," she said. "Would you mind terribly giving us the address of this facility—Oren North, was it?"

Collins bristled a little, still sore from Vega's demand. He glanced up at Cap for his approval.

"It would be really helpful," Cap added.

Collins wiped his hands on his pants and picked up his phone from the desk.

"I sent you directions," he said to Cap. "You're not going to find it on Google Maps. I'll let them know you're coming, too," Collins added, feeling magnanimous now. "The guy you want to see is Steve McConnell. I'm the only one in this field office with his info."

"Yeah?" said Cap. "Why's that?"

"It's federally classified information. I'm the only one who needs to know, so I know. That's why Mackey reached out to me."

He tapped the screen with his index finger, then set the phone back down. He took another loud slurp of coffee and stared at the phone.

"Delivered," he said. "You should be all set."

Vega turned around in her chair, asked Cap a question with her eyes.

Cap glanced around the office. Most of the cubes were empty; a couple of people here and there on the phone and tapping at keyboards.

One person in one of the offices with the door closed. He was changing his shoes.

Cap looked back at Vega and gave her an encouraging nod.

"That it?" said Collins, impatient now.

"Think so," said Cap.

Vega stood, and Collins began to stand as well but Vega knocked his mug over, the coffee splattering onto his lap.

"Fuck!" he yelled.

"I'm sorry," she said. "I'm so clumsy."

"*What is wrong with you?*" he said, grabbing his thighs.

"There you go. You *do* know how to ask questions," she said.

Cap looked mildly satisfied and headed out of the cubicle.

"Get the hell outta here!" Collins yelled at her.

He stood and hurried, stiff-legged, out of the cubicle and toward the restroom.

Vega looked down and saw the mug staring up at her. She lifted her right knee high as it would go and brought her foot down hard, shattering the thing into five or six dull pieces.

Cap didn't see any other cars on the interstate. They were past Salton and El Centro, less than a mile north of the Mexican border. He peered out his window and the side mirror and rearview. There was nothing out there. He didn't even know if he could call it the desert because it just looked like dirt with brushy shrubs here and there.

But it was getting warmer with each mile they went inland. Even though the sky was Easter blue, there was an ominous feeling he couldn't shake.

"Vega," he said, trepidatious.

"Yeah?" she said, studying the directions on her phone.

"We're going to ask the six girls at this facility if they know anything about where Mackey is with the other four, right?"

"Yeah," said Vega. "McConnell, too. He may have something that can help us."

"Right," said Cap. "So let's say we find the four girls, the girls Perez is looking for. We're not just going to hand them over to him, right? This is not something we can do," he said, not sounding as confident as he had hoped.

Vega removed her jacket and laid it on her lap. Cap saw her face lightly glossed with sweat. He could only see the corner of one of her eyes from behind her sunglasses, soft flutter of her lashes.

"I have no intention of handing any girl over to Javier," said Vega. "He will have to go through me. Take my eyes and my tongue and whatever else he needs to. He's not getting those girls. Not one."

"Not one," Cap repeated.

He thought of Nell and hoped he'd see her again, hoped that he wouldn't die in California, in the desert that may well have been Mars. But he also knew he agreed with Vega. He knew it like he knew his daughter's name.

They drove in silence for another ten minutes or so. FIFTEEN MILES TO YUMA read a sign.

"We have to be close," said Cap. "We're not going to Arizona, right?"

"Right," said Vega. "Collins said there should be an unmarked road."

Cap could see a billboard-size sign about a hundred feet away reading THANKS FOR VISITING CALIFORNIA AND COME BACK SOON! He slowed down and looked out his window. He didn't see the road immediately but saw a rectangular structure in the distance. It was hard to tell how far it was from the interstate, the flat land creating the illusion of it being quite close, but considering how small it appeared, about the size of a brick, it had to be at least five miles north.

"There's the road," said Vega, pointing to a dirt path just big enough for a bus to fit through, tire marks on either side.

"I guess you could call it that," said Cap.

He turned onto the unmarked road and drove toward the building. As they got closer he could see a tall chain-link fence, curls of barbed wire running along the top. Also an observation tower, presumably for a guard. Cap accelerated, suddenly anxious.

"What is this place?" he said.

"I don't know," said Vega, removing her sunglasses. "Looks like a prison to me."

Cap slowed just a bit as they approached the facility. Up close they could see that it was not one building but two rows of khaki-colored tents close together, with four white trailers on either side. There was no parking lot or security booth. Cap pulled the car up to the section of fence where there was what appeared to be a handwritten sign: EAST CA. PROCESSING.

He parked, and they got out. Cap went right up to the sign.

"Someone make this in their basement?" he said.

Vega didn't answer, just wandered to the fence and looked at everything. She saw a line of people—kids, looked to be on the young side of their teens, all boys. Guards walked in front of them and behind them, handguns holstered on their hips.

"I'm going to wait in the car. Just watch for a while, okay?" she said.

"Okay," said Cap, placing his hand on the fence.

Vega walked back to the car and got in.

Cap watched the line of boys trailing into a tent. Most of them wore brightly colored T-shirts but some wore gray shirts with ISC printed on the back.

"Jeff Collins send you?" said a voice from behind him.

Cap turned around, and there was a guard with an AR-15 slung over his shoulder. He was in a blue uniform, ISC printed over the breast pocket.

"That's right," said Cap curtly. "Where's Steve McConnell?"

The guard was unfazed by Cap's attitude.

"This way," he answered.

Cap followed him as he unlocked a padlock on the fence and opened it. He led them to one of the trailers.

The guard knocked three times on the trailer door and then opened it. Inside it was an office space—one small conference table, three desks, wheeled chairs. No windows but there was slightly cooler air than outside circulating from a portable AC unit and a loud rotating steel fan in the corner.

A man was there on his phone. Fifties, gray hair blending into blond on his head. Taller than Cap by an inch or two and thin but not necessarily fit. Wrinkled shirt, visible pit circles. He held up one finger to Cap.

Cap didn't sit in any of the seats around the conference table, stood by the door.

McConnell said a few words, some yeps and thanks, then finally, "Bye." He took the phone away from his ear and set it on the desk closest to him.

"Sorry about that. Special Agent Steve McConnell," he said, leaning over the table, shaking Cap's hand.

"Max Caplan," Cap said quietly through his teeth so he would keep his temper in check.

"Pleasure," McConnell said, all business.

He stayed behind the table like he was about to give a presentation. He didn't sit, didn't ask Cap to either.

"What can I do for you?" he said.

"I need to speak to the six girls that Jeff Collins dropped off here yesterday," said Cap, taking care to speak slowly, calmly.

McConnell's eyes searched Cap's face.

"Why would you need to do that?" he asked.

"I'm working with SDPD, as I'm sure Collins told you," said Cap. "My partner and I need to question those girls with regard to an ongoing homicide investigation."

"Okay," he said. "You have their names?"

"We don't know their names," said Cap. "They are the six girls that Collins dropped off yesterday."

McConnell leaned on the desk, tilted his head to one side, stretching.

"We have a lot of kids coming in," he said. "Hard to keep track."

"Were you here yesterday?"

"I'm here every day," said McConnell. "Even on the weekends."

"Then you must remember six girls," said Cap, even slower, even quieter. "They were in their underwear. Does this ring a bell for you?"

McConnell stood up straight, set his hands on his hips above his belt.

"Yeah, I think so," he conceded, didn't seem about to offer up anything else.

"Good," said Cap. "I'm sure you're aware, then, that they had all experienced weeks, if not months, of continual sexual assault. Do you have medical resources available here?"

McConnell sniffed loudly.

"We have a doctor come in once a week," he said.

"Once a week," Cap echoed, stunned.

"Correct," said McConnell. "The girls who were admitted yesterday did not appear to require immediate medical attention so we saw no need to call our MD in early."

Cap felt heat spread on his brow. He clenched and unclenched his fists to get the blood going in his fingers.

"Where are they? The six girls."

McConnell crossed his arms.

"Can I ask what this ongoing case is regarding?" he said.

"You can't, actually," said Cap plainly. "It's confidential. Look, it's my understanding that ISC gets out of the PD's and the DEA's way. I'm working with the PD and the DEA. You can call Commander Roland Otero or Agent Christian Boyce any time you'd like for verification. My partner and I speaking with these girls is vital in preventing other girls being harmed."

Cap tapped the table with two fingers as he spoke. McConnell didn't respond right away. The fan oscillated back and forth.

"You can have an hour," said McConnell dismissively, leaving Cap speechless again. "It's not good for the kids if they're out of their daily routine for any longer than that."

"Yeah?" said Cap. "Their daily routine looks remarkably similar to that of prisoners."

"Don't get overexcited," said McConnell, patronizing. "We're under orders from DHS. You can name it whatever you like. These kids get three square a day and beds. It's probably more than a lot of them had before."

Cap laughed. He was sweating everywhere now, a sheet down his back. His eyes jumped from the desks to the corners of the room and he realized something: There was no paperwork anywhere, no file cabinets, no computers.

"Do you have some kind of admissions process?" he asked.

McConnell licked the corners of his mouth, and Cap realized he was sweating a lot too, the circles under his arms grown to the diameters of dinner plates. He did not answer Cap's question.

"You don't know these kids' names, do you?" Cap said, nausea pressing down on his chest.

"Not your concern," said McConnell, visibly flustered, not meeting his eye.

"Do you have any files? Anywhere?" Cap said, his volume rising steadily.

"Yes, of course we have files. We have a system in place when kids come in and out."

"Yeah? Where is it, McConnell? This trailer isn't that big," Cap said, his eyes wildly searching the space. He pointed to the bare surfaces of the desks and continued: "You have no files, no computer." The unease shifted to anger and disbelief. "What the hell is this place? Who are all of those kids and where are their parents?"

McConnell pushed past his momentary sheepishness and seemed to steel himself, hands pressed on the table in front of him like he was guarding a door.

"You're not here to do oversight, Mr. Caplan. I'm under no obligation to assist you in any way except to provide limited access to the six detainees you wish to interview."

"Detainees," Cap said, the word stumbling on his tongue. "You know, I have a suggestion to propose if you need some help keeping track of your detainees."

McConnell was silent and crossed his arms in a display of willfulness.

"Since you're having such a hard time recording their names, maybe you could give each of them a number," Cap said, preposterously upbeat. "And you know, kids can never remember stuff like that so maybe you could just, you know, write it down on their shirts." Cap scratched his head, continuing his little bit of theater. "But, now that I think about it, you're going to have to wash the shirts, so maybe you could have someone tattoo the numbers on their arms, like right here, for example," Cap said, presenting his left forearm.

McConnell was stoic.

Cap put both hands on the table and leaned forward.

"Find the girl named Missy who got here yesterday and she'll know the other five," he said, his voice shaky with rage.

He couldn't be sure that Missy, the terrified girl whom Davis had matched him with at the Salton house, was one of the six at the facility, but it was worth a shot.

McConnell's scowl had grown larger than the confines of his narrow face, his fair eyebrows arched, mouth pinched and puckered. He came around the conference table and went past Cap, leaving less than an inch between them. McConnell opened the door and yelled, "Sam!"

Cap imagined Nell's face throughout her history: baby, toddler, age ten, age twelve. Sometimes those images were the only hope of him remaining calm.

Vega watched the guard with the AR-15 for a while. It became clear to her that he was not used to carrying one, the way he had it slung over his shoulder like a messenger bag. She also kept an eye on the observation tower and did not see anyone standing at the top of it. It was not a particularly tall tower either, only about fifty feet high, made of wood with a ladder built in down the side. It reminded Vega of the lookout towers people had built in her county after a rash of wildfires the year before.

The trailer door opened, and a tall blond man, whom Vega suspected was McConnell, leaned out and yelled something to the guard with the AR-15. The guard jogged toward the fence and entered the main camp.

She took one last look at the fence held closed by the padlock and then got out of the car, headed toward the trailer.

. . .

Missy was first through the door. When she saw Cap, she smiled tentatively and went right to him. She didn't hug him but stood directly in front of him as if the proximity was intimate enough.

"*Policía,*" she said quietly.

"Missy," said Cap.

Her smile grew now, more secure.

"Are you okay?" said Cap in English.

Missy looked around at McConnell standing by the table and Sam leaning against the door. Then she nodded.

Cap didn't recognize the five other girls, but he knew it was only because he had not interacted with them the way he had with Missy. Three of them appeared to be closer to Missy's age, and the other two were a little bit older, closer to Nell's. They all wore baggy gray ISC shirts and jeans, which also looked too big, rolled up at the ankles on the younger girls.

McConnell and Sam stood in their respective places watching the girls with what Cap thought was an inappropriate degree of suspicion.

"You guys can go," said Vega, who leaned against the wall next to the open door.

McConnell shrugged his shoulders like a frustrated teen and came around the table.

"You got sixty minutes," he said to Vega.

"You're the boss," said Vega.

McConnell and Sam left, slamming the door behind them, the trailer shaking with the force of it.

Cap pulled out a chair at the conference table for Missy and gestured for her to sit. The other five girls were already sitting, taking in their surroundings. Vega pulled a wheeled chair over from one of the desks and rolled it to Cap, then grabbed one for herself and sat at the corner of the table.

"Are you all okay?" she said in Spanish.

Missy nodded first. Four others did, one by one. The girl at the end, older with a burn on her temple just like Cap's, did not respond. Vega recognized the girl next to her as the one covered in blood from Mitch's gunshot wound, the girl with the unusually sharp and accurate answers with regard to the head count and number of weapons. She nudged the girl on the end with the burn mark and whispered something to her. Finally the girl with the burn mark nodded.

"Is anyone hurt?"

Shakes of the head all around the table.

"Are they giving you food and water here?"

Nods.

Vega looked at Cap. What first?

"Their names," said Cap. "Let's get them down."

Vega pulled her phone from her pocket and tapped opened a notes app.

"Please tell us your names. Your real names."

One by one they did.

Missy started: "Melisenda Cantiñero."

"Yolanda Torres."

"Rosa María Silva."

"Francisca Santana."

"Dalena Cortez," said the girl who had been Fat Mitch's hostage.

She nudged the girl on the end, who shook her head again.

Dalena said, "She's Isabel Benitez."

Vega wrote them all down on her phone.

"Do you know the names of the other four girls?" Vega asked.

"Ara, Nati," said Missy, who paused.

"María Elena," added Francisca. Her hair was cut a little shorter than the others', and her arms were thin, no muscle and no fat, more like a preteen boy than a girl.

"Catalina," said Dalena, and then, "Chicago."

Vega finished typing the names into her notes and looked back up at Cap. Where to, next.

"I guess we start with the biggest first," said Cap.

Vega nodded.

"Do any of you know Michael Mackey?" she asked.

The girls had blank expressions. Some of them looked at one another, but no one answered.

"Do we have a picture?" said Cap.

"Yeah," said Vega, scrolling on her phone. She brought up a photo that Otero had sent and passed the phone to Missy, who nodded.

"He was waiting for the other girls yesterday, before we came here," she said.

"Did you ever see him before that?" asked Vega.

"He was at the house sometimes," said the girl named Rosa María in a voice so high and quiet Vega thought she had to be even younger than she looked. "He talked to Coyote Ben."

Vega translated for Cap, who said, "You want to confirm what Collins told us?" he said.

"Did any of you see where the other four girls were dropped off yesterday, to this man, Michael Mackey?" Vega said, holding up the phone so they could still see the photo.

"We saw them get off the bus," said Francisca. "The driver said some of us were going with the man," she said, pointing at the phone.

"The man had a van, and the girls got in," Missy added. "Then the bus brought us here."

"Do any of you remember what color the man's van was?" Vega asked.

She hoped only to get the color. She knew most witnesses who had not been through repeated and extensive trauma and had a passing familiarity with English wouldn't remember any details; it was unrealistic to expect that any of them could identify the make or model.

"Blue?" said Missy hopefully.

"I think it was black," said Francisca.

"No, it was dark blue," added Yolanda.

"That's fine," Vega said kindly. "Black or blue."

She said it in English for Cap's benefit.

Dalena, the older girl who had spoken for Isabel Benitez, raised her hand like she was in a classroom.

"Yes, Dalena, right?" said Vega.

Dalena nodded.

"Do you want the license plate number?" she asked politely, saying "license plate" in English.

Cap almost fell off his chair. He and Vega looked at each other.

"Yes, I do," said Vega earnestly. "You remember the license plate number?"

Dalena nodded.

"6GLV478," she recited.

Vega typed it on the phone and then flipped it so Dalena could see the screen.

"Is that right?"

Dalena nodded again. Vega handed her phone to Cap, who began a text to McTiernan.

"Thank you," said Vega to Dalena. Then she looked around the table at the group. "Thank all of you."

"Excuse me," said Rosa María, painfully polite. "How long will we stay here?"

"Do you know where my mother is?" said Missy right away.

Then they all began speaking at once, suddenly overflowing with questions and details, addressing both Vega and Cap. All of them except Isabel, who stared at a point on the table.

"I'm sorry," Vega said over them. "We have to leave now because we need to find the other four girls and make sure they're okay. But we will come back, and we will have answers to your questions."

"Please don't leave," Missy implored Cap.

She wasn't crying but there was fear in her face. It reminded him of how she'd looked back in the cell of a room in the Salton basement. He longed to hug her or at least place his hand on top of hers to console her but didn't dare. She was not his to touch.

"You'll be safe here," he said.

Vega translated, and Missy nodded bravely.

Then a stark sound burst from Dalena's mouth.

"Sorry," she said, her hand on her throat. "I have a cough."

Cap continued to console Missy and the other girls. Even though he spoke English, they all listened to him intently.

Vega smiled at Dalena, who weakly smiled back. She looked away quickly, though, and Vega couldn't be sure because she'd heard it for only a second, but she could swear it hadn't been a cough at all. It was a laugh.

23

CAP DROVE A CLEAN NINETY ON THE INTERSTATE TOWARD THEIR
hotel. He gripped the wheel and ground his teeth together, fury still
rushing over him like the rash of a fever.

Vega had McTiernan on speaker, as they updated each other.

McTiernan spoke in a hushed voice: "Montalvo's guys are in the
tunnel. They're on motorbikes, like scooters, you know. Otero thinks it
will take them a couple of hours at most. Usually takes people sixteen
hours on foot."

"Good," said Vega. "Let us know when you get a hit on the plates."

"Will do. What was the story at the ISC facility?"

Vega glanced at Cap, who stared straight ahead, still mute with anger.

"We have to hit pause on that," she said, still watching Cap. "We'll
deal with it after we find Mackey. The girls don't appear to be in immediate danger there."

She and McTiernan said their goodbyes and hung up. Cap didn't
speak, didn't look like he would start speaking soon.

"Caplan," said Vega. "They're not in immediate danger there, yes?"

Cap's eyes searched the horizon, stinging from the bleachy dryness
of the air. He made himself blink a couple of times.

"Yes," he said.

They continued the ride in silence. Soon there were more on- and
off-ramps, cars appearing around them on the freeway, gas stations,
strip malls. Cap pulled off at the exit for the hotel and drove to the lot.
He parked the car.

"I'll wait," he said.

He didn't appear to be seething anymore, Vega thought, but fatigue
had replaced his anger, his face drawn.

"I'll be right back," Vega said.

She got out of the car and ran up the stairs. Cap watched her go into the room and shut the door. He leaned his head down and rested it on the steering wheel, closed his eyes. He thought maybe he could fall asleep like that, his shoulders hunching forward. He imagined Nell again, then Missy's frightened face.

Vega's phone on her seat buzzed, and Cap twitched and sat up. He grabbed the phone and read the first line of a long text from McTiernan: "Surf Motel, 68 Beachfront."

Vega came down the stairs with the bolt cutters over her shoulder and a duffel bag in her hand. She got back into the car, and Cap handed her the phone.

"We got a hit on the van plates," he said.

Vega laid the bolt cutters across her lap and placed the duffel bag at her feet.

She read the text and said, "It's a Hertz minivan, rented by Michael Mackey yesterday morning from a lot near the airport. And now the plates have come up registered at the Surf Motel. Near the beach."

Vega sent a text to McTiernan and Otero, and then her phone buzzed with a call. Vega tapped the speaker and turned up the volume.

"Boyce and I are meeting shortly," Otero said. "We think your earlier proposal about using the tunnels made sense. We need to meet at the station and then we can all go check out this motel?"

Vega looked at Cap, who had his hand on the wheel, staring at the dashboard. He rubbed his eyes.

"I don't think we should wait that long, Commander," said Vega. "We know where Mackey is; Cap and I can bring him in."

"Wait a second," said Otero, stern. "Let's think this through. Mackey is a trained agent, and we don't need this spinning into a hostage situation."

"It's already a hostage situation," said Vega. "He's holed up at a motel with the girls, and he's not thinking the clearest right now."

She shook her head as if Otero could see her.

"If we have a lock on a location, we need to take advantage of it. I would rate Mackey pretty high on the possibility of flight risk."

"Ms. Vega," said Otero, Cap getting the feeling he was straining to control his volume. "I realize no order I give you holds since you're not a police officer, but we are working together on this, and we need each other. I strongly advise waiting for us to get there so we can maximize the chances of a positive outcome."

Vega shut her eyes and winced sharply, as if she'd just grabbed a hot pan handle without a towel.

"Fair enough," Cap cut in, sounding beaten. "In two, three hours we'll meet you at the station and work out a strategy, unless you need us sooner."

"Not necessary," said Otero, the relief plainly audible in his voice. "At the station, two or three hours. Ms. Vega, please feel free to call Mr. Castán."

They said a few more things and then hung up. Cap turned the key in the ignition, and Vega reached over and turned it off again. Cap leaned back out of her way.

"What the hell?" said Vega, her voice cracking, the betrayal fresh on her face.

"Vega," said Cap wearily.

He gently brushed her hand away from the key and started the car again.

"Do you really think I'm going to let those girls wait any longer?"

Vega reared back in her seat, surprised. Cap turned to her.

"This is that half hour," he said.

Vega remembered saying it to him in the woods, which felt like ten years ago now. She remembered the wet leaves on her feet, the bright blurry sun through the naked branches of the white birch trees, the unmistakable taste of blood in the back of her throat being pushed up from her rapidly pounding heart. She remembered Cap's lips on hers, their kinetic warmth, his skin coated with cool sweat.

She had done it to disarm him, of course, but also because she had damn well wanted to. And even though they didn't know it when she kissed him, they could have died that day in the woods.

Maybe they did, she thought now. Maybe they did get shot by meth heads that day, and everything since then was the last gasp of neurological activity before death. Maybe their bodies lay side by side in the woods, still under that cold, clear sky.

"Yeah, it is," she said.

Cap looked at her, something daring and young behind his eyes, and she knew they were not still in the woods. They were right here.

They made good time driving to the Surf Motel, just beating the afternoon rush hour. The rooms were laid out in a long strip on the beach, a line of parking spaces facing them on the street side. Cap cruised the lot, looking for Mackey's van. It was not difficult; the lot was mostly empty, and they saw it at the far end of the strip, no cars on either side. Cap made a U and parked close by the entrance, next to a bungalow with a CHECK-IN sign on the door.

Vega dialed the numbers on Javier's business card. The phone rang once, and then he picked up.

"Miss Vega," he said, his voice like a growl. "You have good news for me."

Statement, not a question.

"I have a place to meet in two hours. Can you and your people be there?"

"Of course," he said, amused.

Vega gave him the coordinates.

"You will bring the four girls and Mr. Mackey to me then," he said.

"That's right," said Vega.

"And what about this Rafa," Javier said. "Do you have him as well?"

"Like I said, he's in police custody in a hospital. You're going to have to employ someone else to help you with him."

She didn't breathe, waited for him to respond.

"Hm," he said. "I suppose I can do that." He paused and exhaled, satisfied. "Very well. I will meet you in two hours. Please don't be late, and also, Ms. Vega?"

He paused again, waiting for her acknowledgment.

"Yes?" she said.

"You should not be joking about this," he said. "This is not a thing to joke about."

"I will be there in two hours," Vega said.

"Yes, you will. Goodbye."

Vega tapped the red button on her phone and sighed.

"Ready?" said Cap.

Vega nodded.

They unbuckled their seatbelts and got out of the car. Vega set the bolt cutters and the duffel bag on the hood and unzipped the bag. Cap leaned forward from his side of the hood and peered inside the bag, which looked to be full of chains. Vega pulled out a thin steel tool, about a foot long, with a circular head on the top. Cap considered himself moderately handy around the house but didn't recognize this particular piece.

"Torque wrench?" said Vega, like she was offering dessert. "I also have a tow chain with grab hooks and a steel drilling hammer."

Cap nodded toward the wrench, and Vega passed it to him. It was heavier than it looked, top-heavy from the head.

"You want to knock on the door, see how far you get?" said Vega, tossing the duffel back into the car.

Cap nodded.

"I'm going around to the beach side. On the website it looks like there are decks for all the rooms with glass doors," she said. "See what condition he's in. You can try to talk to him. Maybe he's ready to break."

"And if he's not?" asked Cap, knowing the answer.

"Then I'll be right there," said Vega, lifting the bolt cutters off the car. "Unless he's totally looped I don't think he'll shoot first. But you should switch the safety off on your Sig just in case."

"Good idea," Cap agreed.

He took out the Sig and flipped the safety, returned it to the holster. He slid the torque wrench into his belt on his side.

"Um, excuse me?" came a scratchy voice.

It was a leathery, tanned woman in a floral print dress and Havaianas flip-flops. She stood at the open door of the check-in bungalow. Cap wasn't sure if she'd seen the gun or not, but he knew she did see Vega resting the bolt cutters on her shoulder and Cap wearing the torque wrench on his hip.

"Can I help you?" the woman said tentatively.

"No thanks," said Cap. "We're good."

The woman retreated into the bungalow.

"She's probably calling the cops," said Cap.

Vega shrugged.

"More, the merrier," she said.

They headed to the end of the strip and stopped three doors from the last room, two doors from where Mackey's van was parked.

"Fourteen, fifteen, sixteen," said Cap, reading the numbers off the doors. "Got to be one of those."

They stood side by side, not moving for a moment.

"It'll take me a minute to get there," said Vega. "Watch your back."

Then she took off, striding through the parking lot toward the road and then to the left, toward the entrance to the beach.

Cap rolled his shoulders back and took a hearty breath through his nose. He could smell the clean salt of the ocean. Then he took a few steps and knocked on the door marked 14.

. . .

Vega walked down a concrete ramp to the sand. There were two signs
at the end: OCEAN BEACH, with an arrow to the left, toward the Surf
Motel and others like it, and DOG BEACH, with an arrow to the right.
DOGS NEED NOT BE LEASHED.

Past a red thatched fence running perpendicular to the ocean, Vega
did see some dogs, kicking up sand clouds and splashing in the water,
their owners throwing balls and sticks. She saw two gray, stout-legged
dogs with long, strong jaws wrestling, their heads big as helmets.

"Aw, you love your sister, don't you?" said their owner, taking pictures of them with his phone.

Vega walked on the sand to the motel. The decks of the rooms were
on stilts, but they were higher than she'd expected, about ten feet. But
the stilt structure was wood, and there were plenty of angled braces on
the posts leading to the beams of the decks. The question was could she
climb up one-handed while holding the bolt cutters in the other.

She jumped once to get used to the feel of the sand under her boots,
holding the bolt cutters down at her side in her left hand and reaching
her right high in the air. She tried a couple more jumps, her fingers just
scraping the brace, wet and sandy from the beach, and on the third
grabbed it hard, the muscles in her fingers locking, nails digging into
the soft wood. She pulled up with her right hand and hiked her legs
around the standing post.

She gasped and slung the bolt cutters up across the brace, placed
one hand at the end of the handles and the other on the jaws and used
it for leverage as she pulled her whole body up. She sat on the brace,
balancing, bolt cutters on her lap, and then carefully leaned backward,
grabbed one of the rails on the platform above, and peered out, onto
the deck surface of the corner room, number 16. She couldn't see inside
the room, just the patio chairs and small round table on the deck. She
slid the bolt cutters through the rails onto the surface of the deck and
climbed up.

Cap knocked three times quickly on the door to room 14 to make it
sound like he was bringing fresh towels instead of being about to raid
the place like a SWAT agent. He waited another minute, moved down
to 15, and knocked. Blackout curtains hung in the window, no space

in the middle or at the edges. Cap knocked on the door again and got close to the window, bringing his hands around his eyes to block the light and see inside, but he couldn't make anything out beyond static dark shapes.

He stepped back from the window and continued to the next and last door, room 16.

Vega crouched in the corner of the deck against the wall. The sliding glass door was a foot to her left. She hadn't leaned forward enough to look inside, didn't want to show her hand just yet. She knew it would all have to happen quickly—she'd have to look, assess, and swing.

She felt the mist from the ocean on her face and wiped her chin on her shoulder. She stood slowly, holding the bolt cutters with both hands by the handles, jaws aiming down, like it was a weighted bat and she was in the bull pen.

Cap knocked on 16. He waited, knocked again. He had a strong feeling Mackey had to be in one of them, so Mackey was either not there at the moment, asleep, or just not answering. So, Cap thought, he would have to check that box, move on to the next plan. He bent down to examine the doorknob, which didn't look exceptionally sturdy, and thought the head of the torque wrench would easily crack it open. There was a dead-bolt cylinder above the knob as well, so Cap figured he would have to knock the doorknob off and then jam the wrench into the cylinder. Subtle.

He pulled out his phone, texted Vega: "No answer 14 15 16."

Then he heard the thick snap of a dead bolt unlocking. He turned and reached for his Sig at the same time but wasn't quick enough. Mackey was there, at the door of room 15, open just a few inches but wide enough for him to point what appeared to be a .50 caliber handgun at Cap's head. Cap recognized the gun as a Marlin. His former partner used to call them IBD pistols. Itty-bitty-dick guns for guys who needed to compensate. He could make fun of it all he wanted, but at that range, about a yard away, Cap knew that kind of round could blow through his skull as if it were an eggshell. He slowly raised his hands.

.   .   .

Vega felt her phone hum in her pocket but didn't look. She took a step away from the wall and could see only a sliver of room 16 through the glass door. She breathed deep, loaded her lungs with air, and stepped in front of the glass, holding the bolt cutters high above her right shoulder, starting to swing.

She stopped short and stumbled backward when she saw the room was empty, and she knew it had to be one of the others, either 14 or 15.

Mackey looked tired. That was the first thing Cap noticed. The second was that there were no girls, just a double bed, which took up most of the room and looked like it hadn't been touched in some time.

"They're not dead," said Mackey, watching Cap's gaze wander.

"Okay."

The room was warm and muggy, the air-conditioning struggling.

"Where's your partner?" he said.

"She's not here," said Cap.

Mackey looked him up and down.

"You have a semiautomatic handgun holstered under your jacket," he said. "You seem smart enough not to make a move for it."

Cap kept his hands up, near his shoulders.

"Where are the girls?"

Mackey nodded toward the connecting door to room 14.

"They can't talk right now."

"How do you expect this all to end?" Cap asked honestly.

Mackey cocked his head to the side and twisted up his mouth as if the question had really gotten under his skin. Were his eyes watering with tears? Cap couldn't tell. The room was gray, vertical blinds rippling slightly over the glass door.

"How do you think?" Mackey said, suddenly petulant. "You don't know me, Mr. Caplan."

Mackey paused, swept his tongue down over his lower lip feverishly like he had little muscle control.

"Maybe not," said Cap. "But this isn't going to end well for any of us if you hurt those girls."

Mackey sighed, moved his tongue around inside his mouth now, from one cheek to the other, like he was trying to stretch them out.

"I'm an optimistic guy, Mr. Caplan. I've worked on the federal level of law enforcement my entire adult life because I believe in the fairness of it."

Cap labored to stay calm, breathed deep through his nose.

"I busted my ass in college, master's in criminal justice, top of my class every time. Outlasted everyone to get the right internships—and DEA came for me, you understand?" he said to Cap, as if he'd doubted this. "They recruited *me* out of school. I didn't come to them." He paused to swipe his tongue over his bottom lip again. "I've given them my whole life, and I barely crack one twenty-five a year."

"That's a lot of money to some people," said Cap.

"Not to me," said Mackey. "I risk my life, Mr. Caplan. Every day."

Cap felt his ears and neck grow hot, the anger roiling in his chest.

"That's what public servants do, Mackey," he said, as calmly as he could. "They serve."

"It wasn't good enough for you though, right?" Mackey said, taunting him. "You were a cop. You got out and probably make a very nice living in the private sector. That's all I want, too," he said earnestly, as if he were talking straight now, law enforcement brother to brother.

"But here's where we're a little different, Mackey," Cap said, straining not to shout. "My private sector work is legal. You're trafficking little girls for Mexico's biggest cartel boss."

"The girls are fine," Mackey snapped. "Do you know how much Perez paid me to watch them?"

Cap didn't speak, didn't want to indulge Mackey with a guess.

"Two hundred K apiece," he said, his eyes glassy with the thought of it.

"I guess you shouldn't have let that psycho kill two of them then," said Cap.

Mackey's face went white. He swallowed, bared his teeth.

"That was not my fault."

His resolve was weakening, Cap thought. Maybe they could all get out clean. Switch tactics.

"This could be an opportunity," Cap said, his voice softer. "Right now you owe Perez four hundred K for Maricel Villareal and Dulce Díaz, right?"

"Plus penalties," said Mackey, appearing depleted.

"Okay," said Cap. "Make a run for it. Just go. Keep the money, and I'll keep the girls."

Mackey took a step closer to Cap, now about a foot away.

Cap watched his face. Big pupils, sweat coating the skin, tongue still licking the lips. He pictured himself on the floor of the motel room, skull blown open, blood seeping into the powder blue carpet. Vega, he thought to himself, now would be a good time.

Vega lifted one leg over the railing, then the other. She pressed her back against the wall, leaned her head forward, and tried to see through the sliding glass door of room 15. The vertical blinds were drawn but not tightly, the strips waving from the gusts of air-conditioning or a fan inside.

She could make out only shapes at first. It was dark in the room, and the sun was beginning its drift downward. She took a small step closer, and pressed her forehead against the glass, tried to see between the swaying blinds.

Near the door, there was Cap with hands up, and Mackey pointing a gun at him. Vega stared at Cap's face. If he was nervous he didn't look it, trying to talk, stall. Vega knew even if Mackey was desperate, it would take a fair amount of narcotics or severe psychosis to undo the years of law enforcement training. If he heard a loud noise behind him, he would probably not just discharge his weapon. His instinct would be to turn toward the source, not fire at the current target, which was Cap's head. Right? she thought.

Right.

Keep him talking, Cap thought. Make him angry, make him sad, just make him talk a minute more. Cap didn't dare look at the glass, didn't want to give Mackey any hints.

"You married, Mackey?" he asked.

"Divorced," Mackey answered, indulging Cap for the moment.

"Me, too," said Cap. "It's rough."

Mackey shrugged gently.

"She was a real cunt," he said.

Cap winced.

Mackey smirked.

"What—you don't like that word?" he said. "It's an accurate descriptor."

"Kids?" said Cap.

"No."

"I have one," said Cap. "She's seventeen. I am mostly worried about her most of the time."

Mackey wasn't listening, Cap could tell. He was weighing his options. If he killed Cap, would it make more trouble for him or less?

He appeared to decide quickly; he stepped right up to Cap now, pressed the nose of the gun in the middle of his forehead. All of Cap's muscles seized up on reflex. He raised his hands higher, scrunched his shoulders up around his neck, knew that if Mackey fired now it wouldn't just be his skull blown to bits; he wouldn't have a face anymore, possibly not even a whole tooth to identify.

"Her name is Nell," he said. "I call her Bug—that's a nickname."

Cap shut his eyes for just a second, then opened them and let his gaze drift to the glass. He saw Vega's face in the corner, her eyes on him.

"But she likes it. Even though she's growing up fast, she still likes that I call her that. But I hate to break it to you, Mackey, for the most part—"

Cap turned to look at the glass now, didn't hide the fact that he was looking at all. Vega's face was gone.

Mackey turned too, confused.

Cap continued: "Women really don't like it when you call them names."

She aimed for the single pane of the glass door instead of the double. She spun around fast, full 360 to build the momentum like a shot put thrower, and smashed the jaws of the bolt cutters right in the middle, shutting her eyes the second before she made contact.

The glass shattered, sprayed in a shower of shards and splinters into the room, back-splashing jagged chips onto Vega's face and chest.

Vega dropped the bolt cutters and leaped to the ground, made her body flat right after she heard the shots.

Cap remembered as a young cop there were situations when he wasn't sure he would make it out with his limbs and his head intact, and the moments would slow down, crawl by at an almost painful rate, but as he got older the inverse seemed to be true. Things went fast now, sucked through a wormhole, the clock's counter on anabolic steroids, racing through the minutes.

He thought about that in less than a second, as the glass exploded into the room. Mackey had already begun to turn toward the noise, and Cap couldn't see Vega clearly, the blinds blowing in the wind from the ocean, bits of glass flying through the air onto the bed. Cap could feel it blow into his hair and the side of his face like gravel. He pulled out the Sig and saw Mackey shield his eyes with his arm and fire the Marlin twice at the waving blinds.

Cap couldn't see straight, a speck of glass hitting his left eyelid, but he fired anyway at Mackey, who ran to the deck. Cap went after him, pushed the blinds aside, the glass crunching under his shoes, saw Mackey jump the railing that connected room 15's deck to room 16's and run to the end of the platform.

Cap aimed the Sig at Mackey but then heard his name.

"Caplan!"

It was Vega on the beach below. She was fine, sweaty, sandy, dots of blood lining her arms from the glass chips.

"The girls are in Fourteen!" Cap called, picking up the bolt cutters from the deck.

"You stay. I've got him," said Vega.

Cap watched Mackey jump off the deck onto the beach, and Vega took off after him, the Springfield in her hand.

As soon as the shots stopped, she'd log-rolled fast toward the end of the deck. Caked in glass, she'd gone off the edge, no vertical railings here, and did her best to jackknife in midair so she landed on her haunches and hands and tumbled sideways in the sand. Her wrists were a little jammed, but she was still able to hold her gun.

Now she watched Mackey run, but he was limping. She ran at full speed, pumping her arms and sprinting on the toes so she wouldn't sink. Mackey seemed to slow down even more as he reached the red thatched fence that bordered the dog beach. Vega saw a thin, dark trail in the sand behind him, realized he was bleeding, that Cap must have hit him.

He jumped over the fence and stumbled, and one of the dogs, the mutts Vega had seen when she'd first come onto the beach, ran at Mackey, barking wildly, the owner yelling, "Rosie!" Vega was close to Mackey now, about ten feet away, and she watched as he shot the dog, blew the animal's hind leg apart.

The owner's scream ripped through the air as he crumpled around the injured dog. Vega walked with purpose, stretching the gun out in front of her. She knew she had to shoot Mackey because now he was shooting and probably wouldn't stop. He'd come undone; the blocks he'd been stacking in his little tower for weeks and months had collapsed. He was injured; he was mad.

Also she was pissed about the dog. She'd had one as a child and had a lot of feelings about it.

She aimed for his right shoulder and fired. He didn't make a sound but dropped the gun and fell on his hands and knees. Vega moved closer, aimed for his right forearm in case he reached for the gun.

The dog owner wept and held the bleeding dog on his lap, the dog's chest moving up and down rapidly. The owner started screaming again but Vega's hearing was a little tweaked—it was a different name now.

"Daisy, Daisy, Daisy, no!" he yelled.

It was the other dog, the sister of the injured one. She jumped in the air and onto Mackey's leg, latching onto his thigh with her boxy jaws. Mackey screamed and tried to pull the dog off, pushing at her head, but she wouldn't let go, jaws locked. She shook her giant head back and forth like Mackey's leg was a twisted rope chew toy, tearing through his pants, blood spraying up from it in an arched stream.

Did she just know where the femoral artery was, thought Vega. Was that just instinct?

Vega lowered her gun slowly with the sun on the back of her neck, watched Mackey bleed to death and didn't do a goddamn thing.

24

CAP WALKED BACK INTO THE ROOM, THROUGH THE BLINDS, AROUND the bed, over the glass. He flipped the lock on the knob of the connecting door to room 14 and opened it. This room was even darker than Mackey's; it took a moment for Cap's eyes to adjust. Then he saw her—a girl, probably sixteen, lying on the bed on her stomach. She had a circular burn on her temple just like Isabel Benitez's, just like his. She still wore her underwear and lingerie from the Salton house. The TV was on, a Spanish-language hospital show playing.

She barely glanced at him, digging one hand into a bag of potato chips, while the other hung over the side of the bed awkwardly, as if it were weighted.

"Hello?" Cap said to her.

She didn't answer but jerked her arm up, and Cap saw that it was indeed weighted—it was connected by a pair of handcuffs at the wrist to another girl, who scrambled out from under the bed and stared at him with a mix of fear and shock.

"*Policía*," Cap said softly, tapping his chest.

"Nati!" called the girl over her shoulder, and then she sat on the bed next to the girl with the burn mark, still solely focused on the TV.

The bathroom door opened, and two more girls emerged, both about twelve or thirteen. One of them looked even younger than Missy.

"Who you?" she said in English. Her eyebrows were dark and almost connected above her nose.

"You speak English?" said Cap.

She nodded.

"I learn school."

"My name's Max," he said to her. He looked around to the other girls. "Max," he said again, pointing to himself. "What's your name?" he said to the English-speaking girl.

"Nati," she said. "Where the man?"

"He's gone," said Cap assuredly, though he did not know himself how he sounded so confident.

"Where Dalena?" asked Nati.

The girl with the burn made a screeching sound, a sort of cackle, her eyes still on the screen, and then she spoke rapid Spanish in Nati's direction. Cap only picked up "Dalena" and "barman" and he thought he heard "Coyote Ben."

"Dalena Cortez?" he said.

Nati nodded.

"She's safe," Cap said, choking on the word a little, picturing the ISC facility. "All the others are safe."

"She say she saves us," said Nati. "She say she come."

"It's okay," said Cap. He glanced around again at all of the girls. "You're all okay now."

He leaned forward and said gently, "Give me your hands."

Nati appeared apprehensive but then focused on the bolt cutters and understood. She said something in Spanish to the girl next to her, and then they both carefully extended their arms toward Cap.

He opened the jaws of the bolt cutters and set the blades on the chain of the cuffs that linked the girls together.

"Don't move, okay?" he said.

Nati nodded, translated for her friend.

Cap held tightly to the handle grips and brought them together forcefully, felt a soft resistance for less than a second before the link broke. The chain came apart like a toy, and the girls stared at their newly freed hands, the cuffs still on their wrists.

Cap drove to the tunnel in the desert, Vega in the passenger seat, the girls squeezed into the back, wrapped in blankets from the Surf Motel. Nati sat on the lap of the other older girl, called María Elena. They stared out the side window, craned their heads to peer out the rear. No one spoke.

There was a white cargo van parked on the side of the road, and a figure standing next to it. As Cap drove closer he could make out who it was. He let his breath out, hadn't realized he'd been holding it.

"There's McT," he said, even though he knew Vega could see him too.

Cap pulled up and parked behind the van. McTiernan held up his hand in a wave. He appeared relieved to see them as well.

Vega turned around to speak to the girls. They seemed nervous, glancing at McTiernan and the van, alarmed that they might end up in it, Vega assumed. Only Chicago, sitting in the middle, squinted toward the window disinterestedly.

"We need to talk to our friend," said Vega in Spanish. "Please wait here, okay?"

The three who were listening nodded. Vega and Cap got out of the car and walked toward McTiernan.

"Are you okay?" he said to them.

Cap looked down at his clothes, wrinkled and sweaty.

"Honestly, I don't know," he said. "Can I answer later?"

"Where's Otero and Boyce?" said Vega.

"At the motel, cleaning up," said McTiernan.

"They planning to stay there?"

McTiernan nodded.

"What's the timing here like?" Vega asked.

McTiernan looked at his watch.

"I'd say within the hour," he said, nodding toward the tunnel's opening. "What about Castán?"

"Hour fifteen," said Vega. Then she turned to Cap. "You should leave first."

"'Scuse me?" he said.

"You should . . . leave first," she said, quieter. "I don't want the girls to see the others," she said, nodding to the van.

Cap followed her gaze to the van and then back at the girls in the car. He hadn't thought it all through until that moment.

"That's fine, but I'm not leaving you here," he said. "McT can take the girls and pick up Rodrigo."

"I'm not leaving either of you here," said McTiernan, incredulous.

"You can't be here," Vega said to McTiernan. "As a cop. You can't see what's about to happen."

"I'm such a good liar, though," said McTiernan.

"You, Otero, Boyce—none of you can have your eyes on this," said Vega.

McTiernan scratched behind his ear, looked like a little kid. Vega knew he knew it was true. She turned to Cap, who shrugged, held his arms out as if to present himself.

"I'm not a cop," he said.

"You can't be here, either," she said gently.

"Vega, these guys . . ." he began, then he stopped.

"These guys know where Nell is," she said.

She took a step toward Cap. McTiernan retreated slowly toward the van, allowing them a spot of privacy. Vega got up close to Cap now but didn't look in his eyes, put her face almost right next to his and looked straight over his shoulder.

"You know it's true," she said, her breath hot on his ear.

"Vega," said Cap, putting his arms on her shoulders and positioning her directly in front of him so she had to look at his face. "One or more people are going to die right here."

"So you want to stay and add to those numbers?" she said. "Why do you have to argue with me all the time?"

Cap was almost angry at how soothing her voice was. He was sure she was placing him under some sort of hypnosis.

"Please listen to me," she said softly, and then, even softer, "don't make me break your femur."

Cap was too tired to laugh so he sighed.

Vega continued: "Get Rodrigo and wait for me to text you."

He didn't protest, but he wasn't moving from where he stood.

"Two hours," he said.

"Two hours," she repeated.

He turned away from her then and got into the car. He said something to the girls in the backseat, and then started the engine, switched on the lights. He made a U in the middle of the road, Nati watching Vega through the window as they sped off the way they'd come.

Vega stared as the car got smaller. She turned back to McTiernan when she heard him unlock the back doors of the van. He latched the handles to hooks on either side of the doors so they stayed open, wiped the sweat from his forehead with the back of his hand, and placed his hands on his hips.

"I'll go in, yeah?" he said.

He didn't wait for her to answer and climbed onto the bed of the van. Vega stepped forward and stood at the doors. There were the two white bags, all zipped up.

"Which one's which?" said Vega.

McTiernan thought about it.

"My left is Maricel Villareal. Right is Dulce Díaz."

"Maricel first," said Vega.

"On two," said McTiernan, crouching, sliding his hands under his end of the bag. "One . . ."

Vega laced her fingers under the bag. She could feel Maricel's legs, light like paper towel tubes in her arms.

"Two."

They lifted the bag. Vega backed up, and McTiernan stepped down from the van bed onto the road.

"Where do you want to go?" he asked her.

"Just over here," she answered, leading him to a patch of cactus-free dirt a dozen feet from the road.

They lowered the bag, then went back for the other. They lined the two bags up, side by side. McTiernan gazed down at them.

"I don't want to leave you here, either," he said to Vega.

"You have to get past that," she said, looking toward the sun.

"And just trust you?"

"You don't have to," said Vega, shrugging.

"But you know what you're doing, right?" McTiernan said, growing anxious.

"Think so," said Vega.

"You *think* so?" said McTiernan.

"Yeah, McT. My near-death count's at three for the day. I think so."

McTiernan rubbed his nose, sweat flying into the air.

Vega peered toward the mouth of the tunnel, then cast her line of vision toward the road and squinted.

"They'll all be here soon," she said. "You should go."

McTiernan nodded, looked about to throw up. As he walked past Vega, he placed his hand on her shoulder for a second, then removed it quickly and kept going. He closed the back doors of the van, and went around to the driver's side and got in, started the engine. He made a U and went in the same direction as Cap had gone.

Vega didn't watch the van shrink. She turned toward the sun, which was heading down but still hot on her face. She kept her eyes on the tunnel's opening, just a black pocket in the sand, the bodies of the dead girls at her feet.

Soon she heard the rattle of a small engine, and she started toward the tunnel. As soon as she saw the first man come up with a kerchief covering the bottom half of his face and a rifle slung over his shoulder, she raised her hands up as far as they would go.

The sun was still not down when Castán's SUV came into view. It was low enough, though, for the headlights to be on, the sky darkening to the color of blue glass. The SUV pulled over and parked at the side of the road.

First the driver stepped out, then the man with the gun named Memo came from the passenger's side. They glanced at Vega in passing, then at the white bags on the ground, about ten feet away from where she stood. Memo stood next to the hood, pointing his gun in Vega's direction, almost casually. The driver, meanwhile, opened the rear door on the passenger side, and Javier Castán got out.

He waved at Vega and approached her, Memo and the driver flanking him on either side.

"Miss Vega," he called cheerily.

Then he made a small circle in the air with his index finger toward her, indicating the driver should move forward.

Vega raised her arms preemptively, and the driver patted her down and removed her Springfield from the holster.

"This is encouraging," said Castán, gesturing to the white bags on the ground.

Then he held his arms out.

"I wonder where are the other four," he said calmly.

"They'll be here soon," said Vega.

Castán checked his watch, the face gold and chunky.

"I hope so," he said, allowing a wince to cross his face. "Have you had any pain today, from the accident?"

Vega shook her head.

Castán shrugged.

"I have been in a few car accidents. The first two or three, nothing. As I get older, I feel it the next day in my back, my neck," he said, gesturing to the areas.

Vega stared at him.

"Getting old is no fun, Miss Vega," he said. "But better than nothing, you'll agree?"

Vega kept her eyes on him, didn't respond.

Castán nodded toward the white bags, and the driver walked toward them. He held Vega's Springfield at his side, an afterthought.

Vega stared at Memo's gun, still on her. She heard the driver unzipping the first bag, and without thinking about it, looked toward the sound, tilting her head the slightest bit.

Then she noticed Castán's expression change, from amused to another thing entirely. The artificial friendliness washed right out of his face, and suddenly it was like he was connected to an unseen power source underground, his arms straight at his sides, his eyes black and hard.

"You should learn to control what you look at, Miss Vega," he said, his voice hollow.

Then one of the men from the tunnel burst through the opening of Maricel Villareal's body bag and fired three quick shots from a semi-automatic rifle across the driver's torso.

Memo fired a messy shot in the direction of the man in the bag and missed. He ran at the bags as a second man ripped through the top of Dulce Díaz's bag and fired a single shot into Memo's face.

Vega didn't even have a second before Castán yanked her by the wrist and turned her around so she was right in front of him, both of them facing the horizon. Castán was strong and clearly had plenty of practice yanking women by the wrist. She could also tell he knew what he was doing, spiraling the wrist backward—he would just have to make one quick snap, and there would go a bone and some tendons. Instinctively her other arm went behind her back also, her fingers digging into Castán's arm.

Could she get away if she tried? Probably not, if she were being honest. But she could struggle, and that she chose not to do. Not just yet.

"Your eyes, I mean," he whispered to her. "You should control your eyes."

And with that he pressed the point of a thin blade against the corner of her eye, so close to the tear duct she could feel it begin to leak and wondered if the liquid was blood.

"Or you'll lose them."

She prepared herself the best she could for the shock of the knife detaching her retina from the socket like an oyster from a shell. Then there was a shot from an unseen gun, the sound so loud and the origin so deceptive, it seemed like it was coming from above them, dropping from the sky.

Castán released the knife and Vega's wrist instantly, and his body fell to the ground. Vega looked down to see that the bullet had drilled a canal along the side of his head above his right ear, the dark hair matted with blood. He was alive, though. His limbs convulsed, blood bubbling up from his mouth as he moved his lips, trying to speak.

His knife glimmered in the dirt, and Vega picked it up. It was clean. Then she touched the corner of her eye—no blood.

The two men with the kerchiefs on their faces climbed out of the white bags, ran to Castán, and pointed their weapons at his head, standing on either side of Vega.

"Wait!" came a voice in Spanish.

It was the man who had fired the shot into Castán's head. He had been hiding in the mouth of the tunnel, in the dark, and now he was coming closer. His name was César Villareal.

He was not tall but his chest was wide and thick, and he held a military-grade sniper rifle in one hand as naturally as most people would carry their car keys. Eight more men followed behind him.

"Back up," he said to the men with the kerchiefs, who did as they were told.

Even though Vega knew he wasn't speaking to her directly, she did the same.

Villareal peered down at Castán and pointed the sniper rifle at his face, pressed the barrel tip against his cheek. Castán continued to choke, the muscles surrounding his mouth contracting. Vega was fairly certain he was still cognizant of what was happening. She was also certain that was exactly how Villareal wanted him.

Villareal kept the gun on Castán, then gestured to one of the men behind him, who came forward. This man was tall, his hair tied into a ponytail. He was also holding a foot-long bowie knife in each hand.

Vega continued to back away, as did the men with the kerchiefs. They all kept their distance as Villareal and Marco Díaz, the fathers of Maricel and Dulce—the two Janes—went to work on Castán. It took only a few minutes, steam rising in the nearly night air as they opened him up.

Cap sped up as he saw Javier Castán's SUV on the side of the road, his throat constricting in some kind of emotional anaphylactic shock. He scanned the scene frantically, looking for her. He saw the scooters, along with ten or so men dressed in dark shirts, jeans, and cowboy boots, some of them with kerchiefs over the bottom halves of their faces, some tying up full black garbage bags with rope. They all carried guns—rifles on straps and handguns in holsters.

Finally Cap saw Vega standing with one of the men, her arms folded, watching it all. He pulled over.

"Papi," said the girl closest to the window, called Areceli, placing her fingers on the glass.

Nati and the girl who hid under the bed, María Elena, clambered over each other to get closer to the window, and then they along with

Areceli began yelling at once. Rodrigo, sitting in the passenger seat, powered the window down.

"Papá!" he called.

The man standing with Vega began to run toward the car.

Cap unlocked the doors, and Rodrigo and the girls spilled out, all but Catalina Checado, the girl called Chicago, running to their fathers. One of the men ran and swept Nati up off the ground. Then two others came forward and clutched and hugged Areceli and María Elena, all of them crying and kissing one another's faces.

Chicago walked unsteadily onto the sand, the blanket falling from her shoulders. She didn't make a move to pick it up. A tall man with a mustache went to her.

"Lina," he said, and he pushed his rifle to the side of his body and hugged her.

Chicago let herself be hugged but didn't move her arms in return. Her father spoke rapidly, what Cap imagined were questions followed by pledges of love, but Chicago didn't respond, even when her father pulled her out of the embrace and held her face in his hands.

Rodrigo and his father hugged and gripped each other's backs and shoulders, and Cap felt the space in his esophagus shrink even smaller.

It became almost nonexistent as Vega approached him.

"You all right?" she said to him. "You look like you're about to pass out."

He nodded, coughed bravely into his fist.

"Are you okay?" he asked.

She nodded distractedly, her eyes on Villareal, who squeezed his son for another minute before turning to Vega and Cap.

"Thank you," he said in English, shaking their hands. "I'm taking my son home now." He cast his gaze toward the men with the kerchiefs, who were carrying two white body bags and three black garbage bags wound with duct tape toward the tunnel's opening. "And my daughter," he added.

Then he turned back to address Vega.

"My boss sends his thanks as well."

He laughed suddenly then, though his eyes remained static.

"He's a good person to have in your debt. Perro Perez will know it was us who did this. We will be ready for that."

He glanced back at the men with the kerchiefs going into the tunnel, the ghost of the sun in a yellow strip behind them.

Villareal continued: "But if Perez finds out about you, he will kill you and anyone you have even thought about loving," he said calmly. Merely an observation.

"I guess no one should tell him about me, then," said Vega.

Villareal smiled broadly.

"I guess you're right."

He turned around then and spoke quietly to Rodrigo. He put his arm around his son's shoulders and they headed toward the tunnel.

"*Adios,* Vega," called Villareal over his shoulder.

The men with the kerchiefs had already carried the bags into the tunnel, then Montalvo's men with their girls who were still alive went next, wheeling the scooters inside. Nati's arms were still slung around her father's neck, while Chicago's father led her like a blind person. Villareal and Rodrigo were the last.

Vega and Cap watched all those people disappear into the tunnel, one by one. Rodrigo paused and turned around before going inside. He was too far away for Vega and Cap to make out the exact expression on his face; they couldn't tell if he was smiling or stoic but they could see him lift a finger to his temple, either in a salute goodbye or, Cap thought, in a corroboration that what happened was committed to memory. Right here, he seemed to be saying with his finger to his head: everything is right in here.

Then he was gone, into the tunnel, and Vega and Cap stood for a few minutes as it got colder and darker in the desert. Eventually they got in their car and left too, and it was like none of them were ever there.

25

THE NEXT MORNING McTIERNAN MET THEM AT THE HOTEL. HE stood in the parking lot leaning against a minivan, waving a white envelope as Cap and Vega descended the stairs.

"Fresh from the district court," he said. "Order to release the six girls from the Oren North facility to police custody."

Cap wasn't feeling like himself, if he was admitting things. He'd been so tired and sore and had crashed so hard from all the adrenaline blasts of the day before that his memory after they'd left the tunnel was spotty at best. He'd told Vega she should drive, not trusting his reflexes, and he'd dozed on the way to the hotel, sporadically filling Vega in on his exchange with the girls at the Surf Motel. He barely recalled climbing the stairs to his room, and he fell asleep in his clothes, waking up only when the sun tore through the curtains at 6:15.

But he knew this was good news, even through the dust.

They all got into the minivan, McTiernan driving, Cap in the passenger seat, and Vega in the row behind them. McTiernan put on a sports radio station and he and Cap talked about players and stats and games, Cap lamenting the Mets' Series loss in '15, and McTiernan lamenting the Padres not even getting close since '06.

Cap felt an unfamiliar buoyancy—even though their work wasn't done, there was somehow cause to feel optimistic. He and McTiernan laughed easily and often, and Cap checked Vega in the side mirror. He saw her leaning her head against the window, eyes shut. But he knew better than to think she was actually sleeping; he knew she was thinking, that the path was narrowing, and soon they would come to the last locked door with a fresh-cut key.

· · ·

The light gleamed red on the backs of her eyelids. She listened to Cap and McTiernan talk about baseball but was also replaying the conversation she and Cap had had the night before, when he'd been half-asleep in the car from the tunnel back to the hotel. He had, in turn, been recalling the interactions with Mackey and then the Montalvo girls at the Surf Motel: how Mackey acted like an entitled little brat; how Chicago was just like Isabel Benitez, numb from trauma, train off the tracks; how none of the girls had thought to attempt escape even though they were only handcuffed to each other and not to some immovable object; how Nati asked for Dalena Cortez, and Cap was unexpectedly moved by that, heartened by the sign that the girls were looking out for one another.

Now McTiernan was telling a story as he drove: "When I was a beat cop, I got this call from Carmel Valley—it's pretty upscale, and me and my partner get there, and the wife had hit her husband with a fungo."

They both laughed.

"She must not have been that angry," said Cap, still laughing.

"Right?" said McTiernan. "If he'd really pissed her off, she would've hit him with a standard bat."

"Who in hell has a fungo lying around?"

Vega opened her eyes and interrupted: "What's a fungo?"

The men glanced at her in the backseat, surprised she was listening, eager to let her in.

"It's a short, skinny bat that coaches use for practice," said McTiernan.

"They can hit the ball further with it," Cap added. "Don't they use it for bunting, too?" he asked McTiernan.

Vega stopped listening then, shut off her interest in the conversation like she was switching radio stations. She pictured what a fungo would look like next to a regulation baseball bat, and how it would not be unlike what a paring knife would look next to a handmade hunting knife.

Steve McConnell held the sheet of paper in his hands for a solid three minutes, his eyes scurrying over the words like house mice, back and forth, back and forth.

They were in the trailer, McTiernan standing directly opposite McConnell, the conference table between them. Cap was right behind

McTiernan with his hand over his mouth, trying to physically pull the grin off his face so it wasn't so obvious. Vega and Sam the guard stood on either side of the closed door.

"Mr. McConnell, we're on a tight schedule here so we'd appreciate if we could move the process along," said McTiernan, polite and firm.

"This is a federally run facility. You'll have to run this through DHS," said McConnell, not sounding particularly convinced about it himself.

"And that's why we went through a federal district court," said McTiernan. "Those six girls are potential witnesses for an ongoing homicide and human trafficking police investigation. If you don't release them to us now, I can look into having you arrested for kidnapping."

Cap grinned openly now, felt like McTiernan's little brother on the school yard. Yeah, what he said.

McConnell stared at McTiernan for another moment, as if to make his reticence known by pausing. Then he looked at Sam the guard, who stepped forward.

"Those six," said McConnell, handing Sam the paper. "*Only* those six," he said to the room, as if McTiernan would try to shove a few more kids in his pockets on the way out.

After Sam left, McConnell sighed and said, "There anything else I can help you with?"

"Yeah, I have to interview one of the girls again," said Vega, still standing by the door. "Dalena Cortez. Could you have your guard bring her here?"

Cap was a little surprised but pretended not to be; this had not been discussed in the van. McConnell sneered, his gray eyes filmy.

"Fine," he said, not moving.

"I'd like to talk to my partner and Detective McTiernan first," she said. "If you'll excuse us."

Now they all stared at McConnell, who realized he was being ousted from his office.

"If you could make it quick," he mumbled, grabbed a pair of sunglasses from his desk, and left the trailer.

As soon as the door shut, Cap said, "That was maybe a little too enjoyable."

McTiernan took his phone out and began taking pictures of the trailer.

"Federally run, my ass," McTiernan said. "There's no way any brass would sign off on this. People are going to get fired at ISC, that's all I'm saying."

McTiernan walked around the table, still taking pictures. He held the phone up to a small window at the rear of the trailer and took pictures of the camp.

Cap turned to Vega and asked, "Why do you need to talk to Dalena?"

"I think she might have seen an exchange between Davis and Mackey that she didn't know was meaningful at the time," said Vega.

Cap nodded, got the distinct feeling she wasn't telling him the whole story. He glanced at McTiernan, still taking pictures at the window.

"You want to tell me what you're looking for?" he said to her, leaning in a little.

Vega leaned in too. Now their foreheads almost touched.

"Not really, Caplan," she said.

He smiled and stepped back.

"Okay, Ms. Vega," he said, raising his hands.

Then he and McTiernan left the trailer. Cap stood on the steps outside as he shut the door and watched Vega sit at the conference table and knock on it twice, tilt her head toward it like she was expecting a response.

Dalena came in, still wearing the baggy ISC shirt, jeans, tennis shoes with no laces. She appeared expectant and not afraid, her eyes alert. She sat in the chair across from Vega without being told to.

"Hi, Dalena. How are you?" said Vega.

Dalena shrugged.

"Where are you taking us?" she said, not particularly suspicious.

"Well, right now we're taking you to the police station, and you're going to meet with people from a group, an organization that helps girls from other countries. They might be able to contact your families," Vega explained.

Dalena thought about it for a moment.

"Will they send us back?" she said.

"I don't know," Vega said honestly. "It's strange in this country right now. I can't say for sure what's going to happen."

Dalena didn't appear distressed. Her eyes left Vega's and searched the room behind her.

"Where are you from exactly?" asked Vega, keeping her tone casual.

"Chiapas," said Dalena. Then she smiled. "A nowhere town. That's what they call them. Farms between towns that have no address. Nowhere towns. I am from there."

"How did you get here?"

Dalena brought her eyes back to Vega. They were deep and brown.

"My parents sent me with my little sister and some other kids. One of the others had a cousin who was older, so he was the leader. We walked a long way. Then we took a bus."

She stopped speaking. It was like she had hit a pothole.

"My sister got sick. I don't know what it was but her throat was swollen and she couldn't talk. Then she died on the bus. Coyote Ben was there when we got off the bus, and we went with him. Along the Tijuana River."

She listed the events without a lot of attachment to any of it, like she had recalled the experience to herself many times before.

"I'm sorry about your sister," said Vega.

Dalena shrugged again, moved her mouth around, did not cry.

Vega leaned in toward the table and folded her hands.

"Dalena, do you know what a fingerprint is?" she asked.

Dalena looked confused. She didn't answer.

Vega held up her hand and pointed to her index fingertip.

"It's like a stamp. Everyone's is different. And whatever you touch, you leave your stamp."

Vega placed her hand palm down on the table.

"So right now, my fingerprints are on this table, and police can know I was here."

Dalena's breath was steady. She kept her eyes on Vega.

"The police have all the things from the house in Salton in boxes. All the loose things from the bedrooms and the bathrooms and the kitchen. They will know who touched what things because of the fingerprints. Do you understand?"

Dalena didn't nod or shake her head. She stared at Vega, frozen.

"So if there's a weapon, like a knife from the kitchen, that was used to cut the limes for the drinks for the men who came to the house, the police will be able to tell who touched that knife."

Dalena continued to stare. She didn't answer.

"Do you know anything about a knife like that?" asked Vega.

Still no answer. Vega was having trouble reading her. She couldn't tell if Dalena didn't understand or was simply staying stoic.

Finally she spoke: "Coyote Ben let me use it for the drinks."

"How long were you in the house?" Vega asked.

"A year, maybe," Dalena said. "The city girls got there and didn't know anything. Chicago got her brains burned out because she used to cry all the time."

Dalena stopped. Another pothole.

"Was Maricel Villareal like that, too? Did she cry all the time?" asked Vega.

"Oh yes," said Dalena. "Missy cried, too, but she knew how to keep it quiet, but the city girls, they didn't know. Maricel and Dulce with the good hair, all they do is cry."

"So what happened to them?" Vega said quietly. "The girls that cried."

"Rafa took Dulce first," said Dalena. Now her eyes were blank, the movie screen of memory showing in front of her. "She was screaming at everyone but then when she looks at me she screams words: 'Help me.' Just for me she said that. She thought I could help her."

"Because Coyote Ben liked you?" Vega ventured.

Dalena snapped free from her reverie and looked at Vega like she was crazy.

"Coyote Ben didn't like me. He tried me out," she spat.

Vega nodded, afraid she'd overstepped.

"What happened when she got back from the shed with Rafa?" said Vega quietly, hoping to redirect the girl's focus.

Dalena shook her head, derisive.

"She wasn't there anymore," she said. "We had to hold her hand to pull her around, because she wouldn't just walk. And she didn't understand what anyone said.

"I slept next to her and one night I wake up. I was all wet because she peed everywhere. So that day I took the knife with me."

"Fat Mitch didn't notice?" said Vega.

"He ate candy and drank tequila. Rafa smoked drugs and pounded the walls. They couldn't watch all of us all the time," Dalena said.

She paused, examined her hands, the tips of her fingers and her nails. Looking for the prints, Vega thought.

"What did you do, Dalena?" Vega said, her voice quiet, rising only a little above the fan in the corner. "What did you do with the knife?"

Dalena stopped looking at her hands, dropped them in her lap.

"I put a towel over Dulce's mouth and stuck in the knife, right here," she said, placing her hand on her side. "I saw my father do that with javelinas. I know if I don't kill her, they will. Or a worse thing."

"What about Maricel Villareal?" said Vega, just north of a whisper.

"I know Rafa will take her next. She cries while she is in the rooms downstairs with the men. The men complain. She watched TV and saw you on it. She watched TV, and I watched her. I saw you on TV, too," said Dalena. "You saved a little boy, but I know you can't save us. Maricel and the city girls, they say they can't go back home because their fathers are in trouble. Their fathers are all big men."

Dalena smiled then, a little laugh.

"My father's not big. Missy's father, not big. But in the house it doesn't matter who your father is. No one will see her father again. I know Maricel's going with Rafa soon, so I do the same thing to her." She paused, then added, "Only I'm better at it the second time."

Dalena's voice remained steady, not a lot of emotion seeping out. Vega didn't think she was showing off, just telling the truth. Vega had met a couple of sociopaths, recognized the cool lack of remorse, but didn't think Dalena fit in that box.

"Dalena," said Vega, gently as she could. "You know that killing a human being is not a good thing to do, right?"

Dalena put her hands on the table and leaned forward.

"It was a good thing to do for those girls. They would have had a worse thing happen to them."

Her nostrils flared and her pupils grew. She bared her teeth as she spoke.

"What do you know? Nothing. You have money and guns," she said. She sat back in her chair, continued: "They had no home to go to anymore."

"They did," said Vega quietly. "Catalina, Nati, Areceli, María Elena. Their fathers aren't in trouble anymore, and they came to get them. Maricel's and Dulce's fathers came with them, too. They were waiting for their daughters."

Dalena turned her head to the side but kept her eyes on Vega. She was breathing quicker now, starting to feel trapped.

"You're lying," she said, not very persuasively.

"I'm not," said Vega.

Dalena looked at her hands again and clenched them slowly into fists. She brought them to her forehead.

"My head is on fire," she said hoarsely.

Vega looked at all of her: the dirt under her thumbnails, the vertical hash marks on her chapped lips, the natural gloss of her young skin, her long straight hair unbrushed but not matted, lying over her shoulders like a dark cloak. The terror in her eyes. Vega saw her living every second of what she had done again and feeling it slip away from her like a coin dropped off a cliff, deeper and further into the past, so far now she could not reach it even if she jumped in after it. Lost.

Vega thought about reaching for Dalena's hands but thought better of it.

So she said all she could say, which was "I know it is."

The girls were happy.

In the van, McTiernan put on a Spanish music station, and the girls were singing and laughing with one another. Cap watched them from the front seat and noticed it was really only four of them who were engaged. Isabel Benitez stared out the window blankly, and Dalena Cortez was pretending to be asleep—Cap could tell because she would periodically open one eye to see if the others were watching her.

Vega was locked in with her phone, not noticing anyone. Cap tried to catch her eye in the side mirror but she refused to look up. She'd spent only a few minutes in the trailer with Dalena and hadn't said anything more to Cap than "I'll fill you in later" when they'd emerged.

But at this moment it was difficult for him to sulk. They had found all the girls, every one, and the guy who'd killed the two Janes was handcuffed to a hospital bed, and the architect of the whole mess was dead due in large part to his own hubris. And on top of everything, he and Vega got to keep their eyeballs. Always a plus. It would all make a great story for Nell, and Cap couldn't wait to call her and tell her everything, good and bad. And big bad, as Vega would say.

The girls erupted in laughter, and Cap turned to see McTiernan laughing but trying not to.

"What?" said Cap.

"They're comparing us to animals. They said Vega's a fox, and I'm a bear, and you're . . ."

McTiernan paused.

"I'm a what?" Cap said, turning almost all the way around to look at them.

The four burst into hysterics again.

"You're a goat, dude," said McTiernan.

"What?" said Cap, incredulous. "Why a goat?"

"Because, um, your hair's a little curly on top and one of them said you have tiny eyes."

"Tiny eyes?"

The girls were now apoplectic with laughter.

"It's because I'm tired. These are bags," Cap said defensively, pointing to them. "How do you say 'bags'?" he said to McTiernan.

"*Las bolsas*," McTiernan said, almost unable to get the word out.

"*Bol-sas*," said Cap to the girls, enunciating.

They howled and cried with laughter. Cap loved the way Missy looked as she laughed with her mouth wide open, her crooked teeth. It was such a glorious image of her compared with how small and terrified she'd been in the room downstairs at the Salton house. Even Isabel Benitez was smiling now, but Cap thought she was just mimicking the others, mirroring their faces the way babies did to see if they could form their features the same way.

Vega, still focused on her phone, let a smile sneak onto her lips. She glanced at Cap quickly.

Only Dalena Cortez stayed out of it, still pretending to sleep, eyes squeezed shut so hard Cap thought she might bruise the lids.

Soon the girls calmed down, and Cap started seeing signs for El Centro exits. Vega leaned over and forward so she was between Cap and McTiernan.

"McT, could you stop at the hotel? I need some more time with Dalena," she said.

"Yeah, of course," said McTiernan. "What's going on?"

Cap turned his head to watch Vega's face while she spoke. He wasn't even sure what he was looking for, just knew she was about to tell them only the select cut she thought they needed to know.

"She might have overheard something about Lara that'll help wrap up his case."

"Definitely. Take all the time you need," said McTiernan. "We're not going to be in any rush at the station. And GATO, the organization, is based downtown. They have some beds where they'll probably put the girls at least for a few nights. You can always drop her off tonight."

Vega thanked him and sat back in her seat.

Cap knew she was lying. He also knew she was trying to protect him from something, and even though he knew that, he still didn't like it.

He tried to meet her eye again in the side mirror but she put her sunglasses on and looked out the window, and then he knew she didn't like lying to him either.

26

MUCH LATER, CAP STOOD ON THE WALKWAY OUTSIDE HIS HOTEL room on the phone. He was in his bare feet wearing jeans and an Eagles T-shirt, drinking a can of beer he'd bought from a 7-Eleven. The sun was setting behind him, and the air was clear and warm. He watched planes overhead and talked to Nell, answered every question she had, which were many. He was tired but awake.

"You have to go to a doctor as soon as you get back, Dad," said Nell. "You have to get an MRI or a CT scan."

"I will, Bug, I promise."

She sighed forcefully.

"I mean, you don't know what kind of long-lasting damage that guy caused. I saw this *Nova* where this guy hit his head when he was in his twenties and then when he was like fifty all he did was hear music, which sounds nice but it's absolutely not nice, it's like torture when you can't sleep because music is blasting in your brain."

"I don't think that's going to happen to me," said Cap, folding his toes under his foot and cracking the knuckles.

She was quiet, sniffling.

"You okay, Bug?" said Cap.

"Yeah," she said, her voice small. "I'm just worried about you."

"I'll be home tomorrow or the next day, okay?" he said. "Don't worry about me. I know this is all really intense, but Vega and me, we're both okay."

"Of course I'm going to worry about you," she said, indignant. "I worry about you, you worry about me. That's what people in families do. They worry themselves sick."

Cap smiled.

"Dad, I've been thinking about something," Nell said.

Cap braced himself and said, "Shoot."

"I think I want you to take that job with Vera Quinn. I mean, you should do what you want to do. Next year I'll be in school somewhere so it's not like you'll need to report to me or anything, but working with Vega, it's just pretty dangerous. That's my official recommendation."

"Noted," said Cap. "We'll talk about it when I get home. Right now all I want to do is sleep for about a week."

"That we can accommodate," said Nell, her tone growing stronger. "And I've got more good news," she whispered.

"What's that?"

"Mom made you a scarf. It's dark blue."

Cap laughed very hard.

"Wow, that's something," he said.

"I'm sure it means you guys are getting back together," Nell said, and then she started laughing.

Both of them continued to laugh, and it reminded Cap of the girls in the car that morning, before they got to the station and met the people from GATO, the nonprofit, who seemed perfectly nice and genuinely interested in the girls and their well-being. But Cap couldn't shake saying goodbye to Missy, how concerned she seemed that he was leaving.

"You're going to be okay now," he'd said to her, knowing that she wouldn't understand, except the word "okay."

She'd nodded confidently, but Cap had the feeling she was doing it to reassure him.

"Get some sleep, Dad," Nell said now, finally curbing the giggles. "Don't do that thing when you drink too many beers and fall asleep and then wake up at three and can't go back to sleep, okay?"

"Yes, Chief," he said, not even pretending to protest.

They said goodbye and I love you, and hung up. Cap finished one beer and opened another, told himself it would be the last one, to pay attention to Nell's warning.

The sun seemed to be taking a while to go down, and Cap enjoyed the last of the light, the near-tropic blue of the sky as it transitioned into black, the still of the palm trees and the cars racing under them.

Soon he saw the undercover loaner pull into the lot and park. Vega got out. Cap thought his eyes were tricking him a little but then he stared and saw that she wore different clothes: a baggy shirt, strange faded jeans, sneakers.

She was wearing Dalena Cortez's clothes.

She carried her Springfield under her arm, the holster wrapped around it, and she came up the stairs slowly. She walked down the walkway toward him, and he stayed right where he was, leaning on the railing, still looking at the trees and the cars. She leaned on the railing next to him the opposite way, facing the room doors.

"You want a beer?" he said.

"Sure."

She reached down to the plastic bag on the mat in front of his room and pulled a can out of it, snapped it open, took a sip.

They were quiet for a few minutes.

"Your text said you were leaving a while ago," said Cap, trying not to sound reproachful. "I was starting to get worried."

"Sorry, Caplan," said Vega. "I had to take care of some things."

Cap nodded.

"Where's Dalena, Vega?" he said quietly. "Why are you wearing her clothes?"

Vega took a deep breath through her nose and sipped her beer. She held the cool can to her forehead.

"I'm going to tell you the first part. Then you can tell me the rest, okay?" she said.

"Okay."

"Rafa didn't kill the Janes. Neither did Davis, or Mitch, or Mackey. Dalena did," said Vega.

Cap pushed off the railing, looked at her.

"What do you mean?"

"She was in charge of the drinks for the guests at the house. She cut the limes with a paring knife and she killed Dulce Díaz because Rafa fried her brain. Then she killed Maricel Villareal because Dalena knew she was next on the table."

Cap felt pins in his skin, on his neck and ears. He bent over, put his hands on thighs, and breathed deeply.

"Shit," he said. "She told you all that?"

Vega nodded.

"She saw no reason to hide it from me. Now, do you think you can tell me the rest?"

Cap stood up straight and leaned back on the railing, facing the room doors like Vega was. He looked at her clothes again and thought.

Then he just started talking, like he was reading from a book: "I think you gave her your clothes, your boots. Some money. I think you put her on a bus or a train or a plane. Maybe back to Mexico or maybe somewhere else.

"You did it because you don't think she deserves any more punishment than she's already had, and you couldn't take the chance that someone will lift her prints off the knife when they find it, which, if she goes through the naturalization process, she'll have to provide.

"You did it because there's not a lot of justice happening right now, and you had to make your own."

Vega didn't respond. She took dainty sips from her beer. Cap watched her profile as the walkway lights fluttered on.

Even though she wasn't trying, she was still this beautiful thing.

"What should we tell McT and Otero and Boyce?" Cap said.

Vega shrugged once. Up and down.

"The truth," she said. "Nobody's going to notice one undocumented girl's name crossed off a court order."

Cap nodded thoughtfully.

"You're probably right," he said. "When do you think I should book my ticket home?"

Vega shrugged again.

"We can do paperwork tomorrow, so you could do the red-eye if you want. I'll drive home at night."

"You think we'll be done by then?" Cap asked, stifling a yawn.

"That's the upside of working an unofficial case," she said, allowing a tired grin.

Cap smiled too. He felt like he had a lot to say but didn't know quite where to start. He pictured an arrow on a board game. Start here.

Then they heard some music. It was a trumpet, and it sounded close. They looked at each other and laughed, perplexed.

"I think it's coming from one of the rooms down below," Cap said, leaning further over the railing.

The trumpet player was not untalented. He played a tune that sounded like part of a larger piece with a larger band, stopping and starting. Cap recognized the rhythm from the way Nell practiced her snare for marching band—a lot of action and then a break. They listened to it for a few minutes and drank their beers.

Then Vega said, "I'm going to take a shower and go to sleep, Caplan."

"Yeah, I think I will, too," he said.

"Thanks for the beer," she said, lifting it toward him in a toast. "Good night."

"Good night, Vega."

He watched her walk away from him again and disappear behind another closed door.

Vega stuffed Dalena's clothes in the small cylindrical trash can in the bathroom and took a shower. She got out, toweled dry, and changed her bandages.

She slid into a tank top and carefully pulled it down over her abdomen. She lay on the bed and realized every muscle was sore, all of them at once.

She could still hear the trumpet now and then, but it was muted and not nearly enough to keep her awake. Her lids glided down over her eyes swiftly. She was not quite asleep, but very close, a rogue thought like the smallest feather tracing figure eights on her toe preventing her from falling into the black.

Cap brushed his teeth. Now that the pressure of the case was off, he felt more inclined to his normal routine, so he did the thing that he did at home after brushing his teeth and before going to bed. He pressed his palms to his cheeks and dragged them down, making himself look like a bulldog, to just confirm that he was forty-three and nearing senior citizenship.

He turned off the light in the bathroom and lay on top of the bedspread. He knew he was tired but suddenly felt unable to sleep. His thoughts clustered and wrestled for space, one on top of another, and he tried to sort them, drop them into drawers and files, but was having difficulty. He shut his eyes hard and turned onto his side, compressed the pillow into a puffy ravioli shape as if it would help.

Then the phone rang. The strange thing was it wasn't his cell phone; it was the landline phone in the room, and Cap sat up with a start, confused. He picked up the receiver cautiously.

"Uh, hello?"

"Hey, it's me," said Vega.

"Oh, hi," said Cap. "You okay?"

"Yeah, I think so," she said. "I wanted to tell you something. I let Mackey die on the beach. I shot him and I watched the dog attack him, and I didn't do anything about it."

She paused, and Cap pictured her on the other side of the wall, lying on her bed the way he had been. He thought he should say something.

"Okay," he said.

"I've never done that before," she said, not defensively. "I've never had the chance to save someone and not done it, or at least tried to."

"Vega," he said. "There aren't any rules to this. It's not clean math. You got all those girls out of that house, and the day after tomorrow, after we do paperwork, you're going to do it again, and you're going to keep doing it. You understand what I'm saying?"

"Yeah," she said.

He listened to her breathe.

"You have to let yourself rest, okay?" he said.

"I just wanted you to know that. So there wasn't a thing you didn't know between us."

He felt a pang somewhere deep in his chest. It was almost like hunger but he couldn't imagine consuming food at that moment.

Then she hung up. It was abrupt. He stared at the receiver in his hand, thought maybe she had gotten disconnected by mistake. He began to dial her room number, and there were three quick knocks at the door.

He hung up the phone and got off the bed and opened the door.

It was Vega. She was wearing a tank top and yoga shorts. Her hair was down.

"Hi," Cap said.

She walked toward him and angled her face up to his, and he didn't have time to think about what would be the best way to kiss her, even though he'd planned it over four thousand times since she kissed him in the woods, so he leaned his head down but she came forward too quickly and stood on her toes at the last second, and they clunked foreheads.

"Ow," said Cap.

"Shit," said Vega. "Sorry."

She turned around and shut the door. Then she walked back to him and kissed the place on his forehead where they'd collided. He put his hands on her face, the back of her neck, threaded his fingers through her hair. Then she kissed the burn mark on his temple, then the ridges of his bad ear. Then she kissed him on the lips, and he felt like lips were insufficient, that there was somehow not enough of him to kiss her but he was going to give it his best shot.

He kissed her chin and her arms; he bent down a little and lifted her tank top and kissed her stomach. She kissed the top of his head, put her nose deep in his hair, and he kissed the skin all around the bandage that covered her cut.

And after they kissed all the broken pieces of each other, then they kissed all the pieces that worked just fine.

27

OUR GIRL IS IN A CITY SHE DOESN'T KNOW. IT'S COLD, THAT'S FOR sure, and the air is wet but the sun is shining when she steps off the bus.

Right away a man asks for money in Spanish. He has red blotches on his face but is dressed in clean clothes and new sneakers, so our girl shakes her head and puts on her sunglasses.

She walks past the bus shelters toward the cabs and waits in line. She wiggles her toes in the boots that are just a little too big for her. After a few minutes, she gets into a cab and hands a note to the driver with the address she's going to.

"Outer Sunset, right?" he says.

Our girl nods, even though she doesn't understand the words. She looks out the window, and the buildings turn into single-story houses next to one another with no space in between. Then houses stacked on hills like boxes, tan and brown and white with a pop of red or green here or there. Wires stretch overhead, connecting block to block. There is a green lake surrounded by trees. Our girl can't quite believe it is all part of the same city.

The ride takes about a half hour. The driver drops her off in front of a powder blue house with scallop marks on the façade, like it was just molded out of clay. There is a driveway with a car in it, a gravel path on either side.

She walks up a flight of stairs—a mosaic of earth-toned pebbles—and presses a small white button next to the door at the top. She waits, looks around. All up and down the street are houses similar to this one. She sees no people, and she's relieved. She knows it's still early in the morning, though; she was on the bus most of the night.

Then a woman opens the door. She's young, and her skin is a shade or two lighter than our girl's. Her hair is black and straight and cut at an angle, the longest tips touching her shoulders. She wears glasses and clothes that seem too big for her—a sweater like a sack and pants so wide with legs long it looks like she has no feet.

"Hi," says the woman in English. "You're Vega's friend?"

Our girl hears only "Vega" and nods. She can't tell if the woman is Latina. Her eyes are black liquid dots.

"*Sí*," our girl says. "*¿Habla español?*"

"*Poquito*," says the woman, pinching her fingers together to indicate the amount. "Got plenty of Tagalog though." Once she sees our girl doesn't understand she shakes her head, as if to say never mind, and says, "Come in."

She gestures for our girl to enter, so she does, into a room filled with electronic equipment. There is a long white table covered with laptop computers and machinery, cords crossed and connected through a console in the center blinking.

The woman picks up a camera and says to our girl, "Stand over here, okay? *Aquí*," she says, pointing toward a wall.

Our girl does as she's told and stands still. The woman presses buttons on the camera, and it clicks and whirs.

"Good," says the woman. "You can sit down," she says, pointing to a chair. "This will take a couple of minutes. *Dos minutos*."

Our girl nods and sits, watches the woman plug the camera into another machine along the wall.

"You want some *café*?" the woman asks, making a drinking motion with her hand.

Our girl shakes her head. She's not sure what she wants. She waits a couple of minutes. The woman is busy, walking from one machine to another, tapping a few keys on one laptop, then another.

The woman gathers some papers and cards and brings them to our girl.

"Here is your social security card, birth certificate, state ID. Vega said to give you these, and you can get a passport and driver's license if you want."

Our girl takes the paper and the cards, examines her new name.

The woman hands her another card, gold, with silver numbers.

"Here's your bank card. You have twenty thousand US. *Veinte mil*."

Our girl stares at the card. She understands what it means.

"I can give you a ride to a motel," says the woman.

Our girl hears only "motel" and nods. Vega had told her that the woman would drive her.

"Thank you," says our girl in English.

The woman shrugs like it's any other day for her.

"No worries," she says.

"What . . . is . . . your . . . name?" our girl asks haltingly.

"Me?" the woman says, somewhat surprised. "Joy. My name's Joy."

"Dalena," says our girl, placing her hand on her chest.

"Not anymore you're not," says Joy, laughing. "That's you now," she says, pointing to the documents.

Our girl smiles, confused, and looks down at her face on the ID.

"That's okay, you'll get used to it," says Joy. "I have *dos nombres,* too. Most people call me the Bastard. *El Bastardo,*" she says, rolling the "r."

Our girl likes Joy. She thinks she will like this strange town as well with the houses close together.

Joy grabs a jacket and some keys and puts on sunglasses.

"You ready, girl?" she says.

Our girl puts on her sunglasses too and nods. She's ready.

ACKNOWLEDGMENTS

AGAIN, I COULD NOT HAVE DONE THIS WITHOUT THE SUPPORT AND kindness of the following people. I am in a constant state of gratitude to all of them:

Agent Supreme, part-time psychologist and el perro duro, Mark Falkin—I cannot believe how lucky I am that you continue to be in my corner. Don't ever think about retiring, or I will have to take certain steps.

Mr. Rob Bloom—it's a toss-up as to who understands these characters better, me or you. Your patience and humor have once again made this process rewarding and invigorating. You can also never retire, I'm afraid, and the threat's a little more real than the one for Mark since you and I live in the same town. Sorry!

The nonstop hardworking folks at Doubleday—Todd Doughty, Sarah Englemann, John Fontana, Nora Grubb, Mandy Licata, Rachel Molland, Charlotte O'Donnell, Victoria Pearson, Bill Thomas, Andrew Weber. You all make this biz look easy.

Dr. Judy Melinek—many thanks for fielding my forensic pathology queries. In my next life, hopefully I can be your assistant.

Anna Quindlen and Samantha Irby—thanks upon thanks for spreading the good word about Vega to so many of your readers. You have very bright futures in this business.

My brother, Zach—your continued optimism and encouragement are greatly appreciated. You're a nice person!

JP and Florie—you guys keep me going. Thanks for not minding when I, for example, burn out the car battery, or forget to pack the spaghetti in the thermos for lunch and leave it in the microwave all day. These are just examples of things that could happen. Thank you for being proud of me and full of good advice and love. All the love.